BESTSELLING AUTHOR COLLECTION

In our Bestselling Author Collection, Harlequin Books is proud to offer classic novels from today's superstars of women's fiction. These authors have captured the hearts of millions of readers around the world, and earned their place on the *New York Times, USA TODAY* and other bestseller lists with every release.

As a bonus, each volume also includes a full-length novel from a rising star of series romance. Bestselling authors in their own right, these talented writers have captured the qualities Harlequin is famous for—heart-racing passion, edge-of-your-seat entertainment and a satisfying happily-ever-after.

Don't miss any of the books in the collection!

BESTSELLING AUTHOR COLLECTION

New York Times and *USA TODAY* Bestselling Author

LINDA LAEL MILLER

PART OF THE *Bargain*

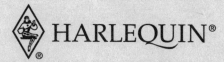

HARLEQUIN®

TORONTO • NEW YORK • LONDON
AMSTERDAM • PARIS • SYDNEY • HAMBURG
STOCKHOLM • ATHENS • TOKYO • MILAN • MADRID
PRAGUE • WARSAW • BUDAPEST • AUCKLAND

Recycling programs
for this product may
not exist in your area.

ISBN-13: 978-0-373-38993-3

PART OF THE BARGAIN

Copyright © 2010 by Harlequin Books S.A.

The publisher acknowledges the copyright holders
of the individual works as follows:

PART OF THE BARGAIN
Copyright © 1985 by Linda Lael Miller

TO WED AND PROTECT
Copyright © 2002 by Carla Bracale

CONTENTS

In loving and grateful memory of Laura Mast.

PART OF THE BARGAIN

New York Times and *USA TODAY* Bestselling Author

Linda Lael Miller

LINDA LAEL MILLER

The daughter of a town marshal, Linda Lael Miller is a *New York Times* and *USA TODAY* bestselling author of more than eighty historical and contemporary novels. Raised in Northport, Washington, the self-confessed barn goddess now lives in Spokane, Washington.

Dedicated to helping others, Linda personally finances her Linda Lael Miller Scholarships for Women, awarded annually to women seeking to improve their lot in life through education. More information about Linda, her novels and her scholarships is available at www.lindalaelmiller.com. She also loves to hear from readers by mail at P.O. Box 19461, Spokane, WA 99219.

Chapter 1

The landing gear made an unsettling *ka-thump* sound as it snapped back into place under the small private airplane. Libby Kincaid swallowed her misgivings and tried not to look at the stony, impassive face of the pilot. If he didn't say anything, she wouldn't have to say anything either, and they might get through the short flight to the Circle Bar B ranch without engaging in one of their world-class shouting matches.

It was a pity, Libby thought, that at the ages of thirty-one and thirty-three, respectively, she and Jess still could not communicate on an adult level.

Pondering this, Libby looked down at the ground below and was dizzied by its passing as they swept over the small airport at Kalispell, Montana, and banked eastward, toward the Flathead River. Trees so green that they had a blue cast carpeted the majestic mountains rimming the valley.

Womanhood being what it is, Libby couldn't resist watching Jess Barlowe surreptitiously out of the corner of her eye. He was like a lean, powerful mountain lion waiting to pounce, even though he kept his attention strictly on the controls and the thin air traffic sharing the big Montana sky that spring morning. His eyes were hidden behind a pair of mirrored sunglasses, but Libby knew that they would be dark with the animosity that had marked their relationship for years.

She looked away again, trying to concentrate on the river, which coursed beneath them like a dusty-jade ribbon woven into the fabric of a giant tapestry. Behind those mirrored glasses, Libby knew Jess's eyes were the exact same shade of green as that untamed waterway below.

"So," he said suddenly, gruffly, "New York wasn't all the two-hour TV movies make it out to be."

Libby sighed, closed her eyes in a bid for patience and then opened them again. She wasn't going to miss one bit of that fabulous view—not when her heart had been hungering for it for several bittersweet years.

Besides, Jess had been to New York dozens of times on corporation business. Who did he think he was fooling?

"New York was all right," she said, in the most inflamatory tone she could manage. *Except that Jonathan died,* chided a tiny, ruthless voice in her mind. *Except for that nasty divorce from Aaron.* "Nothing to write home about," she added aloud, realizing her blunder too late.

"So your dad noticed," drawled Jess in an undertone that would have been savage if it hadn't been so carefully modulated. "Every day, when the mail came, he fell on it like it was manna from heaven. He never stopped hoping—I'll give him that."

"Dad knows I hate to write letters," she retorted defensively. But Jess had made his mark, all the same—Libby felt real pain, picturing her father flipping eagerly through the mail and trying to hide his disappointment when there was nothing from his only daughter.

"Funny—that's not what Stace tells me."

Libby bridled at this remark, but she kept her composure. Jess was trying to trap her into making some foolish statement about his older brother, no doubt, one that he could twist out of shape and hold over her head. She raised her chin and choked back the indignant diatribe aching in her throat.

The mirrored sunglasses glinted in the sun as Jess turned to look at her. His powerful shoulders were taut beneath the blue cotton fabric of his workshirt, and his jawline was formidably hard.

"Leave Cathy and Stace alone, Libby," he warned with blunt savagery. "They've had a lot of problems lately, and if you do anything to make the situation worse, I'll see that you regret it. Do I make myself clear?"

Libby would have done almost anything to escape his scrutiny just then, short of thrusting open the door of that small four-passenger Cessna and jumping out, but her choices were undeniably limited. Trembling just a little, she turned away and fixed her attention on the ground again.

Dear heaven, did Jess really think that she would interfere in Cathy's marriage—or any other, for that matter? Cathy was her *cousin*—they'd been raised like sisters!

With a sigh, Libby faced the fact that there was every chance that Jess and a lot of other people would believe she had been involved with Stacey Barlowe. There had, after all, been that exchange of correspondence, and Stace had even visited her a few times, in the thick of her traumatic divorce, though in actuality he had been in the city on business.

"Libby?" prodded Jess sharply, when the silence grew too long to suit him.

"I'm not planning to vamp your brother!" she snapped. "Could we just drop this, please?"

To her relief and surprise, Jess turned his concentration on piloting the plane. His suntanned jaw worked with suppressed annoyance, but he didn't speak again.

The timbered land below began to give way to occasional patches of prairie—cattle country. Soon they would be landing on the small airstrip serving the prosperous 150,000-acre Circle Bar B, owned by Jess's father and overseen, for the most part, by Libby's.

Libby had grown up on the Circle Bar B, just as Jess had, and her mother, like his, was buried there. Even though she couldn't call the ranch home in the legal sense of the word, it was *still* home to her, and she had every right to go there—especially now, when she needed its beauty and peace and practical routines so desperately.

The airplane began to descend, jolting Libby out of her reflective state. Beside her, Jess guided the craft skillfully toward the paved landing strip stretched out before them.

The landing gear came down with a sharp snap, and Libby drew in her breath in preparation. The wheels of the plane screeched and grabbed as they made contact with the asphalt, and then the Cessna was rolling smoothly along the ground.

When it came to a full stop, Libby wrenched at her seat belt, anxious to put as much distance as possible between herself and Jess Barlowe. But his hand closed over her left wrist in a steel-hard grasp. "Remember, Lib—these people aren't the sophisticated if-it-feels-good-do-it types you're used to. No games."

Games. *Games?* Hot color surged into Libby's face and pounded there in rhythm with the furious beat of her heart. "Let go of me, you bastard!" she breathed.

If anything, Jess's grip tightened. "I'll be watching you," he warned, and then he flung Libby's wrist from his hand and turned away to push open the door on his side and leap nimbly to the ground.

Libby was still tugging impotently at the handle on her own door when her father strode over, climbed deftly onto the wing and opened it for her. She felt such a surge of love and relief at the sight of him that she cried out softly and flung herself into his arms, nearly sending both of them tumbling to the hard ground.

Ken Kincaid hadn't changed in the years since Libby had seen him last—he was still the same handsome, rangy cowboy that she remembered so well, though his hair, while as thick as ever, was iron-gray now, and the limp he'd acquired in a long-ago rodeo accident was more pronounced.

Once they were clear of the plane, he held his daughter at arm's length, laughed gruffly, and then pulled her close again. Over his shoulder she saw Jess drag her suitcases and portable drawing board out of the Cessna's luggage compartment and fling them unceremoniously into the back of a mud-speckled truck.

Nothing if not perceptive, Ken Kincaid turned slightly, assessed Senator Cleave Barlowe's second son, and grinned. There was mischief in his bright blue eyes when he faced Libby again. "Rough trip?"

Libby's throat tightened unaccountably, and she wished she could explain *how* rough. She was still stung by Jess's insulting opinion of her morality, but how could she tell her father that? "You know that it's always rough going where Jess and I are concerned," she said.

Her father's brows lifted speculatively as Jess got behind the wheel of the truck and sped away without so much as a curt nod or a halfhearted so-long. "You two'd better watch out," he mused. "If you ever stop butting heads, you might find out you like each other."

"Now, that," replied Libby with dispatch, "is a horrid thought if I've ever heard one. Tell me, Dad—how have you been?"

He draped one wiry arm over her shoulders and guided her in the direction of a late-model pickup truck. The door on the driver's side was emblazoned with the words CIRCLE BAR B RANCH, and Yosemite Sam glared from both the mud flaps shielding the rear tires. "Never mind how I've been, dumplin'. How've *you* been?"

Libby felt some of the tension drain from her as her father opened the door on the passenger side of the truck and helped her inside. She longed to shed her expensive tailored linen suit for jeans and a T-shirt, and—oh, heaven—her sneakers would be a welcome change from the high heels she was wearing. "I'll be okay," she said in tones that were a bit too energetically cheerful.

Ken climbed behind the wheel and tossed one searching, worried look in his daughter's direction. "Cathy's waiting over at the house, to help you settle in and all that. I was hoping we could talk...."

Libby reached out and patted her father's work-worn hand, resting now on the gearshift knob. "We can talk tonight. Anyway, we've got lots of time."

Ken started the truck's powerful engine, but his wise blue eyes had not strayed from his daughter's face. "You'll stay here awhile, then?" he asked hopefully.

Libby nodded, but she suddenly found that she had to look away. "As long as you'll let me, Dad."

The truck was moving now, jolting and rattling over the rough ranch roads with a pleasantly familiar vigor. "I expected you before this," he said. "Lib..."

She turned an imploring look on him. "Later, Dad—okay? Could we please talk about the heavy stuff later?"

Ken swept off his old cowboy hat and ran a practiced arm

across his forehead. "Later it is, dumplin'." Graciously he changed the subject. "Been reading your comic strip in the funny papers, and it seems like every kid in town's wearing one of those T-shirts you designed."

Libby smiled; her career as a syndicated cartoonist was certainly safe conversational ground. And it had all started right here, on this ranch, when she'd sent away the coupon printed on a matchbook and begun taking art lessons by mail. After that, she'd won a scholarship to a prestigious college, graduated, and made her mark, not in portraits or commercial design, as some of her friends had, but in cartooning. Her character, Liberated Lizzie, a cave-girl with modern ideas, had created something of a sensation and was now featured not only in the Sunday newspapers but also on T-shirts, greeting cards, coffee mugs and calendars. There was a deal pending with a poster company, and Libby's bank balance was fat with the advance payment for a projected book.

She would have to work hard to fulfill her obligations— there was the weekly cartoon strip to do, of course, and the panels for the book had to be sketched in. She hoped that between these tasks and the endless allure of the Circle Bar B, she might be able to turn her thoughts from Jonathan and the mess she'd made of her personal life.

"Career-wise, I'm doing fine," Libby said aloud, as much to herself as to her father. "I don't suppose I could use the sunporch for a studio?"

Ken laughed. "Cathy's been working for a month to get it ready, and I had some of the boys put in a skylight. All you've got to do is set up your gear."

Impulsively Libby leaned over and kissed her father's beard-stubbled cheek. "I love you!"

"Good," he retorted. "A husband you can dump—a daddy you're pretty well stuck with."

The word "husband" jarred Libby a little, bringing an unwelcome image of Aaron into her mind as it did, and she didn't speak again until the house came into sight.

Originally the main ranch house, the structure set aside for the general foreman was an enormous, drafty place with plenty of Victorian scrollwork, gabled windows and porches. It overlooked a sizable spring-fed pond and boasted its own sheltering copse of evergreens and cottonwood trees.

The truck lurched a little as Ken brought it to a stop in the gravel driveway, and through the windshield Libby could see glimmering patches of the silver-blue sparkle that was the pond. She longed to hurry there now, kick off her shoes on the grassy bank and ruin her stockings wading in the cold, clear water.

But her father was getting out of the truck, and Cathy Barlowe, Libby's cousin and cherished friend, was dashing down the driveway, her pretty face alight with greeting.

Libby laughed and stood waiting beside the pickup truck, her arms out wide.

After an energetic hug had been exchanged, Cathy drew back in Libby's arms and lifted a graceful hand to sign the words: "I've missed you so much!"

"And I've missed you," Libby signed back, though she spoke the words aloud, too.

Cathy's green eyes sparkled. "You haven't forgotten how to sign!" she enthused, bringing both hands into play now. She had been deaf since childhood, but she communicated so skillfully that Libby often forgot that they weren't conversing verbally. "Have you been practicing?"

She had. Signing had been a game for her and Jonathan to play during the long, difficult hours she'd spent at his hospital bedside. Libby nodded and tears of love and pride gathered in her dark blue eyes as she surveyed her cousin—physically, she and Cathy bore no resemblance to each other at all.

Cathy was petite, her eyes wide, mischievous emeralds, her hair a glistening profusion of copper and chestnut and gold that reached almost to her waist. Libby was of medium height, and her silver-blond hair fell just short of her shoulders.

"I'll be back later," Ken said quietly, signing the words as he spoke so that Cathy could understand, too. "You two have plenty to say to each other, it looks like."

Cathy nodded and smiled, but there was something sad trembling behind the joy in her green eyes, something that made Libby want to scurry back to the truck and beg to be driven back to the airstrip. From there she could fly to Kalispell and catch a connecting flight to Denver and then New York....

Good Lord—surely Jess hadn't been so heartless as to share his ridiculous suspicions with Cathy!

The interior of the house was cool and airy, and Libby followed along behind Cathy, her thoughts and feelings in an incomprehensible tangle. She was glad to be home, no doubt about it. She'd yearned for the quiet sanity of this place almost from the moment of leaving it.

On the other hand, she wasn't certain that she'd been wise to come back. Jess obviously intended to make her feel less than welcome, and although she had certainly never been intimately involved with Stacey Barlowe, Cathy's husband, sometimes her feelings toward him weren't all that clearly defined.

Unlike his younger brother, Stace was a warm, outgoing person, and through the shattering events of the past year and a half, he had been a tender and steadfast friend. Adrift in waters of confusion and grief, Libby had told Stacey things that she had never breathed to another living soul, and it was true that, as Jess had so bitterly pointed out, she had written to the man when she couldn't bring herself to contact her own father.

But she wasn't in love with Stace, Libby told herself

firmly. She had always looked up to him, that was all—like an older brother. Maybe she'd become a little too dependent on him in the bargain, but that didn't mean she cared for him in a romantic way, did it?

She sighed, and Cathy turned to look at her pensively, almost as though she had heard the sound. That was impossible, of course, but Cathy was as perceptive as anyone Libby had ever known, and she often *felt* sounds.

"Glad to be home?" the deaf woman inquired, gesturing gently.

Libby didn't miss the tremor in her cousin's hands, but she forced a weary smile to her face and nodded in answer to the question.

Suddenly Cathy's eyes were sparkling again, and she caught Libby's hand in her own and tugged her through an archway and into the glassed-in sunporch that overlooked the pond.

Libby drew in a swift, delighted breath. There was indeed a skylight in the roof—a big one. A drawing table had been set up in the best light the room offered, along with a lamp for night work, and there were flowering plants hanging from the exposed beams in the ceiling. The old wicker furniture that had been stored in the attic for as long as Libby could remember had been painted a dazzling white and bedecked with gay floral-print cushions. Small rugs in complementary shades of pink and green had been scattered about randomly, and there was even a shelving unit built into the wall behind the art table.

"Wow!" cried Libby, overwhelmed, her arms spread out wide in a gesture of wonder. "Cathy, you missed your calling! You should have been an interior decorator."

Though Libby hadn't signed the words, her cousin had read them from her lips. Cathy's green eyes shifted quickly from Libby's face, and she lowered her head. "Instead of what?" she motioned sadly. "Instead of Stacey's wife?"

Libby felt as though she'd been slapped, but she recovered quickly enough to catch one hand under Cathy's chin and force her head up. "Exactly what do you mean by that?" she demanded, and she was never certain afterward whether she had signed the words, shouted them, or simply thought them.

Cathy shrugged in a miserable attempt at nonchalance, and one tear slid down her cheek. "He went to see you in New York," she challenged, her hands moving quickly now, almost angrily. "You wrote to him."

"Cathy, it wasn't what you think—"

"Wasn't it?"

Libby was furious and wounded, and she stomped one foot in frustration. "Of course it wasn't! Do you really think I would do a thing like that? Do you think Stacey would? He *loves* you!" *And so does Jess,* she lamented in silence, without knowing why that should matter.

Stubbornly Cathy averted her eyes again and shoved her hands into the pockets of her lightweight cotton jacket—a sure signal that as far as she was concerned, the conversation was over.

In desperation, Libby reached out and caught her cousin's shoulders in her hands, only to be swiftly rebuffed by an eloquent shrug. She watched, stricken to silence, as Cathy turned and hurried out of the sunporch-turned-studio and into the kitchen beyond. Just a moment later the back door slammed with a finality that made Libby ache through and through.

She ducked her head and bit her lower lip to keep the tears back. That, too, was something she had learned during Jonathan's final confinement in a children's hospital.

Just then, Jess Barlowe filled the studio doorway. Libby was aware of him in all her strained senses.

He set down her suitcases and drawing board with an unsympathetic thump. "I see you're spreading joy and good cheer as usual," he drawled in acid tones. "What, pray tell, was *that* all about?"

Libby was infuriated, and she glared at him, her hands resting on her trim rounded hips. "As if you didn't know, you heartless bastard! How could you be so mean...so thought-less..."

The fiery green eyes raked Libby's travel-rumpled form with scorn. Ignoring her aborted question, he offered one of his own. "Did you think your affair with my brother was a secret, princess?"

Libby was fairly choking on her rage and her pain. "What affair, dammit?" she shouted. "We didn't *have* an affair!"

"That isn't what Stacey says," replied Jess with impervious savagery.

Libby felt the high color that had been pounding in her face seep away. *"What?"*

"Stace is wildly in love with you, to hear him tell it. You need him and he needs you, and to hell with minor stumbling blocks like his wife!"

Libby's knees weakened and she groped blindly for the stool at her art table and then sank onto it. "My God..."

Jess's jawline was tight with brutal annoyance. "Spare me the theatrics, princess—I know why you came back here. Dammit, *don't you have a soul?*"

Libby's throat worked painfully, but her mind simply refused to form words for her to utter.

Jess crossed the room like a mountain panther, terrifying in his grace and prowess, and caught both her wrists in a furious, inescapable grasp. With his other hand he captured Libby's chin.

"Listen to me, you predatory little witch, and listen well," he hissed, his jade eyes hard, his flesh pale beneath his deep rancher's tan. "Cathy is good and decent and she loves my brother, though I can't for the life of me think why she condescends to do so. And I'll be *damned* if I'll stand by and watch you and Stacey turn her inside out! Do you understand me?"

Tears of helpless fury and outraged honor burned like fire in Libby's eyes, but she could neither speak nor move. She could only stare into the frightening face looming only inches from her own. It was a devil's face.

When Jess's tightening grasp on her chin made it clear that he would have an answer of some sort, no matter what, Libby managed a small, frantic nod.

Apparently satisfied, Jess released her with such suddenness that she nearly lost her balance and slipped off the stool.

Then he whirled away from her, his broad back taut, one powerful hand running through his obsidian hair in a typical gesture of frustration. "Damn you for ever coming back here," he said in a voice no less vicious for its softness.

"No problem," Libby said with great effort. "I'll leave."

Jess turned toward her again, this time with an ominous leisure, and his eyes scalded Libby's face, the hollow of her throat, the firm roundness of her high breasts. "It's too late," he said.

Still dazed, Libby sank back against the edge of the drawing table, sighed and covered her eyes with one hand. "Okay," she began with hard-won, shaky reason, "why is that?"

Jess had stalked to the windows; his back was a barrier between them again, and he was looking out at the pond. Libby longed to sprout claws and tear him to quivering shreds.

"Stacey has the bit in his teeth," he said at length, his voice low, speculative. "Wherever you went, he'd follow."

Since Libby didn't believe that Stacey had declared himself to be in love with her, she didn't believe that there was any danger of his following her away from the Circle Bar B, either. "You're crazy," she said.

Jess faced her quickly, some scathing retort brewing in his eyes, but whatever he had meant to say was lost as Ken strode into the room and demanded, "What the hell's going on in here? I just found Cathy running up the road in tears!"

"Ask your daughter!" Jess bit out. "Thanks to her, Cathy has just gotten *started* shedding tears!"

Libby could bear no more; she was like a wild creature goaded to madness, and she flung herself bodily at Jess Barlowe, just as she had in her childhood, fists flying. She would have attacked him gladly if her father hadn't caught hold of her around the waist and forcibly restrained her.

Jess raked her with one last contemptuous look and moved calmly in the direction of the door. "You ought to tame that little spitfire, Ken," he commented in passing. "One of these days she's going to hurt somebody."

Libby trembled in her father's hold, stung by his double meaning, and gave one senseless shriek of fury. This brought a mocking chuckle from a disappearing Jess and caused Ken to turn her firmly to face him.

"Good Lord, Libby, what's the *matter* with you?"

Libby drew a deep, steadying breath and tried to quiet the raging ten-year-old within her, the child that Jess had always been able to infuriate. "I hate Jess Barlow," she said flatly. "I hate him."

"Why?" Ken broke in, and he didn't look angry anymore. Just honestly puzzled.

"If you knew what he's been saying about me—"

"If it's the same as what Stacey's been mouthing off about, I reckon I do."

Libby stepped back, stunned. "What?"

Ken Kincaid sighed, and suddenly all his fifty-two years showed clearly in his face. "Stacey and Cathy have been having trouble the last year or so. Now he's telling everybody who'll listen that it's over between him and Cathy and he wants you."

"I don't believe it! I—"

"I wanted to warn you, Lib, but you'd been through so much, between losing the boy and then falling out with your husband after that. I thought you needed to be home, but I knew you wouldn't come near the place if you had any idea what was going on."

Libby's chin trembled, and she searched her father's honest, weathered face anxiously. "I...I haven't been fooling around with C-Cathy's husband, Dad."

He smiled gently. "I know that, Lib—knew it all along. Just never mind Jess and all the rest of them—if you don't run away, this thing'll blow over."

Libby swallowed, thinking of Cathy and the pain she had to be feeling. The betrayal. "I can't stay here if Cathy is going to be hurt."

Ken touched her cheek with a work-worn finger. "Cathy doesn't really believe the rumors, Libby—think about it. Why would she work so hard to fix a studio up for you if she did? Why would she be waiting here to see you again?"

"But she was crying just now, Dad! And she as much as accused me of carrying on with her husband!"

"She's been hurt by what's been said, and Stacey's been acting like a spoiled kid. Honey, Cathy's just testing the waters, trying to find out where you stand. You can't leave her now, because except for Stace, there's nobody she needs more."

Despite the fact that all her instincts warned her to put the Circle Bar B behind her as soon as humanly possible, Libby saw the sense in her father's words. As incredible as it seemed, Cathy would need her—if for nothing else than to lay those wretched rumors to rest once and for all.

"These things Stacey's been saying—surely he didn't unload them on Cathy?"

Ken sighed. "I don't think he'd be that low, Libby. But you know how it is with Cathy, how she always knows the score."

Libby shook her head distractedly. "Somebody told her, Dad—and I think I know who it was."

There was disbelief in Ken's discerning blue eyes, and in his voice, too. "*Jess?* Now, wait a minute…"

Jess.

Libby couldn't remember a time when she had gotten along well with him, but she'd been sure that he cared deeply for Cathy. Hadn't he been the one to insist that Stace and Libby learn signing, as he had, so that everyone could talk to the frightened, confused little girl who couldn't hear? Hadn't he gifted Cathy with cherished bullfrogs and clumsily made valentines and even taken her to the high-school prom?

How could Jess, of all people, be the one to hurt Cathy, when he knew as well as anyone how badly she'd been hurt by her handicap and the rejection of her own parents? How?

Libby had no answer for any of these questions. She knew only that she had separate scores to settle with both the Barlowe brothers.

And settle them she would.

Chapter 2

Libby sat at the end of the rickety swimming dock, bare feet dangling, shoulders slumped, her gaze fixed on the shimmering waters of the pond. The lines of her long, slender legs were accentuated, rather than disguised, by the old blue jeans she wore. A white eyelet suntop sheltered shapely breasts and a trim stomach and left the rest of her upper body bare.

Jess Barlowe studied her in silence, feeling things that were at wide variance with his personal opinion of the woman. He was certain that he hated Libby, but something inside him wanted, nonetheless, to touch her, to comfort her, to know the scent and texture of her skin.

A reluctant grin tilted one corner of his mouth. One tug at the top of that white eyelet and...

Jess caught his skittering thoughts, marshaled them back into stern order. As innocent and vulnerable as Libby Kincaid looked at the moment, she was a viper, willing to betray her own cousin to get what she wanted.

Jess imagined Libby naked, her glorious breasts free and welcoming. But the man in his mental scenario was not himself—it was Stacey. The thought lay sour in Jess's mind.

"Did you come to apologize, by any chance?"

The question so startled Jess that he flinched; he had not noticed that Libby had turned around and seen him, so caught up had he been in the vision of her giving herself to his brother.

He scowled, as much to recover his wits as to oppose her. It was and always had been his nature to oppose Libby Kincaid, the way electricity opposes water, and it annoyed him that, for all his travels and his education, he didn't know why.

"Why would I want to do that?" he shot back, more ruffled by her presence than he ever would have admitted.

"Maybe because you were a complete ass," she replied in tones as sunny as the big sky stretched out above them.

Jess lifted his hands to his hips and stood fast against whatever it was that was pulling him toward her. *I want to make love to you,* he thought, and the truth of that ground in his spirit as well as in his loins.

There was pain in Libby's navy blue eyes, as well as a cautious mischief. "Well?" she prodded.

Jess found that while he could keep himself from going to her, he could not turn away. Maybe her net reached farther than he'd thought. Maybe, like Stacey and that idiot in New York, he was already caught in it.

"I'm not here to apologize," he said coldly.

"Then why?" she asked with chiming sweetness.

He wondered if she knew what that shoulderless blouse of hers was doing to him. Damn. He hadn't been this tongue-tied since the night of his fifteenth birthday, when Ginny Hillerman had announced that she would show him hers if he would show her his.

Libby's eyes were laughing at him. "Jess?"

"Is your dad here?" he threw out in gruff desperation.

One shapely, gossamer eyebrow arched. "You know perfectly well that he isn't. If Dad were home, his pickup truck would be parked in the driveway."

Against his will, Jess grinned. His taut shoulders rose in a shrug. The shadows of cottonwood leaves moved on the old wooden dock, forming a mystical path—a path that led to Libby Kincaid.

She patted the sun-warmed wood beside her. "Come and sit down."

Before Jess could stop himself, he was striding along that small wharf, sinking down to sit beside Libby and dangle his booted feet over the sparkling water. He was never entirely certain what sorcery made him ask what he did.

"What happened to your marriage, Libby?"

The pain he had glimpsed before leapt in her eyes and then faded away again, subdued. "Are you trying to start another fight?"

Jess shook his head. "No," he answered quietly, "I really want to know."

She looked away from him, gnawing at her lower lip with her front teeth. All around them were ranch sounds—birds conferring in the trees, leaves rustling in the wind, the clear pond water lapping at the mossy pilings of the dock. But no sound came from Libby.

On an impulse, Jess touched her mouth with the tip of one index finger. Water and electricity—the analogy came back to him with a numbing jolt.

"Stop that," he barked, to cover his reactions.

Libby ceased chewing at her lip and stared at him with

wide eyes. Again he saw the shadow of that nameless, shifting ache inside her. "Stop what?" she wanted to know.

Stop making me want to hold you, he thought. *Stop making me want to tuck your hair back behind your ears and tell you that everything will be all right.* "Stop biting your lip!" he snapped aloud.

"I'm sorry!" Libby snapped back, her eyes shooting indigo sparks.

Jess sighed and again spoke involuntarily. "Why did you leave your husband, Libby?"

The question jarred them both: Libby paled a little and tried to scramble to her feet; Jess caught her elbow in one hand and pulled her down again.

"Was it because of Stacey?"

She was livid. "No!"

"Someone else?"

Tears sprang up in Libby's dark lashes and made then spiky. She wrenched free of his hand but made no move to rise again and run away. "Sure!" she gasped. "'If it feels good, do it'—that's my motto! By God, I *live* by those words!"

"Shut up," Jess said in a gentle voice.

Incredibly, she fell against him, wept into the shoulder of his blue cotton workshirt. And it was not a delicate, calculating sort of weeping—it was a noisy grief.

Jess drew her close and held her, broken on the shoals of what she was feeling even though he did not know its name. "I'm sorry," he said hoarsely.

Libby trembled beneath his arm and wailed like a wounded calf. The sound solidified into a word usually reserved for stubborn horses and income-tax audits.

Jess laughed and, for a reason he would never understand, kissed her forehead. "I love it when you flatter me," he teased.

Miraculously, Libby laughed, too. But when she tilted her

head back to look up at him, and he saw the tear streaks on her beautiful, defiant face, something within him, something that had always been disjointed, was wrenched painfully back into place.

He bent his head and touched his lips to hers, gently, in question. She stiffened, but then, at the cautious bidding of his tongue, her lips parted slightly and her body relaxed against his.

Jess pressed Libby backward until she lay prone on the shifting dock, the kiss unbroken. As she responded to that kiss, it seemed that the sparkling water-light of the pond danced around them both in huge, shimmering chips, that they were floating inside some cosmic prism.

His hand went to the full roundness of her left breast. Beneath his palm and the thin layer of white eyelet, he felt the nipple grow taut in that singular invitation to passion.

Through the back of his shirt, Jess was warmed by the heat of the spring sun and the tender weight of Libby's hands. He left her mouth to trail soft kisses over her chin, along the sweet, scented lines of her neck.

All the while, he expected her to stiffen again, to thrust him away with her hands and some indignant—and no doubt colorful—outburst. Instead, she was pliant and yielding beneath him.

Enthralled, he dared more and drew downward on the uppermost ruffle of her suntop. Still she did not protest.

Libby arched her back and a low, whimpering sound came from her throat as Jess bared her to the soft spring breeze and the fire of his gaze.

Her breasts were heavy golden-white globes, and their pale rose crests stiffened as Jess perused them. When he offered a whisper-soft kiss to one, Libby moaned and the other peak pouted prettily at his choice. He went to it, soothed it to fury with his tongue.

Libby gave a soft, lusty cry, shuddered and caught her hands in his hair, drawing him closer. He needed more of her and positioned his body accordingly, careful not to let his full weight come to bear. Then, for a few dizzying moments, he took suckle at the straining fount of her breast.

Recovering himself partially, Jess pulled her hands from his hair, gripped them at the wrists, pressed them down above her head in gentle restraint.

Her succulent breasts bore his assessment proudly, rising and falling with the meter of her breathing.

Jess forced himself to meet Libby's eyes. "This is me," he reminded her gruffly. "Jess."

"I know," she whispered, making no move to free her imprisoned hands.

Jess lowered his head, tormented one delectable nipple by drawing at it with his lips. "This is real, Libby," he said, circling the morsel with just the tip of his tongue now. "It's important that you realize that."

"I do…oh, God…Jess, *Jess*."

Reluctantly he left the feast to search her face with disbelieving eyes. "Don't you want me to stop?"

A delicate shade of rose sifted over her high cheekbones. Her hands still stretched above her, her eyes closed, she shook her head.

Jess went back to the breasts that so bewitched him, nipped at their peaks with gentle teeth. "Do you…know how many…times I've wanted…to do this?"

The answer was a soft, strangled cry.

He limited himself to one nipple, worked its surrendering peak into a sweet fervor with his lips and his tongue. "So… many…times. My God, Libby…you're so beautiful…."

Her words were as halting as his had been. "What's happening to us? We h-hate each other."

Jess laughed and began kissing his way softly down over her rib cage, her smooth, firm stomach. The snap on her jeans gave way easily—and was echoed by the sound of car doors slamming in the area of the house.

Instantly the spell was broken. Color surged into Libby's face and she bolted upright, nearly thrusting Jess off the end of the dock in her efforts to wrench on the discarded suntop and close the fastening of her jeans.

"Broad daylight…" she muttered distractedly, talking more to herself than to Jess.

"Lib!" yelled a jovial masculine voice, approaching fast. "Libby?"

Stacey. The voice belonged to Stacey.

Sudden fierce anger surged, white-hot, through Jess's aching, bedazzled system. Standing up, not caring that his thwarted passion still strained against his jeans, visible to anyone who might take the trouble to look, he glared down at Libby and rasped, "I guess reinforcements have arrived."

She gave a primitive, protesting little cry and shot to her feet, her ink-blue eyes flashing with anger and hurt. Before Jess could brace himself, her hands came to his chest like small battering rams and pushed him easily off the end of the dock.

The jolting cold of that spring-fed pond was welcome balm to Jess's passion-heated flesh, if not his pride. When he surfaced and grasped the end of the dock in both hands, he knew there would be no physical evidence that he and Libby had been doing anything other than fighting.

Libby ached with embarrassment as Stacey and Senator Barlowe made their way down over the slight hillside that separated the backyard from the pond.

The older man cast one mischievously baleful look at his

younger son, who was lifting himself indignantly onto the dock, and chuckled, "I see things are the same as always," he said.

Libby managed a shaky smile. *Not quite,* she thought, her body remembering the delicious dance Jess's hard frame had choreographed for it. "Hello, Senator," she said, rising on tiptoe to kiss his cheek.

"Welcome home," he replied with gruff affection. Then his wise eyes shifted past her to rest again on Jess. "It's a little cold yet for a swim, isn't it, son?"

Jess's hair hung in dripping ebony strands around his face, and his eyes were jade-green flares, avoiding his father to scald Libby's lips, her throat, her still-pulsing breasts. "We'll finish our...discussion later," he said.

Libby's blood boiled up over her stomach and her breasts to glow in her face. "I wouldn't count on that!"

"I would," Jess replied with a smile that was at once tender and evil. And then, without so much as a word to his father and brother, he walked away.

"What the hell did he mean by that?" barked Stacey, red in the face.

The look Libby gave the boyishly handsome, caramel-eyed man beside her was hardly friendly. "You've got some tall explaining to do, Stacey Barlowe," she said.

The senator, a tall, attractive man with hair as gray as Ken's, cleared his throat in the way of those who have practiced diplomacy long and well. "I believe I'll go up to the house and see if Ken's got any beer on hand," he said. A moment later he was off, following Jess's soggy path.

Libby straightened her shoulders and calmly slapped Stacey across the face. "How dare you?" she raged, her words strangled in her effort to modulate them.

Stacey reddened again, ran one hand through his fashionably cut wheat-colored hair. He turned, as if to follow his father. "I could use a beer myself," he said in distracted, evasive tones.

"Oh, no you don't!" Libby cried, grasping his arm and holding on. The rich leather of his jacket was smooth under her hand. "Don't you *dare* walk away from me, Stacey—not until you explain why you've been lying about me!"

"I haven't been lying!" he protested, his hands on his hips now, his expensively clad body blocking the base of the dock as he faced her.

"You have! You've been telling everyone that I… That we…"

"That we've been doing what you and my brother were doing a few minutes ago?"

If Stacey had shoved Libby into the water, she couldn't have been more shocked. A furious retort rose to the back of her throat but would go no further.

Stacey's tarnished-gold eyes flashed. "Jess was making love to you, wasn't he?"

"What if he was?" managed Libby after a painful struggle with her vocal cords. "It certainly wouldn't be any of your business, would it?"

"Yes, it would. I love you, Libby."

"You love *Cathy!*"

Stacey shook his head. "No. Not anymore."

"Don't say that," Libby pleaded, suddenly deflated. "Oh, Stacey, don't. Don't do this…."

His hands came to her shoulders, fierce and strong. The topaz fever in his eyes made Libby wonder if he was sane. "I love you, Libby Kincaid," he vowed softly but ferociously, "and I mean to have you."

Libby retreated a step, stunned, shaking her head. The

reality of this situation was so different from what she had imagined it would be. In her thoughts, Stacey had laughed when she confronted him, ruffled her hair in that familiar brotherly way of old, and said that it was all a mistake. That he loved Cathy, wanted Cathy, and couldn't anyone around here take a joke?

But here he was declaring himself in a way that was unsettlingly serious.

Libby took another step backward. "Stacey, I need to be here, where my dad is. Where things are familiar and comfortable. Please...don't force me to leave."

Stacey smiled. "There is no point in leaving, Lib. If you do, I'll be right behind you."

She shivered. "You've lost your mind!"

But Stacey looked entirely sane as he shook his handsome head and wedged his hands into the pockets of his jacket. "Just my heart," he said. "Corny, isn't it?"

"It's worse than corny. Stacey, you're unbalanced or something. You're fantasizing. There was never anything between us—"

"No?" The word was crooned.

"No! You need help."

His face had all the innocence of an altar boy's. "If I'm insane, darlin', it's something you could cure."

Libby resisted an urge to slap him again. She wanted to race into the house, but he was still barring her way, so that she could not leave the dock without brushing against him. "Stay away from me, Stacey," she said as he advanced toward her. "I mean it—stay away from me!"

"I can't, Libby."

The sincerity in his voice was chilling; for the first time in all the years she'd known Stacey Barlowe, Libby was afraid of him. Discretion kept her from screaming, but just barely.

Stacey paled, as though he'd read her thoughts. "Don't look at me like that, Libby—I wouldn't hurt you under any circumstances. And I'm not crazy."

She lifted her chin. "Let me by, Stacey. I want to go into the house."

He tilted his head back, sighed, met her eyes again. "I've frightened you, and I'm sorry. I didn't mean to do that."

Libby couldn't speak. Despite his rational, settling words, she was sick with the knowledge that he meant to pursue her.

"You must know," he said softly, "how good it could be for us. You needed me in New York, Libby, and now I need you."

The third voice, from the base of the hillside, was to Libby as a life preserver to a drowning person. "Let her pass, Stacey."

Libby looked up quickly to see Jess, unlikely rescuer that he was. His hair was towel-rumpled and his jeans clung to muscular thighs—thighs that only minutes ago had pressed against her own in a demand as old as time. His manner was calm as he buttoned a shirt, probably borrowed from Ken, over his broad chest.

Stacey shrugged affably and walked past his brother without a word of argument.

Watching him go, Libby went weak with relief. A lump rose in her throat as she forced herself to meet Jess's gaze. "You were right," she muttered miserably. "You were *right.*"

Jess was watching her much the way a mountain cat would watch a cornered rabbit. For the briefest moment there was a look of tenderness in the green eyes, but then his expression turned hard and a muscle flexed in his jaw. "I trust the welcome-home party has been scheduled for later—after Cathy has been tucked into her bed, for instance?"

Libby gaped at him, appalled. Had he interceded only to torment her himself?

Jess's eyes were contemptuous as they swept over her. "What's the matter, Lib? Couldn't you bring yourself to tell your married lover that the welcoming had already been taken care of?"

Rage went through Libby's body like an electric current surging into a wire. "You don't seriously think that I would... That I was—"

"You even managed to be alone with him. Tell me, Lib— how did you get rid of my father?"

"G-get rid..." Libby stopped, tears of shock and mortification aching in her throat and burning behind her eyes. She drew a deep, audible breath, trying to assemble herself, to think clearly.

But the whole world seemed to be tilting and swirling like some out-of-control carnival ride. When Libby closed her eyes against the sensation, she swayed dangerously and would probably have fallen if Jess hadn't reached her in a few strides and caught her shoulders in his hands.

"Libby..." he said, and there was anger in the sound, but there was a hollow quality, too—one that Libby couldn't find a name for.

Her knees were trembling. Too much, it was all too much. Jonathan's death, the ugly divorce, the trouble that Stacey had caused with his misplaced affections—all of those things weighed on her, but none were so crushing as the blatant contempt of this man. It was apparent to Libby now that the lovemaking they had almost shared, so new and beautiful to her, had been some sort of cruel joke to Jess.

"How could you?" she choked out. "Oh, Jess, how could you?"

His face was grim, seeming to float in a shimmering mist.

Instead of answering, Jess lifted Libby into his arms and carried her up the little hill toward the house.

She didn't remember reaching the back door.

* * *

"What the devil happened on that dock today, Jess?" Cleave Barlowe demanded, hands grasping the edge of his desk.

His younger son stood at the mahogany bar, his shoulders stiff, his attention carefully fixed on the glass of straight Scotch he meant to consume. "Why don't you ask Stacey?"

"Goddammit, I'm asking *you!*" barked Cleave. "Ken's mad as hell, and I don't blame him—that girl of his was shattered!"

Girl. The word caught in Jess's beleaguered mind. He remembered the way Libby had responded to him, meeting his passion with her own, welcoming the greed he'd shown at her breasts. Had it not been for the arrival of his father and brother, he would have possessed her completely within minutes. "She's no 'girl,'" he said, still aching to bury himself in the depths of her.

The senator swore roundly. "What did you say to her, Jess?" he pressed, once the spate of unpoliticianly profanity had passed.

Jess lowered his head. He'd meant the things he'd said to Libby, and he couldn't, in all honesty, have taken them back. But he knew some of what she'd been through in New York, her trysts with Stacey notwithstanding, and he was ashamed of the way he'd goaded her. She had come home to heal—the look in her eyes had told him that much—and instead of respecting that, he had made things more difficult for her.

Never one to be thwarted by silence, no matter how eloquent, Senator Barlowe persisted. "Dammit, Jess, I might expect this kind of thing from Stacey, but I thought you had more sense! You were harassing Libby about these blasted rumors your brother has been spreading, weren't you?"

Jess sighed, set aside the drink he had yet to take a sip from, and faced his angry father. "Yes," he said.

"Why?"

Stubbornly, Jess refused to answer. He took an interest in the imposing oak desk where his father sat, the heavy draperies that kept out the sun, the carved ivory of the fireplace.

"All right, mulehead," Cleave muttered furiously, "don't talk! Don't explain! And don't go near Ken Kincaid's daughter again, damn you. That man's the best foreman I've ever had and if he gets riled and quits because of you, Jess, you and I are going to come to time!"

Jess almost smiled, though he didn't quite dare. Not too many years before the phrase "come to time," when used by his father, had presaged a session in the woodshed. He wondered what it meant now that he was thirty-three years old, a member of the Montana State Bar Association, and a full partner in the family corporation. "I care about Cathy," he said evenly. "What was I supposed to do—stand by and watch Libby and Stace grind her up into emotional hamburger?"

Cleave gave a heavy sigh and sank into the richly upholstered swivel chair behind his desk. "I love Cathy, too," he said at length, "but Stacey's behind this whole mess, not Libby. Dammit, that woman has been through hell from what Ken says—she was married to a man who slept in every bed but his own, and she had to watch her nine-year-old stepson die by inches. Now she comes home looking for a little peace, and what does she get? Trouble!"

Jess lowered his head, turned away—ostensibly to take up his glass of Scotch. He'd known about the bad marriage—Ken had cussed the day Aaron Strand was born often enough—but he hadn't heard about the little boy. My God, he hadn't known about the boy.

"Maybe Strand couldn't sleep in his own bed," he said, urged on by some ugliness that had surfaced inside him since Libby's return. "Maybe Stacey was already in it."

"Enough!" boomed the senator in a voice that had made presidents tremble in their shoes. "I like Libby and I'm not going to listen to any more of this, either from you or from your brother! Do I make myself clear?"

"Abundantly clear," replied Jess, realizing that the Scotch was in his hand now and feeling honor-bound to take at least one gulp of the stuff. The taste was reminiscent of scorched rubber, but since the liquor seemed to quiet the raging demons in his mind, he finished the drink and poured another.

He fully intended to get drunk. It was something he hadn't done since high school, but it suddenly seemed appealing. Maybe he would stop hardening every time he thought of Libby, stop craving her.

Too, after the things he'd said to her that afternoon by the pond, he didn't want to remain sober any longer than necessary. "What did you mean," he ventured, after downing his fourth drink, "when you said Libby had to watch her stepson die?"

Papers rustled at the big desk behind him. "Stacey says the child had leukemia."

Jess poured another drink and closed his eyes. *Oh, Libby,* he thought, *I'm sorry. My God, I'm sorry.* "I guess Stacey would know," he said aloud, with bitterness.

There was a short, thunderous silence. Jess expected his father to explode into one of his famous tirades, was genuinely surprised when the man sighed instead. Still, his words dropped on Jess's mind like a bomb.

"The firewater isn't going to change the fact that you love Libby Kincaid, Jess," he said reasonably. "Making her life and your own miserable isn't going to change it, either."

Love Libby Kincaid? Impossible. The strange needs possessing him now were rooted in his libido, not his heart. Once he'd had her—and have her he would, or go crazy—her hold on him would be broken. "I've never loved a woman in my life," he said.

"Fool. You've loved one woman—Libby—since you were seven years old. Exactly seven years old, in fact."

Jess turned, studying his father quizzically. "What the hell are you talking about?"

"Your seventh birthday," recalled Cleave, his eyes far away. "Your mother and I gave you a pony. First time you saw Libby Kincaid, you were out of that saddle and helping her into it."

The memory burst, full-blown, into Jess's mind. A pinto pony. The new foreman arriving. The little girl with dark blue eyes and hair the color of winter moonlight.

He'd spent the whole afternoon squiring Libby around the yard, content to walk while she rode.

"What do you suppose Ken would say if I went over there and asked to see his daughter?" Jess asked.

"I imagine he'd shoot you, after today."

"I imagine he would. But I think I'll risk it."

"You've made enough trouble for one day," argued Cleave, taking obvious note of his son's inebriated state. "Libby needs time, Jess. She needs to be close to Ken. If you're smart, you'll leave her alone until she has a chance to get her emotional bearings again."

Jess didn't want his father to be right, not in this instance, anyway, but he knew that he was. Much as he wanted to go to Libby and try to make things right, the fact was that he was the last person in the world she needed or wanted to see.

"Better?"

Libby smiled at Ken as she came into the kitchen, freshly showered and wrapped in the cozy, familiar chenille robe she'd found in the back of her closet. "Lots better," she answered softly.

Her father was standing at the kitchen stove stirring something in the blackened cast-iron skillet.

Libby scuffled to the table and sat down. It was good to be home, so good. Why hadn't she come sooner? "Whatever you're cooking there smells good," she said.

Ken beamed. In his jeans and his western shirt, he looked out of place at that stove. He should, Libby decided fancifully, have been crouching at some campfire on the range, stirring beans in a blue enamel pot. "This here's my world-famous red-devil sauce," he grinned, "for which I am known and respected."

Libby laughed, and tears of homecoming filled her eyes. She went to her father and hugged him, needing to be a little girl again, just for a moment.

Chapter 3

Libby nearly choked on her first taste of Ken's taco sauce. "Did you say you were known and respected for this stuff, or known and feared?"

Ken chuckled roguishly at her tear-polished eyes and flaming face. "My calling it 'red devil' should have been a clue, dumplin'."

Libby muttered an exclamation and perversely took another bite from her bulging taco. "From now on," she said, chewing, "I'll do the cooking around this spread."

Her father laughed again and tapped one temple with a calloused index finger, his pale blue eyes twinkling.

"You deliberately tricked me!" cried Libby.

He grinned and shrugged. "Code of the West, sweetheart. Grouse about the chow, and presto—you're the cook!"

"Actually," ventured Libby with cultivated innocence, "this sauce isn't too bad."

"Too late," laughed Ken. "You already broke the code."

Libby lowered her taco to her plate and lifted both hands in a gesture of concession. "All right, all right—but have a little pity on me, will you? I've been living among dudes!"

"That's no excuse."

Libby shrugged and took up her taco again. "I tried. Have you been doing your own cooking and cleaning all this time?"

Ken shook his head and sat back in his chair, his thumbs hooked behind his belt buckle. "Nope. The Barlowes' housekeeper sends her crew down here once in a while."

"What about the food?"

"I eat with the boys most of the time, over at the cook shack." He rose, went to fill two mugs from the coffeepot on the stove. When he turned around again, his face was serious. "Libby, what happened today? What upset you like that?"

Libby averted her eyes. "I don't know," she lied lamely.

"Dammit, you *do* know. You fainted, Libby. When Jess carried you in here, I—"

"I know," Libby broke in gently. "You were scared. I'm sorry."

Carefully, as though he feared he might drop them, Ken set the cups of steaming coffee on the table. "What happened?" he persisted as he sat down in his chair again.

Libby swallowed hard, but the lump that had risen in her throat wouldn't go down. Knowing that this conversation couldn't be avoided forever, she managed to reply, "It's complicated. Basically, it comes down to the fact that Stacey's been telling those lies."

"And?"

"And Jess believes him. He said…he said some things to me and…well, it must have created some kind of emotional overload. I just gave out."

Ken turned his mug idly between his thumb and index

finger, causing the liquid to spill over and make a coffee stain on the tablecloth. "Tell me about Jonathan, Libby," he said in a low, gentle voice.

The tears that sprang into Libby's eyes were not related to the tang of her father's red-devil taco sauce. "He died," she choked miserably.

"I know that. You called me the night it happened, remember? I guess what I'm really asking you is why you didn't want me to fly back there and help you sort things out."

Libby lowered her head. Jonathan hadn't been her son, he'd been Aaron's, by a previous marriage. But the loss of the child was a raw void within her, even though months had passed. "I didn't want you to get a firsthand look at my marriage," she admitted with great difficulty—and the shame she couldn't seem to shake.

"Why not, Libby?"

The sound Libby made might have been either a laugh or a sob. "Because it was terrible," she answered.

"From the first?"

She forced herself to meet her father's steady gaze, knew that he had guessed a lot about her marriage from her rare phone calls and even rarer letters. "Almost," she replied sadly.

"Tell me."

Libby didn't want to think about Aaron, let alone talk about him to this man who wouldn't understand so many things. "He had…he had lovers."

Ken didn't seem surprised. Had he guessed that, too? "Go on."

"I can't!"

"Yes, you can. If it's too much for you right now, I won't press you. But the sooner you talk this out, Libby, the better off you're going to be."

She realized that her hands were clenched in her lap and

tried to relax them. There was still a white mark on her finger where Aaron's ostentatious wedding ring had been. "He didn't care," she mourned in a soft, distracted whisper. "He honestly didn't care...."

"About you?"

"About Jonathan. Dad, he didn't care about his own son!"

"How so, sweetheart?"

Libby dashed away tears with the back of one hand. "Th-things were bad between Aaron and me b-before we found out that Jonathan was sick. After the doctors told us, it was a lot worse."

"I don't follow you, Libby."

"Dad, Aaron wouldn't have anything to do with Jonathan from the moment we knew he was dying. He wasn't there for any of the tests and he never once came to visit at the hospital. Dad, that little boy cried for his father, and Aaron wouldn't come to him!"

"Did you talk to Aaron?"

Remembered frustration made Libby's cheeks pound with color. "I *pleaded* with him, Dad. All he'd say was, 'I can't handle this.'"

"It would be a hell of a thing to deal with, Lib. Maybe you're being too hard on the man."

"Too hard? *Too hard?* Jonathan was terrified, Dad, and he was in pain—constant pain. All he asked was that his own father be strong for him!"

"What about the boy's mother? Did she come to the hospital?"

"Ellen died when Jonathan was a baby."

Ken sighed, framing a question he was obviously reluctant to ask. "Did you ever love Aaron Strand, Libby?"

Libby remembered the early infatuation, the excitement that had never deepened into real love and had quickly been

quelled by the realities of marriage to a man who was funda-
mentally self-centered. She tried, but she couldn't even recall
her ex-husband's face clearly—all she could see in her mind
was a pair of jade-green eyes, dark hair. Jess. "No," she finally
said. "I thought I did when I married him, though."

Ken stood up suddenly, took the coffeepot from its back
burner on the stove, refilled both their cups. "I don't like
asking you this, but—"

"No, Dad," Libby broke in firmly, anticipating the question
all too well, "I don't love Stacey!"

"You're sure about that?"

The truth was that Libby *hadn't* been sure, not entirely. But
that ill-advised episode with Jess at the end of the swimming
dock had brought everything into clear perspective. Just remembering how willingly she had submitted to him made her
throb with embarrassment. "I'm sure," she said.

Ken's strong hand came across the table to close over hers.
"You're home now," he reminded her, "and things are going
to get better, Libby. I promise you that."

Libby sniffled inelegantly. "Know something, cowboy? I
love you very much."

"Bet you say that to all your fathers," Ken quipped. "You
planning to work on your comic strip tomorrow?"

The change of subject was welcome. "I'm six or eight
weeks ahead of schedule on that, so I'm not worried about
my deadline. I think I'll go riding, if I can get Cathy to go with
me."

"I was looking forward to watching you work. What's
your process?"

Libby smiled, feeling sheltered by the love of this strong
and steady man facing her. She explained how her cartoons
came into being, thinking it was good to talk about work, to
think about work.

Disdainful as he had been about her career, it was the one thing Aaron had not been able to spoil for her.

Nobody's fool, Ken drew her out on the subject as much as he could, and she found herself chattering on and on about cartooning and even her secret hope to branch out into portraits one day.

They talked, father and daughter, far into the night.

"You deserve this," Jess Barlowe said to his reflection in the bathroom mirror. A first-class hangover pounded in his head and roiled in his stomach, and his face looked drawn, as though he'd been hibernating like one of the bears that sometimes troubled the range stock.

Grimly he began to shave, and as he wielded his disposable razor, he wondered if Libby was awake yet. Should he stop at Ken's and talk to her before going on to the main house to spend a day with the corporation accountants?

Jess wanted to go to Libby, to tell her that he was sorry for baiting her, to try to get their complex relationship—if it *was* a relationship—onto some kind of sane ground. However, all his instincts told him that his father had been right the day before: Libby needed time.

His thoughts strayed to Libby's stepson. What would it be like to sit by a hospital bed, day after day, watching a child suffer and not being able to help?

Jess shuddered. It was hard to imagine the horror of something like that. At least Libby had had her husband to share the nightmare.

He frowned as he nicked his chin with the razor, blotted the small wound with tissue paper. If Libby had had her husband during that impossible time, why had she needed Stacey?

Stacey. Now, there was someone he could talk to. Granted,

Jess had not been on the best of terms with his older brother of late, but the man had a firsthand knowledge of what was happening inside Libby Kincaid, and that was reason enough to approach him.

Feeling better for having a plan, Jess finished his ablutions and got dressed. Normally he spent his days on the range with Ken and the ranch hands, but today, because of his meeting with the accountants, he forwent his customary blue jeans and cotton workshirt for a tailored three-piece suit. He was still struggling with his tie as he made his way down the broad redwood steps that led from the loftlike second floor of his house to the living room.

Here there was a massive fireplace of white limestone, taking up the whole of one wall. The floors were polished oak and boasted a number of brightly colored Indian rugs. Two easy chairs and a deep sofa faced the hearth, and Jess's cluttered desk looked out over the ranchland and the glacial mountains beyond.

Striding toward the front door, in exasperation he gave up his efforts to get the tie right. He was glad he didn't have Stacey's job; not for him the dull task of overseeing the family's nationwide chain of steak-house franchises.

He smiled. Stacey liked playing the dude, doing television commercials, traveling all over the country.

And taking Libby Kincaid to bed.

Jess stalked across the front lawn to the carport and climbed behind the wheel of the truck he'd driven since law school. One of these times, he was going to have to get another car—something with a little flash, like Stacey's Ferrari.

Stacey, Stacey. He hadn't even seen his brother yet, and already he was sick of him.

The truck's engine made a grinding sound and then huffed to life. Jess patted the dusty dashboard affectionately and grinned. A car was a car was a car, he reflected as he backed the notorious wreck out of his driveway. The function of a car was to transport people, not impress them.

Five minutes later, Jess's truck chortled to an asthmatic stop beside his brother's ice-blue Ferrari. He looked up at the modernistic two-story house that had been the senator's wedding gift to Stacey and Cathy and wondered if Libby would be impressed by the place.

He scowled as he made his way up the curving white-stone walk. What the hell did he care if Libby was impressed?

Irritated, he jabbed one finger at the special doorbell that would turn on a series of blinking lights inside the house. The system had been his own idea, meant to make life easier for Cathy.

His sister-in-law came to the door and smiled at him somewhat wanly, speaking with her hands. "Good morning."

Jess nodded, smiled. The haunted look in the depths of Cathy's eyes made him angry all over again. "Is Stacey here?" he signed, stepping into the house.

Cathy caught his hand in her own and led him through the cavernous living room and the formal dining room beyond. Stacey was in the kitchen, looking more at home in a three-piece suit than Jess ever had.

"You," Stacey said tonelessly, setting down the English muffin he'd been slathering with honey.

Cathy offered coffee and left the room when it was politely declined. Distractedly Jess reflected on the fact that her life had to be boring as hell, centering on Stacey the way it did.

"I want to talk to you," Jess said, scraping back a chrome-and-plastic chair to sit down at the table.

Stacey arched one eyebrow. "I hope it's quick—I'm

leaving for the airport in a few minutes. I've got some business to take care of in Kansas City."

Jess was impatient. "What kind of man is Libby's ex-husband?" he asked.

Stacey took up his coffee. "Why do you want to know?"

"I just do. Do I have to have him checked out, or are you going to tell me?"

"He's a bastard," said Stacey, not quite meeting his brother's eyes.

"Rich?"

"Oh, yes. His family is old-money."

"What does he do?"

"Do?"

"Yeah. Does he work, or does he just stand around being rich?"

"He runs the family advertising agency; I think he has a lot of control over their other financial interests, too."

Jess sensed that Stacey was hedging, wondered why. "Any bad habits?"

Stacey was gazing at the toaster now, in a fixed way, as though he expected something alarming to pop out of it. "The man has his share of vices."

Annoyed now, Jess got up, helped himself to the cup of coffee he had refused earlier, sat down again. "Pulling porcupine quills out of a dog's nose would be easier than getting answers out of you. When you say he has vices, do you mean women?"

Stacey swallowed, looked away. "To put it mildly," he said.

Jess settled back in his chair. "What the hell do you mean by that?"

"I mean that he not only liked to run around with other women, he liked to flaunt the fact. The worse he could make Libby feel about herself, the happier he was."

"Jesus," Jess breathed. "What else?" he pressed, sensing, from Stacey's expression, that there was more.

"He was impotent with Libby."

"Why did she stay? Why in God's name did she stay?" Jess mused distractedly, as much to himself as to his brother.

A cautious but smug light flickered in Stacey's topaz eyes. "She had me," he said evenly. "Besides, Jonathan was sick by that time and she felt she had to stay in the marriage for his sake."

The spacious sun-filled kitchen seemed to buckle and shift around Jess. "Why didn't she tell Ken, at least?"

"What would have been the point in that, Jess? He couldn't have made the boy well again or transformed Aaron Strand into a devoted husband."

The things Libby must have endured—the shame, the loneliness, the humiliation and grief, washed over Jess in a dismal, crushing wave. No wonder she had reached out to Stacey the way she had. No wonder. "Thanks," he said gruffly, standing up to leave.

"Jess?"

He paused in the kitchen doorway, his hands clasping the woodwork, his shoulders aching with tension. "What?"

"Don't worry about Libby. I'll take care of her."

Jess felt a despairing sort of anger course through him. "What about Cathy?" he asked, without turning around. "Who is going to take care of her?"

"You've always—"

Jess whirled suddenly, staring at his brother, almost hating him. "I've always *what?*"

"Cared for her." Stacey shrugged, looking only mildly unsettled. "Protected her…"

"Are you suggesting that I sweep up the pieces after you shatter her?" demanded Jess in a dangerous rasp.

Stacey only shrugged again.

Because he feared that he would do his brother lasting harm if he stayed another moment, Jess stormed out of the house. Cathy, dressed in old jeans, boots and a cotton blouse, was waiting beside the truck. The pallor in her face told Jess that she knew much more about the state of her marriage than he would have hoped.

Her hands trembled a little as she spoke with them. "I'm scared, Jess."

He drew her into his arms, held her. "I know, baby," he said, even though he knew she couldn't hear him or see his lips. "I know."

Libby opened her eyes, yawned and stretched. The smells of sunshine and fresh air swept into her bedroom through the open window, ruffling pink eyelet curtains and reminding her that she was home again. She tossed back the covers on the bed and got up, sleepily making her way into the bathroom and starting the water for a shower.

As she took off her short cotton nightshirt, she looked down at herself and remembered the raging sensations Jess Barlowe had ignited in her the day before. She had been stupid and self-indulgent to let that happen, but after several years of celibacy, she supposed it was natural that her passions had been stirred so easily—especially by a man like Jess.

As Libby showered, she felt renewed. Aaron's flagrant infidelities had been painful for her, and they had seriously damaged her self-esteem in the bargain.

Now, even though she had made a fool of herself by being wanton with a man who could barely tolerate her, many of Libby's doubts about herself as a woman had been eased, if not routed. She was not as useless and undesirable as Aaron had made her feel. She had caused Jess Barlowe to want her, hadn't she?

Big deal, she told the image in her mirror as she brushed her teeth. *How do you know Jess wasn't out to prove that his original opinion of you was on target?*

Deflated by this very real possibility, Libby combed her hair, applied the customary lip gloss and light touch of mascara and went back to her room to dress. From her suit-cases she selected a short-sleeved turquoise pullover shirt and a pair of trim jeans. Remembering her intention to find Cathy and persuade her to go riding, she ferreted through her closet until she found the worn boots she'd left behind before moving to New York, pulling them on over a pair of thick socks.

Looking down at those disreputable old boots, Libby imagined the scorn they would engender in Aaron's jet-set crowd and laughed. Problems or no problems, Jess or no Jess, it was good to be home.

Not surprisingly, the kitchen was empty. Ken had probably left the house before dawn, but there was coffee on the stove and fruit in the refrigerator, so Libby helped herself to a pear and sat down to eat.

The telephone rang just as she was finishing her second cup of coffee, and Libby answered cheerfully, thinking that the caller would be Ken or the housekeeper at the main house, relaying some message for Cathy.

She was back at the table, the receiver pressed to her ear, before Aaron spoke.

"When are you coming home?"

"Home?" echoed Libby stupidly, off-balance, unable to believe that he'd actually asked such a question. "I *am* home, Aaron."

"Enough," he replied. "You've made your point, exhibited your righteous indignation. Now you've got to get back here because I need you."

Libby wanted to hang up, but it seemed a very long way from her chair to the wall, where the rest of the telephone was. "Aaron, we are divorced," she reminded him calmly, "and I am never coming back."

"You have to," he answered, without missing a beat. "It's crucial."

"Why? What happened to all your…friends?"

Aaron sighed. "You remember Betty, don't you? Miss November? Well, Betty and I had a small disagreement, as it happens, and she went to my family. I am, shall we say, exposed as something less than an ideal spouse.

"In any case, my grandmother believes that a man who cannot run his family—she was in Paris when we divorced, darling—cannot run a company, either. I have six months to bring you back into the fold and start an heir, or the whole shooting match goes to my cousin."

Libby was too stunned to speak or even move; she simply stood in the middle of her father's kitchen, trying to absorb what Aaron was saying.

"That," Aaron went on blithely, "is where you come in, sweetheart. You come back, we smile a lot and make a baby, my grandmother's ruffled feathers are smoothed. It's as simple as that."

Sickness boiled into Libby's throat. "I don't believe this!" she whispered.

"You don't believe what, darling? That I can make a baby? May I point out that I sired Jonathan, of whom you were so cloyingly fond?"

Libby swallowed. "Get Miss November pregnant," she managed to suggest. And then she added distractedly, more to herself than Aaron, "I think I'm going to be sick."

"Don't tell me that I've been beaten to the proverbial

draw," Aaron remarked in that brutally smooth, caustic way of his. "Did the steak-house king already do the deed?"

"You are disgusting!"

"Yes, but very practical. If I don't hand my grandmother an heir, whether it's mine or the issue of that softheaded cowboy, I stand to lose millions of dollars."

Libby managed to stand up. A few steps, just a few, and she could hang up the telephone, shut out Aaron's voice and his ugly suggestions. "Do you really think that I would turn any child of mine over to someone like you?"

"There is a child, then," he retorted smoothly.

"No!" Five steps to the wall, six at most.

"Be reasonable, sweetness. We're discussing an empire here. If you don't come back and attend to your wifely duties, I'll have to visit that godforsaken ranch and try to persuade you."

"I am not your wife!" screamed Libby. One step. One step and a reach.

"Dear heart, I don't find the idea any more appealing than you do, but there isn't any other way, is there? My grandmother likes you—sees you as sturdy peasant stock—and she wants the baby to be yours."

At last. The wall was close and Libby slammed the receiver into place. Then, dazed, she stumbled back to her chair and fell into it, lowering her head to her arms. She cried hard, for herself, for Jonathan.

"Libby?"

It was the last voice she would have wanted to hear, except for Aaron's. "Go away, Stacey!" she hissed.

Instead of complying, Stacey laid a gentle hand on her shoulder. "What happened, Libby?" he asked softly. "Who was that on the phone?"

Fresh horror washed over Libby at the things Aaron had requested, mixed with anger and revulsion. God, how self-centered and insensitive that man was! And what gall he had, suggesting that she return to that disaster of a marriage, like some unquestioning brood mare, to produce a baby on order!

She gave a shuddering cry and motioned Stacey away with a frantic motion of her arm.

He only drew her up out of the chair and turned her so that he could hold her. She hadn't the strength to resist the intimacy and, in her half-hysterical state, he seemed to be the old Stacey, the strong big brother.

Stacey's hand came to the back of her head, tangling in her freshly washed hair, pressing her to his shoulder. "Tell me what happened," he urged, just as he had when Libby was a child with a skinned knee or a bee sting.

From habit, she allowed herself to be comforted. For so long there had been no one to confide in except Stacey, and it seemed natural to lean on him now. "Aaron…Aaron called. He wanted me to have his…his baby!"

Before Stacey could respond to that, the door separating the kitchen from the living room swung open. Instinctively Libby drew back from the man who held her.

Jess towered in the doorway, pale, his gaze scorching Libby's flushed, tear-streaked face. "You know," he began in a voice that was no less terrible for being soft, "I almost believed you. I almost had myself convinced that you were above anything this shabby."

"Wait—you don't understand.…"

Jess smiled a slow, vicious smile—a smile that took in his startled brother as well as Libby. "Don't I? Oh, princess, I wish I didn't." The searing jade gaze sliced menacingly to Stacey's face. "And it seems I'm going to be an uncle. Tell me, brother—what does that make Cathy?"

To Libby's horror, Stacey said nothing to refute what was obviously a gross misunderstanding. He simply pulled her back into his arms, and her struggle was virtually imperceptible because of his strength.

"Let me go!" she pleaded, frantic.

Stacey released her, but only grudgingly. "I've got a plane to catch," he said.

Libby was incredulous. "Tell him! Tell Jess that he's wrong," she cried, reaching out for Stacey's arm, trying to detain him.

But Stacey simply pulled free and left by the back door.

There was a long, pulsing silence, during which both Libby and Jess seemed to be frozen. He was the first to thaw.

"I know you were hurt, Libby," he said. "Badly hurt. But that didn't give you the right to do something like this to Cathy."

It infuriated Libby that this man's good opinion was so important to her, but it was, and there was no changing that. "Jess, I didn't do anything to Cathy. Please listen to me."

He folded his strong arms and rested against the door jamb with an ease that Libby knew was totally feigned. "I'm listening," he said, and the words had a flippant note.

Libby ignored fresh anger. "I am not expecting Stacey's baby, and this wasn't a romantic tryst. I don't even know why he came here. I was on the phone with Aaron and he—"

A muscle in Jess's neck corded, relaxed again. "I hope you're not going to tell me that your former husband made you pregnant, Libby. That seems unlikely."

Frustration pounded in Libby's temples and tightened the already constricted muscles in her throat. "I am not pregnant!" she choked out. "And if you are going to eavesdrop, Jess Barlowe, you could at least pay attention! Aaron wanted me

to come back to New York and have his baby so that he would
have an heir to present to his grandmother!"

"You didn't agree to that?"

"Of course I didn't agree! What kind of monster do you
think I am?"

Jess shrugged with a nonchalance that was belied by the
leaping green fire in his eyes. "I don't know, princess, but rest
assured—I intend to find out."

"I have a better idea!" Libby flared. "Why don't you just
leave me the hell alone?"

"In theory that's brilliant," he fired back, "but there is one
problem—I want you."

Involuntarily Libby remembered the kisses and caresses
exchanged by the pond the day before, relived them. Hot
color poured into her face. "Am I supposed to be honored?"

"No," Jess replied flatly, "you're supposed to be kept so
busy that you won't have time to screw up Cathy's life any
more than you already have."

If Libby could have moved, she would have rushed across
that room and slapped Jess Barlowe senseless. Since she
couldn't get her muscles to respond to the orders of her mind,
she was forced to watch in stricken silence as he gave her a
smoldering assessment with his eyes, executed a half salute
and left the house.

Chapter 4

When the telephone rang again, immediately after Jess's exit from the kitchen, Libby was almost afraid to answer it. It would be like Aaron to persist, to use pressure to get what he wanted.

On the other hand, the call might be from someone else, and it could be important.

"Hello?" Libby dared, with resolve.

"Ms. Kincaid?" asked a cheerful feminine voice. "This is Marion Bradshaw, and I'm calling for Mrs. Barlowe. She'd like you to meet her at the main house if you can, and she says to dress for riding."

Libby looked down at her jeans and boots and smiled. In one way, at least, she and Cathy were still on the same wavelength. "Please tell her that I'll be there as soon as I can."

There was a brief pause at the other end of the line, followed by, "Mrs. Barlowe wants me to ask if you have a car down there. If not, she'll come and pick you up in a few minutes."

Though there was no car at her disposal, Libby declined the offer. The walk to the main ranch house would give her a chance to think, to prepare herself to face her cousin again.

As Libby started out, striding along the winding tree-lined road, she ached to think that she and Cathy had come to this. Fresh anger at Stacey quickened her step.

For a moment she was mad at Cathy, too. How could she believe such a thing, after all they'd been through together? How?

Firmly Libby brought her ire under control. *You don't get mad at a handicapped person,* she scolded herself.

The sun was already high and hot in the domelike sky, and Libby smiled. It was warm for spring, and wasn't it nice to look up and see clouds and mountaintops instead of tall buildings and smog?

Finally the main house came into view. It was a rambling structure of red brick, and its many windows glistened in the bright sunshine. A porch with marble steps led up to the double doors, and one of them swung open even as Libby reached out to ring the bell.

Mrs. Bradshaw, the housekeeper, stepped out and enfolded Libby in a delighted hug. A slender middle-aged woman with soft brown hair, Marion Bradshaw was as much a part of the Circle Bar B as Senator Barlowe himself. "Welcome home," she said warmly.

Libby smiled and returned the hug. "Thank you, Marion," she replied. "Is Cathy ready to go riding?"

"She's gone ahead to the stables—she'd like you to join her there."

Libby turned to go back down the steps but was stopped by the housekeeper. "Libby?"

She faced Marion, again, feeling wary.

"I don't believe it of you," said Mrs. Bradshaw firmly.

Libby was embarrassed, but there was no point in trying to pretend that she didn't get the woman's meaning. Probably everyone on the ranch was speculating about her supposed involvement with Stacey Barlowe. "Thank you."

"You stay right here on this ranch, Libby Kincaid," Marion Bradshaw rushed on, her own face flushed now. "Don't let Stacey or anybody else run you off."

That morning's unfortunate scene in Ken's kitchen was an indication of how difficult it would be to take the housekeeper's advice. Life on the Circle Bar B could become untenable if both Stacey and Jess didn't back off.

"I'll try," she said softly before stepping down off the porch and making her way around the side of that imposing but gracious house.

Prudently, the stables had been built a good distance away. During the walk, Libby wondered if she shouldn't leave the ranch after all. True, she needed to be there, but Jonathan's death had taught her that sometimes a person had to put her own desires aside for the good of other people.

But would leaving help, in the final analysis? Suppose Stacey did follow her, as he'd threatened to do? What would that do to Cathy?

The stables, like the house, were constructed of red brick. As Libby approached them, she saw Cathy leading two horses out into the sun—a dancing palomino gelding and the considerably less prepossessing pinto mare that had always been Libby's to ride.

Libby hesitated; it had been a long, long time since she'd ridden a horse, and the look in Cathy's eyes was cool. Distant. It was almost as though Libby were a troublesome stranger rather than her cousin and confidante.

As if to break the spell, Cathy lifted one foot to the stirrup of the Palomino's saddle and swung onto its back. Though she gave no sign of greeting, her eyes bade Libby to follow suit.

The elderly pinto was gracious while Libby struggled into the saddle and took the reins in slightly shaky hands. A moment later they were off across the open pastureland behind the stables, Cathy confident in the lead.

Libby jostled and jolted in the now unfamiliar saddle, and she felt a fleeting annoyance with Cathy for setting the brisk pace that she did. Again she berated herself for being angry with someone who couldn't hear.

Cathy rode faster and faster, stopping only when she reached the trees that trimmed the base of a wooded hill. There she turned in the saddle and flung a look back at the disgruntled Libby.

"You're out of practice," she said clearly, though her voice had the slurred meter of those who have not heard another person speak in years.

Libby, red-faced and damp with perspiration, was not surprised that Cathy had spoken aloud. She had learned to talk before the childhood illness that had made her deaf, and when she could be certain that no one else would overhear, she often spoke. It was a secret the two women kept religiously.

"Thanks a lot!" snapped Libby.

Deftly Cathy swung one trim blue-jeaned leg over the neck of her golden gelding and slid to the ground. The fancy bridle jingled musically as the animal bent its great head to graze on the spring grass. "We've got to talk, Libby."

Libby jumped from the pinto's back and the action engendered a piercing ache in the balls of her feet. "You've got that right!" she flared, forgetting for the moment her earlier resolve to respect Cathy's affliction. "Were you trying to get me killed?"

Watching Libby's lips, Cathy grinned. "Killed?" she echoed in her slow, toneless voice. "You're my cousin. That's important, isn't it? That we're cousins, I mean?"

Libby sighed. "Of course it's important."

"It implies a certain loyalty, don't you think?"

Libby braced herself. She'd known this confrontation was coming, of course, but that didn't mean she wanted it or was ready for it. "Yes," she said somewhat lamely.

"Are you having an affair with my husband?"

"No!"

"Do you want to?"

"What the hell kind of person do you think I am, Cathy?" shouted Libby, losing all restraint, flinging her arms out wide and startling the horses, who nickered and danced and tossed their heads.

"I'm trying to find that out," said Cathy in measured and droning words. Not once since the conversation began had her eyes left Libby's mouth.

"You already know," retorted her cousin.

For the first time, Cathy looked ashamed. But there was uncertainty in her expression, too, along with a great deal of pain. "It's no secret that Stacey wants you, Libby. I've been holding my breath ever since you decided to come back, waiting for him to leave me."

"Whatever problems you and Stacey have, Cathy, I didn't start them."

"What about all his visits to New York?"

Libby's shoulders slumped, and she allowed herself to sink to the fragrant spring-scented ground, where she sat cross-legged, her head down. With her hands she said, "You knew about the divorce, and about Jonathan. Stacey was only trying to help me through—we weren't lovers."

The lush grass moved as Cathy sat down too, facing Libby. There were tears shining in her large green eyes, and her lower lip trembled. Nervously she plied a blade of grass between her fingers.

"I'm sorry about your little boy," she said aloud.

Libby reached out, calmer now, and squeezed Cathy's hands with her own. "Thanks."

A lonely, haunted look rose in Cathy's eyes. "Stacey wanted us to have a baby," she confided.

"Why didn't you?"

Sudden color stained Cathy's lovely cheeks. "I'm deaf!" she cried defensively.

Libby released her cousin's hands to sign, "So what? Lots of deaf people have babies."

"Not me!" Cathy signaled back with spirited despair. "I wouldn't know when it cried!"

Libby spoke slowly, her hands falling back to her lap. "Cathy, there are solutions for that sort of problem. There are trained dogs, electronic devices—"

"Trained dogs!" scoffed Cathy, but there was more anguish in her face than anger. "What kind of woman needs a dog to help her raise her own baby?"

"A deaf woman," Libby answered firmly. "Besides, if you don't want a dog around, you could hire a nurse."

"No!"

Libby was taken aback. "Why not?" she signed after a few moments.

Cathy clearly had no intention of answering. She bolted to her feet and was back in the palomino's saddle before Libby could even rise from the ground.

After that, they rode without communicating at all. Knowing that things were far from settled between herself and her cousin, Libby tried to concentrate on the scenery. A shadow moved across the sun, however, and a feeling of impending disaster unfolded inside her.

Jess glared at the screen of the small computer his father placed so much store in and resisted a caveman urge to strike its side with his fist.

"Here," purred a soft feminine voice, and Monica Summers, the senator's curvaceous assistant, reached down to move the mouse and tap the keyboard in a few strategic places.

Instantly the profit-and-loss statement Jess had been trying to call up was prominently displayed on the screen.

"How did you do that?"

Monica smiled her sultry smile and pulled up a chair to sit down beside Jess. "It's a simple matter of command," she said, and somehow the words sounded wildly suggestive.

Jess's collar seemed to tighten around his throat, but he grinned, appreciating Monica's lithe, inviting body, her profusion of gleaming brown hair, her impudent mouth and soft gray eyes. Her visits to the ranch were usually brief, but the senator's term of office was almost over, and he planned to write a long book—with which Monica was slated to help. Until that project was completed, she would be around a lot.

The fact that the senior senator did not intend to campaign for reelection didn't seem to faze her—it was common knowledge that she had a campaign of her own in mind.

Monica had made it clear, time and time again, that she was available to Jess for more than an occasional dinner date and subsequent sexual skirmish. And before Libby's return, Jess had seriously considered settling down with Monica.

He didn't love her, but she was undeniably beautiful, and

the promises she made with her skillfully made-up eyes were not idle ones. In addition to that, they had a lot of ordinary things in common—similar political views, a love of the outdoors, like tastes in music and books.

Now, even with Monica sitting so close to him, her perfume calling up some rather heated memories, Jess Barlowe was patently unmoved.

A shower of anger sifted through him. He *wanted* to be moved, dammit—he wanted everything to be the way it was before Libby's return. Return? It was an invasion! He thought about the little hellion day and night, whether he wanted to or not.

"What's wrong, Jess?" Monica asked softly, perceptively, her hand resting on his shoulder. "It's more than just this computer, isn't it?"

He looked away. The sensible thing to do would be to take Monica by the hand, lead her off somewhere private and make slow, ferocious love to her. Maybe that would exorcise Libby Kincaid from his mind.

He remembered passion-weighted breasts, bared to him on a swimming dock, remembered their nipples blossoming sweetly in his mouth. Libby's breasts.

"Jess?"

He forced himself to look at Monica again. "I'm sorry," he said. "Did you say something?"

Mischief danced in her charcoal eyes. "Yes. I offered you my body."

He laughed.

Instead of laughing herself, Monica gave him a gentle, discerning look. "Mrs. Bradshaw tells me that Libby Kincaid is back," she said. "Could it be that I have some competition?"

Jess cleared his throat and diplomatically fixed his attention on the computer screen. "Show me how you made this monster cough up that profit-and-loss statement," he hedged.

"Jess." The voice was cool, insistent.

He made himself meet Monica's eyes again. "I don't know what I feel for Libby," he confessed. "She makes me mad as hell, but…"

"But," said Monica with rueful amusement, "you want her very badly, don't you?"

There was no denying that, but neither could Jess bring himself to openly admit to the curious needs that had been plaguing him since the moment he'd seen Libby again at the small airport in Kalispell.

Monica's right index finger traced the outline of his jaw, tenderly. Sensuously. "We've never agreed to be faithful to each other, Jess," she said in the silky voice that had once enthralled him. "There aren't any strings tying you to me. But that doesn't mean that I'm going to step back and let Libby Kincaid have a clear field. I want you myself."

Jess was saved from answering by the sudden appearance of his father in the study doorway.

"Oh, Monica—there you are," Cleave Barlowe said warmly. "Ready to start working on that speech now? We have to have it ready before we fly back to Washington, remember."

Gray eyes swept Jess's face in parting. "More than ready," she replied, and then she was out of her chair and walking across the study to join her employer.

Jess gave the computer an unloving look and switched it off, taking perverse pleasure in the way the images on the screen dissolved. "State of the art," he mocked, and then stood up and strode out of the room.

The accountants would be angry, once they returned from

their coffee break, but he didn't give a damn. If he didn't do something physical, he was going to go crazy.

Back at the stables, Libby surrendered her horse to a ranch hand with relief. Already the muscles in her thighs were aching dully from the ride; by morning they would be in savage little knots.

Cathy, who probably rode almost every day, looked breezy and refreshed, and from her manner no one would have suspected that she harbored any ill feelings toward Libby. "Let's take a swim," she signed, "and then we can have lunch."

Libby would have preferred to soak in the hot tub, but her pride wouldn't allow her to say so. Unless a limp betrayed her, she wasn't going to let Cathy know how sore a simple horseback ride had left her.

"I don't have a swimming suit," she said, somewhat hopefully.

"That's okay," Cathy replied with swift hands. "It's an indoor pool, remember?"

"I hope you're not suggesting that we swim naked," Libby argued aloud.

Cathy's eyes danced. "Why not?" she signed impishly. "No one would see us."

"Are you kidding?" Libby retorted, waving one arm toward the long, wide driveway. "Look at all these cars! There are *people* in that house!"

"Are you so modest?" queried Cathy, one eyebrow arched.

"Yes!" replied Libby, ignoring the subtle sarcasm.

"Then we'll go back to your house and swim in the pond, like we used to."

Libby recalled the blatant way she'd offered herself to Jess Barlowe in that place and winced inwardly. The peaceful solace of that pond had probably been altered forever, and it was going to be some time before she could go there comfortably again. "It's spring, Cathy, not summer. We'd catch pneumonia! Besides, I think it's going to rain."

Cathy shrugged. "All right, all right. I'll borrow a car and we'll drive over and get your swimming suit, then come back here."

"Fine," Libby agreed with a sigh.

She was to regret the decision almost immediately. When she and Cathy reached the house they had both grown up in, there was a florist's truck parked out front.

On the porch stood an affable young man, a long, narrow box in his hands. "Hi, Libby," he said.

Libby recognized Phil Reynolds, who had been her classmate in high school. *Go away, Phil,* she thought, even as she smiled and greeted him.

Cathy's attention was riveted on the silver box he carried, and there was a worried expression on her face.

Phil approached, beaming. "I didn't even know you were back until we got this order this morning. Aren't you coming into town at all? We got a new high school.…"

Simmonsville, a dried-up little community just beyond the south border of the Circle Bar B, hadn't even entered Libby's thoughts until she'd seen Phil Reynolds. She ignored his question and stared at the box he held out to her as if it might contain something squirmy and vile.

"Wh-who sent these?" she managed, all too conscious of the suspicious way Cathy was looking at her.

"See for yourself," Phil said brightly, and then he got back into his truck and left.

Libby took the card from beneath the red ribbon that bound the box and opened it with trembling fingers. The flowers couldn't be from Stacey, please God, they couldn't!

The card was typewritten. *Don't be stubborn, sweetness,* the message read. *Regards, Aaron.*

For a moment Libby was too relieved to be angry. "Aaron," she repeated. Then she lifted the lid from the box and saw the dozen pink rosebuds inside.

For one crazy moment she was back in Jonathan's hospital room. There had been roses there, too—along with mums and violets and carnations. Aaron and his family had sent costly bouquets and elaborate toys, but not one of them had come to visit.

Libby heard the echo of Jonathan's purposefully cheerful voice. *Daddy must be busy,* he'd said.

With a cry of fury and pain, Libby flung the roses away, and they scattered over the walk in a profusion of long-stemmed delicacy. The silver box lay with them, catching the waning sunlight.

Cathy knelt and began gathering up the discarded flowers, placing them gently back in their carton. Once or twice she glanced up at Libby's livid face in bewilderment, but she asked no questions and made no comments.

Libby turned away and bounded into the house. By the time she had found a swimming suit and come back downstairs again, Cathy was arranging the rosebuds in a cut-glass vase at the kitchen sink.

She met Libby's angry gaze and held up one hand to stay the inevitable outburst. "They're beautiful, Libby," she said in a barely audible voice. "You can't throw away something that's beautiful."

"Watch me!" snapped Libby.

Cathy stepped between her cousin and the lush bouquet. "Libby, at least let me give them to Mrs. Bradshaw," she pleaded aloud. "Please?"

Glumly Libby nodded. She supposed she should be

grateful that the roses hadn't been sent by Stacey in a fit of ardor, and they *were* too lovely to waste, even if she herself couldn't bear the sight of them.

Libby remembered the words on Aaron's card as she and Cathy drove back to the main house. *Don't be stubborn.* A tremor of dread flitted up and down her spine.

Aaron hadn't been serious when he'd threatened to come to the ranch and "persuade" her to return to New York with him, had he? She shivered.

Surely even Aaron wouldn't have the gall to do that, she tried to reassure herself. After all, he had never come to the apartment she'd taken after Jonathan's death, never so much as called. Even when the divorce had been granted, he had avoided her by sending his lawyer to court alone.

No. Aaron wouldn't actually come to the Circle Bar B. He might call, he might even send more flowers, just to antagonize her, but he wouldn't come in person. Despite his dismissal of Stacey as a "soft-headed cowboy," he was afraid of him.

Cathy was drawing the car to a stop in front of the main house by the time Libby was able to recover herself. To allay the concern in her cousin's eyes, she carried the vase of pink roses into the kitchen and presented them to Mrs. Bradshaw, who was puzzled but clearly pleased.

Inside the gigantic, elegantly tiled room that housed the swimming pool and the spacious hot tub, Libby eyed the latter with longing. Thus, it was a moment before she realized that the pool was already occupied.

Jess was doing a furious racing crawl from one side of the deep end to the other, his tanned, muscular arms cutting through the blue water with a force that said he was trying to work out some fierce inner conflict. Watching him admiringly from the poolside, her slender legs dangling into the water, was a pretty dark-haired woman with beautiful gray eyes.

The woman greeted Cathy with an easy gesture of her hands, though her eyes were fixed on Libby, seeming to assess her in a thorough, if offhand, fashion.

"I'm Monica Summers," she said, as Jess, apparently oblivious of everything other than the furious course he was following through the water, executed an impressive somersault turn at the poolside and raced back the other way.

Monica Summers. The name was familiar to Libby, and so, vaguely, was the perfect fashion-model face.

Of course. Monica was Senator Barlowe's chief assistant. Libby had never actually met the woman, but she had seen her on television newscasts and Ken had mentioned her in passing, on occasion, over long-distance telephone.

"Hello," Libby said. "I'm—"

The gray eyes sparkled. "I know," Monica broke in smoothly. "You're Libby Kincaid. I enjoy your cartoons very much."

Libby felt about as sophisticated, compared to this woman, as a Girl Scout selling cookies door-to-door. And Monica's subtle emphasis on the word "cartoons" had made her feel defensive.

All the same, Libby thanked her and forced herself not to watch Jess's magnificent body moving through the bright blue water of the pool. It didn't bother her that Jess and Monica had been alone in this strangely sensual setting. It didn't.

Cathy had moved away, anxious for her swim.

"I'm sorry if we interrupted something," Libby said, and hated herself instantly for betraying her interest.

Monica smiled. Clearly she had not been in swimming herself, for her expensive black swimsuit was dry, and so was her long, lush hair. Her makeup, of course, was perfect. "There are always interruptions," she said, and then she turned away to take up her adoring-spectator position again, her gaze following the play of the powerful muscles in Jess's naked back.

My thighs are too fat, mourned Libby, in petulant despair. She took a seat on a lounge far removed from Jess and his lovely friend and tried to pretend an interest in Cathy's graceful backstroke.

Was Jess intimate with Monica Summers? It certainly seemed so, and Libby couldn't understand, for the life of her, why she was so brutally surprised by the knowledge. After all, Jess was a handsome, healthy man, well beyond the age of handholding and fantasies-from-afar. Had she really ever believed that he had just been existing on this ranch in some sort of suspended animation?

Cathy roused her from her dismal reflection by flinging a stream of water at her with both hands. Instantly Libby was drenched and stung to an annoyance out of all proportion to the offense. Surprising even herself, she stomped over to the hot tub, flipped the switch that would make the water bubble and churn, and after hurling one scorching look at her unrepenting cousin, slid into the enormous tile-lined tub.

The heat and motion of the water were welcome balm to Libby's muscles, if not to her spirit. She had no right to care who Jess Barlowe slept with, no right at all. It wasn't as though she had ever had any claim on his affections.

Settling herself on a submerged bench, Libby tilted her head back, closed her eyes, and tried to pretend that she was alone in that massive room with its sloping glass roof, lush plants and lounges.

The fact that she was sexually attracted to Jess Barlowe was undeniable, but it was just a physical phenomenon, certainly. It would pass.

All she had to do to accelerate the process was allow

herself to remember how very demeaning Aaron's lovemaking had been. And remember she did.

After Libby had caught her husband with the first of his lovers, she had moved out of his bedroom permanently, remaining in his house only because Jonathan, still at home then, had needed her so much.

Before her brutal awakening, however, she had tried hard to make the rapidly failing marriage work. Even then, bedtime had been a horror.

Libby's skin prickled as she recalled the way Aaron would ignore her for long weeks and then pounce on her with a vicious and alarming sort of determination, tearing her clothes, sometimes bruising her.

In retrospect, Libby realized that Aaron must have been trying to prove something to himself concerning his identity as a man, but at the time she had known only that sex, much touted in books and movies, was something to be feared.

Not once had Libby achieved any sort of satisfaction with Aaron—she had only endured. Now, painfully conscious of the blatantly masculine, near-naked cowboy swimming in the pool nearby, Libby wondered if lovemaking would be different with Jess.

The way that her body had blossomed beneath his seemed adequate proof that it would be different indeed, but there was always the possibility that she would be disappointed in the ultimate act. Probably she had been aroused only because Jess had taken the time to offer her at least a taste of pleasure. Aaron had never done that, never shown any sensitivity at all.

Shutting out all sight and sound, Libby mentally decried her lack of experience. If only she'd been with even one man besides Aaron, she would have had some frame of reference, some inkling of whether or not the soaring releases she'd read about really existed.

The knowledge that so many people thought she had been carrying on a torrid affair with Stacey brought a wry smile to her lips. If only they knew.

"What are you smiling about?"

The voice jolted Libby back to the here and now with a thump. Jess had joined her in the hot tub at some point; indeed, he was standing only inches away.

Startled, Libby stared at him for a moment, then looked wildly around for Cathy and the elegant Ms. Summers.

"They went in to have lunch," Jess informed her, his eyes twinkling. Beads of water sparkled in the dark down that matted his muscular chest, and his hair had been towel-rubbed into an appealing disarray.

"I'll join them," said Libby in a frantic whisper, but the simple mechanics of turning away and climbing out of the hot tub eluded her.

Smelling pleasantly of chlorine, Jess came nearer. "Don't go," he said softly. "Lunch will wait."

Anger at Cathy surged through Libby. Why had she gone off and left her here?

Jess seemed to read the question in her face, and it made him laugh. The sound was soft—sensuously, wholly male. Overhead, spring thunder crashed in a gray sky.

Libby trembled, pressing back against the edge of the hot tub with such force that her shoulder blades ached. "Stay away from me," she breathed.

"Not on your life," he answered, and then he was so near that she could feel the hard length of his thighs against her own. The soft dark hair on his chest tickled her bare shoulders and the suddenly alive flesh above her swimsuit top. "I intend to finish what we started yesterday beside the pond."

Libby gasped as his moist lips came down to taste hers, to tame and finally part them for a tender invasion. Her hands went up, of their own accord, to rest on his hips.

He was naked. The discovery rocked Libby, made her try to twist away from him, but his kiss deepened and subdued her struggles. With his hands, he lifted her legs, draped them around the rock-hard hips she had just explored.

The imposing, heated length of his desire, now pressed intimately against her, was powerful proof that he meant to take her.

Chapter 5

Libby felt as though her body had dissolved, become part of the warm, bubbling water filling the hot tub. When Jess drew back from his soft conquering of her mouth, his hands rose gently to draw down the modest top of her swimsuit, revealing the pulsing fullness of her breasts to his gaze.

It was not in Libby to protest: she was transfixed, caught up in primal responses that had no relation to good sense or even sanity. She let her head fall back, saw through the transparent ceiling that gray clouds had darkened the sky, promising a storm that wouldn't begin to rival the one brewing inside Libby herself.

Jess bent his head, nipped at one exposed, aching nipple with cautious teeth.

Libby drew in a sharp breath as a shaft of searing pleasure went through her, so powerful that she was nearly convulsed by it. A soft moan escaped her, and she tilted her head even further back, so that her breasts were still more vulnerable to the plundering of his mouth.

Inside Libby's swirling mind, a steady voice chanted a litany of logic: she was behaving in a wanton way—Jess didn't really care for her, he was only trying to prove that he could conquer her whenever he desired—this place was not private, and there was a very real danger that someone would walk in at any moment and see what was happening.

Thunder reverberated in the sky, shaking heaven and earth. And none of the arguments Libby's reason was offering had any effect on her rising need to join herself with this impossible, overbearing man feasting so brazenly on her breast.

With an unerring hand, Jess found the crux of her passion, and through the fabric of her swimsuit he stroked it to a wanting Libby had never experienced before. Then, still greedy at the nipple he was attending, he deftly worked aside the bit of cloth separating Libby's womanhood from total exposure.

She gasped as he caught the hidden nubbin between his fingers and began, rhythmically, to soothe it. Or was he tormenting it? Libby didn't know, didn't care.

Jess left her breast to nibble at her earlobe, chuckled hoarsely when the tender invasion of his fingers elicited a throaty cry of welcome.

"Go with it, Libby," he whispered. "Let it carry you high…higher.…"

Libby was already soaring, sightless, mindless, conscious only of the fiery marauding of his fingers and the strange force inside her that was building toward something she had only imagined before. "Oh," she gasped as he worked this new and fierce magic. "Oh, Jess…"

Mercilessly he intensified her pleasure by whispering outrageously erotic promises, by pressing her legs wide of each other with one knee, by caressing her breast with his other hand.

A savage trembling began deep within Libby, causing her breath to quicken to a soft, lusty whine.

"Meet it, Libby," Jess urged. "Rise to meet it."

Suddenly Libby's entire being buckled in some ancient, inescapable response. The thunder in the distant skies covered her final cry of release, and she convulsed again and again, helpless in the throes of her body's savage victory.

When at last the ferocious clenching and unclenching had ceased, Libby's reason gradually returned. Forcing wide eyes to Jess's face, she saw no demand there, no mockery or revulsion. Instead, he was grinning at her, as pleased as if he'd been sated himself.

Wild embarrassment surged through Libby in the wake of her passion. She tried to avert her face, but Jess caught her chin in his hand and made her look at him.

"Don't," he said gruffly. "Don't look that way. It wasn't wrong, Libby."

His ability to read her thoughts so easily was as unsettling as the knowledge that she'd just allowed this man unconscionable liberties in a hot tub. "I suppose you think…I suppose you want…"

Jess withdrew his conquering hand, tugged her swimsuit back into place. "I think you're beautiful," he supplied, "and I want you—that's true. But for now, watching you respond like that was enough."

Libby blushed again. She was still confused by the power of her release, and she had expected Jess to demand his own satisfaction. She was stunned that he could give such fierce fulfillment and ask nothing for himself.

"You've never been with any man besides your husband, have you, Libby?"

The outrageous bluntness of that question solidified Libby's jellylike muscles, and she reached furiously for one of the towels Mrs. Bradshaw had set nearby on a low shelf. "I've been with a thousand men!" she snapped in a harsh whisper. "Why, one word from any man, and I let him…I let him…"

Jess grinned again. "You've never had a climax before," he observed.

How could he guess a thing like that? It was uncanny. Libby knew that the hot color in her face belied her sharp answer. "Of course I have! I've been married—did you think I was celibate?"

The rapid-fire hysteria of her words only served to amuse Jess, it seemed. "We both know, Libby Kincaid, that you are, for all practical intents and purposes, a virgin. You may have lain beneath that ex-husband of yours and wished to God that he would leave you alone, but until a few minutes ago you had never even guessed what it means to be a woman."

Libby wouldn't have thought it possible to be as murderously angry as she was at that moment. "Why, you arrogant, *insufferable*…"

He caught her hand at the wrist before it could make the intended contact with his face. "You haven't seen anything yet, princess," he vowed with gentle force. "When I take you to bed—and I assure you that I will—I'll prove that everything I've said is true."

While Libby herself was outraged, her traitorous body yearned to lie in his bed, bend to his will. Having reached the edges of passion, it wanted to go beyond, into the molten core. "You egotistical bastard!" Libby hissed, breaking away from him to lift herself out of the hot tub and land on its edge with an inelegant, squishy plop, "You act as if you'd invented sex!"

"As far as you're concerned, little virgin, I did. But have no fear—I intend to deflower you at the first opportunity."

Libby stood up, wrapped her shaky, nerveless form in a towel the size of a bedsheet. "Go to hell!"

Jess rose out of the water, not the least bit self-conscious of his nakedness. The magnitude of his desire for her was all too obvious.

"The next few hours will be just that," he said, reaching for a towel of his own. Naturally, the one he selected barely covered him.

Speechless, Libby imagined the thrust of his manhood, imagined her back arching to receive him, imagined a savage renewal of the passion she had felt only minutes before.

Jess gave her an amused sidelong glance, as though he knew what she was thinking, and intoned, "Don't worry, princess. I'll court you if that's what you want. But I'll have you, too. And thoroughly."

Having made this incredible vow, he calmly walked out of the room, leaving Libby alone with a clamoring flock of strange emotions and unmet needs.

The moment Jess was gone, she stumbled to the nearest lounge chair and sank onto it, her knees too weak to support her. *Well, Kincaid,* she reflected wryly, *now you know. Satisfied?*

Libby winced at the last word. Though she might have wished otherwise, given the identity of the man involved, she was just that.

With carefully maintained dignity, Jess Barlowe strode into the shower room adjoining the pool and wrenched on one spigot. As he stepped under the biting, sleetlike spray, he gritted his teeth.

Gradually his body stopped screaming and the stubborn

evidence of his passion faded. With relief, Jess dived out of the shower stall and grabbed a fresh towel.

A hoarse chuckle escaped him as he dried himself with brisk motions. Good God, if he didn't have Libby Kincaid soon, he was going to die of pneumonia. A man could stand only so many plunges into icy ponds, only so many cold showers.

A spare set of clothes—jeans and a white pullover shirt—awaited Jess in a cupboard. He donned them quickly, casting one disdainful look at the three-piece suit he had shed earlier. His circulation restored, to some degree at least, he toweled his hair and then combed it with the splayed fingers of his left hand.

A sweet anguish swept through him as he remembered the magic he had glimpsed in Libby's beautiful face during that moment of full surrender. *My father was right,* Jess thought as he pulled on socks and old, comfortable boots. *I love you, Libby Kincaid. I love you.*

Jess was not surprised to find that Libby wasn't with Cathy and Monica in the kitchen—she had probably made some excuse to get out of joining them for lunch and gone off to gather her thoughts. God knew, she had to be every bit as undone and confused as he was.

Mostly to avoid the sad speculation in Monica's eyes, Jess glanced toward the kitchen windows. They were already sheeted with rain.

A crash of thunder jolted him out of the strange inertia that had possessed him. He glanced at Cathy, saw an impish light dancing in her eyes.

"You can catch her if you hurry," she signed, cocking her head to one side and grinning at him.

Did she know what had happened in the hot tub? Some of the heat lingering in Jess's loins rose to his face as he bolted out of the room and through the rest of the house.

His truck, an eyesore among the other cars parked in front of the house, patently refused to start. Annoyed, Jess "borrowed" Monica's sleek green Porsche without a moment's hesitation, and his aggravation grew as he left the driveway and pulled out onto the main road.

What the hell did Libby think she was doing, walking in this rain? And why had Cathy let her go?

He found Libby near the mailboxes, slogging despondently along, soaked to the skin.

"Get in!" he barked, furious in his concern.

Libby lifted her chin and kept walking. Her turquoise shirt was plastered to her chest, revealing the outlines of her bra, and her hair hung in dripping tendrils.

"Now!" Jess roared through the window he had rolled down halfway.

She stopped, faced him with indigo fury sparking in her eyes. "Why?" she yelled over the combined roars of the deluge and Monica's car engine. "Is it time to teach me what it means to be a woman?"

"How the hell would I know what it means to be a woman?" he shouted back. "Get in this car!"

Libby told him to do something that was anatomically impossible and then went splashing off down the road again, ignoring the driving rain.

Rasping a swearword, Jess slipped the Porsche out of gear and wrenched the emergency brake into place. Then he shoved open the door and bounded through the downpour to catch up with Libby, grasp her by the shoulders and whirl her around to face him.

"If you don't get your backside into that car *right now,*" he bellowed, "I swear to God I'll *throw* you in!"

She assessed the Porsche. "Monica's car?"

Furious, Jess nodded. Christ, it was raining so hard that his clothes were already saturated and she was standing there talking details!

An evil smile curved Libby's lips and she stalked toward the automobile, purposely stepping in every mud puddle along the way. Jess could have sworn that she enjoyed sinking, sopping wet, onto the heretofore spotless suede seat.

"Home, James," she said smugly, folding her arms and grinding her mud-caked boots into the lush carpeting on the floorboard.

Jess had no intention of taking Libby to Ken's place, but he said nothing. Envisioning her lying in some hospital bed, wasted away by a case of rain-induced pneumonia, he ground the car savagely back into gear and gunned the engine.

When they didn't take the road Libby expected, the smug look faded from her face and she stared at Jess with wide, wary eyes. "Wait a minute…"

Jess flung an impudent grin at her and saluted with one hand. "Yes?" he drawled, deliberately baiting her.

"Where are we going?"

"My place," he answered, still angry. "It's the classic situation, isn't it? I'll insist you get out of those wet clothes, then I'll toss you one of my bathrobes and pour brandy for us both. After that, lady, I'll make mad love to you."

Libby paled, though there was a defiant light in her eyes. "On a fur rug in front of your fireplace, no doubt!"

"No doubt," Jess snapped, wondering why he found it impossible to deal with this woman in a sane and reasonable way. It would be so much simpler just to tell her straight out that he loved her, that he needed her. But he couldn't quite bring himself to do that, not just yet, and he was still mad as hell that she would walk in the pouring rain like that.

"Suppose I tell you that I don't want you to 'make mad love' to me, as you so crudely put it? Suppose I tell you that

I won't give in to you until the first Tuesday after doomsday, if then, brandy and fur rugs notwithstanding?"

"The way you didn't give in in the hot tub?" he gibed, scowling.

Libby blushed. "That was different!"

"How so?"

"You…you *cornered* me, that's how."

His next words were out of his mouth before he could call them back. "I know about your ex-husband, Libby."

She winced, fixed her attention on the overworked windshield wipers. "What does he have to do with anything?"

Jess shifted to a lower gear as he reached the road leading to his house and turned onto it. "Stacey told me about the women."

The high color drained from Libby's face and she would not look at him. She appeared ready, in fact, to thrust open the door on her side of the car and leap out. "I don't want to talk about this," she said after an interval long enough to bring them to Jess's driveway.

"Why not, Libby?" he asked, and his voice was gentle, if a bit gruff.

One tear rolled over the wet sheen on her defiant rainpolished face, and Libby's chin jutted out in a way that was familiar to him, at once maddening and appealing. "Why do you want to talk about Aaron?" she countered in low, ragged tones. "So you can sit there and feel superior?"

"You know better."

She glared at him, her bruised heart in her eyes, and Jess ached for her. She'd been through so much, and he wished that he could have taken that visible, pounding pain from inside her and borne it himself.

"I don't know better, Jess," she said quietly. "We haven't exactly been kindred spirits, you and I. For all I know, you

just want to torture me. To throw all my mistakes in my face
and watch me squirm."

Jess's hands tightened on the steering wheel. It took great
effort to reach down and shut off the Porsche's engine. "It's
cold out here," he said evenly, "and we're both wet to the skin.
Let's go inside."

"You won't take me home?" Her voice was small.

He sighed. "Do you want me to?"

Libby considered, lowered her head. "No," she said after
a long time.

The inside of Jess's house was spacious and uncluttered.
There were skylights in the ceiling and the second floor
appeared to be a loft of some sort. Lifting her eyes to the
railing above, Libby imagined that his bed was just beyond
it and blushed.

Jess seemed to be ignoring her; he was busy with newspa-
per and kindling at the hearth. She watched the play of the
muscles in his back in weary fascination, longing to feel them
beneath her hands.

The knowledge that she loved Jess Barlowe, budding in her
subconscious mind since her arrival in Montana, suddenly
burst into full flower. But was the feeling really new?

If Libby were to be honest with herself—and she tried to
be, always—she had to admit that the chances were good that
she had loved Jess for a very long time.

He turned, rose from his crouching position, a small fire
blazing and crackling behind him. "How do you like my
house?" he asked with a half smile.

Between her newly recognized feelings for this man and the
way his jade eyes seemed to see through all her reserve to the
hurt and confusion hidden beneath, Libby felt very vulnerable.

Trusting in an old trick that had always worked in the past, she looked around in search of something to be angry about.

The skylights, the loft, the view of the mountains from the windows beyond his desk—all of it was appealing. Masculine. Quietly romantic.

"Perfect quarters for a wealthy and irresponsible playboy," she threw out in desperation.

Jess stiffened momentarily, but then an easy grin creased his face. "I think that was a shot, but I'm not going to fire back, Libby, so you might as well relax."

Relax? Was the man insane? Half an hour before, he had blithely brought her to climax in a hot tub, for God's sake, and now they were alone, the condition of their clothes necessitating that they risk further intimacies by stripping them off, taking showers. If they couldn't fight, what *were* they going to do?

Before Libby could think of anything to say in reply, Jess gestured toward the broad redwood stairs leading up to the loft. "The bathroom is up there," he said. "Take a shower. You'll find a robe hanging on the inside of the door." With that, he turned away to crouch before the fire again and add wood.

Because she was cold and there seemed to be no other options, Libby climbed the stairs. It wasn't until she reached the loft that her teeth began to chatter.

There she saw Jess's wide unmade bed. It was banked by a line of floor-to-ceiling windows, giving the impression that the room was open to the outdoors, and the wrinkled sheets probably still bore that subtle, clean scent that was Jess's alone....

Libby took herself in hand, wrenched her attention away from the bed. There was a glass-fronted wood-burning stove in one corner of the large room, and a long bookshelf on the other side was crammed with everything from paperback mysteries to volumes on veterinary medicine.

Libby made her way into the adjoining bathroom and kicked off her muddy boots, peeled away her jeans and shirt, her sodden underwear and socks. Goosebumps leapt out all over her body, and they weren't entirely related to the chill.

The bathtub was enormous, and like the bed, it was framed by tall uncurtained windows. Bathing here would be like bathing in the high limbs of a tree, so sweeping was the view of mountains and grassland beyond the glass.

Trembling a little, Libby knelt to turn on the polished brass spigots and fill the deep tub. The water felt good against her chilled flesh, and she was submerged to her chin before she remembered that she had meant to take a quick shower, not a lingering, dreamy bath.

Libby couldn't help drawing a psychological parallel between this tub and the larger one at the main house, where she had made such a fool of herself. Was there some mysterious significance in the fact that she'd chosen the bathtub over the double-wide shower stall on the other side of the room?

Now you're really getting crazy, Kincaid, she said to herself, settling back to soak.

Somewhere in the house, a telephone rang, was swiftly answered.

Libby relaxed in the big tub and tried to still her roiling thoughts and emotions. She would not consider what might happen later. For now, she wanted to be comforted, pampered. Deliciously warm.

She heard the click of boot heels on the stairs, though, and sat bolt upright in the water. A sense of sweet alarm raced through her system. Jess wouldn't come in, actually *come in,* would he?

Of course he would! Why would a bathroom door stop a man who would make such brazen advances in a hot tub?

With frantic eyes Libby sought the towel shelf. It was

entirely too far away, and so was the heavy blue-and-white velour robe hanging on the inside of the door. She sank into the bathwater until it tickled her lower lip, squeezed her eyes shut and waited.

"Lib?"

"Wh-what?" she managed. He was just beyond that heavy wooden panel, and Libby found herself hoping…

Hoping what? That Jess would walk in, or that he would stay out? She honestly didn't know.

"That was Ken on the phone," Jess answered, making no effort to open the door. "I told him you were here and that I'd bring you home after the rain lets up."

Libby reddened, there in the privacy of that unique bathroom, imagining the thoughts that were probably going through her father's mind. "Wh-what did he say?"

Jess chuckled, and the sound was low, rich. "Let me put it this way—I don't think he's going to rush over here and defend your virtue."

Libby was at once pleased and disappointed. Wasn't a father *supposed* to protect his daughter from persuasive lechers like Jess Barlowe?

"Oh," she said, her voice sounding foolish and uncertain. "D-do you want me to hurry? S-so you can take a shower, I mean?"

"Take your time," he said offhandedly. "There's another bathroom downstairs—I can shower there."

Having imparted this conversely comforting and disenchanting information, Jess began opening and closing drawers. Seconds later, Libby again heard his footsteps on the stairs.

Despite the fact that she would have preferred to lounge in that wonderful bathtub for the rest of the day, Libby shot out of the water and raced to the towel bar. This was her chance to get dried off and dressed in something before Jess could incite her to further scandalous behavior.

She was wrapped in his blue-and-white bathrobe, the belt securely tied, and cuddled under a knitted afghan by the time Jess joined her in the living room, looking reprehensibly handsome in fresh jeans and a green turtleneck sweater. His hair, like her own, was still damp, and there was a smile in his eyes, probably inspired by the way she was trying to burrow deeper into her corner of the couch.

"There isn't any brandy after all," he said with a helpless gesture of his hands. "Will you settle for chicken soup?"

Libby would have agreed to anything that would get Jess out of that room, even for a few minutes, and he would have to go to the kitchen for soup, wouldn't he? Unable to speak, she nodded.

She tried to concentrate on the leaping flames in the fireplace, but she could hear the soft thump of cupboard doors, the running of tapwater, the singular whir of a microwave oven. The sharp *ting* of the appliance's timer bell made her flinch.

Too soon, Jess returned, carrying two mugs full of steaming soup. He extended one to Libby and, to her eternal gratitude, settled in a chair nearby instead of on the couch beside her.

Outside, the rain came down in torrents, making a musical, pelting sound on the skylights, sliding down the windows in sheets. The fire snapped and threw out sparks, as if to mock the storm that could not reach it.

Jess took a sip of the hot soup and grinned. "This doesn't exactly fit the scenario I outlined in the car," he said, lifting his cup.

"You got everything else right," Libby quipped, referring to the bath she'd taken and the fact that she was wearing his robe. Instantly she realized how badly she'd slipped, but it was too late to call back her words, and the ironic arch of Jess's brow and the smile on his lips indicated that he wasn't going to let the comment pass.

"Everything?" he teased. "There isn't any fur rug, either."

Libby's cheekbones burned. Unable to say anything, she lowered her eyes and watched the tiny noodles colliding in her mug of soup.

"I'm sorry," Jess said softly.

She swallowed hard and met his eyes. He did look contrite, and there was nothing threatening in his manner. Because of that, Libby dared to ask, "Do you really mean to…to make love to me?"

"Only if you want me to," he replied. "You must know that I wouldn't force you, Libby."

She sensed that he meant this and relaxed a little. Sooner or later, she was going to have to accept the fact that all men didn't behave in the callous and hurtful way that Aaron had. "You believe me now—don't you? About Stacey, I mean?"

If that off-the-wall question had surprised or nettled Jess, he gave no indication of it. He simply nodded.

Some crazy bravery, carrying her forward like a reckless tide, made Libby put aside her carefully built reserve and blurt out, "Do you think I'm a fool, Jess?"

Jess gaped at her, the mug of soup forgotten in his hands. "A fool?"

Libby lowered her eyes. "I mean…well…because of Aaron."

"Why should I think anything like that?"

Thunder exploded in the world outside the small cocoon-like one that held only Libby and Jess. "He was…he…"

"He was with other women," supplied Jess quietly. Gently.

Libby nodded, managed to look up.

"And you stayed with him." He was setting down the mug, drawing nearer. Finally he crouched before her on his haunches and took the cup from her hands to set it aside. "You couldn't leave Jonathan, Libby. I understand that. Besides, why should the fact that you stuck with the marriage have any bearing on my attitude toward you?"

"I just thought…"

"What?" prodded Jess when her sentence fell away. "What did you think, Libby?"

Tears clogged her throat. "I thought that I couldn't be very desirable if my o-own husband couldn't…wouldn't…"

Jess gave a ragged sigh. "My God, Libby, you don't think that Aaron was unfaithful because of some lack in you?"

That was exactly what she'd thought, on a subliminal level at least. Another woman, a stronger, more experienced, more alluring woman, might have been able to keep her husband happy, make him want her.

Jess's hands came to Libby's shoulders, gentle and insistent. "Lib, talk to me."

"Just how terrific could I be?" she erupted suddenly, in the anguish that would be hidden no longer. "Just how desirable? My husband needed other women because he couldn't bring himself to make love to me!"

Jess drew her close, held her as the sobs she had restrained at last broke free. "That wasn't your fault, Libby," he breathed, his hand in her hair now, soothing and strong. "Oh, sweetheart, it wasn't your fault."

"Of course it was!" she wailed into the soft green knit of his sweater, the hard strength of the shoulder beneath. "If I'd been better…if I'd known how…"

"Shhh. Baby, don't. Don't do this to yourself."

Once freed, Libby's emotions seemed impossible to check. They ran as deep and wild as any river, swirling in senseless currents and eddies, causing her pride to founder.

Jess caught her trembling hands in his, squeezed them reassuringly. "Listen to me, princess," he said. "These doubts that you're having about yourself are understandable, under the circumstances, but they're not valid. You are desirable." He paused, searched her face with tender, reproving eyes. "I can swear to that."

Libby still felt broken, and she hadn't forgotten the terrible things Aaron had said to her during their marriage—that she was cold and unresponsive, that he hadn't been impotent before he'd married her. Time and time again he had held up Jonathan as proof that he had been virile with his first wife, taken cruel pleasure in pointing out that none of his many girl-friends found him wanting.

Wrenching herself back to the less traumatic present, Libby blurted out, "Make love to me, Jess. Let me prove to myself—"

"No," he said with cold, flat finality. And then he released her hands, stood up and turned away as if in disgust.

Chapter 6

"I thought you wanted me," Libby said in a small, broken voice.

Jess's broad back stiffened, and he did not turn around to face her. "I do."

"Then, why…?"

He went to the fireplace, took up a poker, stoked the blazing logs within to burn faster, hotter. "When I make love to you, Libby, it won't be because either one of us wants to prove anything."

Libby lowered her head, ashamed. As if to scold her, the wind and rain lashed at the windows and the lightning flashed, filling the room with its eerie blue-gold light. She began to cry again, this time softly, wretchedly.

And Jess came to her, lifted her easily into his arms. Without a word, he carried her up the stairs, across the storm-shadowed loft room to the bed. After pulling back the covers with one hand, he lowered her to the sheets. "Rest," he said, tucking the blankets around her.

Libby gaped at him, amazed and stricken. She couldn't help thinking that he wouldn't have tucked Monica Summers into bed this way, kissed *her* forehead as though she were some overwrought child needing a nap.

"I don't want to rest," Libby said, insulted. And her hands moved to pull the covers down.

Jess stopped her by clasping her wrists. A muscle knotted in his jaw, and his jade-green eyes flashed, their light as elemental as that of the electrical storm outside. "Don't Libby. Don't tempt me."

She *had* been tempting him—if he hadn't stopped her when he did, she would have opened the robe, wantonly displayed her breasts. Now, she was mortally embarrassed. What on earth was making her act this way?

"I'm sorry," she whispered. "I don't know what's the matter with me."

Jess sat down on the edge of the bed, his magnificent face etched in shadows, his expression unreadable. "Do we have to go into that again, princess? Nothing is wrong with you."

"But—"

Jess laid one index finger to her lips to silence her. "It would be wrong if we made love now, Libby—don't you see that? Afterward, you'd be telling yourself what a creep I was for taking advantage of you when you were so vulnerable."

His logic was unassailable. To lighten the mood, Libby summoned up a shaky grin. "Some playboy you are. Chicken soup. Patience. Have you no passion?"

He laughed. "More than I know what to do with," he said, standing up, walking away from the bed. At the top of the stairs he paused. "Am I crazy?"

Libby didn't answer. Smiling, she snuggled down under

the covers—she was just a bit tired—and placidly watched the natural light show beyond the windows. Maybe later there would be fireworks of another sort.

Downstairs, Jess resisted a fundamental urge to beat his head against the wall. Libby Kincaid was up there in his bed, for God's sake, warm and lush and wanting him.

He ached to go back up the stairs and finish what they'd begun that morning in the hot tub. He couldn't, of course, because Libby was in no condition, emotionally, for that kind of heavy scene. If he did the wrong thing, said the wrong thing, she could break, and the pieces might not fit together again.

In a fit of neatness, Jess gathered up the cups of cold chicken soup and carried them into the kitchen. There he dumped their contents into the sink, rinsed them, and stacked them neatly in the dishwasher.

The task was done too quickly. What could he do? He didn't like the idea of leaving Libby alone, but he didn't dare go near her again, either. The scent of her, the soft disarray of her hair, the way her breasts seemed to draw at his mouth and the palms of his hands—all those things combined to make his grasp on reason tenuous.

Jess groaned, lifted his eyes to the ceiling and wondered if he was going to have to endure another ice-cold shower. The telephone rang, startling him, and he reached for it quickly. Libby might already be asleep, and he didn't want her to be disturbed.

"Hello?"

"Jess?" Monica's voice was calm, but there was an undercurrent of cold fury. "Did you take my car?"

He sighed, leaning back against the kitchen counter. "Yeah. Sorry. I should have called you before this, but—"

"But you were busy."

Jess flinched. Exactly what could he say to that? "Monica—"

"Never mind, Jess." She sighed the words. "I didn't have any right to say that. And if you helped yourself to my car, you must have had a good reason."

Why the hell did she have to be so reasonable? Why didn't Monica yell at him or something, so that he could get mad in good conscience and stop feeling like such an idiot? "I'm afraid the seats are a little muddy," he said.

"Muddy? Oh, yes—the rain. Was Libby okay?"

Again Jess's gaze lifted to the ceiling. Libby was not okay, thanks to him and Stacey and her charming ex-husband. But then, Monica was just making polite conversation, not asking for an in-depth account of Libby's emotional state. "She was drenched."

"So you brought her there, got her out of her wet clothes, built a fire—"

The anger Jess had wished for was suddenly there. "Monica."

She drew in a sharp breath. "All right, all right—I'm sorry. I take it our dinner date is off?"

"Yeah," Jess answered, turning the phone cord between his fingers. "I guess it is."

Monica was nothing if not persistent—probably that quality accounted for her impressive success in political circles. "Tomorrow night?"

Jess sighed. "I don't know."

There was a short, uncomfortable silence. "We'll talk later," Monica finally said brightly. "Listen, is it okay if I send somebody over there to get my car?"

"I'll bring it to you," Jess said. It was, after stealing it, the least he could do. He'd check first, to make sure that Libby really was sleeping, and with luck, he could be back before she woke up.

"Thanks," sang Monica in parting.

Jess hung up the phone and climbed the stairs, pausing at the edge of the bedroom. He dared go no farther, wanting that rumple-haired little hellion the way he did. "Libby?"

When there was no answer, Jess turned and went back down the stairs again, almost grateful that he had somewhere to go, something to do.

Monica hid her annoyance well as she inspected the muddy splotches on her car's upholstery. Overhead, the incessant rain pummeled the garage roof.

"I'm sorry," Jess said. It seemed that he was always apologizing for one thing or another lately. "My truck wouldn't start, and I was in a hurry...."

Monica allowed a flicker of anger to show in her gray eyes. "Right. When there is a damsel to be rescued, a knight has to grab the first available charger."

Having no answer for that, Jess shrugged. "I'll have your car cleaned," he offered when the silence grew too long, and then he turned to walk back out of the garage and down the driveway to his own car, which refused to start.

He got out and slammed the door. "Damn!" he bellowed, kicking yet another dent into the fender.

"Problems?"

Jess hadn't been aware of Ken until that moment, hadn't noticed the familiar truck parked nearby. "It would take all day to list them," he replied ruefully.

Ken grinned a typical sideways grin, and his blue eyes twinkled. He seemed oblivious of the rain pouring off the brim of his ancient hat and soaking through his denim jacket and jeans. "I think maybe my daughter might be at the top of the list. Is she all right?"

"She's..." Jess faltered, suddenly feeling like a high-school kid. "She's sleeping."

Ken laughed. "Must have been real hard to say that," he observed, "me being her daddy and all."

"It isn't... I didn't..."

Again Ken laughed. "Maybe you should," he said.

Jess was shocked—so shocked that he was speechless.

"Take my truck if you need it," Ken offered calmly, his hand coming to rest on Jess's shoulder. "I'll get a ride home from somebody here. And, Jess?"

"What?"

"Don't hurt Libby. She's had enough trouble and grief as it is."

"I know that," Jess replied, as the rain plastered his hair to his neck and forehead and made his clothes cling to his flesh in sodden, clammy patches. "I swear I won't hurt her."

"That's good enough for me," replied Libby's father, and then he pried the truck keys out of his pocket and tossed them to Jess.

"Ken..."

The foreman paused, looking back, his eyes wise and patient. How the hell was Jess going to ask this man what he had to ask, for Libby's sake?

"Spit it out, son," Ken urged. "I'm getting wet."

"Clothes—she was...Libby was caught in the rain, and she needs dry clothes."

Ken chuckled and shrugged his shoulders. "Stop at our place and get some of her things then," he said indulgently.

Jess was suddenly as confused by this man as he was by his daughter. What the hell was Ken doing, standing there taking this whole thing so calmly? Didn't it bother him, knowing what might happen when Jess got back to that house?

"See ya," said Ken in parting.

Completely confused, Jess got into Ken's truck and drove away. It wasn't until he'd gotten a set of dry clothes for Libby and reached his own house again that he understood. Ken trusted him.

Jess let his forehead rest on the truck's steering wheel and groaned. He couldn't stand another cold shower, dammit. He just couldn't.

But Ken trusted him. Libby was lying upstairs in his bed, and even if she was, by some miracle, ready to handle what was destined to happen, Jess couldn't make love to her. To do so would be to betray a man who had, in so many ways, been as much a father to him as Cleave Barlowe had.

The problem was that Jess couldn't think of Libby as a sister.

Jess sat glumly at the little table in the kitchen, making patterns in his omelet with a fork. Tiring of that, he flung Libby a beleaguered look and sneezed.

She felt a surge of tenderness. "Aren't you hungry?"

He shook his head. "Libby…"

It took all of her forbearance not to stand up, round the table, and touch Jess's forehead to see if he had a fever. "What?" she prompted softly.

"I think I should take you home."

Libby was hurt, but she smiled brightly. "Well, it *has* stopped raining," she reasoned.

"And I've got your dad's truck," added Jess.

"Um-hmm. Thanks for stopping and getting my clothes, by the way."

Outside, the wind howled and the night was dark. Jess gave the jeans and loose pink sweater he had picked up for Libby a distracted look and sneezed again. "You're welcome."

"And you, my friend, are sick."

Jess shook his head, went to the counter to pour coffee from the coffeemaker there. "Want some?" he asked, lifting the glass pot.

Libby declined. "Were you taking another shower when I got up?" she ventured cautiously. The peace between them, for all its sweet glow, was still new and fragile.

Libby would have sworn that he winced, and his face was unreadable. "I'm a clean person," he said, averting his eyes.

Libby bit the inside of her lower lip, suddenly possessed by an untimely urge to laugh. Jess had been shivering when he came out of that bathroom and unexpectedly encountered his newly awakened houseguest.

"Right," she said.

Jess sneezed again, violently. Somehow, the sound unchained Libby's amusement and she shrieked with laughter.

"What is so goddamn funny?" Jess demanded, setting his coffee cup down with an irritated thump and scowling.

"N-nothing," cried Libby.

Suddenly Jess was laughing, too. He pulled Libby out of her chair and into his arms, and she deliberately pressed herself close to him, delighting in the evidence of his desire, in the scent and substance and strength of him.

She almost said that she loved him.

"You wanted my body!" she accused instead, teasing.

Jess groaned and tilted his head back, ostensibly to study the ceiling. Libby saw a muscle leap beneath his chin and wanted to kiss it, but she refrained.

"You were taking a cold shower, weren't you, Jess?"

"Yes," he admitted with a martyrly sigh. "Woman, if I die of pneumonia, it will be your fault."

"On the contrary. I've done everything but throw myself at your feet, mister, and you haven't wanted any part of me."

"Wrong." Jess grinned wickedly, touching the tip of her breast with an index finger. "I want this part…" The finger trailed away, following an erotic path. "And this part…"

It took all of Libby's courage to say the words again, after his brisk rejection earlier. "Make love to me, Jess."

"My God, Libby—"

She silenced him by laying two fingers to his lips. Remembering the words he had flung at her in the Cessna the day of her arrival, she said saucily, "If it feels good, do it."

Jess gave her a mock scowl, but his arms were around her now, holding her against him. "You were a very mean little kid," he muttered, "and now you're a mean adult. Do you know what you're doing to me, Kincaid?"

Libby moved her hips slightly, delighting in the contact and the guttural groan the motion brought from Jess. "I have some vague idea, yes."

"Your father trusts me."

"My father!" Libby stared up at him, amazed. "Is that what you've been worried about? What my father will think?"

Jess shrugged, and his eyes moved away from hers. Clearly he was embarrassed. "Yes."

Libby laughed, though she was not amused. "You're not serious!"

His eyes came back to meet hers and the expression in their green depths was nothing if not serious. "Ken is my best friend," he said.

"Shall I call him up and ask for permission? Better yet, I could drive over there and get a note!"

The taunts caused Jess to draw back a little, though their thighs and hips were still touching, still piping primitive messages one to the other. "Very funny!" he snapped, and a muscle bunched in his neck, went smooth again.

Libby was quietly furious. "You're right—it isn't funny. This is my body, Jess—mine. I'm thirty-one years old and I make my own living and I *damned well* don't need my daddy's permission to go to bed with a man!"

The green eyes were twinkling with mischief. "That's a healthy attitude if I've ever heard one," he broke in. "However, before we go up those stairs, there is one more thing I want to know. Are you using me, Libby?"

"Using you?"

"Yes. Do I really mean something to you, or would any man do?"

Libby felt as though she'd just grabbed hold of a high-voltage wire; in a few spinning seconds she was hurled from pain to rage to humiliation.

Jess held her firmly. "I see the question wasn't received in the spirit in which it was intended," he said, his eyes serious now, searching her burning, defiant face. "What I meant to ask was, are we going to be making love, Libby, or just proving that you can go the whole route and respond accordingly?"

Libby met his gaze bravely, though inside she was still shaken and angry. "Why would I go to all this trouble, Jess, if I didn't want you? After all, I could have just stopped someone on the street and said, 'Excuse me, sir, but would you mind making love to me? I'd like to find out if I'm frigid or not.'"

Jess sighed heavily, but his hands were sliding up under the back of Libby's pink sweater, gently kneading the firm flesh there. The only sign that her sarcasm had rankled him was the almost imperceptible leaping of the pulsepoint beneath his right ear.

"I guess I'm having a little trouble understanding your sudden change of heart, Libby. For years you've hated my guts. Now, after confiding that your ex-husband put you through some kind of emotional wringer and left you feeling about as attractive as a sink drain, you want to share my bed."

Libby closed her eyes. The motion of his hands on her back was hypnotic, making it hard for her to breathe, let alone think. When she felt the catch of her bra give way, she shivered.

She should tell him that she loved him, that maybe, despite outward appearances, she'd always loved him, but she didn't dare. This was a man who had thought the worst of her at every turn, who had never missed a chance to get under her skin. Allowing him inside the fortress where her innermost emotions were stored could prove disastrous.

His hands came slowly around from her back to the aching roundness of her breasts, sliding easily, brazenly under the loosened bra.

"Answer me, Libby," he drawled, his voice a sleepy rumble.

She was dazed; his fingers came to play a searing symphony at her nipples, plying them, drawing at them. "I...I want you. I'm not trying to p-prove anything."

"Let me look at you, Libby."

Libby pulled the pink sweater off over her head, stood perfectly still as Jess dispensed with her bra and then stepped back a little way to admire her.

He outlined one blushing nipple with the tip of his finger, progressed to wreak the same havoc on the other. Then, with strong hands, he lifted Libby up onto a counter, so that her breasts were on a level with his face.

She gasped as he took languid, tentative suckle at one peak, then trailed a path with the tip of his tongue to the other, conquering it with lazy ease.

She was desperate now. "Make love to me," she whispered again in broken tones.

"Make love to me, *Jess*," he prompted, nibbling now, driving her half-wild with the need of him.

Libby swallowed hard, closed her eyes. His teeth were scraping gently at her nipple now, rousing it to obedience. "Make love to me, Jess," she repeated breathlessly.

He withdrew his mouth, cupping her in his hands, letting

his thumbs do the work his lips and teeth had done before. "Open your eyes," he commanded in a hoarse rumble. "Look at me, Libby."

Dazed, her very soul spinning within her, Libby obeyed.

"Tell me," he insisted raggedly, "that you're not seeing Stacey or your misguided ex-husband. Tell me that you see *me,* Libby."

"I do, Jess."

He lifted her off the counter and into his arms, and his mouth came down on hers, cautious at first, then almost harshly demanding. Libby was electrified by the kiss, by the searching fierceness of his tongue, by the moan of need that came from somewhere deep inside him. Finally he ended the kiss, and his eyes were smiling into hers.

Feeling strangely giddy, Libby laughed. "Is this the part where you make love to me?"

"This is it," he replied, and then they were moving through the house toward the stairs. Lightning crackled and flashed above the skylights, while thunder struck a booming accompaniment.

"The earth is moving already," said Libby into the Jess-scented wool of his sweater.

Jess took the stairs two at a time. "Just wait," he replied.

In the bedroom, which was lit only by the lightning that was sundering the night sky, he set Libby on her feet. For a moment they just stood still, looking at each other. Libby felt as though she had become a part of the terrible storm that was pounding at the tall windows, and she grasped Jess's arms so that she wouldn't be blown away to the mountaintops or flung beyond the angry clouds.

"Touch me, Libby," Jess said, and somehow, even over the renewed rage of the storm, she heard him.

Cautiously she slid her hands beneath his sweater, splaying

her fingers so that she could feel as much of him as possible. His chest was hard and broad and softly furred, and he groaned as she found masculine nipples and explored them.

Libby moved her hands down over his rib cage to the sides of his waist, up his warm, granite-muscled back. *I love you,* she thought, and then she bit her lower lip lest she actually say the words.

At some unspoken urging from Jess, she caught his sweater in bunched fists and drew it up over his head. Silver-blue lightning scored the sky and danced on the planes of his bare chest, his magnificent face.

Libby was drawn to him, tasting one masculine nipple with a cautious tongue, suckling the other. He moaned and tangled his fingers in her hair, pressing her close, and she knew that he was experiencing the same keen pleasure she had known.

Presently he caught her shoulders in his hands and held her at arm's length, boldly admiring her bare breasts. "Beautiful," he rasped. "So beautiful."

Libby had long been ashamed of her body, thinking it inadequate. Now, in this moment of storm and fury, she was proud of every curve and hollow, every pore and freckle. She removed her jeans and panties with graceful motions.

Jess's reaction was a low, rumbling groan, followed by a gasp of admiration. He stood still, a western Adonis, as she undid his jeans, felt the hollows of his narrow hips, the firmness of his buttocks. Within seconds he was as naked as Libby.

She caught his hands in her own, drew him toward the bed. But instead of reclining with her there, he knelt at the side, positioned Libby so that her hips rested on the edge of the mattress.

His hands moved over every part of her—her breasts, her

shoulders, her flat, smooth stomach, the insides of her trembling thighs.

"Jess…"

"Shh, it's all right."

"But…" Libby's back arched and a spasm of delight racked her as he touched the curls sheltering the core of her passion, first with his fingers, then with his lips. "Oh…wait…oh, Jess, no…"

"Yes," he said, his breath warm against her. And then he parted her and took her fully into his mouth, following the instinctive rising and falling of her hips, chuckling at the soft cry she gave.

A violent shudder went through Libby's already throbbing body, and her knees moved wide of each other, shaking, made of no solid substance.

Frantic, she found his head, tangled her fingers in his hair. "Stop," she whimpered, even as she held him fast.

Jess chuckled again and then went right on consuming her, his hands catching under her knees, lifting them higher, pressing them farther apart.

Libby was writhing now, her breath harsh and burning, her vision blurred. The storm came inside the room and swept her up, up, up, beyond the splitting skies. She cried out in wonder as she collided with the moon and bounced off, to be enfolded by a waiting sun.

When she came back inside herself, Jess was beside her on the bed, soothing her with soft words, stroking away the tears that had somehow gathered on her face.

"I've never read…" she whispered stupidly. "I didn't know…"

Jess was drawing her up, so that she lay full on the bed, naked and sated at his side. "Look it up," he teased, kissing her briefly, tenderly. "I think it would be under O."

Libby laughed, and the sound was a warm, soft contrast to the tumult of the storm. "What an ego!"

With an index finger, Jess traced her lips, her chin, the moist length of her neck. Small novas flashed and flared within her as her pulsing senses began to make new demands.

When his mouth came to her breast again, Libby arched her back and whimpered. "Jess…Jess…"

He circled the straining nipple with a warm tongue. "What, babe?"

No coherent words would come to Libby's beleaguered mind. "I don't know," she managed finally. "I don't know!"

"I do," Jess answered, and then he suckled in earnest.

Powerless under the tyranny of her own body, Libby gave herself up to sensation. It seemed that no part of her was left untouched, unconquered or unworshiped.

When at last Jess poised himself above her, strong and fully a man, his face reflected the flashing lightning that seemed to seek them both.

"I'm Jess," he warned again in a husky whisper that betrayed his own fierce need.

Libby drew him to her with quick, fevered hands. "I know," she gasped, and then she repeated his name like some crazy litany, whispering it first, sobbing it when he thrust his searing magnificence inside her.

He moved slowly at first, and the finely sculptured planes of his face showed the cost of his restraint, the conflicting force of his need. "Libby," he pleaded. "Oh, God…Libby…"

She thrust her hips upward in an instinctive, unplanned motion that shattered Jess's containment and caused his great muscular body to convulse once and then assert its dominance in a way that was at once fierce and tender. It seemed that he sought some treasure within her, so deeply did he delve, some shimmering thing that he would perish without.

His groans rose above the sound of thunder, and as his pace accelerated and his passion was unleashed, Libby moved in rhythm with him, one with him, his.

Their bodies moved faster, agile in their quest, each glistening with the sheen of sweet exertion, each straining toward the sun that, this time, would consume them both.

The tumult flung them high, tore them asunder, fused them together again. Libby sobbed in the hot glory of her release and heard an answering cry from Jess.

They clung together, struggling for breath, for a long time after the slow, treacherous descent had been made. Twice, on the way, Libby's body had paused to greedily claim what had been denied it before.

She was flushed, reckless in her triumph. "I did it," she exalted, her hands moving on the slackened muscles in Jess's back. "I did it…I responded…"

Instantly she felt those muscles go taut, and Jess's head shot up from its resting place in the curve where her neck and shoulder met.

"What?"

Libby stiffened, knowing now, too late, how grave her mistake had been. "I mean, *we* did it…" she stumbled lamely.

But Jess was wrenching himself away from her, searching for his clothes, pulling them on. "Congratulations!" he yelled.

Libby sat up, confused, wildly afraid. Dear God, was he going to walk out now? Was he going to hate her for a few thoughtless words?

"Jess, wait!" she pleaded, clutching the sheet to her chest. "Please!"

"For what, Libby?" he snapped from the top of the stairs. "Exhibit B? Is there something else you want to prove?"

"Jess!"

But he was storming down the stairs, silent in his rage, bent on escaping her.

"Jess!" Libby cried out again in fear, tears pouring down her face, her hands aching where they grasped the covers.

The only answer was the slamming of the front door.

Chapter 7

Ken Kincaid looked up from the cards in his hand as the lights flickered, went out, came on again. Damn, this was a hell of a storm—if the rain didn't let up soon, the creeks would overflow and they'd have range calves drowning right and left.

Across the table, Cleave Barlowe laid down his own hand of cards. "Quite a storm, eh?" he asked companionably. "Jess bring your truck back yet?"

"I don't need it," said Ken, still feeling uneasy.

Lightning creased the sky beyond the kitchen window, and thunder shook the old house on its sturdy foundations. Cleave grinned. "He's with Libby, then?"

"Yup," said Ken, smiling himself.

"Think they know the sky's turning itself inside out?"

There was an easing in Ken; he laughed outright. "Doubt it," he replied, looking at his cards again.

For a while the two men played the two-handed poker

they had enjoyed for years, but it did seem that luck wasn't running with either one of them. Finally they gave up the effort and Cleave went home.

With his old friend gone, Ken felt apprehensive again. He went around the house making sure all the windows were closed against the rain, and wondered why one storm should bother him that way, when he'd seen a thousand and never found them anything more than a nuisance.

He was about to shut off the lamp in the front room when he saw the headlights of his own truck swing into the driveway. Seconds later, there was an anxious knock at the door.

"Jess?" Ken marveled, staring at the haggard, rain-drenched man standing on the front porch. "What the hell...?"

Jess looked as though he'd just taken a first-rate gut punch. "Could I come in?"

"That's a stupid question," retorted Ken, stepping back to admit his unexpected and obviously distraught visitor. "Is Libby okay?"

Jess's haunted eyes wouldn't quite link up with Ken's. "She's fine," he said, his hands wedged into the pockets of his jeans, his hair and sweater dripping rainwater.

Ken arched an eyebrow. "What'd you do, anyway—ride on the running board of that truck and steer from outside?"

Jess didn't answer; he didn't seem to realize that he was wet to the skin. There was a distracted look about him that made Ken ache inside.

In silence Ken led the way into the kitchen, poured a dose of straight whiskey into a mug, added strong coffee.

"You look like you've been dragged backward through a knothole," he observed when Jess was settled at the table. "What happened?"

Jess closed his hands around the mug. "I'm in love with your daughter," he said after a long time.

Ken sat down, allowed himself a cautious grin. "If you drove over here in this rain just to tell me that, friend, you got wet for nothing."

"You knew?" Jess seemed honestly surprised.

"Everybody knew. Except maybe you and Libby."

Jess downed the coffee and the potent whiskey almost in a single gulp. There was a struggle going on in his face, as though he might be fighting hard to hold himself together.

Ken rose to put more coffee into Jess's mug, along with a lot more whiskey. If ever a man needed a drink, this one did.

"Maybe you'd better put on some dry clothes," the older man ventured.

Jess only shook his head.

Ken sat back in his chair and waited. When Jess was ready to talk, he would. There was, Ken had learned, no sense in pushing before that point was reached.

"Libby's beautiful, you know," Jess remarked presently, as he started on his third drink.

Ken smiled. "Yeah. I've noticed."

Simple and ordinary though they were, the words triggered some kind of emotional reaction in Jess, broke down the barriers he had been maintaining so carefully. His face crumbled, he lowered his head to his arms, and he cried. The sobs were deep and dry and ragged.

Hurting because Jess hurt, Ken waited.

Soon enough, his patience was rewarded. Jess began to talk, brokenly at first, and then with stone-cold reason.

Ken didn't react openly to anything he said; much of what Jess told him about Libby's marriage to Aaron Strand came as no real surprise. He was wounded, all the same, for his daughter and for the devastated young man sitting across the table from him.

The level of whiskey in Ken's bottle went down as the hour

grew later. Finally, when Jess was so drunk that his words started getting all tangled up with each other, Ken half led, half carried him up the stairs to Libby's room.

In the hallway, he paused, reflecting. Life was a hell of a thing, he decided. Here was Jess, sleeping fitfully in Libby's bed, all alone. And just up the hill, chances were, Libby was tossing and turning in Jess's bed, just as lonely.

Not for the first time, Ken Kincaid felt a profound desire to get them both by the hair and knock their heads together.

Libby cried until far into the night and then, exhausted, she slept. When she awakened, shocked to find herself in Jess Barlowe's bed, she saw that the world beyond the windows had been washed to a clean sparkle.

The world inside her seemed tawdry by comparison.

Her face feeling achy and swollen, Libby got out of bed, stumbled across the room to the bathroom. Jess was nowhere in the house; she would have sensed it if he were.

As Libby filled the tub with hot water, she wondered whether she was relieved that he wasn't close by, or disappointed. A little of both, she concluded as she slid into her bath and sat there in miserable reverie.

Facing Jess now would have been quite beyond her. Why, why had she said such a foolish thing, when she might have known how Jess would react? On the other hand, why had *he* made such a big deal out of a relatively innocuous remark?

More confused than ever, Libby finished her bath and climbed out to dry herself with a towel. In short order she was dressed and her hair was combed. Because she had no toothbrush—Jess had forgotten that when he picked up her things—she had to be content with rinsing her mouth.

Downstairs, Libby stood staring at the telephone, willing herself to call her father and confess that she needed a ride home. Pride wouldn't allow that, however, and she had made up her mind to walk the distance when she heard a familiar engine outside, the slam of a truck door.

Jess was back, she thought wildly. Where had he been all night? With Monica? What would she say to him?

The questions were pointless, for when Libby forced herself to go to the front door and open it, she saw her father striding up the walk, not Jess.

Fresh embarrassment stained Libby's cheeks, though there was no condemnation in Ken's weathered face, no anger in his understanding eyes. "Ride home?" he said.

Unable to speak, Libby only nodded.

"Pretty bad night?" he ventured in his concise way when they were both settled in the truck and driving away.

"Dismal," replied Libby, fixing her eyes on the red Hereford cattle grazing in the green, rain-washed distance.

"Jess isn't in very good shape, either," commented Ken after an interval.

Libby's eyes were instantly trained on her father's profile. "You've seen him?"

"Seen him?" Ken laughed gruffly. "I poured him into bed at three this morning."

"He was drunk?" Libby was amazed.

"He had a nip or two."

"How is he now?"

Ken glanced at her, turned his eyes back to the rutted, winding country road ahead. "Jess is hurting," he said, and there was a finality in his tone that kept Libby from asking so much as one more question.

Jess is hurting. What the devil did that mean? Was he hung over? Had the night been as miserable for him as it had been for her?

Presently the truck came to a stop in front of the big Victorian house that had been "home" to Libby for as long as she could remember. Ken made no move to shut off the engine, and she got out without saying goodbye. For all her brave words of the night before, about not needing her father's approval, she felt estranged from him now, subdued.

After forcing down a glass of orange juice and a slice of toast in the kitchen, Libby went into the studio Cathy and her father had improvised for her and did her best to work. Even during the worst days in New York, she had been able to find solace in the mechanics of drawing her cartoon strip, forgetting her own troubles to create comical dilemmas for Liberated Lizzie.

Today was different.

The panels Libby sketched were awkward, requiring too many erasures, and even if she had been able to get the drawings right, she couldn't have come up with a funny thought for the life of her.

At midmorning, Libby decided that her career was over and paced from one end of the studio to the other, haunted by thoughts of the night before.

Jess had made it clear, in his kitchen, that he didn't want to make love just to let Libby prove that she was "normal." And what had she done? She'd *gloated.*

Shame ached in Libby's cheeks as she walked. *I did it,* she'd crowed, as though she were Edison and the first electric light had just been lit. God, how could she have been so stupid? So insensitive?

"You did have a little help, you know," she scolded herself out loud. And then she covered her face with both hands and cried. It had been partly Jess's fault, that scene—he had definitely overreacted, and on top of that, he had been unreasonable. He had stormed out without giving Libby a chance to make things right.

Still, it was all too easy to imagine how he'd felt. Used. And the truth was that, without intending to, Libby had used him.

Small, strong hands were suddenly pulling Libby's hands away from her face. Through the blur, she saw Cathy watching her, puzzled and sad.

"What's wrong?" her cousin asked. "Please, Libby, tell me what's wrong."

"Everything!" wailed Libby, who was beyond trying to maintain her dignity now.

Gently Cathy drew her close, hugged her. For a moment they were two motherless little girls again, clinging to each other because there were some pains that even Ken, with his gruff, unswerving devotion, couldn't ease.

The embrace was comforting, and after a minute or two Libby recovered enough to step back and offer Cathy a shaky smile. "I've missed you so much, Cathy," she said.

"Don't get sloppy," teased Cathy, using her face to give the toneless words expression.

Libby laughed. "What are you doing today, besides being one of the idle rich?"

Cathy tilted her head to one side. "Did you really stay with Jess last night?" she asked with swift hands.

"Aren't we blunt today?" Libby shot back, both speaking and signing. "I suppose the whole ranch is talking about it!"

Cathy nodded.

"Damn!"

"Then it's true!" exalted Cathy aloud, her eyes sparkling.

Some of Libby's earlier remorse drained away, pushed aside by feelings of anger and betrayal. "Has Jess been bragging?" she demanded, her hands on her hips, her indignation warm and thick in her throat.

"He isn't the type to do that," Cathy answered in slow, carefully formed words, "and you know it."

Libby wasn't so certain—Jess had been very angry, and his pride had been stung. Besides, the only other person who had known was Ken, and he was notoriously tight-lipped when it came to other people's business. "Who told you?" she persisted, narrowing her eyes.

"Nobody had to," Cathy answered aloud. "I was down at the stables, saddling Banjo, and one of the range crews was there—ten or twelve men, I guess. Anyway, there was a fight out front—Jess punched out one of the cowboys."

Libby could only gape.

Cathy gave the story a stirring finale. "I think Jess would have killed that guy if Ken hadn't hauled him off."

Libby found her voice. "Was Jess hurt? Cathy, did you see if he was hurt?"

Cathy grinned at her cousin's undisguised concern. "Not a scratch. He got into an argument with Ken and left."

Libby felt a strong need to find her father and ask him exactly what had happened, but she knew that the effort would be wasted. Even if she could find Ken, which was unlikely considering the size of the ranch and all the places he could be, he wouldn't explain.

Cathy was studying the messy piece of drawing paper affixed to the art board. "You're not going to work?" she signed.

"I gave up," Libby confessed. "I couldn't keep my mind on it."

"After a night with Jess Barlowe, who could?"

Libby suddenly felt challenged, defensive. She even thought that, perhaps, there was more to the deep closeness between Jess and Cathy than she had guessed. "What do you know about spending the night with Jess?" she snapped before she could stop herself.

Cathy rolled her beautiful green eyes. "*Nothing.* For better or worse, and mostly it's been better, I'm married to Jess's brother—remember?"

Libby swallowed, feeling foolish. "Where is Stacey, anyway?" she asked, more to make conversation than because she wanted to know.

The question brought a shadow of sadness to Cathy's face. "He's away on one of his business trips."

Libby sat down on her art stool, folded her hands. "Maybe you should have gone with him, Cathy. You used to do that a lot, didn't you? Maybe if you two could be alone…talk…"

The air suddenly crackled with Cathy's anger and hurt. "*He* talks!" she raged aloud. "I just move my hands!"

Libby spoke softly, gently. "You could talk to Stacey, Cathy—really talk, the way you do with me."

"No."

"Why not?"

"I know I sound like a record playing on the wrong speed, that's why!"

"Even if that were so, would it matter?" signed Libby, frowning. "Stacey knew you were deaf before he married you, for heaven's sake."

Cathy's head went down. "He must have felt sorry for me or something."

Instantly Libby was off her stool, gripping Cathy's shoulders in firm, angry hands. "He loves you!"

Tears misted the emerald-green eyes and Cathy's lower lip trembled. "No doubt that's why he intends to divorce me and marry you, Libby."

"No," insisted Libby, giving her cousin a slight shake. "No, that isn't true. I think Stacey is confused, Cathy. Upset. Maybe it's this thing about your not wanting to have a baby. Or maybe he feels that you don't need him, you're so independent."

"Independent? Don't look now, Libby Kincaid, but *you're* the independent one! You have a career…you can hear—"

"Will you stop feeling sorry for yourself, dammit!" Libby almost screamed. "I'm so tired of hearing how you suffer! For God's sake, stop whining and fight for the man you love!"

Cathy broke free of Libby's grasp, furious, tears pouring down her face. "It's too late!" she cried. "You're here now, and it's too late!"

Libby sighed, stepped back, stricken by her own outburst and by Cathy's, too. "You're forgetting one thing," she reasoned quietly. "I'm not in love with Stacey. And it would take two of us to start anything, wouldn't it?"

Cathy went to the windows and stared out at the pond, her chin high. Knowing that her cousin needed this interval to restore her dignity and assemble her thoughts, Libby did not approach her.

Finally Cathy sniffled and turned back to offer a shaky smile. "I didn't come over here to fight with you," she said clearly. "I'm going to Kalispell, and I wanted to know if you would like to come with me."

Libby agreed readily, and after changing her clothes and leaving a quick note for Ken, she joined Cathy in the shiny blue Ferrari.

The ride to Kalispell was a fairly long one, and by the time Cathy and Libby reached the small city, they had reestablished their old, easy relationship.

They spent the day shopping, had lunch in a rustic steak house bearing the Circle Bar B brand, and then started home again.

"Are you really going to give that to Jess?" Cathy asked, her eyes twinkling when she cast a look at the bag in Libby's lap.

"I may lose my courage." Libby frowned, wondering what had possessed her to buy a T-shirt with such an outlandish saying printed on it. She supposed she'd hoped that the gesture would penetrate the barrier between herself and Jess, enabling them to talk.

"Take my advice," said Cathy, guiding the powerful car off the highway and onto the road that led to the heart of the ranch. "Give him the shirt."

"Maybe," said Libby, looking off into the sweeping, endless blue sky. A small airplane was making a graceful descent toward the Circle Bar B landing strip.

"Who do you suppose that is?" Libby asked, catching Cathy's attention with a touch on her arm.

The question was a mistake. Cathy, who had not, of course, heard the plane's engine, scanned the sky and saw it. "Why don't we find out?"

Libby scrunched down in her seat, sorry that she had pointed out the airplane now. Suppose Stacey was aboard, returning from his business trip, and there was another uncomfortable scene at the airstrip? Suppose it was Jess, and he either yelled at Libby or, worse yet, pretended that she wasn't there?

"I'd rather go home," she muttered.

But Cathy's course was set, and the Ferrari bumped and jostled over the road to the landing strip as though it were a pickup truck.

The plane came to a smooth stop as Cathy parked at one side of the road and got out of the car, shading her eyes with one hand, watching. Libby remained in her seat.

She had, it seemed, imagined only part of the possible scenario. The pilot was Jess, and his passenger was a wan, tight-lipped Stacey.

"Oh, God," said Libby, sinking even farther into the car seat. She would have kept her face hidden in her hand forever, probably, if it hadn't been for the crisp, insistent tap at her window.

Having no other choice, she rolled the glass down and squinted into Jess Barlowe's unreadable, hard-lined face. "Come with me," he said flatly.

Libby looked through the Ferrari's windshield, saw Stacey and Cathy standing nearby, a disturbing distance between them. Cathy was glaring angrily into Stacey's face, and Stacey was casting determined looks in Libby's direction.

"They need some time alone," Jess said, his eyes linking fiercely, warningly, with Libby's as he opened the car door for her.

Anxious not to make an obviously unpleasant situation any worse, Libby gathered up her bags and her purse and got out of the car, following along behind Jess's long strides. His truck, which she hadn't noticed before, was parked close by.

Without looking back at Stacey and Cathy, Libby slid gratefully into the dusty front seat and closed her eyes. Not until the truck was moving did she open them, and even then she couldn't quite bring herself to look at the man behind the wheel.

"That was touching," he said in a vicious rasp.

Libby stiffened in the seat, staring at Jess's rock-hard profile now. "What did you say?"

The powerful shoulders moved in an annoying shrug. "Your wanting to meet Stacey on his triumphant return."

It took Libby a moment to absorb what he was implying. When she had, she slammed him with the paper bag that contained the T-shirt she'd bought for him in Kalispell and hissed, "You bastard! I didn't know Stacey was going to be on that plane, and if I had, I certainly wouldn't have been there at all!"

"Sure," he drawled, and even though he was grinning and

looking straight ahead at the road, there was contempt in his tone and a muscle pulsing at the base of his jaw.

Libby felt tears of frustration rise in her eyes. "I thought you believed me," she said.

"I thought I did, too," Jess retorted with acid amusement. "But that was before you showed up at the landing strip at such an opportune moment."

"It was Cathy's idea to meet the plane!"

"Right."

The paper bag crackled as Libby lifted it, prepared to swing.

"Do that again and I'll stop this car and raise blisters on your backside," Jess warned, without so much as looking in her direction.

Libby lowered the bag back to her lap, swallowed miserably, and turned her attention to the road. She did not believe Jess's threat for one moment, but she felt childish for trying to hit him with the bag. "Cathy told me there was a fight at the stables this morning," she dared after a long time. "What happened?"

Another shrug, as insolent as the first, preceded his reply. "One of Ken's men said something I didn't like."

"Like what?"

"Like didn't it bother me to sleep with my brother's mistress."

Libby winced, sorry for pressing the point. "Oh, God," she said, and she was suddenly so tired, so broken, and so frustrated that she couldn't hold back her tears anymore. She covered her face with both hands and turned her head as far away from Jess as she could, but the effort was useless.

Jess stopped the truck at the side of the road, turned Libby easily toward him. Through a blur, she saw the Ferrari race past.

"Let go of me!"

Jess not only didn't let go, he pulled her close. "I'm sorry," he muttered into her hair. "God, Libby, I don't know what comes over me, what makes me say things to hurt you."

"Garden-variety hatred!" sniffled Libby, who was already forgiving him even though it was against her better judgment.

He chuckled. "No. I couldn't ever hate you, Libby."

She looked up at him, confused and hopeful. Before she could think of anything to say, however, there was a loud *pop* from beneath the hood of the truck, followed by a sizzle and clouds of steam.

"Goddammit!" rasped Jess.

Libby laughed, drunk on the scent of him, the closeness of him, the crazy paradox of him. "This crate doesn't exactly fit your image, you know," she taunted. "Why don't you get yourself a decent car?"

He turned from glowering at the hood of the truck to smile down into her face. "If I do, Kincaid, will you let me make love to you in the backseat?"

She shoved at his immovable chest with both hands, laughing again. "No, no, a thousand times no!"

Jess nibbled at her jawline, at the lobe of her ear, chuckled huskily as she tensed. "How many times no?"

"Maybe," said Libby.

Just when she thought she would surely go crazy, Jess drew back from his brazen pursuits and smiled lazily. "It is time I got a new car," he conceded, with an evil light glistening in his jade eyes. "Will you come to Kalispell and help me pick it out, Libby?"

A thrill skittered through Libby's body and flamed in her face. "I was just there," she protested, clutching at straws.

"It shouldn't—" Jess bent, nipped at the side of her neck with gentle teeth "—take long. A couple of days at the most."

"A couple of days!"

"And nights." Jess's lips were scorching their way across

the tender hollow of her throat. "Think about it, Lib. Just you and me. No Stacey. No Cathy. No problems."

Libby shivered as a knowledgeable hand closed over one of her breasts, urging, reawakening. "No p-problems?" she echoed.

Jess undid the top button of her blouse.

Libby's breath caught in her throat; she felt heat billowing up inside her, foaming out, just as it was foaming out of the station wagon's radiator. "Wh-where would we s-stay?"

Another button came undone.

Jess chuckled, his mouth on Libby's collarbone now, tasting it, doing nothing to cool the heat that was pounding within her. "How about—" the third button gave way, and Libby's bra was displaced by a gentle hand "—one of those motels…with the…vibrating beds?"

"Tacky," gasped Libby, and her eyes closed languidly and her head fell back as Jess stroked the nipple he'd just found to pebble-hard response.

"My condo, then," he said, and his lips were sliding down from her collarbone, soft, soft, over the upper rounding of her bare breast.

Libby gasped and arched her back as his lips claimed the distended, hurting peak. "Jess…oh, God…this is a p-public road!"

"Umm," Jess said, lapping at her now with the tip of his tongue. "Will you go with me, Libby?"

Wild need went through her as he stroked the insides of her thighs, forcing her blue-jeaned legs apart. And all the while he plied her nipple into a panic of need. "Yes!" she gasped finally.

Jess undid the snap of her jeans, slid his hand inside, beneath the scanty lace of her panties.

"Damn you," Libby whispered hoarsely, "s-stop that! I said I'd go—"

He told her what else she was about to do. And one glorious, soul-scoring minute later, she did.

Red in the face, still breathing heavily, Libby closed her jeans, tugged her bra back into place, buttoned her blouse. God, what if someone had come along and seen her letting Jess…letting him play with her like that?

All during the ride home, she mentally rehearsed the blistering diatribe he deserved to hear. He could just go to Kalispell by *himself,* she would tell him. If he thought for one damned minute that he was going to take her to his condo and make love to her, he was sadly mistaken, she would say.

"Be ready in half an hour," Jess told her at her father's front door.

"Okay," Libby replied.

After landing the Cessna in Kalispell and making arrangements to rent a car, which turned out to be a temperamental cousin to Jess's truck, they drove through the small city to an isolated tree-dense property beyond. There were at least a million stars in the sky, and as the modest rental rattled over a narrow wooden bridge spanning a creek, Libby couldn't help giving in a little to the romance of it all.

Beyond the bridge, there were more trees—towering ponderosa pines, whispering, shiny-leaved birches. They stopped in the driveway of a condominium that stood apart from several others. Jess got out of the car, came around to open Libby's door for her.

"Let's get rid of the suitcases and go out for something to eat," he said.

Libby's stomach rumbled inelegantly, and Jess laughed as he caught her hand in his and drew her up the darkened walk to the front door of the condominium. "That shoots my plans for a little fun before dinner," he teased.

"There's always after," replied Libby, lifting her chin.

Chapter 8

The inside of the condominium was amazingly like Jess's house on the ranch. There was a loft, for instance, this one accessible by both stairs and, of all things, a built-in ladder. Too, the general layout of the rooms was much the same.

The exceptions were that the floors were carpeted rather than bare oak, and the entire roof was made of heavy glass. *When we make love here, I'll be able to look up and see the stars,* Libby mused.

"Like it?" Jess asked, setting the suitcases down and watching her with discerning, mirthful green eyes.

Libby was uncomfortable again, doubting the wisdom of coming here now that she was faced with the realities of the situation. "Is this where you bring all your conquests?"

Jess smiled, shrugged.

"Well?" prodded Libby, annoyed because he hadn't even had the common decency to offer a denial.

He sat down on the stone ledge fronting the fireplace, wrapped his hands around one knee. "The place does happen to be something of a love nest, as a matter of fact."

Libby was stung. Dammit, how unchivalrous could one man be? "Oh," she said loftily.

"It's my father's place," Jess said, clearly delighting in her obvious curiosity and the look of relief she couldn't quite hide.

"Your father's?"

Jess grinned. "He entertains his mistress here, from time to time. In his position, he has to be discreet."

Libby was gaping now, trying to imagine the sedate, dignified Senator Barlowe cavorting with a woman beneath slanted glass roofs, climbing ladders to star-dappled lofts.

Jess's amused gaze had strayed to the ladder. "It probably puts him in mind of the good old days—climbing into the hayloft, and all that."

Libby blushed. She was still quite disturbed by that ladder, among other things. "You did ask the senator's permission to come here, didn't you?"

Jess seemed to know that she had visions of Cleave Barlowe carrying some laughing woman over the threshold and finding the place already occupied. "Yes," he assured her in a teasing tone, rising and coming toward her. "I said, 'Mind if I take Libby to your condo, dear old dad, and take her to bed?' And he said—"

"Jess!" Libby howled, in protest.

He laughed, caught her elbows in his hands, kissed her playfully, his lips sampling hers, tugging at them in soft entreaty. "My father is in Washington," he said. "Stop worrying."

Libby pulled back, her face hot, her mind spinning. "I'm hungry!"

"Umm," replied Jess, "so am I."

Why did she feel like a sixteen-year-old on the verge of big trouble? "Please…let's go now."

Jess sighed.

They went, but they were back, arms burdened with cartons of Chinese food, in less than half an hour.

While Jess set the boxes out on the coffee table, Libby went to the kitchen for plates and silverware. Scribbled on a blackboard near the sink, she saw the surprising words: "Thanks, Ken. See you next week. B."

A soft chuckle simmered up into Libby's throat and emerged as a giggle. Could it be that her father, her serious, hardworking father, had a ladyfriend who visited him here in this romantic hideaway? Tilting her head to one side, she considered, grinned again. "Naaaah!"

But Libby's grin wouldn't fade as she carried plates, forks, spoons and paper napkins back into the living room.

"What's so funny?" Jess asked, trying to hide the hunk of sweet-and-sour chicken he had just purloined from one of the steaming cartons.

"Nothing," said Libby, catching his hand and raising it to his mouth. Sheepishly he popped the tidbit of chicken onto his tongue and chewed.

"You lie," Jess replied, "but I'm too hungry to press the point."

While they ate, Libby tried to envision what sort of woman her father would be drawn to—tall, short? Quiet, talkative?

"You're mulling over more than the chow mein," accused Jess presently in a good-natured voice. "Tell me, what's going on in that gifted little head?"

Libby shrugged. "Romance."

He grinned. "That's what I like to hear."

But Libby was thinking seriously, following her thoughts

through new channels. In all the years since her mother's death, just before Cathy had come to live on the ranch, she had never imagined Ken Kincaid caring about another woman. "It isn't as though he's old," she muttered, "or unattractive."

Jess set down his plate with a mockingly forceful thump. "That does it. Who are you talking about, Kincaid?" he demanded archly, his wonderful mouth twitching in the effort to suppress a grin.

She perused him with lofty disdain. "Am I correct in assuming that you are jealous?"

"Jealous as hell," came the immediate and not-so-jovial response.

Libby laughed, laid a hand on his knee. "If you must know, I was thinking about my father. I've always kept him in this neat little cubicle in my mind, marked 'Dad.' If you can believe it, it has just now occurred to me that he's a man, with a life, and maybe even a love, of his own."

Mirth danced in Jess's jade eyes, but if he knew anything about Ken's personal life, he clearly wasn't going to speak of it. "Pass the eggroll," he said diplomatically.

When the meal was over, Libby's reflections began to shift to matters nearer the situation at hand.

"I don't know what I'm doing here," she said pensively as she and Jess cleared the coffee table and started toward the kitchen with the debris. "I must be out of my mind."

Jess dropped the cartons and the crumpled napkins into the trash compactor. "Thanks a lot," he said, watching her attentively as she rinsed the plates and silverware and put them into the dishwasher.

Wearing tailored gray slacks and a lightweight teal-blue sweater, he was devastatingly attractive. Still, the look Libby gave him was a serious, questioning one. "What is it with us,

Jess? What makes us behave the way we do? One minute, we're yelling at each other, or not speaking at all, and the next we're alone in a place like this."

"Chemistry?"

Libby laughed ruefully. "More like voodoo. So what kind of car are you planning to buy?"

Jess drew her to him; his fingertips were butterfly-light on the small of her back. "Car?" he echoed, as though the word were foreign.

There was a soft, quivering ache in one corner of Libby's heart. Why couldn't things always be like this between them? Why did they have to wrangle so fiercely before achieving this quiet accord? "Stop teasing me," she said softly. "We did come here to buy a car, you know."

Jess's hands pulled her blouse up and out of her slacks, made slow-moving, sensuous circles on her bare back. "Yes," he said in a throaty rumble. "A car. But there are lots of different kinds of cars, aren't there, Libby? And a decision like this can't be made in haste."

Libby closed her eyes, almost hypnotized by the slow, languid meter of his words, the depth of his voice. "N-no," she agreed.

"Definitely not," he said, his mouth almost upon hers. "It could take two—or three—days to decide."

"Ummm," agreed Libby, slipping deeper and deeper under his spell.

Jess had pressed her back against a counter, and his body formed an impassable barricade, leaning, hard and fragrant, into hers. He was tracing the length of her neck with soft, searing lips, tasting the hollow beneath her ear.

Finally he kissed her, first with tenderness, then with fervor, his tongue seeking and being granted sweet entry. This preliminary joining made Libby's whole entity pulse with an awareness of the primitive differences between his body and her own. Where she was soft and yielding, he was fiercely hard. Her nipples pouted into tiny peaks, crying out for his attention.

Seeming to sense that, Jess unbuttoned her blouse with deft, brazen fingers that felt warm against her skin. He opened the front catch on her bra, admired the pink-tipped lushness that seemed to grow richer and rounder under his gaze.

Idly he bent to kiss one peak into ferocious submission, and Libby groaned, her head falling back. Etched against the clear roof, she saw the long needles of ponderosa pines splintering the spring moonlight into shards of silver.

After almost a minute of pleasure so keen that Libby was certain she couldn't bear it, Jess turned to the other breast, kissing, suckling, nipping softly with his teeth. And all the while, he worked the opposite nipple skillfully with his fingers, putting it through delicious paces.

Libby was almost mindless by the time she felt the snap and zipper of her jeans give way, and her hands were still tangled in his dark hair as he knelt. Down came the jeans, her panties with them.

She could manage no more than a throaty gasp as his hands stroked the smooth skin of her thighs, the V of curls at their junction. She felt his breath there, warm, promising to cherish.

Libby trembled as he sought entrance with a questioning kiss, unveiled her with fingers that would not await permission.

As his tongue first touched the tenderness that had been hidden, his hands came to Libby's hips, pressing her down onto this fiery, inescapable glory. Only when she pleaded did he tug her fully into his mouth and partake of her.

Jess enjoyed Libby at his leisure, demanding her essence, showing no mercy even when she cried out and shuddered upon him in a final, soaring triumph. When her own chants of passion had ceased, she was conscious of his.

Jess still knelt before her, his every touch saying that he was worshiping, but there was sweet mastery in his manner, too. After one kiss of farewell, he gently drew her jeans and panties back into place and stood.

Libby stared at him, amazed at his power over her. He smiled at her wonder, though there was a spark of that same emotion deep in his eyes, and then lifted her off her feet and into his arms.

Say "I love you," Libby thought with prayerful fervor.

"I need you," he said instead.

And, for the moment, it was enough.

Stars peeked through the endlessly varied patterns the fallen pine needles made on the glass roof, as if to see and assess the glory that glowed beneath. Libby preened under their celestial jealousy and cuddled closer to Jess's hard, sheet-entangled frame.

"Why didn't you ever marry, Jess?" she asked, tracing a soft path across his chest with her fingers.

The mattress shifted as he moved to put one arm around Libby and draw her nearer still. "I don't know. It always seemed that marriage could wait."

"Didn't you even come close?"

Jess sighed, his fingers moving idly in her hair. "A couple of times I seriously considered it, yes. I guess it bothered me, subliminally, that I was looking these women over as though they were livestock or something. This one would have beautiful children, that one would like living on the ranch—that sort of thing."

"I see."

Jess stiffened slightly beneath the patterns she was making in the soft swirls of hair on his chest, and she felt the question coming long before he uttered it.

"What attracted you to Aaron Strand?"

Libby had been pondering that mystery herself, ever since her marriage to Aaron had begun to dissolve. Now, suddenly, she was certain that she understood. Weak though he might be, Aaron Strand was tall, dark-haired, broad in the shoulders. He had given the impression of strength and self-assurance, qualities that any woman would find appealing.

"I guess I thought he was strong, like Dad," she said, because she couldn't quite amend the sentence to a full truth and admit that she had probably superimposed Jess's image over Aaron's in the first place.

"Ummm," said Jess noncommittally.

"Of course, he is actually very weak."

Jess offered no comment.

"I guess my mistake," Libby went on quietly, "was in seeing myself through Aaron's eyes. He made me feel so worthless.…"

"Maybe that made him feel better about himself."

"Maybe. But I still hate him, Jess—isn't that awful? I still hate him for leaving Jonathan in the lurch like that, especially."

"It isn't awful, it's human. It appears that you and Jonathan needed more than he had to give. Unconsciously, you probably measured him against Ken, and whatever else he is, your dad is a hard act to follow, Libby."

"Yes," said Libby, but she was thinking: *I didn't measure Aaron against Dad. God help me, Jess, I measured him against you.*

Jess turned over in a graceful, rolling motion, so that he was above her, his head and shoulders blocking out the light of the stars. "Enough heavy talk, woman. I came here to—"

"Buy a car?" broke in Libby, her tone teasing and full of love.

He nuzzled his face between her warm, welcoming breasts. "My God," he said, his voice muffled by her satin flesh, "what an innocent you are, Libby Kincaid!" One of his hands came down, gentle and mischievous, to squeeze her bottom. "Nice upholstery."

Libby gasped and arched her back as his mouth slid up over the rounding of her breast to claim its peak. "Not much mileage," she choked out.

Jess laughed against the nipple he was tormenting so methodically. "A definite plus." His hand moved between her thighs to assert an ancient mastery, and his breath quickened at Libby's immediate response. "Starts easily," he muttered, sipping at her nipple now, tugging it into an obedient little point.

Libby was beyond the game now, rising and falling on the velvet swells of need he was stirring within her. "I… Oh, God, Jess…what are you…ooooh!"

Somehow, Jess managed to turn on the bedside lamp without interrupting the searing pace his right hand was setting for Libby's body. "You are a goddess," he said.

The fevered dance continued, even though Libby willed herself to lie still. Damn him, he was watching her, taking pleasure from the unbridled response she could not help giving. Her heart raced with exertion, blood boiled in every vein, and Jess's lazy smile was lost in a silver haze.

She sobbed out his name, groping for his shoulders with her hands, holding on. Then, shuddering violently, she tumbled into some chasm where there was no sound but the beat of her own heart.

"You like doing that, don't you?" she snapped when she could see again, breathe again.

"Yes," replied Jess without hesitation.

Libby scrambled into a sitting position, blue eyes shooting flames. "Bastard," she said.

He met her gaze placidly. "What's the matter with you?"

Libby wasn't quite sure of the answer to that question. "It just…it just bothers me that you were…you were looking at me," she faltered, covering her still-pulsing breasts with the bedclothes.

With a deliberate motion of his hands, Jess removed the covers again, and Libby's traitorous nipples puckered in response to his brazen perusal. "Why?" he asked.

Libby's cheeks ached with color, and she lowered her eyes. Instantly Jess caught her chin in a gentle grasp, made her look at him again.

"Sweetheart, you're not ashamed, are you?"

Libby couldn't reply, she was so confused.

His hand slid, soothing, from Libby's chin to the side of her face. "You were giving yourself to me, Libby, trusting me. Is there shame in that?"

She realized that there wasn't, not the way she loved this brazen, tender, outlandish man. If only she dared to tell him verbally what her body already had.

He kissed her softly, sensing her need for greater reassurance. "Exquisite," he said. "Even ordinarily, you are exquisite. But when you let me love you, you go beyond that. You move me on a level where I've never even been touched before."

Say it now, Libby urged silently, *say you love me.*

But she had to be satisfied with what he had already said, for it was immediately clear that there would be no poetic avowals of devotion forthcoming. He'd said she was exquisite, that she moved him, but he'd made no declaration.

For this reason, there was a measure of sadness in the lovemaking that followed.

Long after Jess slept, exhausted, beside her, Libby lay awake, aching. She wanted, needed more from Jess than his readily admitted lust. So much more.

And yet, if a commitment were offered, would Libby want

to accept it? Weren't there already too many conflicts complicating their lives? Though she tried to shut out the memory, Libby couldn't forget that Jess had believed her capable of carrying on with his brother and hurting her cousin and dearest friend in the process. Nor could she forget the wedge that had been driven between them the first time they'd made love, when she'd slipped and uttered words that had made him feel as though she'd used him to prove herself as a woman.

Of course, they had come together again, despite these things, but that was of no comfort to Libby. If they were to achieve any real closeness, more than just their bodies would have to be in accord.

After several hours, Libby fell into a fitful, dream-ridden sleep. When morning came, casting bright sunlight through the expanse of glass overhead, she was alone in the tousled bed.

"Lib!"

She went to the edge of the loft, peering down over the side. "What?" she retorted, petulant in the face of Jess's freshly showered, bright-and-shiny good cheer.

He waved a cooking spatula with a flourish. "One egg or two?"

"Drop dead," she replied flatly, frowning at the ladder.

Jess laughed. "Watch it. You'll get my hopes up with such tender words."

"What's this damned ladder for, anyway?"

"Are you this grouchy every morning?" he countered.

"Only when I've engaged in illicit sex the night before!" Libby snapped, scowling. "I believe I asked you about the ladder?"

"It's for climbing up and down." Jess shrugged.

Libby's head throbbed, and her eyes felt puffy and sore. "Given time, I probably could have figured out that much!"

Jess chuckled and shook his head, as if in sympathy.

Libby grasped the top of the peculiar ladder in question and gave it a vigorous shake. It was immovable. Her puzzlement made her feel even more irritable and, for no consciously conceived reason, she put out her tongue at Jess Barlowe and whirled away from the edge of the loft, out of his view.

His laughter rang out as she stumbled into the bathroom and turned on the water in the shower stall.

Once she had showered and brushed her teeth, Libby began to feel semihuman. With this came contrition for the snappish way she had greeted Jess minutes before. It wasn't his fault, after all, that he was so nauseatingly happy in the mornings.

Grinning a mischievous grin, Libby rummaged through the suitcase she had so hastily packed and found the T-shirt she had bought for Jess the day before, when she'd come to Kalispell with Cathy. She pulled the garment on over her head and, in a flash of daring, swung over the loft to climb down the ladder.

Her reward was a low, appreciative whistle.

"Now I know why that ladder was built," Jess said. "The view from down here is great.

Libby was embarrassed; she'd thought Jess was in the kitchen and thus unable to see her novel descent from the loft. Reaching the floor, she whirled, her face crimson, to glare at him.

Jess read the legend printed on the front of the T-shirt, which was so big that it reached almost to her knees, and laughed explosively. "'If it feels good, do it'?" he marveled.

Libby's glare simply would not stay in place, no matter how hard she tried to sustain it. Her mouth twitched and a chuckle escaped her and then she was laughing as hard as Jess was.

Given the situation, his words came as a shock.

"Libby, will you marry me?"

She stared at him, bewildered, afraid to hope. "What?"

The jade eyes were gentle now, still glistening with residual laughter. "Don't make me repeat it, princess."

"I think the eggs are burning," said Libby in tones made wooden by surprise.

"Wrong. I've already eaten mine, and yours are congealing on your plate. What's your answer, Kincaid?"

Libby's throat ached; something about the size of her heart was caught in it. "I… What…"

"I thought you only talked in broken sentences at the height of passion. Are you really as surprised as all that?"

"Yes!" croaked Libby after a struggle.

The broad shoulders, accentuated rather than hidden by a soft yellow sweater, moved in a shrug. "It seemed like a good solution to me."

"A solution? To what?"

"All our separate and combined problems," answered Jess airily. Persuasively. "Think about it, Lib. Stacey couldn't very well hassle you anymore, could he? And you could stay on the ranch."

Despite the companionable delivery, Jess's words made Libby's soul ache. "Those are solutions for *me*. What problems would marriage solve for *you*?"

"We're good in bed," he offered, shattering Libby with what he seemed to mean as a compliment.

"It takes more than that!"

"Does it?"

Libby was speechless, though a voice inside her kept screaming silly, sentimental things. *What about love? What about babies and leftover meatloaf and filing joint tax returns?*

"You dad would be happy," Jess added, and he couldn't have hurt Libby more if he'd raised his hand and slapped her.

"My dad? My *dad?*"

Jess turned away, seemingly unaware of the effect his convoluted proposal was having on Libby. He looked like exactly what he was: a trained, skillful attorney pleading a weak case. "You want children, don't you? And I know you like living on the ranch."

Libby broke in coldly. "I guess I meet all the qualifications. I do want children. I do like living on the Circle Bar B. So why don't you just hog-tie me and brand me a Barlowe?"

Every muscle in Jess's body seemed to tense, but he did not turn around to face her. "There is one other reason," he offered.

For all her fury and hurt, hope sang through Libby's system like the wind unleashed on a wide prairie. "What's that?"

He drew a deep breath, his hands clasped behind him, courtroom style. "There would be no chance, for now at least, of Cathy being hurt."

Cathy. Libby's knees weakened; she groped for the sofa behind her, fell into it. Good God, was his devotion to Cathy so deep that he would marry the woman he considered a threat to her happiness, just to protect her?

"I am so damned tired of hearing about Cathy," she said evenly, tugging the end of the T-shirt down over her knees for something to do.

Now Jess turned, looked at her with unreadable eyes.

Even though Libby felt the guilt she always did whenever she was even mildly annoyed with Cathy, she stood her ground. "A person doesn't have to be handicapped to hurt, you know," she said in a small and rather uncertain voice.

Jess folded his arms and the sunlight streaming in through the glass ceiling glittered in his dark hair. "I know that," he said softly. "And we're all handicapped in some way, aren't we?"

She couldn't tell whether he was reprimanding her or

offering an olive branch. Huddling on the couch, feeling foolish in the T-shirt she had put on as a joke, Libby knotted her hands together in her lap. "I suppose that remark was intended as a barb."

Jess came to sit beside her on the couch, careful not to touch her. "Libby, it wasn't. I'm tired of exchanging verbal shots with you—that was fine when we had to ride the same school bus every day, but we're adults now. Let's try to act as such."

Libby looked into Jess's face and was thunderstruck by how much she cared for him, needed him. And yet, even a week before, she would have said she despised Jess and meant it. All that rancor they'd borne each other—had it really been passion instead?

"I don't understand any of this."

Jess took one of her hands into both of his. "Do you want to marry me or not?"

Both fear and joy rose within Libby. In order to look inward at her own feelings, she was forced to look away from him. She did love Jess, there was absolutely no doubt of that, and she wanted, above all things, to be his wife. She wanted children and, at thirty-one, she often had the feeling that time was getting short. Dammit, why couldn't he say he loved her?

"Would you be faithful to me, Jess?"

He touched her cheek, turning her face without apparent effort, so that she was again looking into those bewitching green eyes. "I would never betray you."

Aaron had said those words, too. Aaron had been so very good with words.

But this was Jess, Libby reminded herself. Jess, not Aaron. "I couldn't give up my career," she said. "It's a crazy business, Jess, and sometimes there are long stretches of time when I don't do much of anything. Other times, I have to work ten-or twelve-hour days to meet a deadline."

Jess did not seem to be dissuaded.

Libby drew a deep breath. "Of course, I'd go on being known as Libby Kincaid. I never took Aaron's name and I don't see any sense in taking yours—should I agree to marry you, that is."

He seemed amused, but she had definitely touched a sore spot. That became immediately obvious. "Wait a minute, lady. Professionally, you can be known by any name you want. Privately, however, you'll be Libby Barlowe."

Libby was secretly pleased, but because she was angry and hurt that he didn't love her, she lifted her chin and snapped, "You have to have that Circle Bar B brand on everything you consider yours, don't you?"

"You are not a thing, Libby," he replied rationally, "but I want at least that much of a commitment. Call it male ego if you must, but I want my wife to be Mrs. Barlowe."

Libby swallowed. "Fair enough," she said.

Jess sat back on the sofa, folded his arms again. "I'm waiting," he said, and the mischievous glint was back in his eyes.

"For what?"

"An answer to my original question."

Fool, fool! Don't you ever learn, Libby Kincaid? Don't you ever learn? Libby quieted the voice in her mind and lifted her chin. Life was short, and unpredictable in the bargain. Maybe Jess would learn to love her the way she loved him. Wasn't that kind of happiness worth a risk?

"I'll marry you," she said.

Jess kissed her with an exuberance that soon turned to desire.

Jess frowned at the sleek showroom sports car, his tongue making one cheek protrude. "What do you think?" he asked.

Libby assessed the car again. "It isn't you."

He grinned, ignoring the salesman's quiet disappointment. "You're right."

Neither, of course, had the last ten cars they had looked at been "him." The sports cars seemed to cramp his long legs, while the big luxury vehicles were too showy.

"How about another truck?" Libby suggested.

"Do you know how many trucks there already are on the ranch?" he countered. "Besides, some yokel would probably paint on the family logo when I wasn't looking."

Libby deliberately widened her eyes. "That would be truly terrible!"

He made a face at her, but when he spoke, his words were delivered in a touchingly serious way. "We could get a van and fill the seats with kids and dogs."

Libby smiled at the image. "A grungy sort of heaven," she mused.

Jess laughed. "And of course there would be lots of room to make love."

The salesman cleared his throat and discreetly walked away.

Chapter 9

"I think you shocked that salesman," observed Libby, snapping the seat belt into place as Jess settled behind the wheel of their rental car.

Jess shrugged. "By wanting a van?" he teased.

"By wanting *me* in the van," clarified Libby.

Jess turned the key in the ignition and shifted gears. "He's lucky I didn't list all the other places I'd like to have you. The hood, for instance. And then there's the roof...."

Libby colored richly as they pulled into the slow traffic. "Jess!"

He frowned speculatively. "And, of course, on the ladder at the condo."

"The ladder?"

Jess flung her a brazen grin. "Yeah. About halfway up."

"Don't you think about anything but sex?"

"I seem to have developed a fixation, Kincaid—just since you came back, of course."

She couldn't help smiling. "Of course."

Nothing more was said until they'd driven through the quiet, well-kept streets to the courthouse. Jess parked the car and turned to Libby with a comical leer. "Are you up to a blood test and a little small-town bureaucracy, Kincaid?"

Libby felt a wild, twisting thrill in the pit of her stomach. A marriage license. He wanted to get a marriage license. In three short days, she could be bound to Jess Barlowe for life. At least, she *hoped* it would be for life.

After drawing a deep breath, Libby unsnapped her seat belt and got out of the car.

Twenty minutes later, the ordeal was over. The fact that the wedding itself wouldn't take nearly as long struck Libby as an irony.

On the sidewalk, Jess caught her elbow in one hand and helped her back into the car. While he must have noticed that she was preoccupied, he was chivalrous enough not to say so.

"Stop at that supermarket!" Libby blurted when they'd been driving for some minutes.

Jess gave her a quizzical look. "Supermarket?"

"Yes. They sell food there, among other necessary items."

Jess frowned. "Why can't we just eat in restaurants? There are several good ones—"

"Restaurants?" Libby cried with mock disdain. "How can I prove what a great catch I am if I don't cook something for you?"

Jess's right hand left the steering wheel to slide languorously up and down Libby's linen-skirted thigh. "Relax, sweetheart," he said in a rather good imitation of Humphrey Bogart. "I already know you're good in the kitchen."

The obvious reference to last night's episode in that room

unsettled Libby. "You delight in saying outrageous things, don't you?" she snapped.

"I delight in *doing* outrageous things."

"You'll get no argument on that score, fella," she retorted acidly.

The car came to a stop in front of the supermarket, which was in the center of a small shopping mall. Libby noticed that Jess's gaze strayed to a jewelry store down the way.

"I'll meet you inside," he said, and then he was gone.

Though Libby told herself that she was being silly and sentimental, she was pleased to think that Jess might be shopping for a ring.

The giddy, romantic feeling faded when she selected a shopping cart inside the supermarket, however. She was wallowing in gushy dreams, behaving like a seventeen-year-old virgin. Of *course* Jess would buy a ring, but only because it would be expected of him.

Glumly Libby went about selecting items from a mental grocery list she had been composing since she'd checked the refrigerator and cupboards at the condominium and found them all but empty.

Taking refuge in practical matters, she frowned at a display of cabbage and wondered how much food to buy. Jess hadn't said how long they would be staying in Kalispell, beyond the time it would take to find the car he wanted.

Shrugging slightly, Libby decided to buy provisions for three days. Because that was the required waiting period for a marriage license, they would probably be in town at least that long.

She looked down at her slacks and brightly colored top. The wedding ceremony was going to be an informal one, obviously, but she would still need a new dress, and she wanted to buy a wedding band for Jess, too.

She pushed her cart along the produce aisle, woodenly selecting bean sprouts, fresh broccoli, onions. Her first wedding had been a quiet one, too, devoid of lace and flowers and music, and something within her mourned those things.

They hadn't even discussed a honeymoon, and what kind of ceremony would this be, without Ken, without Cathy, without Senator Barlowe and Marion Bradshaw, the housekeeper?

A box seemed to float up out of the cart, but Libby soon saw that it was clasped in a strong sun-browned hand.

"I hate cereals that crunch," Jess said, and his eyes seemed to be looking inside Libby, seeing the dull ache she would rather have kept hidden. "What's wrong, love?"

Libby fought back the sudden silly tears that ached in her throat and throbbed behind her eyes. "Nothing," she lied.

Jess was not fooled. "You want Ken to come to the wedding," he guessed.

Libby lowered her head slightly. "He was hurt when Aaron and I got married without even telling him first," she said.

There was a short silence before a housewife, tagged by two preschoolers, gave Libby's cart a surreptitious bump with her own, tacitly demanding access to the cereal display. Libby wrestled her groceries out of the way and looked up at Jess, waiting for his response.

He smiled, touched her cheek. "Tell you what. We'll call the ranch and let everybody know we're getting married. That way, if they want to be there, they can. And if you want frills and flash, princess, we can have a formal wedding later."

The idea of a second wedding, complete with the trimmings, appealed to Libby's romantic soul. She smiled at the thought. "You would do that? You would go through it all over again, just for show?"

"Not for show, princess. For you."

The housewife made an appreciative sound and Libby started a little, having completely forgotten their surroundings.

Jess laughed and the subject was dropped. They walked up one aisle and down another, dropping the occasional pertinent item into the cart, arguing good-naturedly about who would do the cooking after they were married.

The telephone was ringing as Libby unlocked the front door of the condo, so she left Jess to carry in their bags of groceries and ran to answer it, expecting to hear Ken's voice, or Marion Bradshaw's, relaying some message from Cathy.

A cruel wave of déjà vu washed over her when she heard Aaron's smooth, confident greeting. "Hello, Libby."

"What do you want?" Libby rasped, too stunned to hang up. How on earth had he gotten that number?

"I told you before, dear heart," said Aaron smoothly. "I want a child."

Libby was conscious of Jess standing at her elbow, the shopping bags clasped in his arms. "You're insane!" she cried into the receiver.

"Maybe so, but not insane enough to let my grandmother hand over an empire to someone else. She has doubts, you know, about my dependability."

"I wonder why!"

"Don't be sarcastic, sugarplum. My request isn't really all that unreasonable, considering all I stand to lose."

"It is unreasonable, Aaron! In fact, it's sick!" At this point Libby slammed down the receiver with a vengeance. She was trembling so hard that Jess hastily shunted the grocery bags onto a side table and took her into his arms.

"What was that all about?" he asked when Libby had recovered herself a little.

"He's horrible," Libby answered, distracted and very much afraid. "Oh, Jess, he's a monster—"

"What did he say?" Jess pressed quietly.

"Aaron wants me to have his baby! Jess, he actually had the gall to ask me to come back, just so he can produce an heir and please his grandmother!"

Jess's hand was entangled in her hair now, comforting her. "It's all right, Lib. Everything will be all right."

Then why am I so damned scared? Libby asked herself, but she put on a brave face for Jess and even managed a smile. "Let's call my dad," she said.

Jess nodded, kissed her forehead. And then he took up the grocery bags again and carried them into the kitchen while Libby dialed her father's telephone number.

There was no answer, which was not surprising, considering that it was still early. Ken would be working, and because of the wide range of his responsibilities, he could be anywhere on the 150,000 acres that made up the Circle Bar B.

Sounds from the kitchen indicated that Jess was putting the food away, and Libby wandered in, needing to be near him.

"No answer?" he asked, tossing a package of frozen egg rolls into the freezer.

"No answer," confirmed Libby. "I should have known, I guess."

Jess turned, gave her a gentle grin. "You did know, Libby. But you needed to touch base just then, and going through the motions was better than nothing."

"When did you get so smart?"

"Last Tuesday, I think," he answered ponderously. "Know something? You look a little tired. Why don't you climb up that ladder that bugs you so much and take a nap?"

Libby arched one eyebrow. "While you do what?"

His answer was somewhat disappointing. "While I go back to town for a few hours," he said. "I have some things to do."

"Like what?"

He grinned. "Like picking up some travel brochures, so we can decide where to take our honeymoon."

Libby felt a rush of pleasure despite the weariness she was suddenly very aware of. Had it been there all along, or was she tired simply because this subtle hypnotist had suggested it to her? "Does it matter where we honeymoon?"

"Not really," Jess replied, coming disturbingly close, kissing Libby's forehead. "But I like having you all to myself. I can't help thinking that the farther we get from home right now, the better off we're going to be."

A tremor of fear brushed against Libby's heart, but it was quickly stilled when Jess caught her right earlobe between gentle teeth and then told her in bluntly erotic terms what he had wanted to do to her on the supermarket checkout counter.

When he'd finished, Libby was wildly aroused and, at the same time, resigned to the fact that when she crawled into that sun-washed bed up in the loft, she would be alone. "Rat," she said.

Jess swatted her backside playfully. "Later," he promised, and then calmly left the condo to attend to his errands.

Libby went obediently up to the bedroom, using the stairs rather than the ladder, and yawned as she stripped down to her lacy camisole and panties. She shouldn't be having a nap now, she told herself, when she had things of her own to do—choosing Jess's ring, for one thing, and buying a special dress, for another….

She was asleep only seconds after slipping beneath the covers.

Libby stirred, indulged in a deliciously lazy stretch. Someone was trailing soft, warm kisses across her collarbone—or was she dreaming? Just in case she was, she did not open her eyes.

Cool air washed over her breasts as the camisole was gently displaced. "Ummm," she said.

"Good dream?" asked Jess, moistening one pulsing nipple to crisp attention with his tongue.

"Oooooh," answered Libby, arching her back slightly, her eyes still closed, her head pressed into the silken pillow in eager, soft surrender. "Very good."

Jess left that nipple to subject its twin to a tender plundering that caused Libby to moan with delight. Her hips writhed slightly, calling to their powerful counterpart.

Jess heard their silent plea, slid the satiny panties down, down, away. "You're so warm, Libby," he said in a ragged whisper. "So soft and delicious." The camisole was unlaced, laid aside reverently, like the wrapping on some splendid gift. Kisses rained down on Libby's sleep-warmed, swollen breasts, her stomach, her thighs.

At last she opened her eyes, saw Jess's wondrous nakedness through a haze of sweet, sleepy need. As he ventured nearer and nearer to the silk-sheltered sanction of her womanhood, she instinctively reached up to clasp the brass railings on the headboard of the bed, anchoring herself to earth.

Jess parted the soft veil, admired its secret with a throaty exclamation of desire and a searing kiss.

A plea was wrenched from Libby, and she tightened her grasp on the headboard.

For a few mind-sundering minutes Jess enjoyed the swelling morsel with his tongue. "More?" he asked, teasing her, knowing that she was already half-mad with the need of him.

"More," she whimpered as his fingers strayed to the pebblelike peaks of her breasts, plying them, sending an exquisite lacelike net of passion knitting its way through her body.

Another tormenting flick of his tongue. "Sweet," he said.

And then he lifted Libby's legs, placing one over each of his shoulders, making her totally, beautifully vulnerable to him.

She cried out in senseless delirium as he took his pleasure, and she was certain that she would have been flung beyond the dark sky if not for her desperate grasp on the headboard.

Even after the highest peak had been scaled, Libby's sated body convulsed again and again, caught in the throes of other, smaller releases.

Still dazed, Libby felt Jess's length stretch out upon her, seeking that sweetest and most intimate solace. In a burst of tender rebellion, she thrust him off and demanded loving revenge.

Soon enough, it was Jess who grasped the gleaming brass railings lest he soar away, Jess who chanted a desperate litany.

Wickedly, Libby took her time, savoring him, taking outrageous liberties with him. Finally she conquered him, and his cry of joyous surrender filled her with love almost beyond bearing.

His breathing still ragged, his face full of wonder, Jess drew Libby down, so that she lay beside him. With his hands he explored her, igniting tiny silver fires in every curve and hollow of her body.

This time, when he came to her, she welcomed him with a ferocious thrust of her hips, alternately setting the pace and following Jess's lead. When the pinnacle was reached, each was lost in the echoing, triumphant cry of the other, and bits of a broken rainbow showered down around them.

Sitting cross-legged on the living-room sofa, Libby twisted the telephone cord between her fingers and waited for her father's response to her announcement.

It was a soft chuckle.

"You aren't the least bit surprised!" Libby accused, marveling.

"I figured anybody that fought and jawed as much as you two did had to end up hitched," replied Ken Kincaid in his colorful way. "Did you let Cleave know yet?"

"Jess will, in a few minutes. Will you tell Cathy for me, please?"

Ken promised that he would.

Libby swallowed hard, gave Jess a warning glare as he moved to slide an exploring hand inside the top of her bathrobe. "Aren't you going to say that we're rushing into this or something like that? Some people will think it's too soon—"

"It was damned near too late," quipped Ken. "What time is the ceremony again?"

There were tears in Libby's eyes, though she had never been happier. "Two o'clock on Friday, at the courthouse."

"I'll be there, dumplin'. Be happy."

The whole room was distorted into a joyous blur. "I will, Dad. I love you."

"I love you, too," he answered with an ease that was typical of him. "Take care and I'll see you Friday."

"Right," said Libby, sniffling as she gently replaced the receiver.

Jess chuckled, touched her chin. "Tears? I'm insulted."

Libby made a face and shoved the telephone into his lap. "Call your father," she said.

Jess settled back in the sofa as he dialed the number of the senator's house in Washington, balancing the telephone on one blue-jeaned knee. While he tried to talk to his father in normal tones, Libby ran impudent fingertips over his bare chest, twining dark hair into tight curls, making hard buttons of deliciously vulnerable nipples.

With a mock-glare and a motion of his free arm, Jess tried

to field her blatant advances. She simply knelt astraddle of his lap and had her way with him, her fingers tracing a path of fire around his mouth, along his neck, over his nipples.

Jess caught the errant hand in a desperate hold, only to be immediately assaulted by the other. Mischief flashed in his jade eyes, followed by an I'll-get-you-for-this look. "See you then," he said to his father, his voice a little deeper than usual and very carefully modulated. There was a pause, and then he added, "Oh, don't worry, I will. In about five seconds, I'm going to lay Libby on the coffee table and kiss her in all the best places. Yes, sir, by the time I get through with her, she'll be—"

Falling into the trap, Libby colored, snatched the receiver out of Jess's hand and pressed it to her ear. The line was, of course, dead.

Jess laughed as she assessed him murderously. "You deserved that," he said.

Libby moved to struggle off his lap, still crimson in the face, her heart pounding with embarrassment. But Jess's hands were strong on her upper arms, holding her in place.

"Oh, no you don't, princess. You're not getting out of this so easily."

"What—"

Jess smiled languidly, still holding her fast with one hand, undoing his jeans with the other. "You let this horse out of the barn, lady. Now you're going to ride it."

Libby gasped as she felt him prod her, hard and insistent, and fierce needs surged through her even as she raged at the affront. She was powerless, both physically and emotionally, to break away from him.

Just barely inside her, Jess reached out and calmly untied her bathrobe, baring her breasts, her stomach, her captured hips. His green eyes glittered as he stroked each satiny expanse in turn, allowing Libby more and more of him until she was fully his.

Seemingly unmoved himself, Jess took wicked delight in Libby's capture and began guiding her soft, trim hips up and down, endlessly up and down, upon him. All the while, he used soft words to lead her through flurries of silver snow to the tumultuous release beyond.

When her vision cleared, Libby saw that Jess had been caught in his own treachery. She watched in love and wonder as he gave himself up to raging sensation—his head fell back, his throat worked, his eyes were sightless.

Gruffly Jess pleaded with Libby, and she accelerated the up-and-down motion of her hips until he shuddered violently beneath her, stiffened and growled her name.

"Mess with me, will you?" she mocked, grinning down at him.

Jess began to laugh, between rasping breaths. When his mirth had subsided and he didn't have to drag air into his lungs, he caressed her with his eyes. In fact, it was almost as though he'd said he loved her.

Libby was still incredibly moved by the sweet spectacle she had seen played out in his face as he submitted to her, and she understood then why he so loved to watch her respond while pleasuring her.

Jess reached up, touched away the tear that tickled on her cheek. It would have been a perfect time for those three special words she so wanted to hear, but he did not say them.

Hurt and disappointed, Libby wrenched her bathrobe closed and tried to rise from his lap, only to be easily thwarted. Jess's hands opened the robe again, his eyes perused her and then came back to her face, silently daring her to hide any part of her body or soul from him.

With an insolent finger he brushed the pink buttons at the tips of her full breasts, smiled as they instantly obeyed him. Apparently satisfied with their pert allegiance, Jess moved on to trace patterns of fire on Libby's stomach, the rounding of her hips, the sensitive hollow at the base of her throat.

Jess seemed determined to prove that he could subdue Libby at will, and he only smiled at the startled gasp she gave when it became apparent that all his prowess had returned in full and glorious force.

He slid her robe off her shoulders then and removed it entirely. They were still joined, and Libby shivered as he toyed idly with her breasts, weighing them in his hands, pressing them together, thumbing their aching tips until they performed for him.

Presently Jess left his sumptuous playthings to tamper elsewhere, wreaking still more havoc, eliciting little anxious cries from a bedazzled Libby.

"What do you want, princess?" he asked in a voice of liquid steel.

Libby was wild upon him, her hands clutching desperately at his shoulders, her knees wide. "I want to be…under you. Oh, Jess…under you…"

In a swift and graceful motion, he turned her, was upon her. The movement unleashed the passion Jess had been able to contain until then, and he began to move over her and within her, his thrusts deep and powerful, his words ragged and incoherent.

As their very souls collided and then fused together, imitating their bodies, it was impossible to tell who had prevailed over whom.

Libby awakened first, entangled with Jess, amazed that they could have slept the whole night on that narrow couch.

A smile lifted one corner of her mouth as she kissed Jess's temple tenderly and then disengaged herself, careful not to disturb him. Heaven knew, he had a right to be tired.

Twenty minutes later, when Libby returned from her shower, dressed in sandals, white slacks and a lightweight yellow sweater, Jess was still sleeping. She could empathize, for her own slumber had been fathomless.

"I love you," she said, and then she went to the kitchen and wrote a quick note on the blackboard there, explaining that she had gone shopping and would be back within a few hours.

Getting into the rented car, which was parked in the gravel driveway near the front door, Libby spotted a cluster of colorful travel brochures fanned out on the opposite seat. Each one touted a different paradise: Acapulco, the Bahamas, Maui.

As Libby slid the key into the ignition and started the car, she grinned. She had it on good authority that paradise was only a few yards away, on the couch where Jess lay sleeping.

The day was a rich mixture of blue and green, set off by the fierce green of pine trees and the riotous blooms of crocuses and daffodils in quiet front yards. Downtown, Libby found a parking place immediately, locked the car and hurried on about her business.

Her first stop was a jewelry store, and while she had anticipated a great quandary, the decision of which wedding band to buy for Jess proved an easy one. Her eyes were immediately drawn to one particular ring, forged of silver, inset with polished chips of turquoise.

Once the jeweler had assured her the band could be resized if it didn't fit Jess's finger, Libby bought it.

In an art-supply store she purchased a sketching pad and a gum eraser and some charcoal pencils. Sweet as this interlude with Jess had been, Libby missed her work and her fingers itched to draw. Too, there were all sorts of new ideas for the comic strip bubbling in her mind.

From the art store, Libby pressed on to a good-sized department store. None of the dresses there quite struck her fancy, and she moved on to one boutique and then another.

Finally, in a small and wickedly expensive shop, she found that special dress, that dress of dresses, the one she would wear when she married Jess Barlowe.

It was a clingy creation of burgundy silk, showing off her figure, bringing a glow of color to her cheeks. There were no ruffles of lace or fancy buttons—only a narrow belt made of the same fabric as the dress itself. It was the last word in elegant simplicity, that garment, and Libby adored it.

Carrying the dress box and the heavy bag of art supplies, she hurried back to the car and locked her purchases inside. It was only a little after ten, and Libby wanted to find shoes that would match her dress.

The shoes proved very elusive, and only after almost an hour of searching did she find a pair that would do. Tired of shopping and anxious to see Jess again, Libby started home.

Some intuitive feeling made her uneasy as she drove toward the elegant condominium hidden in the tall trees. After crossing the wooden bridge and making the last turn, she knew why— Stacey's ice-blue Ferrari was parked in the driveway.

Don't be silly, Libby reprimanded herself, but she still felt alarmed. What if Stacey had come to try to talk her out of marrying Jess? What if Cathy was with him, and there was an unpleasant scene?

Determined not to let her imagination get the upper hand, Libby gathered up her loot from the shopping trip and got out of the car. As she approached the house, she caught sight of a familiar face at the window and was surprised all over again. Monica! What on earth was she doing here? Hadn't she left for Washington, D.C., with the senator?

Now Libby really hesitated. She remembered the proprietary looks the woman had given Jess as he swam that day in the pool at the main ranch house. Looks that had implied intimacy.

Libby sighed. So what if Jess and Monica had slept together? She could hardly have expected a man like him to live like a monk, and it wasn't as if Libby hadn't had a prior relationship herself, however unsatisfactory.

Despite the cool sanity of this logic, it hurt to imagine Jess making love with Monica—or with any other woman, for that matter.

Libby grappled with her purchases at the front door, reached for the knob. Before she could clasp it, the door opened.

Jess was standing there, shirtless, wearing jeans, his hair and suntanned chest still damp from a recent shower. Instead of greeting Libby with a smile, let alone a kiss, he scowled at her and stepped back almost grudgingly, as though he had considered refusing her entrance.

Bewildered and hurt, Libby resisted a primal instinct urging her to flee and walked in.

Monica had left the window and was now seated comfortably on the couch, her shapely legs crossed at the knee, a cocktail in her hand.

Libby took in the woman's sleek designer suit and felt shabby by comparison in her casual attire. "Hello, Monica."

"Libby," replied Monica with a polite nod.

The formalities dispensed with, Libby flung a hesitant look at Jess. Why was he glaring at her like that, as though he wanted to do her bodily harm? Why was his jawline so tight, and why was it that he clenched the towel draped around his neck in white-knuckled hands?

Before Libby could voice any of her questions, Stacey came out of the kitchen, raked her with guileless caramel eyes and smiled.

"Hello," he said, as though his very presence, under the circumstances, was not an outrage.

Libby only stared at him. She was very conscious of Jess, seething somewhere on the periphery of her vision, and of Monica, taking in the whole scene with detached amusement.

Suddenly Stacey was coming toward Libby, speaking words she couldn't seem to hear. Then he had the outright gall to kiss her, and Libby's inertia was broken.

She drew back her hand and slapped him, her dress box, purse and bag of art supplies falling to the floor.

Stacey reached out for her, caught her waist in his hands. She squirmed and flung one appealing look in Jess's direction.

Though he looked anything but chivalrous, he did intercede. "Leave Libby alone, Stacey."

Stacey paled. "I've left Cathy," he said, as though that settled everything. "Libby, we can be together now!"

Libby stumbled backward, stunned. Only when she came up against the hard barrier of Jess's soap-scented body did she stop. Wild relief went through her as he enclosed her in a steel-like protective embrace.

"Get out," he said flatly, addressing his brother.

Stacey hesitated, but then he reddened and left the condo in a huff, pulling Monica Summers behind him.

Chapter 10

Furious and shaken, Libby turned to glare at Jess. It was all too clear what had happened—Stacey had been telling more of his outrageous lies and Jess had believed them.

For a few moments he stubbornly returned her angry regard, but then he spread his hands in a gesture of concession and said, "I'm sorry."

Libby was trembling now, but she stooped to pick up her dress box, and the art-store bag. She couldn't look at Jess or he would see the tears that had clouded her eyes. "After all we've done and planned, how could you, Jess? How could you believe Stacey?"

He was near, very near—Libby was conscious of him in every sense. He moved to touch her, instantly stopped himself. "I said I was sorry."

Libby forgot that she'd meant to hide her tears and looked him full in the face. Her voice shook with anger when she spoke. "Sometimes being sorry isn't enough, Jess!" She carried the things she'd bought across the room, tossed them onto the couch. "Is this what our marriage is going to be like? Are we going to do just fine as long as we aren't around Stacey?"

Jess was standing behind her; his hands came to rest on her shoulders. "What can I say, Libby? I was jealous. That may not be right, but it's human."

Perhaps because she wanted so desperately to believe that everything would turn out all right, that a marriage to this wonderful, contradictory man would succeed, Libby set aside her doubts and turned to face Jess. The depth of her love for this erstwhile enemy still staggered her. "What did Stacey tell you?"

Jess drew in an audible breath, and for a moment there was a tightness in his jaw. Then he sighed and said, "He was sharing the glorious details of your supposed affair. And he had a remarkable grasp on what you like in bed, Libby."

The words were wounding, but Libby was strong. "Did it ever occur to you that maybe all women like essentially the same things?"

Jess didn't answer, but Libby could see that she had made her mark, and she rushed on.

"Exactly what was Monica's part in all this?" she demanded hotly. "Was she here to moderate your sexual discussion? Why the hell isn't she in Washington, where she belongs?"

Jess shrugged, obviously puzzled. "I'm not sure why she was here."

"I am! Once you were diverted from your disastrous course—marrying me—she was going to take you by the hand and lead you home!"

One side of Jess's mouth lifted in a grin. "I'm not the only one who is prone to jealousy, it appears."

"You were involved with her, weren't you?"

"Yes."

The bluntness of the answer took Libby unawares, but only for a moment. After all, had Jess said no, she would have known he was lying and that would have been devastating. "Did you love Monica?"

"No. If I had, I would have married her."

The possible portent of those words buoyed Libby's flagging spirits. "Passion wouldn't be enough?" she ventured.

"To base a marriage on? Never. Now, let's see what you bought today."

Let's see what you bought today. Libby's frustration knew no bounds, but she was damned if she was going to pry those three longed-for words out of him—she'd fished enough as it was. "I bought a wedding dress, for your information. And you're not going to see it until tomorrow, so don't pester me about it."

He laughed. "I like a woman who is loyal to her superstitions. What else did you purchase, milady?"

Libby's sense of financial independence, nurtured during the insecure days with Aaron, chafed under the question. "I didn't use your money, so what do you care?" she snapped.

Jess arched one eyebrow. "Another touchy subject rears its ugly head. I was merely curious, my love—I didn't ask for a meeting with your accountant."

Feeling foolish, Libby made a great project of opening the art-store bag and spreading its contents out on the couch.

Jess was grinning as he assessed the array of pencils, the large sketchbook. "Have I been boring you, princess?"

Libby pulled a face at him. "You could be called many things, Jess Barlowe, but you are definitely not boring."

"Thank you—I think. Shall we brave the car dealers of Kalispell again, or are you going to be busy?" The question was guileless, indicating that Jess would have understood if she wanted to stay and block out some of the ideas that had come to her.

After Aaron, who had viewed her cartooning as a childish hobby, Jess's attitude was a luxury. "I think I'd rather go with you," she said with a teasing smile. "If I don't you might come home with some motorized horror that has horns on its hood."

"Your faith in my good taste is positively underwhelming," he replied, walking toward the ladder, climbing its rungs to the loft in search of a shirt.

"You were right!" Libby called after him. "The view from down here is marvelous!"

During that foray into the jungle of car salesmen and gasoline-fed beasts, Libby spent most of her time in the passenger seat of Jess's rented car, sketching. Instead of drawing Liberated Lizzie, her cartoon character, however, she found herself reproducing Jess's image.

She imagined him looking out over the stunning view of prairies and mountains at home and drew him in profile, the wind ruffling his hair, a pensive look to his eyes and the set of his face. Another sketch showed him laughing, and still another, hidden away in the middle of the drawing pad, not meant for anyone else to see, mirrored the way Jess looked when he wanted her.

To field the responses the drawing evoked in her, Libby quickly sketched Cathy's portrait, and then Ken's. After that, strictly from memory, she drew a picture of Jonathan, full face, as he'd looked before his illness, then, on the same piece of paper, in a profile that revealed the full ravages of his disease.

She supposed it was morbid, including this aspect of the child, but to leave out his pain would have meant leaving out his courage, and Jonathan deserved better.

Touching his charcoal image with gentle, remembering fingers, Libby heard the echo of his voice in her mind. *Naturally I'm brave,* he'd told her once, at the end of a particularly difficult day. *I'm a Jedi knight, like Luke Skywalker.*

Smiling through a mist of tears, Libby added another touch to the sketch—a tiny figure of Jonathan, well and strong, wielding a light saber in valiant defense of the Rebel Alliance.

"That's terrific," observed a gentle voice.

Libby looked up quickly, surprised that she hadn't heard Jess get into the car, hadn't sensed his presence somehow. Because she couldn't speak just yet, she bit her lower lip and nodded an acknowledgment of the compliment.

"Could I take a closer look? Please?"

Libby extended the notebook and it was a gesture of trust, for these sketches were different from the panels for her comic strip. They were large pieces of her soul.

Jess was pensive as he examined the portraits of himself, Cathy, Ken. But the study of Jonathan was clearly his favorite, and he returned to it at intervals, taking in each line, each bit of shading, each unspoken cry of grief.

Finally, with a tenderness that made Libby love him even more than she had before, Jess handed the sketchbook back to her. "You are remarkably talented," he said, and then he had the good grace to look away while Libby recomposed herself.

"D-did you find a car you like?" she asked finally.

Jess smiled at her. "Actually, yes. That's why I came back—to get you."

"Me? Why?"

"Well, I don't want to buy the thing without your checking it out first. Suppose you hated it?"

It amazed Libby that such a thing mattered to him. She set the sketchbook carefully in the backseat and opened her car door to get out. "Lead on," she said, and the clean spring breeze braced her as it touched her face.

The vehicle in question was neither car nor truck, but a

Land Rover. It was perfectly suited to the kind of life Jess led, and Libby approved of it with enthusiasm.

The deal was made, much to the relief of a salesman they had been plaguing, on and off, since the day before.

After some discussion, it was decided that they would keep the rental car until after the wedding, in case Libby needed it. Over a luncheon of steak and salad, which did much to settle her shaky nerves, Jess suggested that they start shopping all over again, for a second car.

Practical as it was, the thought exhausted Libby.

"You'll need transportation," Jess argued.

"I don't think I could face all those plaid sport jackets and test drives again," Libby replied with a sigh.

Jess laughed. "But you would like to have a car, wouldn't you?"

Libby shrugged. In New York, she had depended on taxis for transportation, but the ranch was different, of course. "I suppose."

"Aren't you choosy about the make, model—all that?"

"Wheels are wheels," she answered with another shrug.

"Hmmmm," Jess said speculatively, and then the subject was changed. "What about our honeymoon? Any place in particular you'd like to go?"

"Your couch," Libby said, shocked at her own audacity.

Again Jess laughed. "That is patently unimaginative."

"Hardly, considering the things we did there," Libby replied, immediately lifting a hand to her mouth. What was wrong with her? Why was she suddenly spouting these outlandish remarks?

Jess bent forward, conjured up a comical leer. "I wish we were on the ranch," he said in a low voice. "I'd take you somewhere private and make violent love to you."

Libby felt a familiar heat simmering inside her, melting through her pelvis. "Jess."

He drew some bills from his wallet, tossed them onto the table. "Let's get out of here while I can still walk," he muttered.

Libby laughed. "I think it's a good thing we're driving separate cars today," she teased, though secretly she was just as anxious for privacy as Jess was.

He groaned. "One more word, lady, and I'll spread you out on this table."

Libby's heart thudded at the bold suggestion and pumped color over her breasts and into her face. She tried to look indignant, but the fact was that she had been aroused by the remark and Jess knew it—his grin was proof of that.

As they left the restaurant, he bent close to her and described the fantasy in vivid detail, sparing nothing. And later, on the table in the condo's kitchen, he turned it into a wildly satisfying reality.

That afternoon, Libby took another nap. Due to the episode just past, her dreams were deliciously erotic.

As he had before, Jess awakened her with strategic kisses. "Hi," he said when she opened her eyes.

She touched his hair, noted that he was wearing his brown leather jacket. "You've been out." She yawned.

Jess kissed the tip of her nose. "I have indeed. Bought you a present or two, as a matter of fact."

The glee in Jess's eyes made Libby's heart twist in a spasm of tenderness; whatever he'd purchased, he was very pleased with. She slipped languid arms around his neck. "I like presents," she said.

Jess drew back, tugged her camisole down so that her breasts were bared to him. Almost idly he kissed each dusty-rose peak and then covered them again. "Sorry," he muttered, his mouth a fraction of an inch from hers. "I couldn't resist."

That strange, magical heat was surging from Libby's just-greeted breasts to her middle, down into her thighs and even her knees. She felt as though every muscle and bone in her body had melted. "You m-mentioned presents?"

He chuckled, kissed her softly, groaned under his breath. "I was momentarily distracted. Get out of bed, princess. Said presents await."

"Can't you just…bring them here?"

"Hardly." Jess withdrew from the bed to stand at its side and wrench back the covers. His green eyes smoldered as he took in the sleep-pinkened glow of her curves, and he bent to swat her satin-covered backside. "Get up," he repeated.

Libby obeyed, curious about the gifts but disappointed that Jess hadn't joined her in the bed, too. She found a floaty cotton caftan and slipped it on.

Jess looked at her, made a low growling sound in his throat, and caught her hand in his. "Come on, before I give in to my baser instincts," he said, pulling her down the stairs.

Libby looked around curiously as he dragged her across the living room but saw nothing out of the ordinary.

Jess opened the front door, pulled her outside. There, beside his maroon Land Rover, sat a sleek yellow Corvette with a huge rosette of silver ribbon affixed to its windshield.

Libby gaped at the car, her eyes wide.

"Like it?" Jess asked softly, his mouth close to her ear.

"Like it?" Libby bounded toward the car, heedless of her bare feet. "I love it!"

Jess followed, opened the door on the driver's side so that Libby could slide behind the wheel. When she did that, she got a second surprise. Taped to the gearshift knob was a ring of white gold, and the diamond setting formed the Circle Bar B brand.

"I'll hog-tie you later," Jess said.

Libby's hand trembled as she reached for the ring; it

blurred and shifted before her eyes as she looked at it. "Oh, Jess."

"Listen, if you hate it…"

Libby ripped away the strip of tape, slid the ring onto her finger. "Hate it? Sacrilege! It's the most beautiful thing I've ever seen."

"Does it fit?"

The ring was a little loose, but Libby wasn't ready to part with it, not even to let a jeweler size it. "No," she said, overwhelmed, "but I don't care."

Gently Jess lifted her chin with his hand, bent to sample her mouth with his. Beneath the hastily donned caftan and her camisole, Libby's nipples hardened in pert response.

"There's only one drawback to this car," Jess breathed, his lips teasing Libby's, shaping them. "It would be impossible to make love in it."

Libby laughed and pretended to shove him. "Scoundrel!"

"You don't know the half of it," he replied hoarsely, drawing Libby out of the beautiful car and back inside the house.

There she gravitated toward the front windows, where she could alternately admire her new car and watch the late-afternoon sun catch in the very special ring on her finger. Standing behind her, Jess wrapped his arms around her waist and held her close, bending to nip at her earlobe.

"Thank you, Jess," Libby said.

He laughed, and his breath moved in Libby's hair and sent warm tingles through her body. "No need for thanks. I'll nibble on your ears anytime."

"You know what I meant!"

His hands had risen to close over her breasts, fully possessing them. "What? What did you mean?" he teased in a throaty whisper.

Libby could barely breathe. "The car…the ring…"

Letting his hands slip from her breasts to her elbows, Jess ushered Libby over to face the mirror above the fireplace. As she watched his reflection in wonder, he undid the caftan's few buttons and slid it slowly down over her shoulders. Then he drew the camisole up over her head and tossed it away.

Libby saw a pink glow rise over her breasts to shine in her face, saw the passion sparking in her dark blue eyes, saw Jess's hands brush upward over her rib cage toward her breasts. The novelty of watching her own reactions to the sensations he was stirring inside her was erotic.

She groaned as she saw—and felt—masculine fingers rise to her waiting nipples and pluck then gently to attention.

"See?" Jess whispered at her ear. "See how beautiful you are, Libby? Especially when I'm loving you."

Libby had never thought of herself as beautiful, but now, looking at her image in the mirror, seeing how passion darkened her eyes to indigo and painted her cheeks with its own special apricot shade, she felt ravishing.

She tilted her head back against the hard breadth of Jess's shoulder, moaned as he softly plundered her nipples.

He spoke with a gruff, choked sort of sternness. "Don't close your eyes, Libby. Watch. You're beautiful—so beautiful—and I want you to know it."

It was hard for Libby not to close her eyes and give herself up to the incredible sensations that were raging through her, but she managed it even as Jess came from behind her to bend his head and take suckle at one breast.

Watching him do this, watching the heightened color in her own face, gave a new intensity to the searing needs that were like storm winds within Libby. Her eyes were fires of ink-blue, and there was a proud, even regal lift to her chin as she watched herself pleasing the man she loved.

Jess drank deeply of one breast, turned to the other. It was an earthy communion between one man and one woman, each one giving and taking.

Presently Jess's mouth slid down over Libby's slightly damp stomach, and then he was kneeling, no longer visible in the magic mirror. "Don't close your eyes," he repeated, and Libby felt her satiny panties sliding slowly down over her hips, her knees, her ankles.

The wide-eyed sprite in the mirror gasped, and Libby was forced to brace herself with both hands against the mantelpiece, just to keep from falling. Her breathing quickened to a rasp as Jess ran skilled hands over her bare bottom, her thighs, the backs of her knees. He heightened her pleasure by telling her precisely what he meant to do.

And then he did it.

Libby's release was a maelstrom of soft sobs that finally melded together into one lusty cry of pleasure. Jess was right, she thought, in the midst of all this and during the silvery descent that followed: she *was* beautiful.

Standing again, Jess lifted Libby up into his arms. Still feeling like some wanton Gypsy princess, she let her head fall back and gloried in the liberties his mouth took with the breasts that were thrust into easy reach.

Libby was conscious of an otherworldly floating sensation as she and Jess glided downward, together, to the floor.

Rain pattered and danced on the glass ceiling above the bed, a dismal heralding of what promised to be the happiest day of Libby Kincaid's life.

Jess slept beside her, beautifully naked, his breathing deep and even. If he hadn't actually spoken of his love, he had shown it in a dozen ways. So why did the pit of Libby's stomach jiggle, as though something awful was about to happen?

The insistent ringing of the doorbell brought Jess up from

his stomach, push-up style, grumbling. His dark hair hopelessly rumpled, his eyes glazed, he stumbled around the bedroom until he found his robe and managed to struggle into it.

Libby laughed at him as he started down the stairs. "So much for being happy in the mornings, Barlowe," she taunted.

His answer was a terse word that Libby couldn't quite make out.

She heard the door open downstairs, heard Senator Barlowe's deep laugh and exuberant greeting. The sounds eased the feeling of dread that had plagued Libby earlier, and she got out of bed and hurried to the bathroom for a shower.

Periodically, as Libby shampooed her hair and washed, she laughed. Having his father arrive unexpectedly from Washington, probably with Ken and Cathy soon to follow, would certainly throw cold water on any plans the groom might have had for prenuptial frolicking.

When Libby went downstairs, her hair blown dry, her makeup in place, she was delighted to see that Cathy was with the senator. They were both, in fact, seated comfortably on the couch, drinking coffee.

"Where's Dad?" Libby asked when hugs and kisses had been exchanged.

Cleave Barlowe, with his elegant, old-fashioned manners, waited for Libby to sit down before returning to his own seat near Cathy. "He'll be here in time for the ceremony," he said. "When we left the ranch, he was heading out with that bear patrol of his."

Libby frowned and fussed with her crisp pink sundress, feeling uneasy again. Jess had gone upstairs, and she could hear the water running in the shower. "Bear patrol?"

"We've lost a few calves to a rogue grizzly," Cleave said easily, as though such a thing were an everyday occurrence. "Ken and half a dozen of his best men have been tracking him, but they haven't had any luck so far."

Cathy, sitting at her father-in-law's elbow, seemed to sense her cousin's apprehension and signed that she wanted a better look at Libby's ring.

The tactic worked, but as Libby offered her hand, she at last looked into Cathy's face and saw the ravages of her marital problems. There were dark smudges under the green eyes, and a hollow ache pulsed inside them.

Libby reprimanded herself for being so caught up in her own tumultuous romance with Jess as to forget that during his visit the day before, Stacey had said he'd left Cathy. It shamed Libby that she hadn't thought more about her cousin, made it a point to find out how she was.

"Are you all right?" she signed, knowing that Cathy was always more comfortable with this form of communication than with lip reading.

Cathy's responding smile was real, if wan. She nodded and with mischievous interest assessed the ring Jess had had specially designed.

Cleave demanded a look at this piece of jewelry that was causing such an "all-fired" stir and laughed with appreciation when he saw his own brand in the setting.

Cathy lifted her hands. "I want to see your dress."

After Jess had come downstairs, dressed in jeans and the scandalous T-shirt Libby had given him, the two women went up to look at the new burgundy dress.

The haunted look was back in Cathy's eyes as she approved the garment. "I can hardly believe you're marrying Jess," she said in the halting, hesitant voice she would allow only Libby to hear.

Libby sat down on the rumpled bed beside her cousin. "That should settle any doubts you might have had about my relationship with Stacey," she said gently.

Cathy's pain was a visible spasm in her face. "He's living

at the main house now," she confessed. "Libby, Stacey says he wants a divorce."

Libby's anger with Stacey was equal only to her sympathy for his wife. "I'm sure he doesn't mean any of the things he's been saying, Cathy. If only you would talk to him…"

The emerald eyes flashed. "So Stacey could laugh at me, Libby? No, thanks!"

Libby drew a deep breath. "I can't help thinking that this problem stems from a lack of communication and trust," she persisted, careful to face toward her cousin. "Stacey loves you. I know he does."

"How can you be so sure?" whispered Cathy. "How, Libby? Marriages end every day of the week."

"No one knows that better than I do. But some things are a matter of instinct, and mine tells me that Stacey is doing this to make you notice him, Cathy. And maybe because you won't risk having a baby."

"Having a baby would be pretty stupid, wouldn't it? Even if I wanted to take the risk, as you call it. After all, my husband moved out of our house!"

"I'm not saying that you should rush back to the ranch and get yourself pregnant, Cathy. But couldn't you just talk to Stacey, the way you talk to me?"

"I told you—I'd be embarrassed!"

"Embarrassed! You are married to the man, Cathy—you share his bed! How can you be embarrassed to let him hear your voice?"

Cathy knotted her fingers together in her lap and lowered her head. From downstairs Libby could hear Jess and the senator talking quietly about the vote Cleave had cast before coming back to Montana for the wedding.

Finally Cathy looked up again. "I couldn't talk to anyone but you, Libby. I don't even talk to Jess or Ken."

"That's your own fault," Libby said, still angry. "Have you kept your silence all this time—all during the years I've been away?"

Cathy shook her head. "I ride up into the foothills sometimes and talk to the wind and the trees, for practice. Do you think that's silly?"

"No, and stop being so afraid that someone is going to think you're silly, dammit! So what if they do? What do you suppose people thought about me when I stayed with a man who had girlfriends?"

Cathy's mouth fell open. "Girlfriends?"

"Yes," snapped Libby, stung by the memory. "And don't tell my dad. He'd faint."

"I doubt it," replied Cathy. "But it must have hurt terribly. I'm so sorry, Libby."

"And I'm sorry if I was harsh with you," Libby answered. "I just want you to be happy, Cathy—that's all. Will you promise me that you'll talk to Stacey? Please?"

"I…I'll try."

Libby hugged her cousin. "That's good enough for me."

There was again a flash of delight in Cathy's eyes, indicating an imminent change of subject. "Is that car outside yours?"

Libby's answer was a nod. "Isn't it beautiful?"

"Will you take me for a ride in it? When the wedding is over and you're home on the ranch?"

"You know I will. We'll be the terror of the back roads— legends in our own time!"

Cathy laughed. "Legends? We'll be memories if we aren't careful."

Libby rose from her seat on the bed, taking up the pretty burgundy dress, slipping it carefully onto a hanger, hanging it in the back of the closet.

When that was done, the two women went downstairs

together. By this time Jess and his father were embroiled in one of their famous political arguments.

Feeling uneasy again, Libby went to the telephone with as much nonchalance as she could and dialed Ken's number. There was no answer, of course—she had been almost certain that there wouldn't be—but the effort itself comforted her a little.

"Try the main house," Jess suggested softly from just behind her.

Libby glanced back at him, touched by his perception. Consoled by it. "How is it," she teased in a whisper, "that you managed to look elegant in jeans and a T-shirt that says 'If it feels good, do it'?"

Jess laughed and went back to his father and Cathy.

Libby called the main house and got a somewhat flustered Marion Bradshaw. "Hello!" barked the woman.

"Mrs. Bradshaw, this is Libby. Have you seen my father this morning?"

There was a long sigh, as though the woman was relieved to learn that the caller was not someone else. "No, dear, I haven't. He and the crew are out looking for that darned bear. Don't you worry, though—Ken told me he'd be in town for your wedding in plenty of time."

Libby knew that her father's word was good. If he said he'd be there, he would, come hell or high water. Still, something in Mrs. Bradshaw's manner was disturbing. "Is something the matter, Marion?"

Another sigh, this one full of chagrin. "Libby, one of the maids told me that a Mr. Aaron Strand called here, asking where you could be reached. Without so much as a by-your-leave, that woman came right out and told him you were in Kalispell and gave him the number. I'm so sorry."

So that was how Aaron had known where to call. Libby sighed. "It's all right, Marion—it wasn't your fault."

"I feel responsible all the same," said the woman firmly, "but I'll kick myself on my own time. I just wanted to let you know what happened. Did Miss Cathy and the senator get there all right?"

Libby smiled. "Yes, they're here. Any messages?"

"No, but I'd like a word with Jess, if it's all right."

Libby turned and gestured to the man in question. He came to the phone, took the receiver, greeted Marion Bradshaw warmly. Their conversation was a brief one, and when Jess hung up, he was laughing.

"What's so funny?" the senator wanted to know.

Jess slid an arm around Libby and gave her a quick squeeze. "Dare I say it in front of the creator of Liberated Lizzie, cartoon cave-woman? I just got Marion's blessing—she says I branded the right heifer."

Chapter 11

Libby stood at a window overlooking the courthouse parking lot, peering through the gray drizzle, anxiously scanning each vehicle that pulled in.

"He'll be here," Cathy assured her, joining Libby at the rain-sheeted window.

Libby sighed. She knew that Ken would come if he possibly could, but the rain would make the roads hazardous, and there was the matter of that rogue grizzly bear. "I hope so," she said.

Cathy stood back a little to admire the flowing silken lines of Libby's dress. "You look wonderful. Here—let's see if the flowers match."

"Flowers?" Libby hadn't thought about flowers, hadn't thought about much at all, beyond contemplating the wondrous event about to take place. Her reason said that it was insanity to marry again, especially to marry Jess Barlowe, but her heart sang a very different song.

Cathy beamed and indicated a cardboard box sitting on a nearby table.

At last Libby left her post at the window, bemused. "But I didn't…"

Cathy was already removing a cellophane-wrapped corsage, several boutonnieres, an enormous bouquet made up of burgundy rosebuds, baby's breath, and white carnations. "This is yours, of course."

Libby reached out for her bridal bouquet, pleased and very surprised. "Did you order these, Cathy?"

"No," replied Cathy, "but I did nudge Jess in the florist's direction, after seeing what color your dress was."

Moved that such a detail had been taken into consideration, Libby hugged her cousin. "Thank you."

"Thank Jess. He's the one that browbeat the florist into filling a last-minute order." Cathy found a corsage labeled with her name. "Pin this on, will you?"

Libby happily complied. There were boutonnieres for Jess and the senator and Ken, too, and she turned this last one wistfully in her hands. It was almost time for the ceremony to begin—where was her father?

A light tap at the door made Libby's heart do a jittery flip. "Yes?"

"It's me," Jess said in a low, teasing voice. "Are the flowers in there?"

Cathy gathered up the boutonnieres, white carnations wrapped in clear, crackly paper, made her way to the door. Opening it just far enough to reach through, she held out the requested flowers.

Jess chuckled but made no move to step past the barrier and see his bride before the designated moment. "Five minutes, Libby," he said, and then she heard him walking away, his heels clicking on the marble courthouse floor.

Libby went back to the window, spotted a familiar truck racing into the parking lot, lurching to a stop. Two men in rain slickers got out and hurried toward the building.

Ken had arrived, and at last Libby was prepared to join Jess in Judge Henderson's office down the hall. She saw that august room through a haze of happiness, noticing a desk, a flag, a portrait of George Washington. In front of the rain-beaded windows, with their heavy, threadbare velvet draperies, stood Jess and his father.

Everyone seemed to move in slow motion. The judge took his place, and Jess, looking quietly magnificent in a tailored three-piece suit of dark blue, took his. His eyes caressed Libby, even from that distance, and somehow drew her toward him. At his side stood the senator, clearly tired from his unexpected cross-country trip, but proud and pleased, too.

Like a person strolling through a sweet dream, Libby let Jess draw her to him. At her side was Cathy, standing up very straight, her green eyes glistening with joyous tears.

Libby's sense of her father's presence was so strong that she did not need to look back and confirm it with her eyes. She tucked her arm through Jess's and the ceremony began.

When all the familiar words had been said, Jess bent toward Libby and kissed her tenderly. The haze lifted and the bride and groom turned, arm in arm, to face their few but much-loved guests.

Instead of congratulations, they met the pain-filled stares of two cowboys dressed in muddy jeans, sodden shirts and raincoats.

Suddenly frantic, Libby scanned the small chamber for her father's face. She'd been so sure that he was there; he had seemed near enough to touch.

"Where—" she began, but her question was broken off

because Jess left her side to stride toward the emissaries from the ranch, the senator close behind him.

"The bear…" said one of them in answer to Jess's clipped question. "We had him cornered and—" the cowboy's Adam's apple moved up and down in his throat "—and he was a mean one, Mr. Barlowe. Meaner'n the devil's kid brother."

Libby knew what was coming and the worn courthouse carpeting seemed to buckle and shift beneath her high-heeled burgundy sandals. Had it not been for Cathy, who gripped her elbow and maneuvered her into a nearby chair, she would have fallen.

"Just tell us what happened!" Jess rasped.

"The bear worked Ken over pretty good," the second cowboy confessed.

Libby gave a strangled cry and felt Cathy's arm slide around her shoulders.

"Is Ken dead?" demanded Cleave Barlowe, and as far as Libby was concerned, the whole universe hinged on the answer to that question.

"No, sir—we got Mr. Kincaid to the hospital fast as we could. But…but."

"But what?" hissed Jess.

"The bear got away, Mr. Barlowe."

Jess came slowly toward Libby, or at least it seemed so to her. As he crouched before her chair and took her chilled hands into his, his words were gentle. "Are you all right?"

Libby was too frightened and sick to speak, but she did manage a nod. Jess helped her to her feet, supported her as they left the room.

She was conscious of the cowboys, behind her, babbling an account of the incident with the bear to Senator Barlowe, of Cathy's quiet sobs, of Jess's steel arm around her waist.

The trip to the hospital, made in the senator's limousine, seemed hellishly long.

At the hospital's admissions desk, they were told by a harried, soft-voiced nurse that there was no news yet and directed to the nearest waiting room.

Stacey was there, and Cathy ran to him. He embraced her without hesitation, crooning to her, smoothing her hair with one hand.

"Ken?" barked the senator, his eyes anxious on his elder son's pale face.

"He's in surgery," replied Stacey. And though he still held Cathy, his gaze shifted, full of pain and disbelief, to Libby. "It's bad," he said.

Libby shuddered, more afraid than she'd ever been in her life, her arms and legs useless. Jess was holding her up—Jess and some instinct that had lain dormant within her since Jonathan's death. "Were you there when it happened, Stacey?" she asked dully.

Stacey was rocking Cathy gently in his arms, his chin propped in her hair. "Yes," he replied.

Suddenly rage surged through Libby—a senseless, shrieking tornado of rage. "You had guns!" she screamed. "I know you had guns! Why didn't you stop the bear? Why didn't you kill it?"

Jess's arm tightened around her. "Libby—"

Stacey broke in calmly, his voice full of compassion even in the face of Libby's verbal attack. "There was too much chance that Ken would be hit," he answered. "We hollered and fired shots in the air and that finally scared the grizzly off." There was a hollow look in Stacey's eyes as they moved to his father's face and then Jess's, looking for the same understanding he had just given to Libby.

"What about the bear?" the senator wanted to know.

Stacey averted his eyes for a moment. "He got away," he breathed, confirming what one of the cowboys had said earlier at the courthouse. "Jenkins got him in the hind flank, but he got away. Ran like a racehorse, that son of a bitch. Anyway, we were more concerned with Ken at the moment."

The senator nodded, but Jess tensed beside Libby, his gaze fierce. "You sent men after the grizzly, didn't you?"

Stacey looked pained and his hold on Cathy tightened as her sobs ebbed to terrified little sniffles. "I…I didn't think—"

"You didn't think?" growled Jess. "Goddammit, Stacey, now we've got a wounded bear on the loose—"

The senator interceded. "I'll call the ranch and make sure the grizzly is tracked down," he said reasonably. "Stacey got Ken to the hospital, Jess, and that was the most important thing."

An uncomfortable silence settled over the waiting room then. The senator went to the window to stand, hands clasped behind his back, looking out. The cowboys went back to the ranch, and Stacey and Jess maneuvered their stricken wives into chairs.

The sounds and smells peculiar to a hospital were a torment to Libby, who had endured the worst minutes, hours, days, and weeks of her life in just such a place. She had lost Jonathan in an institution like this one—would she lose Ken, too?

"I can't stand it," she whispered, breaking the awful silence.

Jess took her chin in his hand, his eyes locking with hers, sharing badly needed strength. "Whatever happens, Libby, we'll deal with it together."

Libby shivered violently, looked at Jess's tailored suit, her own dress, the formal garb of Cathy and the senator. Only Stacey, in his muddy jeans, boots, shirt and sodden denim jacket, seemed dressed for the horrible occasion. The rest of the party was at ludicrous variance with the situation.

My father may be dying, she thought in quiet hysteria, *and we're wearing flowers.* The smell of her bouquet suddenly sickened Libby, bringing back memories of Jonathan's funeral, and she flung it away. It slid under a couch upholstered in green plastic and cowered there against the wall.

Jess's grip tightened on her hand, but no one made a comment.

Presently the senator wandered out, returning some minutes later with cups of vending-machine coffee balanced on a small tray. "Ken is my best friend," he announced in befuddled tones to the group in general.

The words brought a startling cry of grief from Cathy, who had been huddled in her chair until that moment, behind a curtain of tangled, rain-dampened hair. "I won't let him die!" she shrieked, to the openmouthed amazement of everyone except Libby.

Stacey, draped over the arm and back of Cathy's chair, stared down at her, his throat working. "Cathy?" he choked out.

Because Cathy was not looking at him, could not see her name on his lips, she did not answer. Her small hands flew to cover her face and she wept for the man who had loved her as his own child, raised her as his own, been her strength as well as Libby's.

"She can't hear you," Libby said woodenly.

"But she talked!" gasped Jess.

Libby lifted one shoulder in a broken shrug. "Cathy has been talking for years. To me, anyway."

"Good God," breathed the senator, his gaze sweeping over his shattered daughter-in-law. "Why didn't she speak to any of us?"

Libby was sorry for Stacey, reading the pain in his face, the shock. Of course, it was a blow to him to realize that his own wife had kept such a secret for so long.

"Cathy was afraid," Libby explained quietly. "She is very

self-conscious about the way her voice sounds to hearing people."

"That's ridiculous!" barked Stacey, looking angry now, paler than before. He bolted away from Cathy's chair to stand at the windows, his back to the room. "For God's sake, I'm her husband!"

"Some of us had a few doubts about that," remarked Jess in an acid undertone.

Stacey whirled, full of fury, but the senator stepped between his two sons before the situation could get out of hand. "This is no time for arguments," he said evenly but firmly. "Libby and Cathy don't need it, and neither do I."

Both brothers receded, Stacey lowering his head a little, Jess averting a gaze that was still bright with anger. Libby watched a muscle leap in her husband's jaw and stifled a crazy urge to touch it with her finger, to still it.

"Was Dad conscious when you brought him here?" she asked of Stacey in a voice too calm and rational to be her own.

Stacey nodded, remembering. "He said that bear was almost as tough as a Mexican he fought once, down in Juarez."

The tears Libby had not been able to cry before suddenly came to the surface, and Jess held her until they passed. "Ken is strong," he reminded her. "Have faith in him."

Libby tried to believe the best, but the fact remained that Ken Kincaid was a mortal man, strong or not. And he'd been mauled viciously by a bear. Even if he survived, he might be crippled.

It seemed that Jess was reading her mind, as he so often did. His hand came up to stroke away her tears, smooth her hair back from her face. "Don't borrow trouble," he said gently. "We've got enough now."

Trying to follow this advice, Libby deliberately reviewed pleasant memories: Ken cursing a tangle of Christmas-tree lights; Ken sitting proudly in the audience while

Cathy and Libby accepted their high school diplomas; Ken trying, and somehow managing, to be both mother and father.

More than two hours went by before a doctor appeared in the waiting room doorway, still wearing a surgical cap, his mask hanging from his neck. "Are you people here for Ken Kincaid?" he asked, and the simple words had the electrifying effect of a cattle prod on everyone there.

Both Libby and Cathy stiffened in their chairs, unable to speak. It was Jess who answered the doctor's question.

"Mr. Kincaid was severely injured," the surgeon said, "but we think he'll be all right, if he rests."

Libby was all but convulsed by relief. "I'm his daughter," she managed to say finally. "Do you think I could see him, just for a few minutes?"

The middle-aged physician smiled reluctantly. "He'll be in Recovery for some time," he said. "Perhaps it would be better if you visited your father tomorrow."

Libby was steadfast. It didn't matter that Ken was still under anesthetic; if she could touch his hand or speak to him, he would know that she was near. Another vigil had taught her the value of that. "I must see him," she insisted.

"She won't leave you alone until you say yes," Jess put in, his arm tight around Libby's shoulders.

Before the doctor could answer, Cathy was gripping Libby's hands, searching her cousin's face. "Libby?" she pleaded desperately. "Libby?"

It was clear that Cathy hadn't discerned the verdict on Ken's condition, and Libby's heart ached for her cousin as she freed her hands, quickly motioned the reassurances needed.

When that was done, Libby turned back to the doctor. "My cousin will want to see my father, too."

"Now, just a minute…"

Stubbornly Libby lifted her chin.

Three hours later, Ken Kincaid was moved from the recovery room to a bed in the intensive-care unit. As soon as he had been settled there, Cathy and Libby were allowed into his room.

Ken was unconscious, and there were tubes going into his nostrils, an IV needle in one of his hands. His chest and right shoulder were heavily bandaged, and there were stitches running from his right temple to his neck in a crooked, gruesome line.

"Oh, God," whimpered Cathy.

Libby caught her cousin's arm firmly in her hand and faced her. "Don't you *dare* fall apart in here, Cathy Barlowe," she ordered. "He would sense how upset you are, and that would be bad for him."

Cathy trembled, but she squared her shoulders, drew a deep breath and then nodded. "We'll be strong," she said.

Libby went to the bedside, barely able to reach her father for all the equipment that was monitoring and sustaining him. "I hear you beat up on a bear," she whispered.

There was no sign that Ken had heard her, of course, but Libby knew that humor reached this man as nothing else could, and she went on talking, berating him softly for cruelty to animals, informing him that the next time he wanted to waltz, he ought to choose a partner that didn't have fur.

Before an insistent nurse came to collect Ken's visitors, both Libby and Cathy planted tender kisses on his forehead.

Stacey, Jess and Cleave were waiting anxiously when they reached the waiting room again.

"He's going to live," Libby said, and then the room danced and her knees buckled and everything went dark.

She awakened to find herself on a table in one of the hospital examining rooms, Jess holding her hand.

"Thanks for scaring the hell out of me," he said softly, a relieved grin tilting one corner of his mouth. "I needed that."

"Sorry," Libby managed, touching the wilting boutonniere that was still pinned to the lapel of his suit jacket. "Some wedding day, huh, handsome?"

"That's the wild west for you. We like excitement out here. How do you feel, princess?"

Libby tried to sit up, but the room began to swirl, so she fell back down. "I'm okay," she insisted. "Or I will be in a few minutes. How is Cathy?"

Jess smiled, kissed her forehead. "Cathy reacted a little differently to the good news than you did."

Libby frowned, still worried. "How do you mean?"

"After she'd been assured that you had fainted and not dropped dead of a coronary, she lit into Stacey like a whirlwind. It seems that my timid little sister-in-law is through being mute—once and for all."

Libby's eyes rounded. "You mean she was yelling at him?"

"Was she ever. When they left, he was yelling back."

Despite everything, Libby smiled. "In this case, I think a good loud argument might be just what the doctor ordered."

"I agree. But the condo will probably be a war zone by the time we get there."

Libby remembered that this was her wedding night, and with a little help from Jess, managed to sit up. "The condo? They're staying there?"

"Yes. The couch makes out into a bed, and Cathy wants to be near the hospital."

Libby reached out, touched Jess's strong face. "I'm sorry," she said.

"About what?"

"About everything. Especially about tonight."

Jess's green eyes laughed at her, gentle, bright with understanding. "Don't worry about tonight, princess. There will be plenty of other nights."

"But—"

He stilled her protests with an index finger. "You are in no condition to consummate a marriage, Mrs. Barlowe. You need to sleep. So let's go home and get you tucked into bed—with a little luck, Stacey and Cathy won't keep us awake all night while they throw pots and pans at each other."

Jess's remark turned out to be remarkably apt, for when they reached the condo, Stacey and his wife were bellowing at each other and the floor was littered with sofa pillows and bric-a-brac.

"Don't mind us," Jess said with a companionable smile as he ushered his exhausted bride across the war-torn living room. "We're just mild-mannered honeymooners, passing through."

Jess and Libby might have been invisible, for all the notice they got.

"Maybe we should have stayed in a motel," Libby yawned as she snuggled into Jess's strong shoulder, minutes later, in the loft bed.

Something shattered downstairs, and Jess laughed. "And miss this? No chance."

Cathy and Stacey were yelling again, and Libby winced. "You don't think they'll hurt each other, do you?"

"They'll be all right, princess. Rest."

Too tired to discuss the matter further, Libby sighed and fell asleep, lulled by Jess's nearness and the soft sound of rain on the glass roof overhead. She awakened once, in the depths of the night, and heard the sounds of another kind of passion from the darkened living room. A smile curved her lips as she closed her eyes.

Cathy was blushing as she tried to neaten up the demolished living room and avoid Libby's gaze at the same time.

Stacey, dead to the world, was sprawled out on the sofa bed, a silly smile shaping his mouth.

Libby made her way to the telephone in silence, called the hospital for a report on her father. He was still unconscious, the nurse on duty told her, but his vital signs were strong and stable.

Cathy was waiting, wide-eyed, when Libby turned away from the telephone.

Gently Libby repeated what the nurse had told her. After that, the two women went into the kitchen and began preparing a quick breakfast.

"I'm sorry about last night," Cathy said.

Standing at the stove, spatula in hand, Libby waited for her cousin to look at her and then asked, "Did you settle anything?"

Cathy's cheeks were a glorious shade of hot pink. "You heard!" she moaned.

Libby had been referring to the fight, not the lovemaking that had obviously followed, but there was no way she could clarify this without embarrassing her cousin further. She bit her lower lip and concentrated on the eggs she was scrambling.

"It was crazy," Cathy blurted, remembering. "I was *yelling* at Stacey! I wanted to hurt him, Libby—I really wanted to hurt him!"

Libby was putting slices of bread into the toaster and she offered no comment, knowing that Cathy needed to talk.

"I even threw things at him," confessed Cathy, taking orange juice from the refrigerator and putting it in the middle of the table. "I can't believe I acted like that, especially when Ken had just been hurt so badly."

Libby met her cousin's gaze and smiled. "I don't see what one thing has to do with the other, Cathy. You were angry with your husband—justifiably so, I'd say—and you couldn't hold it in any longer."

"I wasn't even worried about the way I sounded," Cathy reflected, shaking her head. "I suppose what happened to Ken triggered something inside me—I don't know."

"The important thing is that you stood up for yourself," Libby said, scraping the scrambled eggs out of the pan and onto a platter. "I was proud of you, Cathy."

"Proud? I acted like a fool!"

"You acted like an angry woman. How about calling those lazy husbands of ours to breakfast while I butter the toast?"

Cathy hesitated, wrestling with her old fear of being ridiculed, and then squared her shoulders and left the kitchen to do Libby's bidding.

Tears filled Libby's eyes at the sound of her cousin's voice. However ordinary the task was, it was a big step forward for Cathy.

The men came to the table, Stacey wearing only jeans and looking sheepish, Jess clad in slacks and a neatly pressed shirt, his green eyes full of mischief.

"Any word about Ken?" he asked.

Libby told him what the report had been and loved him the more for the relief in his face. He nodded and then executed a theatrical yawn.

Cathy blushed and looked down at her plate, while Stacey glared at his brother. "Didn't you sleep well, Jess?" he drawled.

Jess rolled his eyes.

Stacey looked like an angry little boy; Libby had forgotten how he hated to be teased. "I'll fight with my wife if I want to!" he snapped.

Both Libby and Jess laughed.

"Fight?" gibed Jess good-naturedly. "Was that what you two were doing? Fighting?"

"*Somebody* had to celebrate your wedding night," Stacey retorted, but then he gave in and laughed, too.

When the meal was over, Cathy and Libby left the dirty dishes to their husbands and went off to get ready for the day.

They were allowed only a brief visit with Ken, and even though his doctor assured them that he was steadily gaining ground, they were both disheartened as they returned to the waiting room.

Senator Barlowe was there, with Jess and Stacey, looking as wan and worried as either of his daughters-in-law. Unaware of their approach, he was saying, "We've got every available man tracking that bear, plus hands from the Three Star and the Rocking C. All we've found so far is paw-prints and dead calves."

Libby was brought up short, not by the mention of the bear but by the look on Jess's face. He muttered something she couldn't hear.

Stacey sliced an ironic look in his brother's direction. "I suppose you think you can find that son of Satan when the hands from three of the biggest ranches in the state can't turn up a trace?"

"I know I can," Jess answered coldly.

"Dammit, we scoured the foothills, the ranges…"

Jess's voice was low, thick with contempt. "And when you had the chance to bring the bastard down, you let him trot away instead—wounded."

"What was I supposed to do? Ken was bleeding to death!"

"Somebody should have gone after the bear," Jess insisted relentlessly. "There were more than enough people around to see that Ken got to the hospital."

Stacey swore.

"Were you scared?" Jess taunted. "Did the big bad bear scare away our steak-house cowboy?"

At this, Stacey lunged toward Jess and Jess bolted out of his chair, clearly spoiling for a fight.

Again, as he had before, the senator averted disaster. "Stop it!" he hissed. "If you two have to brawl, kindly do it somewhere else!"

"You can bank on that," Jess said bitterly, his green gaze moving over Stacey and then dismissing him.

"What's gotten into the two of you?" Senator Barlowe rasped in quiet frustration. "This is a hospital! And have you forgotten that you're brothers?"

Libby cleared her throat discreetly, to let the men know that she and Cathy had returned. She was disturbed by the barely controlled hostility between Jess and his brother, but with Ken in the condition that he was, she had no inclination to pursue the issue.

It was later, in the Land Rover, when she and Jess were alone, that Libby voiced a subject that had been bothering her. "You plan to go looking for that bear, don't you?"

Jess appeared to be concentrating on the traffic, but a muscle in his cheek twitched. "Yes."

"You're going back to the ranch and track him down," Libby went on woodenly.

"That's right."

She sank back against the seat and closed her eyes. "Let the others do it."

There was a short, ominous silence. "No way."

Libby swallowed the sickness and fear that roiled in her throat. God in heaven, wasn't it enough that she'd nearly lost her father to that vicious beast? Did she have to risk losing her husband, too? "Why?" she whispered miserably. "Why do you want to do this?"

"It's my job," he answered flatly, and Libby knew that there was no point in trying to dissuade him.

She squeezed her eyes even more tightly shut, but the tears escaped anyway. When they reached the condo again, Stacey's car and Cleave's pulling in behind them, Jess turned to her, brushed the evidence of her fear from her cheeks with gentle thumbs and kissed her.

"I promise not to get killed," he said softly.

Libby stiffened in his arms, furious and full of terror. "That's comforting!"

He kissed the tip of her nose. "You can handle this alone, can't you? Going to the hospital, I mean?"

Libby bit her lower lip. Here was her chance. She could say that she needed Jess now, she could keep him from hunting that bear. She did need him, especially now, but in the end, she couldn't use weakness to hold him close. "I can handle it."

An hour later, when Stacey and the senator left for the ranch, Jess went with them. Libby was now keeping two vigils instead of one.

Understanding Libby's feelings but unable to help, Cathy built a fire in the fireplace, brewed cocoa, and tried to interest her cousin in a closed-caption movie on television.

Libby watched for a while, then got out her sketchbook and began to draw with furious, angry strokes: Jess on horseback, a rifle in the scabbard of his saddle; a full-grown grizzly, towering on its hind legs, ominous muscles rolling beneath its hide, teeth bared. Try though she did, Libby could not bring herself to put Jess and that bear in the same picture, either mentally or on paper.

That evening, when Libby and Cathy went to the hospital, Ken was awake. He managed a weak smile as they came to his bedside to bestow tearful kisses.

"Sorry about missin' the wedding," he said, and for all his obvious pain, there was mirth in his blue eyes.

Libby dashed away the mist from her own eyes and smiled a shaky smile, shrugging. "You've seen one, cowboy, you've seen them all."

Ken laughed and the sound was beautiful.

Chapter 12

Having assured herself that Ken was indeed recovering, Cathy slipped out to allow Libby a few minutes alone with her father.

"Thanks for scaring me half to death," she said.

Ken tried to shrug, winced instead. "You must have known I was too mean to go under," he answered. "Libby, did they get the bear?"

Libby stiffened. The bear, the bear—she was so damned sick of hearing about the bear! "No," she said after several moments, averting her eyes.

Ken sighed. He was pale and obviously tired. "Jess went after him, didn't he?"

Libby fought back tears of fear. Was Jess face to face with that creature even now? Was he suffering injuries like Ken's, or even worse? "Yes," she admitted.

"Jess will be all right, Libby."

"Like you were?" Libby retorted sharply, without thinking.

Ken studied her for a moment, managed a partial grin. "He's younger than I am. Tougher. No grizzly in his right mind would tangle with him."

"But this grizzly isn't in his right mind, is he?" Libby whispered, numb. "He's wounded, Dad."

"All the more reason to find him," Ken answered firmly. "That bear was dangerous before, Libby. He's deadly now."

Libby shuddered. "You'd think the beast would just crawl off and die somewhere."

"That would be real handy, but he won't do it, Lib. Grizzlies have nasty dispositions as it is—their eyesight is poor and their teeth hurt all the time. When they're wounded, they can rampage for days before they finally give out."

"The Barlowes can afford to lose a few cows!"

"Yes, but they can't afford to lose people, Lib, and that's what'll happen if that animal isn't found."

There was no arguing that; Ken was proof of how dangerous a bear could be. "The men from the Three Star and the Rocking C are helping with the hunt, anyway," Libby said, taking little if any consolation from the knowledge.

"That's good," Ken said, closing his eyes.

Libby bent, kissed his forehead and left the room.

Cathy was pacing the hallway, her lower lip caught in her teeth, her eyes wide. Libby chastised herself for not realizing that Stacey was probably hunting the bear too, and that her cousin was as worried as she was.

When Libby suggested a trip to the Circle Bar B, Cathy agreed immediately.

During the long drive, Libby made excuses to herself. She wasn't going just to check on Jess—she absolutely was not. She needed her drawing board, her pens and inks, jeans and blouses.

The fact that she could have bought any or all of these items in Kalispell was carefully ignored.

By the time Libby and Cathy drew the Corvette to a stop in the wide driveway of the main ranch house, the sun was starting to go down. There must have been fifty horsemen converging on the stables, all of them looking tired and discouraged.

Libby's heart wedged itself into her throat when she spotted Jess. He was dismounting, wrenching a high-powered rifle from the scabbard on his saddle.

She literally ran to him, but then she stopped short, her shoes encased in the thick, gooey mud Montanans call gumbo, her vocal cords no more mobile than her feet.

"Ken?" he asked in a hoarse whisper.

Libby was quick to reassure him. "Dad's doing very well."

"Then what are you doing here?"

Libby smiled, pried one of her feet out of the mud, only to have it succumb again when she set it down. "I had to see if you were all right," she admitted. "May I say that you look terrible?"

Jess chuckled, rubbed the stubble of beard on his chin, assessed the dirty clothes he wore in one downward glance. "You should have stayed in town."

Libby lifted her chin. "I'll go back in the morning," she said, daring him to argue.

Jess surrendered his horse to one of the ranch hands, but the rifle swung at his side as he started toward the big, well-lighted house. Libby slogged along at his side.

"Is that gun loaded?" she demanded.

"No," he replied. "Any more questions?"

"Yes. Did you see the bear?"

They had reached the spacious screened-in porch, where Mrs. Bradshaw had prudently laid out newspapers to accommodate dozens of mud-caked boots.

"No," Jess rasped, lifting his eyes to some distant thing that Libby could not see. "That sucker might as well be invisible."

Libby watched as Jess kicked off his boots, flung his sodden denim jacket aside, dispensed with his hat. "Maybe he's dead, Jess," she blurted out hopefully, resorting to the optimism her father had tacitly warned her against. "Maybe he collapsed somewhere—"

"Wrong," Jess bit out. "We found more cattle."

"Calves?"

"A bull and two heifers," Jess answered. "And the hell of it is, he didn't even kill them to eat. He just ripped them apart."

Libby shivered. "He must be enormous!"

"The men that were with Stacey and Ken said he stood over eight feet," Jess replied, and his green eyes moved wearily over Libby's face. "I don't suppose I need to say this, but I will. I don't like having you here, not now. For God's sake, don't go wandering off by yourself—not even to walk down to the mailboxes. The same goes for Cathy."

It seemed ludicrous that one beast could restrict the normal activities of human beings—in fact, the bear didn't seem real to Libby, even after what had happened to Ken. Instead, it was as though Jess was telling one of the delicious, scary stories he'd loved to terrify Libby with when they were children.

"That means, little one," he went on sternly, "that you don't go out to the barn and you don't go over to Ken's to sit and moon by that pond. Am I making myself clear?"

"Too clear," snapped Libby, following him as he carried the rifle through the kitchen, down a long hallway and into the massive billiard room where the gun cabinets were.

Jess locked the weapon away and turned to his wife. "I'm a little bit glad you're here," he confessed with a weary grin.

"Even tough cowboys need a little spoiling now and then,"

she replied, "so hie thyself to an upstairs bathroom, husband of mine, and get yourself a shower. I'll bring dinner to your room."

"And how do you know where my room is, Mrs. Barlowe?"

Libby colored a little. "I used to help Marion Bradshaw with the cleaning sometimes, remember?"

"I remember. I used to watch you bending over to tuck in sheets and smooth pillows and think what a great rear end you had."

She arched one eyebrow. "Had?"

Jess caught her bottom in strong hands, pressed her close to him. "Have," he clarified.

"Go take your shower!" Libby huffed, suddenly conscious of all the cowboys that would be gathering in the house for supper that night.

"Join me?" drawled Jess, persistent to the end.

"Absolutely not. You're exhausted." Libby broke away, headed toward the kitchen.

"Not *that* exhausted," Jess called after her.

Libby did not respond, but as she went in to prepare a dinner tray for her husband, she was smiling.

Minutes later, entering Jess's boyhood bedroom, she set the tray down on a long table under a line of windows. The door of the adjoining bathroom was open and steam billowed out like the mist in a spooky movie.

Presently Libby heard the shower shut off, the rustling sound of a towel being pulled from a rack. She sat down on the edge of Jess's bed and then bounded up again.

"Libby?"

She went cautiously to the doorway, looked in. Jess was peering into a steamy mirror, trying to shave. "Your dinner is getting cold," she said.

After flinging one devilish look at his wife, Jess grabbed

the towel that had been wrapped around his hips and calmly used it to wipe the mirror. "I'll hurry," he replied.

Libby swallowed hard, as stunned by the splendor of his naked, muscle-corded frame as she had been on that first mantelpiece night when they'd made love in the bedroom at Jess's house, the fevered motions of their bodies metered by the raging elements outside.

Jess finished shaving, rinsed his face, turned toward Libby like a proud savage. She could not look away, even though she wanted to. Her eyes were fixed on the rising, swelling shaft of his manhood.

Jess laughed. "I used to fantasize about this."

"What?" Libby croaked, her throat tight.

"Bringing the foreman's pretty daughter up here and having my way with her."

Libby's eyes were, at last, freed, and they shot upward to his face. "Oh, yeah?"

"Yeah."

"I thought you liked Cathy then."

He nodded. "I did. But even before she married Stacey, I thought of her as a sister."

"And what, pray tell, did you think of me as?"

"A hellion. But I wanted to be your lover, all the same. Since I didn't dare, I settled for making your life miserable."

"How very chivalrous of you!"

Jess was walking toward her now, holding her with the scorching assessment of those jade-green eyes even before his hands touched her. "Teenage boys are not chivalrous, Libby."

Libby closed her eyes as he reached her, drew her close. "Neither are men," she managed to say.

Her blouse was coming untucked from her jeans, rising until she felt the steamy air on her stomach and back. Finally it was bunched under her arms and Jess was tracing a brazen finger over the lines of her scanty lace bra. Beneath the fabric, her nipples sprang into full bloom, coy flowers offering their nectar.

"Y-your dinner," she reminded Jess, floating on the sensations he was stirring within her, too bedazzled even to open her eyes.

The bra slipped down, just on one side, freeing a hard-peaked, eager breast. "Yes," Jess breathed evilly, "my dinner."

"Not that. I mean—"

His mouth closed over the delicate morsel, drawing at it softly. With a pleased and somewhat triumphant chuckle, Jess drew back from the tender treat and Libby's eyes flew open as he began removing her blouse and then her bra, leaving her jeans as they were.

He led her slowly to the bed, but instead of laying her down there, as she had expected, Jess stretched out on his back and positioned her so that she was sitting up, astraddle of his hips.

Gripping her waist, he pulled her forward and lifted, so that her breasts were suspended within easy reach of his mouth.

"The age-old quandary," he breathed.

Libby was dazed. "What qu-quandary?"

"Which one," Jess mused. "How like nature to offer two when a man has only one mouth."

Libby blushed hotly as Jess nuzzled a knotted peak, a peak that ached to nourish him. "Oh, God, Jess," she whispered. "Take it...take it!"

He chuckled, flicked the nipple in question with an impertinent tongue. "I love it when you beg."

Both rage and passion moved inside Libby. "I'm...not...begging!" she gasped, but even as she spoke she was bracing herself with her hands, brushing her breast back and forth across Jess's lips, seeking admission.

"You will," he said, and then he caught the pulsing nipple between careful teeth, raking it to an almost unendurable state of wanting.

"Not on your wretched life!" moaned Libby.

"We'll see," he replied.

The opposite breast was found and thoroughly teased and Libby had to bite her lower lip to keep from giving in and pleading senselessly for the suckling Jess promised but would not give. He played with her, using his tongue and his lips, delighting in the rocking motion of her body and the soft whimpers that came from her throat.

The sweet torment became keener, and Libby both loved and hated Jess for being able to drive her to such lengths. "Make love to me…oh, Jess…make love…to me."

The concession elicited a hoarse growl from Jess, and Libby found herself spinning down to lie flat on the bed. Her remaining clothes were soon stripped away, her legs were parted.

Libby gasped and arched her back as he entered her in one ferocious, needing thrust. After gaining this warm and hidden place, Jess paused, his hard frame shuddering with restraint.

As bedazzled as she was, Libby saw her chance to set the pace, to take command, and she took it. Acting on an age-old instinct, she wrapped her legs around his hips in a fierce claiming and muttered, "Give me all of you, Jess—all of you."

He groaned in lusty surrender and plunged deep within her, seeking solace in the velvety heat of her womanhood. They were locked together for several glittering moments, each afraid to move. Soon enough, however, their bodies demanded more and began a desperate, swift rhythm.

Straining together, both moaning in fevered need, Libby and Jess reached their shattering pinnacle at the same moment, crying out as their two souls flared as one golden fire.

Twice after Jess lay still upon her, his broad back moist beneath her hands, Libby convulsed softly, whimpering.

"Some people are really greedy," he teased when, at last, her body had ceased its spasmodic clenching and unclenching.

Libby stretched, sated, cosseted in delicious appeasement. "More," she purred.

"What did I tell you?" Jess sighed. "The lady is greedy."

"Very."

He rolled, still joined with Libby, bringing her with him so that she once again sat astraddle of him. They talked, in hushed and gentle voices, of very ordinary things.

After some minutes had passed, however, Libby began to trace his nipples with feather-light fingertips. "I've always wanted to have my way with the boss's son," she crooned, teasing him as he had teased her earlier.

She bent forward, tasted those hardening nipples, each in turn, with only the merest flick of her tongue. Jess groaned and grew hard within her, by degrees, as she continued to torment him.

"How like nature," she gibed tenderly, "to offer two when a woman has only one mouth."

Jess grasped her hips in inescapable hands and thrust his own upward in a savage demand.

Libby's release came swiftly; it was soft and warm, rather than violent, and its passing left her free to bring Jess to exquisite heights. She set a slow pace for him, delighting in the look in his eyes, the back-and-forth motion of his head on the pillow, the obvious effort it took for him to lie still beneath her.

He pleaded for release, but Libby was impervious, guiding him gently, reveling in the sweet power she held over this man she so completely loved. "I'm going to love you in my own way," she told him. "And in my own time."

His head pressed back into the pillows in magnificent surrender, Jess closed his eyes and moaned. His control was awesome, but soon enough it slipped and he began to move beneath Libby, slowly at first and then quickly. Finally, his hands tangling in her hair, he cried out and his body spasmed as she purposely intensified his pleasure. His triumph seemed endless.

When Jess was still at last, his eyes closed, his body glistening with perspiration, Libby tenderly stroked a lock of hair back from his forehead and whispered, "Some people are really greedy."

Jess chuckled and was asleep before Libby withdrew from him to make her way into the bathroom for a shower of her own.

The dream was very sexy. In it, a blue-gray dawn was swelling at the bedroom windows and Libby's breast was full in Jess's hand, the nipple stroked to a pleading state.

She groaned as she felt his hard length upon her, his manhood seeking to sheathe itself in her warmth. Jess entered her, and his strokes were slow and gentle, evoking an immediate series of tremulous, velvet-smooth responses.

"Good," she sighed, giving herself up to the dream. "So good…"

The easy strokes became demanding thrusts. "Yes," said the dream Jess gruffly. "Good."

"Ooooooh," moaned Libby, as a sudden and piercing release rocked her, thrusting her into wakefulness.

And Jess was there, upon her, his face inches from her own. She watched in wonder and in love as his features grew taut and his splendid body flexed, more rapidly now. She thrust herself up to receive the fullness of his love.

Libby's hands clasped Jess's taut buttocks as he shuddered and delved deep, his manhood rippling powerfully within her, his rasping moan filling Libby's heart.

Minutes later, a languid, hazy sleep overtook Libby and she rolled over onto her stomach and settled back into her dreams. She stirred only slightly when Jess patted her derriere and left the bed.

Hours later, when she awakened fully, Libby was not entirely certain that she hadn't dreamed the whole gratifying episode. As she got out of bed, though, to take a bath and get dressed, Libby knew that Jess had loved her—the feeling of lush well-being she enjoyed was proof of that.

The pampered sensation was short-lived. When Libby went downstairs to search out a light breakfast, she found Monica Summers sitting in the kitchen, sipping coffee and reading a weekly newsmagazine.

Even though Monica smiled, her dark gray eyes betrayed her malice. "Hello…Mrs. Barlowe."

Libby nodded uneasily and opened the refrigerator to take out an apple and a carton of yogurt. "Good morning," she said.

"I was very sorry to hear about your father," Monica went on, the tone of her voice totally belying her expression. "Is he recovering?"

Libby got a spoon for her yogurt and sat down at the table. "Yes, thank you, he is."

"Will you be staying here with us, or going back to Kalispell?"

There was something annoyingly proprietary in the way Monica said the word "us," as though Libby were somehow invading territory where she didn't belong. She lifted her chin and met the woman's stormy-sky gaze directly. "I'll be going back to Kalispell," she said.

"You must hate leaving Jess."

The pit of Libby's stomach developed an unsettling twitch. She took a forceful bite from her apple and said nothing.

"Of course, I'll be happy to…look after him," sighed Monica, striking a flame to the fuse she had been uncoiling. "It's an old habit, you know."

Libby suppressed an unladylike urge to fly over the table, teeth bared, fists flying. "Sometimes old habits have to be broken," she said, sitting very still, reminding herself that she was a grown woman now, not the foreman's little brat. Furthermore, she was Jess's wife and she didn't have to take this kind of subtle abuse in any case.

Monica arched one perfect eyebrow. "Do they?"

Libby leaned forward. "Oh, yes. You see, Ms. Summers, if you mess with my husband, I'll not only break the habit for you, I'll break a few of your bones for good measure."

Monica paled, muttered something about country girls.

"I am not a girl," Libby pointed out. "I'm a woman, and you'd better remember it."

"Oh, I will," blustered Monica, recovering quickly. "But will Jess? That's the question, isn't it?"

If there was one thing in the world Libby had absolutely no doubts about, at that moment anyway, it was her ability to please her husband in the way Monica was referring to. "I don't see how he could possibly forget," she said, and then she finished her apple and her yogurt, dropped the remnants into the trash, and left the room.

Marion Bradshaw was sweeping away residual dried mud when Libby reached the screened porch, hoping for one glimpse of Jess before she had to go back to Kalispell.

He was nowhere in sight, of course—Libby had not really expected him to be.

"How's Ken getting on?" Marion asked.

Libby smiled. "He's doing very well."

The housekeeper sighed, leaning on her broom. "Thank the good Lord for that. Me and Ken Kincaid run this place, and I sure couldn't manage it alone!"

Libby laughed and asked if Cathy was around.

Sheer delight danced in Mrs. Bradshaw's eyes. "She's where she belongs—upstairs in her husband's bed."

Libby blushed. She had forgotten how much this astute woman knew about the goings-on on the ranch. Did she know, too, why Jess had never gotten around to eating his dinner the night before?

"No shame in loving your man," Mrs. Bradshaw twinkled.

Libby swallowed. "Do you know if Stacey went with the others this morning?"

"He did. You go ahead and wake Miss Cathy right now, if you want to."

Libby was grateful for an excuse to hurry away.

Finding Stacey's room from memory, in just the way she'd found Jess's, she knocked briskly at the closed door, realized the foolishness of that, and turned the knob.

Cathy was curled up like a kitten in the middle of a bed as mussed and tangled as the one Libby had shared with Jess.

Libby bent to give Cathy's bare shoulder a gentle shake. Her cousin sat up, mumbling, her face lost behind a glistening profusion of tangled hair. "Libby? What…?"

Libby laughed and signed, "I'm going back to town as soon as I pick up some of my things at the other house. Do you want to go with me?"

Cathy's full lips curved into a mischievous smile and she shook her head.

"Things are going well between you and Stacey, then?"

Cathy's hands moved in a scandalously explicit answer.

"I'm shocked!" Libby signed, beaming. And then she gave her cousin a quick kiss on the forehead, promised to call Mrs. Bradshaw if there was any sort of change in Ken's condition, and left the room.

In Jess's room she found paper and a pen, and probably because of the tempestuous night spent in his bed, dared to write, "Jess. I love you. Sorry I couldn't stay for a proper goodbye, but I've got to get back to Dad. Take care and come to me if you can. Smiles and sunshine, Libby."

On the way downstairs, Libby almost lost her courage and ran back to rip up the note. Telling Jess outright that she loved him! What if he laughed? What if he was derisive or, even worse, pitying?

Libby denied herself the cowardice of hiding her feelings any longer. It was time she took responsibility for her own emotions, wasn't it?

The weather was crisp and bright that day, and Libby hummed as she drove the relatively short distance to her father's house, parked her car behind his truck and went in to get the things she needed.

Fitting extra clothes and her special set of pens and inks into the back of the Corvette proved easy enough, but the drawing board was another matter. She turned it this way and that way and it just wouldn't fit.

Finally Libby took it back inside the house and left it there. She would just have to make do with the kitchen table at the condo for the time being.

Libby was just passing the passenger side of Ken's truck when she heard the sound; it was a sort of shifting rustle, coming from the direction of the lilac hedge on the far side of the yard. There followed a low, ominous grunt.

Instinctively Libby froze, the hair tingling on the nape of her neck. Dear God, it couldn't be… Not here—not when there were men with rifles searching every inch of the ranch.…

She turned slowly, and her heart leapt into her throat and then spun back down into the pit of her stomach. The bear stood within ten feet of her, on its hind legs.

The beast growled and lolled its massive head to one side.

Its mangy, lusterless hide seemed loose over the rolling muscles beneath, and on its flank was a bloodcrusted, seeping wound.

In that moment, it was as though Libby became two people, one hysterically afraid, one calm and in control. Fortunately, it was this second Libby that took command. Slowly, ever so slowly, she eased her hand back behind her, to the door handle, opened it. Just as the bear lunged toward her, making a sound more horrifying than she could ever have imagined, she leapt inside the truck and slammed the door after her.

The raging beast shook the whole vehicle as it flung its great bulk against its side, and Libby allowed herself the luxury of one high-pitched scream before reaching for Ken's CB radio under the dashboard.

Again and again, the furious bear pummeled the side of the truck, while Libby tried frantically to make the CB radio work. She knew that the cowboys would be carrying receivers, in order to communicate with each other, and they were her only hope.

Fingers trembling, Libby finally managed to lift the microphone to her mouth and press the button. Her mind skittered over a series of movies she'd seen, books she'd read. *Mayday,* she thought with triumphant terror. *Mayday!* But the magic word would not come past her tight throat.

Suddenly a giant claw thundered across the windshield, shattering it into a glittering cobweb of cracks. One more blow, just one, and the bear would reach her easily, even though she was now crouching on the floorboard.

At last she found her voice. "Cujo!" she screamed into the radio receiver. "Cujo!" She closed her eyes, gasping, tried to get a hold on herself. *This is not a Stephen King movie,* she reminded herself. *This is reality. And that bear out there is going to tear you apart if you don't do something!*

"Libby!" the radio squawked suddenly. "Libby, come in!" The voice was Jess's. "Th-the bear," she croaked, remembering to hold in the button on the receiver when she talked. "Jess, the bear!"

"Where are you?"

Libby closed her eyes as the beast again threw itself against the truck. "My dad's house—in his truck."

"Hold on. Please, baby, hold on. We're not far away."

"Hurry!" Libby cried, as the bear battered the windshield again and tiny bits of glass rained down on her head.

Another voice came in over the radio, this one belonging to Stacey. "Libby," he said evenly, "honk the horn. Can you do that?"

Libby couldn't speak. There were tears pouring down her face and every muscle in her body seemed inert, but she did reach up to the center of the wheel and press the truck's horn.

The bear bellowed with rage, as though the sound had hurt him, but he stopped striking the truck and withdrew a little way. Libby knew he wasn't gone, for she could hear him lumbering nearby, growling in frustration.

Jess's men converged with Stacey's at the end of the rutted country road leading to Ken's house. When the pickup truck was in sight, they reined in their horses.

"He's mine," Jess breathed, reaching for the rifle in his scabbard, drawing it out, cocking it. He was conscious of the other men and their nervous, nickering horses, but only vaguely. Libby was inside that truck—his whole being seemed to focus on that one fact.

The bear rose up in full view suddenly, its enormous head visible even over the top of the pickup's cab. Even over the repeated honking of the truck's horn, the beast's hideous, echoing growl was audible.

"Sweet Jesus," Stacey whispered.

"Easy," said Jess, to himself more than the men around

him, as he lifted the rifle, sighted in carefully, pulled back the trigger.

The thunderous shot struck the bear in the center of its nose, and the animal shrieked as it went down. The impact of its body was so solid that it seemed to shake the ground.

Instantly Jess was out of the saddle. "Make sure he's dead," he called over one shoulder as he ran toward the truck.

Stacey and several of his men reached the bear just as Jess wrenched open the door on the driver's side.

Libby scrambled out from under the steering wheel, her hair a wild, glass-spattered tangle, to fling herself, sobbing, into his arms. Jess cradled her in his arms, carried her away from the demolished truck and inside the house. His own knees suddenly weak, he fell into the first available chair and buried his face in Libby's neck.

"It's over, sweetheart," he said. "It's over."

Libby shuddered and wailed with terror.

When she was calmer, Jess caught her chin in his hand and lifted it. "What the hell did you mean, yelling 'Cujo! Cujo!'"

Libby sniffled, and the fight was back in her eyes, a glorious, snapping blue. "There was this book about a mad dog…and then there was a movie…"

Jess lifted his eyebrows and grinned.

"Oh, never mind!" hissed Libby.

Chapter 13

Libby froze in the doorway of Ken's room in the intensive-care unit, her mouth open, her heart racing as fast as it had earlier, when she'd been trapped by the bear.

"Where is he?" she finally managed to whisper. "Oh, Jess, where is my father?"

Standing behind Libby, Jess lifted his hands to her shoulders and gently ushered her back into the hallway, out of sight of the empty bed. "Don't panic," he said quietly.

Libby trembled, looked frantically toward the nurses' station. "Jess, what if he…?"

There was a gentle lecture forming in Jess's features, but before he could deliver it, an attractive red-headed nurse approached, trim in her uniform. "Mrs. Barlowe?"

Libby nodded, holding her breath.

"Your father is fine. We moved Mr. Kincaid to another floor earlier today, since he no longer needs such careful monitoring. If you will just come back to the desk with me, I'll be happy to find out which room he's in."

Libby's breath escaped in one long sigh. What with spending perilous minutes cowering inside a truck, with a rogue bear doing its best to get inside and tear her to bits, and then rushing to the hospital to find her father's bed empty, she had had more than enough stress for one day. "Thank you," she said, giving Jess a relieved look.

He got rather familiar during the elevator ride down to the second floor, but desisted when the doors opened again.

"You're incorrigible," Libby whispered, only half in anger.

"Snatching my wife from the jaws of death has that effect on me," he whispered back. "I keep thinking that I might never have gotten the chance to touch you like that again."

Libby paused, in the quest for Room 223, to search Jess's face. "Were you scared?"

"Scared? Sweet thing, I was *terrified.*"

"You seemed so calm!"

He lifted one eyebrow. "Somebody had to be."

Libby considered that and then sighed. "I don't suppose we should tell Dad what actually happened. Not yet, at least."

Jess chuckled. "We'll tell a partial truth—that the bear is dead. The rest had better wait until he's stronger."

"Right," agreed Libby.

When they reached Ken's new room, another surprise was in store. A good-looking dark-haired woman was there plumping the patient's pillows, fussing with his covers. She wore well-cut jeans and a western shirt trimmed with a rippling snow-white fringe, and the way she laughed, low in her throat, said more about her relationship with Ken Kincaid than all her other attentions combined.

"Hello, Becky," said Jess, smiling.

Becky was one of those people, it seemed, who smile not

just with the mouth but with the whole face. "Jess Barlowe," she crowed, "you black-hearted son-of-a-gun! Where ya been?"

Libby drew a deep breath and worked up a smile of her own. Was this the woman who had written that intriguing farewell on the condo's kitchen blackboard?

Deliberately she turned her attention on her father, who looked downright rakish as he favored his startled daughter with a slow grin and a wink.

"Who's this pretty little gal?" demanded Becky, giving Libby a friendly once-over.

For the first time, Ken spoke. "This is my daughter, Libby. Libby, Becky Stafford."

"I'll be!" cried Becky, clearly delighted. "Glad to meet ya!"

Libby found the woman's boisterous good nature appealing, and despite a few lingering twinges of surprise, she responded warmly.

"Did you get that bear?" Ken asked of Jess, once the women had made their exchange.

"Yes," Jess replied, after one glance at Libby.

Ken gave a hoot of delight and triumph. "Nail that son-of-a...nail that devil's hide to the barn door for me, will you?"

"Done," answered Jess with a grin.

A few minutes later, Jess and the energetic Becky left the room to have coffee in the hospital cafeteria. Libby lifted her hands to her hips, fixed her father with a loving glare and demanded, "Is there something you haven't told me?"

Ken laughed. "Maybe. But I'll wager that there are a few things you haven't told me, either, dumplin'."

"Who is Becky, exactly?"

Ken thought for a moment before speaking. "She's a good friend of mine, Libby. An old friend."

For some reason, Libby was determined to find something

to dislike about Becky Stafford, difficult as it was. "Why does she dress like that? Is she a rodeo performer or something?"

"She's a cocktail waitress," Ken replied patiently.

"Oh," said Libby. And then she couldn't sustain her petty jealousy any longer, because Becky Stafford was a nice person and Ken had a right to like her. He was more than just her father, after all, more than just Senator Barlowe's general foreman. He was a man.

There was a brief silence, which Ken broke with a very direct question. "Do you like Becky, Lib?"

Like her? The warmth and humor of the woman still lingered in that otherwise dreary room, as did the earthy, unpretentious scent of her perfume. "Sure I do," said Libby. "Anybody with the perception to call Jess Barlowe a 'black-hearted son-of-a-gun' is okay in my book!"

Ken chuckled, but there was relief in his face, and his expression revealed that he knew how much Libby loved her husband. "How's Cathy?" he asked.

Remembering that morning's brief conversation with her cousin, Libby grinned. "She's doing fine, as far as I can tell. Bad as it was, your tussle with that bear seems to have brought Cathy and Stacey both to a point where they can open up to each other. Cathy actually talked to him."

Ken did not seem surprised by this last; perhaps he'd known all along that Cathy still had use of her voice. "I don't imagine it was peaceable," he observed drily.

"Not in the least," confirmed Libby, "but they're communicating and…and, well, let's just say they're closer."

"That's good," answered Ken, smiling at his daughter's words. "That's real good."

Seeing that her father was getting very tired, Libby quickly kissed him and took her leave. When she reached the cafeteria, Becky was sitting alone at a table, staring sadly into her coffee cup.

Libby scanned the large room for Jess and failed to see him, but she wasn't worried. Probably he had gone back to Ken's room and missed seeing Libby on the way. Noticing the pensive look on Becky's face, she was glad for a few minutes alone with the woman her father obviously liked and perhaps even loved.

"May I sit down?" she asked, standing behind the chair that had probably been Jess's.

Becky looked up, smiled. "Sure," she said, and there was surprise in her dark eyes.

Libby sat down with a sigh. "I hate hospitals," she said, filled to aching with the memory of Jonathan's confinement.

"Me too," answered Becky, but her eyes were watchful. Hopeful, in a touchingly open way.

Libby swallowed. "My…my father has been very lonely, and I'm glad you're his friend."

Becky's smile was almost cosmic in scope. "That's good to hear," she answered. "Lordy, that man did scare the life out of me, going a round with that damned bear that way."

Libby thought of her own chance meeting with the creature and shivered. She hoped that she would never know that kind of numbing fear gain.

Becky's hand came to pat hers. "It's all right now, though, isn't it? That hairy booger is dead, thanks to Jess."

Libby laughed. Indeed, that "hairy booger" was dead, and she did have Jess to thank for her life. When she'd tried to voice her gratitude earlier, he had brushed away her words and said that she was his wife and, therefore, saving her from bears, fire-breathing dragons and the like was just part of the bargain.

As if conjured by her thoughts of him, Jess appeared to take Libby home.

* * *

The coming days were happy ones for Libby, if hectic. She visited her father morning and evening and worked on her cartoon strip and the panels for the book between times, her drawing board having been transported from the ranch by Jess and set up in the middle of the condo's living room.

Jess commuted between Kalispell and the ranch; many of Ken's duties had fallen to him. Instead of being exhausted by the crazy pace, however, he seemed to thrive on it and his reports on the stormy reconciliation taking place between Cathy and Stacey were encouraging. It appeared that, with the help of the marriage counselor they were seeing, their problems might be worked out.

The irrepressible Becky Stafford rapidly became Libby's friend. Vastly different, the two women nevertheless enjoyed each other—Libby found that Becky could draw her out when she became too burrowed down in her work, and just as quickly drive her back if she tried to neglect it.

"You did what?" Jess demanded archly one early-summer evening as he and Libby sat on the living-room floor consuming the take-out Chinese food they both loved.

Libby laughed with glee and a measure of pride. "I rode the mechanical bull at the bar where Becky works," she repeated.

Jess worked up an unconvincing scowl. "Hanging around bars these days, are you?" he demanded, waving a fortune cookie for emphasis.

Libby batted her eyelashes demurely. "Don't you worry one little bit," she said, feigning a musical southern drawl. "Becky guards mah virtue, y'all."

Jess's green eyes slipped to the V neck of Libby's white sweater, which left a generous portion of cleavage in full and enticing view. "Does she now? And where is she, at this very moment, when said virtue is in immediate peril?"

An anticipatory thrill gyrated in the pit of Libby's stomach and warmed her breasts, which were bare beneath her light-weight sweater. Jess had loved her often, and well, but he could still stir that sweet, needing tension with remarkable ease. "What sort of peril am I in, exactly?"

Jess grinned and hooked one finger in the V of her sweater, slid it downward into the warmth between her breasts. "Oh, the most scandalous sort, Mrs. Barlowe."

Libby's breath quickened, despite stubborn efforts to keep it even. "Your attentions are quite unseemly, Mr. Barlowe," she replied.

He moved the wanton finger up and down between the swelling softness that was Libby, and sharp responses ached in other parts of her. "Absolutely," he said. "I mean to do several unseemly things to you."

Libby tensed with delicious sensation as Jess's exploring finger slid aside, explored a still-hidden nipple.

"I want to see your breast, Libby. This breast. Show it to me."

The outrageous request made Libby color slightly, but she knew she would comply. She was a strong, independent person, but now, in this sweet, aching moment, she was Jess's woman. With one motion of her hand, she tugged the sweater's neckline down and to one side, so that it made a sort of sling for the breast that had been softly demanded.

Not touching the rounded pink-tipped treasure in any way, Jess admired it, rewarding it with an approving smile when the confectionlike peak tightened into an enticing point.

Libby was kneeling now, resting on her heels, the cartons littering the coffee table completely forgotten. She was at once too proud to plead for Jess's mouth and too needing of it to cover herself.

Knowing that, Jess chuckled hoarsely and bent to flick at

the exposed nipple with just the tip of his tongue. Libby moaned and let her head fall back, making the captured breast even more vulnerable.

"Unseemly," breathed Jess, nibbling, drawing at the straining morsel with his lips.

Libby felt the universe sway in time with his tender plundering, but she bit down hard on the garbled pleas that were rising in her throat. They escaped through her parted lips, all the same, as small gasps.

Her heartbeat grew louder and louder as Jess finally took suckle; it muffled the sounds of his greed, of the cartons being swept from the surface of the coffee table in a motion of one of his arms.

The coolness of the air battled with the heat of Libby's flesh as she was stripped of her sweater, her white slacks, her panties. Gently he placed her on the coffee table.

Entranced, Libby allowed him to position her legs wide of each other, one on one side of the low table, one on the other. Beyond the glass roof, in the dark, dark sky, a million silvery stars surged toward her and then melted back into the folds of heaven, becoming pinpoints.

Jess found the silken nest of her passion and attended it lovingly, stroking, kissing, finding, losing. Libby's hips moved wildly, struggling even as she gave herself up.

And when she had to have this singular gratification or die, Jess understood and feasted unreservedly, his hands firm under her bottom, lifting her, the breadth of his shoulders making it impossible for her to deny him what he would have from her.

At last, when the tumult broke on a lusty cry of triumph from Libby, she saw the stars above plummet toward her—or had she risen to meet them?

* * *

"Of course you're going to the powwow!" cried Becky, folding her arms and leaning over the platter of french fries in front of her. "You can't miss that and call yourself a Barlowe!"

Libby shrank down a little in the benchlike steak-house seat. As this restaurant was a part of the Barlowe chain, the name drew immediate attention from all the waiters and a number of the other diners, too. "Becky," she began patiently, "even though Dad's getting out of the hospital this afternoon, he won't be up to something like that, and I wouldn't feel right about leaving him behind."

"Leaving Ken behind?" scoffed Becky in a more discreet tone of voice. "You just try keeping him away—he hasn't missed a powwow in fifteen years."

Libby's memories of the last powwow and all-day rodeo she had attended were hardly conducive to nostalgia. She remembered the dust, the hot glare of the summer sun, the seemingly endless rodeo events, the revelers draped over the hoods of parked cars and sprawled on the sidewalks. She sighed.

"Jess'll go," Becky prodded.

Libby had no doubt of that, and having spent so much time away from Jess of late, what with him running the ranch while she stayed in Kalispell, she was inclined to attend the powwow after all.

Becky saw that she had relented and beamed. "Wait'll you see the Sioux doing their war dances," she enthused. "There'll be Blackfoot, too, and Flathead."

Libby consoled herself with the thought of the dances and the powwow finery of feathers and buckskin and beads. She could take her sketchbook along and draw, at least.

Becky wasn't through with her conversation. "Did you tell

Jess how you rode that electric bull over at the Golden Buckle?"

Libby tried to look dignified in the wake of several molten memories. "I told him," she said shyly.

Her friend laughed. "If that wasn't a sight! I wish I woulda took your picture. Maybe you should enter some of the events at the powwow, Libby." Her face took on a disturbingly serious expression. "Maybe barrel racing, or women's calf roping—"

"Hold it," Libby interceded with a grin. "Riding a mechanical bull is one thing and calf roping is quite another. The only sport I'm going to take part in is stepping over drunks."

"Stepping over what?" inquired a third voice, masculine and amused, from the table side.

Libby looked and saw Stacey. "What are you doing here?"

He laughed, turning his expensive silver-banded cowboy hat in both hands. "I own the place, remember?"

"Where's Cathy?" Becky wanted to know. As she had become Libby's friend, she had also become Cathy's—she was even learning to sign.

Stacey slid into the bench seat beside Libby. "She's seeing the doctor," he said, and for all his smiling good manners, he seemed nervous.

Libby elbowed her brother-in-law lightly. "Why didn't you stay there and wait for her?"

"She wouldn't let me."

Just then Becky stood up, saying that she had to get to work. A moment later, eyes twinkling over some secret, she left.

Libby felt self-conscious with Stacey, though he hadn't made any more advances or disturbing comments. She wished that Becky had been able to stay a little longer. "What's going on? Is Cathy sick?"

"She's just having a checkup. Libby…"

Libby braced herself inwardly and moved a little closer to the wall of the enclosed booth, so that Stacey's thigh wasn't touching hers. "Yes?" she prompted when he hesitated to go on.

"I owe you an apology," he said, meeting her eyes. "I acted like a damned fool and I'm sorry."

Knowing that he was referring to the rumors he'd started about their friendship in New York, Libby chafed a little. "I accept your apology, Stacey, but I truly don't understand why you said what you did in the first place."

He sighed heavily. "I love Cathy very much, Libby," he said. "But we do have our problems. At that time, things were a lot worse, and I started thinking about the way you'd leaned on me when you were going through all that trouble in New York. I liked having somebody need me like that, and I guess I worked the whole thing up into more than it was."

Tentatively Libby touched his hand. "Cathy needs you, Stacey."

"No," he answered gruffly, looking at the flickering bowl candle in the center of the table. "She won't allow herself to need me. After some of the things I've put her through, I can't say I blame her."

"She'll trust you again, if you're worthy of it," Libby ventured. "Just be there for Cathy, Stace. The way you were there for me when my whole life seemed to be falling apart. I don't think I could have gotten through those days without you."

At that moment Jess appeared out of nowhere and slid into the seat Becky had occupied before. "Now, that," he drawled acidly, "is really touching."

Libby stared at him, stunned by his presence and by the angry set of his face. Then she realized that both she and Stacey were sitting on the same side of the booth and knew that it gave an impression of intimacy. "Jess…"

He looked down at his watch, a muscle dancing furiously

in his jaw. "Are you going to pick your father up at the hospital, or do you have more interesting things to do?"

Stacey, who had been as shocked by his brother's arrival as Libby had, was suddenly, angrily vocal. The candle leapt a little when he slammed one fist down on the tabletop and hissed, "Dammit, Jess, you're deliberately misunderstanding this!"

"Am I?"

"Yes!" Libby put in, on the verge of tears. "Becky and I were having lunch and then Stacey came in and—"

"Stop it, Libby," Stacey broke in. "You didn't do anything wrong. Jess is the one who's out of line here."

The long muscle in Jess's neck corded, and his lips were edged with white, but his voice was still low, still controlled. "I came here, Libby, because I wanted to be with you when you brought Ken home," he said, and his green eyes, dark with passion only the night before, were coldly indifferent now. "Are we going to collect him or would you rather stay here and carry on?"

Libby was shaking. "Carry on? *Carry on?*"

Stacey groaned, probably considering the scandal a scene in this particular restaurant would cause. "Couldn't we settle this somewhere else?"

"We'll settle it, all right," Jess replied.

Stacey's jaw was rock-hard as he stood up to let a shaken Libby out of the booth. "I'll be on the ranch," he said.

"So will I," replied Jess, rising, taking a firm grip on Libby's arm. "See you there."

"Count on it."

Jess nodded and calmly propelled Libby out of the restaurant and into the bright sunlight, where her shiny Corvette was parked. Probably he had seen the car from the highway and known that she was inside the steak house.

Now, completely ignoring her protests, he dragged her past her car and thrust her into the Land Rover beside it.

"Jess—damn you—will you *listen* to me?"

Jess started the engine, shifted it into reverse with a swift motion of his hand. "I'm afraid storytime will have to wait," he informed her. "We've got to go and get Ken, and I don't want him upset."

"Do you think I do?"

Jess sliced one menacing look in her direction but said nothing.

Libby felt a need to reach him, even though, the way he was acting, he didn't deserve reassurances. "Jess, how can you…after last night, how could you…"

"Last night," he bit out. "Yes. Tell me, Libby, do you do that trick for everybody, or just a favored few?"

It took all her determination not to physically attack him. "Take me back to my car, Jess," she said evenly. "Right now. I'll pick Dad up myself, and we'll go back to his house—"

"Correction, Mrs. Barlowe. *He* will go to his house. You, my little vixen, will go to mine."

"I will not!"

"Oh, but you will. Despite your obvious attraction to my brother, you are still my wife."

"I am not attracted to your brother!"

They had reached the hospital parking lot, and the Land Rover lurched to a stop. Jess smiled insolently and patted Libby's cheek in a way so patronizing that it made her screaming mad. "That's the spirit, Mrs. Barlowe. Walk in there and show your daddy what a pillar of morality you are."

Going into that hospital and pretending that nothing was wrong was one of the hardest things Libby had ever had to do.

* * *

Preparations for Ken's return had obviously been going on for some time. As Libby pulled her reclaimed Corvette in behind Jess's Land Rover, she saw that the front lawn had been mowed and the truck had been repaired.

Ken, still not knowing the story of his daughter, his truck, and the bear, paused after stepping out of Jess's Land Rover, his arm still in a sling. He looked his own vehicle over quizzically. "Looks different," he reflected.

Jess rose to the occasion promptly, smoothly. "The boys washed and waxed it," he said.

To say the very least, thought Libby, who would never forget, try though she might, how that truck had looked before the repair people in Kalispell had fixed and painted it. She opened her mouth to tell her father what had happened, but Jess stopped her with a look and a shake of his head.

The inside of the house had been cleaned by Mrs. Bradshaw and her band of elves; every floor and stick of furniture had been either dusted or polished or both. The refrigerator had been stocked and a supply of the paperback westerns Ken loved to read had been laid in.

As if all this wasn't enough to make Libby's services completely superfluous, it turned out that Becky was there, too. She had strung streamers and dozens of brightly colored balloons from the ceiling of Ken's bedroom.

Her father was obviously pleased, and Libby's last hopes of drumming up an excuse to stay the night, at least, were dashed. Becky, however, was delighted with her surprise.

"I thought you were working!" Libby accused.

"I lied," replied Becky, undaunted. "After I left you and Stacey at the steak house, I got a friend to bring me out here."

Libby shot a glance in Jess's direction, knew sweet triumph as she saw that Becky's words had registered with him. After only a moment's chagrin, however, he tightened his jaw and looked away.

While Becky was getting Ken settled in his room and generally spoiling him rotten, Libby edged over to her husband. "You heard her," she whispered tersely, "so where's my apology?"

"Apology?" Jess whispered back, and there was nothing in his face to indicate that he felt any remorse at all. "Why should I apologize?"

"Because I was obviously telling the truth! Becky said—"

"Becky said that she left you and Stacey at the steak house. It must have been a big relief when she did."

Heedless of everything but the brutal effect of Jess's unfair words, Libby raised one hand and slapped him, hard.

Stubbornly, he refused her the satisfaction of any response at all, beyond an imperious glare, which she returned.

"Hey, do you guys…?" Becky's voice fell away when she became aware of the charged atmosphere of the living room. She swallowed and began again. "I was going to ask if you wanted to stay for supper, but maybe that wouldn't be such a good idea."

"You can say that again," rasped Jess, catching Libby's arm in a grasp she couldn't have broken without making an even more embarrassing scene. "Make our excuses to Ken, will you, please?"

After a moment's hesitation and a concerned look at Libby, Becky nodded.

"You overbearing bastard!" Libby hissed as her husband squired her out of the house and toward his Land Rover.

Jess opened the door, helped her inside, met her fiery blue gaze with one of molten green. Neither spoke to the other, but the messages flashing between them were all too clear anyway.

Jess still believed that Libby had been either planning or carrying on a romantic tryst with Stacey, and Libby was too proud and too angry to try to convince him otherwise. She was also too smart to get out of his vehicle and make a run for hers.

Jess would never hurt her, she knew that. But he would not allow her a dramatic exit, either. And she couldn't risk a screaming fight in the driveway of her father's house.

Because she was helpless and she hated that, she began to cry.

Jess ignored her tears, but he too was considerate of Ken—he did not gun the Land Rover's engine or back out at a speed that would fling gravel in every direction, as he might have at another time.

When they passed his house, with its window walls, and started up a steep road leading into the foothills beyond, Libby was still not afraid. For all his fury, this man was too tender a lover to touch her in anger.

"Where are we going?" she demanded.

He ground the Land Rover into a low gear and left the road, now little more than a cow path, for the rugged hillside. "On our honeymoon, Mrs. Barlowe."

Libby swallowed, unnerved by his quiet rage and the jostling, jolting ascent of the Land Rover itself. "If you take me in anger, Jess Barlowe, I'll never forgive you. Never. That would be rape."

The word "rape" got through Jess's hard armor and stung him visibly. He paled as he stopped the Land Rover with a lurch and wrenched on the emergency brake. "Goddammit, you *know* I wouldn't do anything like that!"

"Do I?" They were parked at an almost vertical angle, it seemed to Libby. Didn't he realize that they were almost straight up and down? "You've been acting like a maniac all afternoon!"

Jess's face contorted and he raised his fists and brought them down hard on the steering wheel. "Dammit it all to hell," he raged, "you drive me crazy! Why the devil do I love you so much when *you drive me crazy?*"

Libby stared at him, almost unable to believe what she had

heard. Not even in their wildest moments of passion had he said he loved her, and if he had found that note she'd left for him, betraying her own feelings, the day the bear was killed, he'd never mentioned it.

"What did you say?"

Jess sighed, tilted his head back, closed his eyes. "That you drive me crazy."

"Before that."

"I said I loved you," he breathed, as though there was nothing out of the ordinary in that.

"Do you?"

"Hell, yes." The muscles in his sun-browned neck corded as he swallowed, his head still back, his eyes still closed. "Isn't that a joke?"

The words tore at Libby's heart. "A joke?"

"Yes." The word came, raw, from deep within him, like a sob.

"You idiot!" yelled Libby, struggling with the door, climbing out of the Land Rover to stalk up the steep hillside. She trembled, and tears poured down her face, and for once she didn't care who saw them.

At the top of the rise, she sat down on a huge log, her vision too blurred to take in the breathtaking view of mountains and prairies and an endless, sweeping sky.

She sensed Jess's approach, tried to ignore him.

"Why am I an idiot, Libby?"

Though the day was warm, Libby shivered. "You're too stupid to know when a woman loves you, that's why!" she blurted out, sobbing now. "Damn! You've had me every way but hanging from a chandelier, and you still don't know!"

Jess straddled the log, drew Libby into his arms and held her. Suddenly he laughed, and the sound was a shout of joy.

Chapter 14

The powwow of the Sioux, Flathead and Blackfoot was a spectacle to remember. Held annually in the same small and otherwise unremarkable town, the meeting of these three tribes was a tradition that reached back to days of mist and shadow, days recorded on no calendar.

Now, on a hot July morning, the erstwhile cow pasture and ramshackle grandstands were churning with activity, and Libby Barlowe's fingers ached to make use of the sketchbook and pencils she carried.

Craning her neck to see the authentic tepees and their colorfully clad inhabitants, she could hardly stand still long enough for the plump woman at the admission gate to stamp her hand.

There was so much noise—laughter, the tinkle of change in the coin box, the neighing and nickering of horses that would be part of the rodeo. Underlying all this was the steady beat of tom-toms and guttural chants of the singers.

"Enjoy yourself now, honey," enjoined the woman tending the cashbox, and Libby jumped, realizing that she was holding up the line behind her. After one questioning look at the hat the woman wore, which consisted of panels cut from various beer cans and crocheted together, she hurried through the gate.

Jess chuckled at the absorbed expression on Libby's face. There was so much to see that a person didn't know where to look first.

"I think I see a fit of creativity coming on," he said.

Libby was already gravitating toward the tepees, plotting light angles and shading techniques as she went. In her heart was a dream, growing bigger with every beat of the tom-toms. "I want to see, Jess," she answered distractedly. "I've got to *see.*"

There was love in the sound of Jess's laughter, but no disdain. "All right, all right—but at least let me get you a hat. This sun is too hot for you to go around bareheaded."

"Get me a hat, get me a hat," babbled Libby, zeroing in on a group of small children as they sat watching fathers, uncles and elder brothers perform the ancient rites for rain or success in warfare or hunting.

Libby was taken with the flash of their coppery skin, the midnight black of their hair, the solemn, stalwart expressions in their dark eyes. Flipping open her sketchbook, she squatted in the lush summer grass and began to rough in the image of one particular little boy.

Her pencil flew, as did her mind. She was thinking in terms of oil paints—vivid shades that would do justice to the child's coloring and the peacock splendor of his headdress.

"Hello," she said when the dark eyes turned to her in dour question. "My name is Libby, what's yours?"

"Jimmy," the little boy responded, but then he must have

remembered the majesty of his ancestry, for he squared his small shoulders and amended, "Jim Little Eagle."

Libby made a hasty note in the corner of his sketch. "I wish I had a name like that," she said.

"You'll have to settle for 'Barlowe,'" put in a familiar voice from behind her, and a lightweight hat landed on the top of her head.

Libby looked up into Jess's face and smiled. "I guess I can make do with that," she answered.

Jess dropped to his haunches, assessed the sketch she'd just finished with admiring eyes. "Wow," he said.

Libby laughed. "I love it when you're profound," she teased. And then she took off the hat he'd given her and inspected it thoroughly. It was a standard western hat, made of straw, and it boasted a trailing tangle of turquoise feathers and crystal beads.

Jess took the hat and put it firmly back on, then arranged the feathers so that they rested on her right shoulder, tickling the bare, sun-gilded flesh there in a pleasant way. "Did you wear that blouse to drive me insane, or are you trying to set a world record for blistering sunburns?" he asked unromantically.

Libby looked down at the brief white eyelet suntop and wondered if she shouldn't have worn a western shirt, the way Becky and Cathy had. The garment she had on had no shoulders or sleeves; it was just a series of ruffles falling from an elasticized band that fitted around her chest, just beneath her collarbone. Not even wanting to think about the tortures of a sunburn, she had liberally applied sunblock to her exposed skin. Not wanting to give Jess the satisfaction, though, she crinkled her nose and said, "I wore it to drive you insane, of course."

Jess was going to insist on being practical; she saw it in his face. "They're selling T-shirts on the fairway—buy one."

"Now?" complained Libby, not wanting to leave the splendors of the recreated Native American village even for a few minutes.

Jess looked down at his watch. "Within half an hour," he said flatly. "I'm going to find Ken and the others in the grandstands, Rembrandt. I'll see you later."

Libby squinted as he rose against the sun, towering and magnificent even in his ordinary jeans and worn cowboy shirt. "No kiss?"

Jess crouched again, kissed her. "Remember. Half an hour."

"Half an hour," promised Libby, turning to a fresh page in her sketchbook and pondering a little girl with coal-black braids and a fringed buckskin shift. She took a new pencil from the case inside her purse and began to draw again, her hand racing to keep up with the pace set by her heart.

When the sketch was finished, Libby thought about what she meant to do and how the syndicate that carried her cartoon strip would react. No doubt they would be furious.

"Portraits!" her agent would cry. "Libby, Libby, there is no *money* in portraits."

Libby sighed, biting her lower lip. Money wasn't a factor really, since she had plenty of that as it was, not only because she had married a wealthy man but also because of prior successes in her career.

She was tired of doing cartoons, yearning to delve into other mediums—especially oils. She wanted color, depth, nuance—she wanted and needed to grow.

"Where the hell is that T-shirt I asked you to buy?"

Libby started, but the dream was still glowing in her face

when she looked up to meet Jess's gaze. "Still on the fairway, I would imagine," she said.

His mouth looked very stern, but Jess's eyes were dancing beneath the brim of his battered western hat. "I don't know why I let you out of my sight," he teased. And then he extended a hand. "Come on, woman. Let's get you properly dressed."

Libby allowed herself to be pulled through the crowd to one of the concession stands. Here there were such thrilling offerings as ashtrays shaped like the state of Montana and gaudy scarves commemorating the powwow itself.

"Your secret is out," she told Jess out of the corner of her mouth, gesturing toward a display of hats exactly like her own. The colors of their feather-and-bead plumage ranged from a pastel yellow to deep, rich purple. "This hat is not a designer original!"

Jess worked up an expression of horrified chagrin and then laughed and began rifling through a stack of colorful T-shirts. "What size do you wear?"

Libby stood on tiptoe, letting her breath fan against his ear, delighting as that appendage reddened visibly. "About the size of the palm of your hand, cowboy."

"Damn," Jess chuckled, and the red moved out from his ear to churn under his suntan. "Unless you want me to drag you off somewhere and make love to you right now, you'd better not make any more remarks like that."

Suddenly Libby was as pink as the T-shirt he was measuring against her chest. Coming from Jess, this was no idle threat—since their new understanding, reached several weeks before on the top of the hill behind his house, they had made love in some very unconventional places. It would be like him to take her to one of the small trailers brought by some of the cowboys from the Circle Bar B and follow through.

Having apparently deemed the pink T-shirt appropriate, Jess bought it and gripped Libby's hand, fairly dragging her across the sawdust-covered fairgrounds. From the grandstands came the deafening shouts and boot-stompings of more than a thousand excited rodeo fans.

Reaching the rest rooms, which were housed in a building of their own, Jess gave an exasperated sigh. There must have been a hundred women waiting to use the facilities, and he clearly didn't want to stand around in the sun just so Libby could exchange her suntop for a T-shirt.

Before she could offer to wait alone so that Jess could go back and watch the rodeo, he was hauling her toward the nest of Circle Bar B trailers at such a fast pace that she had to scramble to keep up with him.

Thrusting her inside the smallest, which was littered with boots, beer cans and dirty clothes, he ordered, "Put on the shirt."

Libby's color was so high that she was sure he could see it, even in the cool darkness of that camper-trailer. "This is Jake Peterson's camper, isn't it? What if he comes back?"

"He won't come back—he's entered in the bull-riding competition. Just change, will you?"

Libby knew only too well what would happen if she removed that suntop. "Jess…"

He closed the camper door, flipped the inadequate-looking lock. Then he reached out, collected her befeathered hat, her sketchbook, her purse. He laid all these items on a small, messy table and waited.

In the distance, over the loudspeaker system, the rodeo announcer exalted, "This cowboy, folks, has been riding bulls longer'n he's been tying his shoes."

There was a thunderous communal cry as the cowboy and his bull apparently came out of their chute, but it was strangely quiet in that tiny trailer where Jess and Libby stood staring at each other.

Finally, in one defiant motion of her hands, Libby wrenched the suntop off over the top of her head and stood still before her husband, her breasts high and proud and completely bare. "Are you satisfied?" she snapped.

"Not yet," Jess retorted.

He came to stand very close, his hands gentle on her breasts. "You were right," he said into her hair. "You just fit the palms of my hands."

"Oh," said Libby in sweet despair.

Jess's hands continued their tender work, lulling her. It was so cool inside that trailer, so intimate and shadowy.

Presently Libby felt the snap on her jeans, and then the zipper, give way. She was conscious of a shivering heat as the fabric glided downward. Protesting was quite beyond her powers now; she was bewitched.

Jess laid her on the narrow camper bed, joining her within moments. Stretched out upon her, he entered her with one deft thrust.

Their triumph was a simultaneous one, reached after they'd both traveled through a glittering mine field of physical and spiritual sensation, and it was of such dizzying scope that it seemed natural for the unknowing crowd in the grandstands to cheer.

Furiously Libby fastened her jeans and pulled on the T-shirt that had caused this situation in the first place. She gathered up her things, plopped her hat onto her head, and glared into Jess's amused face.

He dressed at a leisurely pace, as though they weren't trespassing.

"If Jake Peterson ever finds out about his, I'll die," Libby said, casting anxious, impatient looks at the locked door.

Jess pulled on one boot, then the other, ran a hand through his rumpled hair. His eyes smoldering with mischief and lingering pleasure, he stood up, pulled Libby into his arms and kissed her. "I love you," he said. "And your shameful secret is safe with me, Mrs. Barlowe."

Libby's natural good nature was overcoming her anger. "Sure," she retorted tartly. "All the same, I think you should know that every man who had ever compromised me in a ranch hand's trailer has said that selfsame thing."

Jess laughed, kissed her again, and then released her. "Go back to your drawing, you little hellion. I'll find you later."

"That's what I'm afraid of," Libby tossed back over one shoulder as she stepped out of the camper into the bright July sunshine. Almost before her eyes had adjusted to the change, she was sketching again.

Libby hardly noticed the passing of the hours, so intent was she on recording the scenes that so fascinated her: men festooned with colorful feathers, doing their war and rain dances; women in their worn buckskin dresses, demonstrating the grinding of corn or making their beaded belts and moccasins; children playing games that were almost as old as the distant mountains and the big sky.

Between the residual effects of that scandalous bout of lovemaking in the trailer and the feast of color and sound assaulting her now, Libby's senses were reeling. She was almost relieved when Cathy came and signed that it was time to leave.

As they walked back to find the others in the still-dense crowd, Libby studied her cousin out of the corner of her eye.

Cathy and Stacey were living together again, but there was a wistfulness about Cathy that was disturbing.

There would be no chance to talk with her now—there were too many distractions for that—but Libby made a mental vow to get Cathy alone later, perhaps during the birthday party that was being held on the ranch for Senator Barlowe that evening, and find out what was bothering her.

As the group made plans to stop at a favorite café for an early supper, Libby grew more and more uneasy about Cathy. What was it about her that was different, besides her obviously downhearted mood?

Before Libby could even begin to work out that complex question, Ken and Becky were off to their truck, Stacey and Cathy to their car. Libby was still staring into space when Jess gently tugged at her hand.

She got into the Land Rover, feeling pensive, and laid her sketchbook and purse on the seat.

"Another fit of creativity?" Jess asked quietly, driving carefully through a maze of other cars, staggering cowboys and beleaguered sheriff's deputies.

"I was thinking about Cathy," Libby replied. "Have you noticed a change in her?"

He thought, shook his head. "Not really."

"She doesn't talk to me anymore, Jess."

"Did you have an argument?"

Libby sighed. "No. I've been so busy lately, what with finishing the book and everything, I haven't spent much time with her. I'm ashamed to say that I didn't even notice the change in her until just a little while ago."

Jess gave her a gentle look. "Don't start beating yourself up Libby. You're not responsible for Cathy's happiness or unhappiness."

Surprised, Libby stared at him. "That sounds strange, coming from you."

They were pulling out onto the main highway, which was narrow and almost as choked with cars as the parking area had been. "I'm beginning to think it was a mistake, our being so protective of Cathy. We all meant well, but I wonder sometimes if we didn't hurt her instead."

"Hurt her?"

One of Jess's shoulders lifted in a shrug. "In a lot of ways, Cathy's still a little girl. She's never had to be a grown-up, Libby, because one of us was always there to fight her battles for her. I think she uses her deafness as an excuse not to take risks."

Libby was silent, reflecting on Cathy's fear of being a mother.

As though he'd looked into her mind, Jess went on to say, "Both Cathy and Stacey want children—did you know that? But Cathy won't take the chance."

"I knew she was scared—she told me that. She's scared of so many things, Jess—especially of losing Stacey."

"She loves him."

"I know. I just wish she had something more—something of her own so that her security as a person wouldn't hinge entirely on what Stacey does."

"You mean the way your security doesn't hinge on what I do?" Jess ventured, his tone devoid of any challenge or rancor.

Libby turned, took off her hat and set it down between them with the other things. "I love you very, very much, Jess, but I could live without you. It would hurt unbearably, but I could do it."

He looked away from the traffic only long enough to flash her one devilish grin. "Who would take shameful liberties with your body, if it weren't for me?"

"I guess I would have to do without shameful liberties," she said primly.

"Thank you for sidestepping my delicate male ego," he replied, "but the fact of the matter is, there's no way a woman as beautiful and talented as you are would be alone for very long."

"Don't say that!"

Jess glanced at her in surprise. "Don't say what?"

It was his meaning that had concerned Libby, not his exact words. "I don't even want to think about another man touching me the way you do."

Jess's attention was firmly fixed on the road ahead. "If you're trying to make me feel secure, princess, it's working."

"I'm not trying to make you feel anything. Jess, before we made love that first time, when you said I was really a virgin, you were right. Even the books I've read couldn't have prepared me for the things I feel when you love me."

"It might interest you to know, Mrs. Barlowe, that my feelings toward you are quite similar. Before we made love, sex was just something my body demanded, like food or exercise. Now it's magic."

She stretched to plant a noisy kiss on her husband's cheek. "Magic, is it? Well, you're something of a sorcerer yourself, Jess Barlowe. You cast spells over me and make me behave like a wanton."

He gave an exaggerated evil chuckle. "I hope I can remember the hex that made you give in to me back there at the fairgrounds."

Libby moved the things that were between them into the backseat and slid closer, taking a mischievous nip at his earlobe. "I'm sure you can," she whispered.

Jess shuddered involuntarily and snapped, "Dammit, Libby, I'm driving."

She was exploring the sensitive place just beneath his ear with the tip of her tongue. "Umm. You like getting me into situations where I'm really vulnerable, don't you, Jess?" she breathed, sliding one hand inside his shirt. "Like today, for instance."

"Libby…"

"Revenge is sweet."

And it was.

Shyly Libby extended the carefully wrapped package that contained her personal birthday gift to Senator Barlowe. She had not shown it to anyone else, not even Jess, and now she was uncertain. After all, Monica had given Cleave gold cuff-links and Stacey and Cathy planned to present him with a bottle of rare wine. By comparison, would her offering seem tacky and homemade?

With the gentle smile that had won him so many hearts and so many votes over the years, he took the parcel, which was revealingly large and flat, and turned it in his hands. "May I?" he asked softly, his kind eyes twinkling with affection.

"Please do," replied Libby.

It seemed to take Cleave forever to remove the ribbons and wrapping paper and lift the lid from the box inside, but there was genuine emotion in his face when he saw the framed pen-and-ink drawing Libby had been working on, in secret, for days. "My sons," he said.

"That's us, all right," commented Jess, who had appeared at the senator's side. "Personally, I think I'm considerably handsomer than that."

Cleave was examining the drawing closely. It showed Jess looking forward, Stacey in profile. When the senator looked up, Libby saw the love he bore his two sons in his eyes. "Thank you," he said. "This is one of the finest gifts I've ever received." He assessed the drawing again, and when his gaze came back to meet hers, it was full of mischief. "But where are my daughters? Where are you and Cathy?"

Libby smiled and kissed his cheek. "I guess you'll have to wait until your *next* birthday for that."

"In that case," rejoined the senator, "why not throw in a couple of grandchildren for good measure?"

Libby grinned. "I might be able to come up with one, but a couple?"

"Cathy will just have to do her part," came the immediate reply. "Now, if you'll excuse me, I want to take this picture around and show all my guests what a talented daughter-in-law I have."

Once his father had gone, Jess lifted his champagne glass and one eyebrow. "*Talented* is definitely the word," he said.

Libby knew that he was not referring to her artwork and hastily changed the subject. "You look so splendid in that tuxedo that I think I'd like to dance with you."

Jess worked one index finger under the tight collar of his formal shirt, obviously uncomfortable. "Dance?" he echoed drily. "Lead me to the organ grinder and we're in business."

Laughing, Libby caught at his free hand and dragged him into the spacious living room, which had been prepared for dancing. There was a small string band to provide the music.

Libby took Jess's champagne glass and set it aside, then rested both hands on his elegant satin lapels. The other guests—and there were dozens—might not have existed at all.

"Dance with me," she said.

Jess took her into his arms, his eyes never leaving hers. "You know," he said softly, "you look so wonderful in that silvery dress that I'm tempted to take you home and make damned sure my father gets that grandchild he wants."

"When we start a baby," she replied seriously, "I want it to be for us."

Jess's mouth quirked into a grin and his eyes were alight

with love. "I wasn't going to tape a bow to the little stinker's head and hand it over to him, Libby."

Libby giggled at the picture this prompted in her mind. "Babies are so funny," she dreamed aloud.

"I know," Jess replied. "I love that look of drunken wonder they get when you lift them up high and talk to them. About that time, they usually barf in your hair."

Before she could answer, Ken and Becky came into the magical mist that had heretofore surrounded Libby and Jess.

"All right if I cut in?" Ken asked.

"How soon do you want a grandchild?" Jess countered.

"Sooner the better," retorted Ken. "And, Jess?"

"What?" demanded his son-in-law, eyes still locked with Libby's.

"The music stopped."

Jess and Libby both came to a startled halt, and Becky was so delighted by their expressions that her laughter pealed through the large room.

When the band started playing again, Libby found herself dancing with her father, while Jess and Becky waltzed nearby.

"You look real pretty," Ken said, beaming down at her.

"You're pretty fancy yourself," Libby answered. "In fact, you look downright handsome in that tuxedo."

"She says that to everybody," put in Jess, who happened to be whirling past with Becky.

Ken's laugh was low and throaty. "He never gets too far away from you, does he?"

"About as far as white gets from rice. And I like it that way."

"That's what I figured. Libby…"

The serious, tentative way he'd said her name gave Libby pause. "Yes?"

"Becky and I are going to get married," he blurted out, without taking a single breath.

Libby felt her eyes fill. "You were afraid to tell me that? Afraid to tell me something wonderful?"

Ken stopped, his arms still around his daughter, his blue eyes bright with relief and delight. Then, with a raucous shout that was far more typical of him than tuxedos and fancy parties, her father lifted her so high that she was afraid she would fall out of the top of her dress.

"That was certainly rustic," remarked Monica, five minutes later, at the refreshment table.

Libby saw Jess approaching through the crowd of guests and smiled down at the buttery crab puff in her fingers. "Are you making fun of my father, Ms. Summers?"

Monica sighed in exasperation. "This *is* a formal party, after all—not a kegger at the Golden Buckle. I don't know why the senator insists on inviting the help to important affairs."

Slowly, and with great deliberation, Libby tucked her crab puff into Monica's artfully displayed cleavage. "Will you hold this, please?" she trilled, and then walked toward her husband.

"The foreman's brat strikes again," Jess chuckled, pulling her into another waltz.

Cathy was sitting alone in the dimly lit kitchen, her eyes fixed on something far in the distance. Libby was careful to let her cousin see her, rather than startle her with a touch.

"Hi," she said.

Cathy replied listlessly.

Libby took a chair opposite Cathy's and signed, "I'd like to help if I can."

Cathy's face crumbled suddenly and she gave a soft cry

that tore at Libby's heart. Her hands flew as she replied, "Nobody can help me!"

"Don't I even get to try?"

A tendril of Cathy's hair fell from the soft knot at the back of her head and danced against a shoulder left bare by her Grecian evening gown. "I'm pregnant," she whispered. "Oh, Libby, I'm pregnant!"

Libby felt confusion and just a touch of envy. "Is that so terrible? I know you were scared before, but—"

"I'm still scared!" Cathy broke in, her voice unusually loud.

Libby drew a deep breath. "Why, Cathy? You're strong and healthy. And your deafness won't be the problem you think it will—you and Stacey can afford to hire help, if you feel it's necessary."

"All of that is so easy for you to say, Libby!" Cathy flared with sudden and startling anger. "You can hear! You're a whole person!"

Libby felt her own temper, always suppressed when dealing with her handicapped cousin, surge into life. "You know something?" she said furiously. "I'm sick of your 'Poor Cathy' number! A child is just about the best thing that can happen to a person and instead of rejoicing, you're standing here complaining!"

"I have a reason to complain!"

Libby's arms flew out from her side in a gesture of wild annoyance. "All right! You're deaf, you can't hear! Poor, poor Cathy! Now, can we get past singing your sad song? Dammit, Cathy, I know how hard it must be to live in silence, but can't you look on the positive side for once? You're married to a successful, gentle-hearted man who loves you very much. You have everything!"

"Said the woman who could hear!" shouted Cathy.

Libby sighed and sat back in her chair. "We're all handicapped in some way—Jess told me that once, and I think it's true."

Cathy was not going to be placated. "What's your handicap, Libby?" she snapped. "Your short fingernails? The fact that you freckle in the summer instead of getting tan?"

The derisive sarcasm of her cousin's words stung Libby. "I'm as uncertain of myself at times as you are, Cathy," she said softly. "Aaron—"

"Aaron!" spouted Cathy with contempt. "Don't hand me that, Libby! So he ran around a little—I had to stand by and watch my husband adore my own cousin for months! And I'll bet Jess has made any traumas you had about going to bed with a man all better!"

"Cathy, please…"

Cathy gave a guttural, furious cry of frustration. "I'm so damned tired of you, Libby, with your career and your loving father and your…"

Libby was mad again, and she bounded to her feet. "And my what?" she cried. "I can't help that you don't have a father—Dad tried to make up for that and I think he did a damned good job! As for a career—don't you dare hassle me about that! I worked like a slave to get where I am! If you want a career, Cathy, get off your backside and start one!"

Cathy stared at her, stunned, and then burst into tears. And, of course, Jess chose exactly that moment to walk in.

Giving Libby one scalding, reproachful look, he gathered Cathy into his arms and held her.

Chapter 15

After one moment of feeling absolutely shattered, Libby lifted her chin and turned from Jess's annoyance and Cathy's veiled triumph to walk out of the kitchen with dignity.

She encountered a worried-looking Marion Bradshaw just on the other side of the door. "Libby...Mrs. Barlowe...that man is here!"

Libby drew a deep breath. "What man?" she managed to ask halfheartedly.

"Mr. Aaron Strand, that's who!" whispered Marion. "He had the nerve to walk right up and ring the bell...."

Libby was instantly alert, alive in every part of her being, like a creature being stalked in the wilds. "Where is he now?"

"He's in the senator's study," answered the flushed, quietly outraged housekeeper. "He says he won't leave till he talks with you, Libby. I didn't want a scene, what with all these people here, so I didn't argue."

Wearily Libby patted Marion's shoulder. Facing Aaron Strand, especially now, was the last thing in the world she wanted to do. But she knew that he would create an awful fuss if his request was denied, and besides, what real harm could he do with so many people in the house? "I'll talk to him," she said.

"I'll get Jess," mused Mrs. Bradshaw, "and your daddy, too."

Libby shook her head quickly, and warm color surged up over her face. Jess was busy lending a strong shoulder to Cathy, and she was damned if she was going to ask for his help now, even indirectly. And though Ken was almost fully recovered from his confrontation with the bear, Libby had no intention of subjecting him to the stress that could result from a verbal round with his former son-in-law. "I'll handle this myself," she said firmly, and then, without waiting for a reply, she started for the senator's study.

Aaron was there, tall and handsome in his formal clothes.

"At least when you crash a party, you dress for it," observed Libby drily from the doorway.

Aaron set down the paperweight he had been examining and smiled. His eyes moved over her in a way that made her want to stride across the room and slap him with all her might. "That dress is classy, sugarplum," he said in acid tones. "You're definitely bunkhouse-calendar material."

Libby bit her lower lip, counted mentally until the urge to scream passed. "What do you want, Aaron?" she asked finally.

"Want?" he echoed, pretending pleasant confusion.

"Yes!" hissed Libby. "You flew two thousand miles—you must want something."

He sighed, leaned back against the senator's desk, folded his arms. "Are you happy?"

"Yes," answered Libby with a lift of her chin.

Again he assessed her shiny silver dress, the hint of

cleavage it revealed. "I imagine the cowboy is pretty happy with you, too," he said. "Which Barlowe is it, Libby? The steak-house king or the lawyer?"

Libby's head began to ache; she sighed and closed her eyes for just a moment. "What do you want?" she asked again insistently.

His shoulders moved in a shrug. "A baby," he answered, as though he was asking for a cup of coffee or the time of day. "I know you're not going to give me that, so relax."

"Why did you come here, then?"

"I just wanted a look at this ranch. Pretty fancy spread, Lib. You do know how to land on your feet, don't you?"

"Get out, Aaron."

"Without meeting your husband? Your paragon of a father? I wouldn't think of it, Mrs. Barlowe."

Libby was off balance, trying to figure out what reason Aaron could have for coming all the way to Montana besides causing her added grief. Incredible as it seemed, he had apparently done just that. "You can't hurt me anymore, Aaron," she said. "I won't let you. Now, get out of here, please."

"Oh, no. I lost everything because of you—everything. And I'll have my pound of flesh, Libby—you can be sure of that."

"If your grandmother relieved you of your company responsibilities, Aaron, that's your fault, not mine. I should think you would be glad—now you won't have anything to keep you from your wine, women and song."

Aaron's face was tense. Gone was his easy, gentlemanly manner. "With the company went most of my money, Libby. And let's not pretend, sweetness—I can make your bright, shiny new life miserable, and we both know it."

"How?" asked Libby, poised to turn and walk out of the study.

"By generating shame and scandal, of course. Your father-in-law is a prominent United States senator, isn't he? I should think negative publicity could hurt him very badly—and you know how good I am at stirring that up."

Rage made Libby tremble. "You can't hurt Cleave Barlowe, Aaron. You can't hurt me. Now, get out before I have you thrown out!"

He crossed the room at an alarming speed, had a hold on Libby's upper arms before she could grasp what was happening. He thrust her back against the heavy door of the study and covered her mouth with his own.

Libby squirmed, shocked and repulsed. She tried to push Aaron away, but he had trapped her hands between his chest and her own. And the kiss went on, ugly and wet, obscene because it was forced upon her, because it was Aaron's.

Finally he drew back, smirking down at her, grasping her wrists in both hands when she tried to wriggle away from him. And suddenly Libby was oddly detached, calm even. Mrs. Bradshaw had been right when she'd wanted to let Jess know that Aaron was here, so very right.

Libby had demurred because of her pride, because she was mad at Jess; she'd thought she could handle Aaron Strand. Pride be damned, she thought, and then she threw back her head and gave a piercing, defiant scream.

Aaron chuckled. "Do you think I'm afraid of your husband, Libby?" he drawled. Incredibly, he was about to kiss her again, it appeared, when he was suddenly wrenched away.

Libby dared one look at Jess's green eyes and saw murder flashing there. She reached for his arm, but he shook her hand away.

"Strand," he said, his gaze fixed on a startled but affably recovering Aaron.

Aaron gave a mocking half-bow. It didn't seem to bother

him that Jess was coldly furious, that half the guests at the senator's party, Ken Kincaid included, were jammed into the study doorway.

"Is this the part," Aaron drawled, "where we fight over the fair lady?"

"This is the part," Jess confirmed icily.

Aaron shrugged. "I feel honor-bound to warn you," he said smugly, "that I am a fifth-degree black belt."

Jess spared him an evil smile, but said nothing.

Libby was afraid; again she grasped at Jess's arm. "Jess, he really is a black belt."

Jess did not so much as look at Libby; he was out of her reach, and not just physically. She felt terror thick in her throat, and flung an appealing look at Ken, who was standing beside her, one arm around her waist.

Reading the plea in his daughter's eyes, he denied it with an almost imperceptible shake of his head.

Libby was frantic. As Jess and Aaron drew closer to each other, circling like powerful beasts, she struggled to free herself from her father's restraining arm. For all his weaknesses of character, Aaron Strand was agile and strong, and if he could hurt Jess, he would, without qualms of any kind.

"Jess, no!" she cried.

Jess turned toward her, his jaw tight with cold annoyance, and Aaron struck in that moment. His foot came up in a graceful arc and caught Jess in the side of the neck. Too sick to stand by herself or run away, Libby buried her face in Ken's tuxedo jacket in horror.

There were sounds—terrible sounds. Why didn't someone stop the fight? Why were they all standing around like Romans thrilling to the exploits of gladiators? Why?

When the sounds ceased and Libby dared to look, Jess was

still standing. Aaron was sitting on the floor, groaning theatrically, one corner of his lip bleeding. It was obvious that he wasn't badly hurt, for all his carrying on.

Rage and relief mingled within Libby in one dizzying sweep. "Animals!" she screamed, and when she whirled to flee the ugliness, no one moved to stop her.

Libby sat on the couch in the condo's living room, her arms wrapped around her knees, stubbornly ignoring the ringing of the telephone. She had turned off the answering machine, but she couldn't help counting the rings—that had become something of a game in the two days since she'd left the ranch to take refuge here. Twenty-six rings. It was a record.

She stood up shakily, made her way into the kitchen, where she had been trying to sketch out the panels for her cartoon strip. "Back to the old drawing board," she said to the empty room, and the stale joke fell flat because there was no one there to laugh.

The telephone rang again and, worn down, Libby reached out for the receiver affixed to the kitchen wall and snapped, "Hello!"

"Lib?" The voice belonged to her father, and it was full of concern. "Libby, are you all right?"

"No," she answered honestly, letting a sigh carry the word. "As a matter of fact, I'm not all right. How are you?"

"Never mind me—why did you run off like that?"

"You know why."

"Are you coming back to the ranch?"

"Why?" countered Libby, annoyed. "Am I missing some bloody spectacle?"

Ken gave a gruff sigh. "Dammit, Libby, do you love Jess Barlowe or not?"

Tears stung her eyes. Love him? These two days away from him had been hell, but she wasn't about to admit that. "What does it matter?" she shot back. "He's probably so busy holding Cathy's hand that he hasn't even noticed I'm gone."

"That's it. Cathy. Standing up for her is a habit with Jess, Lib—you know that."

Libby did know; in two days she'd had plenty of time to come to the conclusion that she had overreacted in the kitchen the night of the party when Jess had seemed to take Cathy's part against her. She shouldn't have walked out that way. "There is still the fight—"

"You screamed, Libby. What would you have done, if you'd been in Jess's place?" Without waiting for an answer, her father went on, "You're just being stubborn, and so is Jess. Do you love him enough to make the first move, Lib? Do you have the gumption?"

Libby reached out for a kitchen chair, sank into it. "Where is he?"

There was a smile in her father's voice. "Up on that ridge behind your place," he answered. "He's got a camp up there."

Libby knew mild disappointment; if Jess was camping, he hadn't been calling. She had been ignoring the telephone for two days for nothing. "It's nice to know he misses me so much," she muttered petulantly.

Having said his piece, Ken was silent.

"He does miss me, doesn't he?" demanded Libby.

"He misses you," chuckled Ken. "He wouldn't be doing his hermit routine if he didn't."

Libby sighed. "The ridge, huh?"

"The ridge," confirmed Ken with amusement. And then he hung up.

* * *

I shouldn't be doing this in my condition, Libby complained to herself as she made her way up the steep hillside. *But since the mountain won't come to me…*

She stopped, looked up. The smoke from Jess's campfire was curling toward the sky; the sun was hot and bright. What the devil did he need with a fire, anyway? It was broad daylight, for heaven's sake.

Muttering, holding on to her waning courage tenaciously, Libby made her way up over the rise to the top of the ridge. Jess was standing with his back to her, looking in the opposite direction, but the stiffness of his shoulders revealed that he knew she was there.

And suddenly she was furious. Hadn't she climbed up this cursed mountain, her heart in her throat, her pride God-only-knew-where? Wasn't the current situation as much his fault as her own? Hadn't she found out, the very day after she'd left him, that she was going to have his baby?

"Damn you, Jess Barlowe," she hissed, "don't you dare ignore me!"

He turned very slowly to face her. "I'm sorry," he said stiffly and with annoying effort.

"For what?" pressed Libby. Damned if she was going to make it easy!

Jess sighed, idly kicked dirt over his campfire with one booted foot. There was a small tent pitched a few feet away, and a coffeepot sat on a fallen log, along with a paperback book and a half-eaten sandwich. "For assuming that the scene with Cathy was your fault," he said.

Libby huffed over to the log, which was a fair distance from Jess, and sat down, folding her arms. "Well, praise be!" she murmured. "What about that stupid fistfight in your father's study?"

His green eyes shot to her face. "You'll grow horns, lady, before you hear me apologize for that!"

Libby bit her lower lip. Fighting wasn't the ideal way to settle things, it was true, but she couldn't help recalling the pleasure she herself had taken in stuffing that crab puff down the front of Monica Summers' dress at the party. If Monica had made one move to retaliate, she would have gladly tangled with her. "Fair enough," she said.

There was an uncomfortable silence, which Libby finally felt compelled to break. "Why did you have a fire going in the middle of the day?"

Jess laughed. "I wanted to make damned sure you found my camp," he replied.

"Dad told you I was coming!"

He came to sit beside her on the log and even though he didn't touch her, she was conscious of his nearness in every fiber of her flesh and spirit. "Yeah," he admitted, and he looked so sad that Libby wanted to cry.

She eased closer to him. "Jess?"

"What?" he asked, looking her squarely in the eyes now.

"I'm sorry."

He said nothing.

Libby drew a deep breath. "I'm not only sorry," she went on bravely, "I'm pregnant, too."

He was quiet for so long that Libby feared she'd been wrong to tell him about their child—at least for now. It was possible that he wanted to ask for a separation or even a divorce, but he might stay with her out of duty now that he knew. To hold him in that manner would break Libby's heart.

"When did you find out?" he asked finally, and the lack of emotion in his face and in his voice made Libby feel bereft.

"Day before yesterday. After Cathy said she was pregnant, I got to thinking and realized that I had a few symptoms myself."

Jess was silent, looking out over the trees, the ranges, the far mountains. After what seemed like an eternity, he turned to her again, his green eyes full of pain. "You weren't going to tell me?"

"Of course I was going to tell you, Jess. But, well, the time didn't seem to be right."

"You're not going to leave, are you?"

"Would I have climbed a stupid mountain, for pity's sake, if I wanted to leave you?"

A slow grin spread across Jess's face, and then he gave a startling hoot of delight and shot to his feet, his hands gripping Libby's and pulling her with him. If he hadn't caught her in his arms and held her, she would probably have fallen into the lush summer grass.

"Is it safe to assume you're happy about this announcement?" Libby teased, looking up at him and loving him all the more because there were tears on his face.

He lifted her into his arms, kissed her deeply in reply.

"Excuse me, sir," she said when he drew back, "but I was wondering if you would mind making love to me. You see, I'd like to find out if I'm welcome here."

In answer, Jess carried her to the tent, set her on her feet. "My tent is your tent," he said.

Libby blushed a little and bent to go inside the small canvas shelter. Since there wasn't room enough to stand, she sat on the rumpled sleeping bag and waited as Jess joined her.

She was never sure exactly how it came about, but within moments they were both lying down, facing each other. The weight of his hand was bliss on her breast, and so were the hoarse words he said.

"I love you, Libby. I need you. No matter how mad I make you, please don't leave me again."

Libby traced the strong lines of his jaw with a fingertip. "I won't, Jess. I might scream and yell, but I won't leave. I love you too much to be away from you—if I learned anything in the last two days, it was that."

He was propped up on one elbow now, very close, and he was idly unbuttoning her blouse. "I want you."

Libby feigned shock. "In a tent, sir?"

"And other novel places." He paused, undid the front catch of her bra.

Libby sighed, then gasped as the warmth of his mouth closed over the straining peak of her breast. The sensation was exquisite, sweeping through her, pushing away the weariness and confusion and pain. She tangled her fingers in his rumpled hair, holding him close.

Jess finally left the breast he had so gently plundered to remove his clothes, and then, more slowly, Libby's. When she lay naked before him in the cool shadows of the tiny tent, he took in her waiting body with a look of rapt wonder. "Little enchantress," he breathed, "let me worship you."

Libby could not bear to be separate from him any longer. "Be close to me, Jess," she pleaded softly, "be part of me."

With a groan, he fell to her, his mouth moist and commanding upon hers. His tongue mated with Libby's and his manhood touched her with fire, prodding, taking only partial shelter inside her.

At last Jess broke the kiss and lifted his head, and Libby saw, through a shifting haze, that he was savoring her passion as well as his own. She was aware of every muscle in his body as he struggled to defy forces that do not brook the rebellion of mere mortals.

Finally these forces prevailed, and Jess was thrust, with a raspy cry, into Libby's depths. They moved together wildly, seeking and reaching and finally breaking through the barriers that divide this world from the glories of the next.

* * *

Cathy assessed the large oil painting of Jim Little Eagle, the child Libby had seen at the powwow months before, her hands resting on her protruding stomach.

Libby, whose stomach was as large as Cathy's, was wiping her hands on a rag reserved for the purpose. The painting was a personal triumph, and she was proud of it. "What do you think?" she signed, after setting aside the cloth.

Cathy grinned. "What do I think?" she asked aloud, sitting down on the tall stool behind Libby's drawing board. "I'll tell you what I think. I think you should sell it to me instead of letting that gallery in Great Falls handle it. After all, they've got your pen-and-ink drawings and the other paintings you did."

Libby tried to look stern. "Are you asking for special favors, Cathy Barlowe?"

Cathy laughed. "Yes!" Her sparkling green eyes fell to the sketch affixed to Libby's drawing board and she exclaimed in delighted surprise. "This is great!"

Libby came to stand behind her, but her gaze touched only briefly on the drawing. Instead, she was looking out at the snow through the windows of her studio in Ken and Becky's house.

"What are you going to do with this?" Cathy demanded, tugging at Libby's arm.

Libby smiled, looking at the drawing. It showed her cartoon character, given over to the care of another artist now. Liberated Lizzie was in an advanced state of pregnancy, and the blurb read, "If it feels good, do it."

"I'm going to give it to Jess," she said with a slight blush. "It's a private joke."

Cathy laughed again, then assessed the spacious, well-equipped studio with happy eyes. "I'm surprised you work down here at your dad's place. Especially with Jess home almost every day, doing paperwork and things."

Libby's mouth quirked in a grin. "That's *why* I work down here. If I tried to paint there, I wouldn't get anything done."

"You're really happy, aren't you?"

"Completely."

Cathy enfolded her in a hug. "Me, too," she said. And when her eyes came to Libby's face, they were dancing with mischief. "Of course, you and Jess have to understand that you will never win the Race. Stacey and I are ahead by at least a nose."

Libby stood straight and tried to look imperious. "We will not concede defeat," she said.

Before Cathy could reply to this, Stacey came into the room, pretending to see only Libby. "Pardon me, pudgy person," he began, "but has my wife waddled by lately?"

"Is she kind of short, with long, pretty hair and big green eyes and a stomach shaped rather like a watermelon?"

Stacey snapped his fingers and a light seemed to go on in his face. "That's a pretty good description."

"Haven't seen her," said Libby.

Cathy gave her a delighted shove and flung herself at her husband, laughing. A moment later they were on their way out, loudly vowing to win what Jess and Stacey had dubbed the Great Barlowe Baby Race.

Through with her work for the day and eager to get home to Jess, Libby cleaned her brushes and put them away, washed her hands again, and went out to find her coat. The first pain struck just as she was getting into the car.

At home, Jess was standing pensively in the kitchen, staring out at the heavy layer of snow blanketing the hillside behind the house. Libby came up as close behind him as her stomach would allow and wrapped her arms around his lean waist.

"I've just had a pretty good tip on the Baby Race," she said.

The muscles beneath his bulky woolen sweater tightened,

and he turned to look down at her, his jade eyes dark with wonder. "What did you say?"

"We're on the homestretch, Jess. I need to go to the hospital. Soon."

He paled, this man who had hunted wounded bears and fire-breathing dragons. "My God!" he yelled, and suddenly they were both caught up in a whirlwind of activity. Phone calls were made, suitcases were snatched from the coat-closet floor, and then Jess was dragging Libby toward his Land Rover.

"Wait, I'm sure we have time—"

"I'm not taking any chances!" barked Jess, hoisting her pear-shaped and unwieldy form into the car seat.

"Jess," Libby scolded, grasping at his arm. "You're panick-ing!"

"You're damned right I'm panicking!" he cried, and then they were driving over the snowy, rutted roads of the ranch at the fastest pace he dared.

When they reached the airstrip, the Cessna had been brought out of the small hangar where it was kept and fuel was being pumped into it. After wrestling Libby into the front passenger seat, Jess quickly checked the engine and the landing gear. These were tasks, she had learned, that he never trusted to anyone else.

"Jess, this is ridiculous!" she protested when he scrambled into the pilot's seat and began a preflight test there. "We have plenty of time to drive to the hospital."

Jess ignored her, and less than a minute later the plane was taxiing down the runway. Out of the corner of one eye Libby saw a flash of ice blue.

"Jess, wait!" she cried. "The Ferrari!"

The plane braked and Jess craned his neck to see around

Libby. Sure enough, Stacey and Cathy were running toward them, if Cathy's peculiar gait could be called a run.

Stacey leapt up onto the wing and opened the door. "Going our way?" he quipped, but his eyes were wide and his face was white.

"Get in," replied Jess impatiently, but his eyes were gentle as they touched Cathy and then Libby. "The race is on," he added.

Cathy was the first to deliver, streaking over the finish line with a healthy baby girl, but Libby produced twin sons soon after. Following much discussion, the Great Barlowe Baby Race was declared a draw.

* * * * *

TO WED AND PROTECT

Bestselling Author

Carla Cassidy

CARLA CASSIDY

is an award-winning author who has written more than fifty novels for Harlequin Books. In 1995 she won the Best Silhouette Romance award from *RT Book Reviews* for *Anything for Danny*. In 1998 she also won a Career Achievement Award for Best Innovative Series from *RT Book Reviews*.

Carla believes the only thing better than curling up with a good book to read is sitting down at the computer with a good story to write. She's looking forward to writing many more books and bringing hours of pleasure to readers.

Chapter 1

The place looked as if it had been abandoned for years, but Luke knew it had only stood empty for a little less than a year. However, before abandonment the house and surrounding acreage had been owned by a cantankerous, eccentric old man who, rumor had it, had believed himself from the planet Zutar and spent most of his time attempting to contact fellow space creatures.

But Zutarian Arthur Graham had died almost a year earlier, and as far as Luke Delaney knew, the ramshackle house had not been entered since.

The early morning sun beat relentlessly on Luke's head as he got out of his car and approached the front door. If not for the car sitting out front, Luke would have assumed the house was still vacant. There were certainly no signs of life and no indication that any work at all had been done to make the house look more inviting.

The wood on the house was weathered to a dull gray, and thick weeds choked the path that led to a dangerously sagging front porch.

Luke had received a call the day before from a Mrs. Abigail Graham, asking if he'd be interested in meeting her here first thing this morning to discuss some carpentry work she wanted done on the place.

He'd been surprised. First and foremost because he hadn't heard any rumors that anyone had moved into the old Graham place, and usually the minute a stranger appeared in or around town, the gossipmongers went into action.

Luke had instantly agreed to meet with her, intrigued to see the interior of the place. After all, it wasn't everyday you got to see the living environment of a space alien.

And he had to admit, he was equally intrigued to meet the woman who owned the smoky, deep voice that had called him the day before. That voice had instantly conjured up visions of a lush brunette or a sultry blonde and had reminded Luke that it had been far too long since he'd enjoyed the company of a pretty lady.

Of course, Abigail Graham was probably sixty years old and as crazy as her infamous relative, he thought as he stepped up on the front porch.

With his first step onto the wooden porch, it instantly became apparent how imminent repairs were needed. The wood was rotten, and a hole was just in front of the door, indicating that somebody'd had a foot go completely through the rotten wood.

He carefully maneuvered around the hole and knocked on the door. It was opened immediately. The woman who stood before him was certainly no sixty-year-old. With long dark hair cascading around her slim shoulders and framing her slender face, she was definitely closer to thirty.

"Abigail Graham?" Luke asked, noting that her eyes were the shade of spring…a soft, lovely green that shimmered like the sea in the bright sunshine.

However, one of those beautiful green eyes appeared slightly swollen, and a hint of a bruise peeked beneath make-up at the corner.

"Yes, and you must be Luke Delaney."

He backed up as she stepped out and across the hole. "I'm assuming this is what you called me about?" he asked, gesturing to the porch.

She nodded. "I knew it was rather unstable but didn't realize just how dangerous it was until my son's foot went through it yesterday."

That sexy voice of hers shot a new wave of pleasure through him. Looking at her certainly wasn't difficult, either. Mrs. Abigail Graham, he reminded himself. A married woman sporting the hint of a black eye—and certainly none of his business.

"Was he hurt?" Luke asked, eyeing the hole.

"Thankfully no. His tennis shoe got scuffed and it scared him, but he wasn't hurt." She smiled, and Luke felt the jolt of that gorgeous smile deep in the pit of him, like that lick of heat he got when he took a swallow of good Scotch.

"Why don't you come on inside and we can discuss the repair work," she suggested. She stepped over the hole to the front door.

He followed her into the house and tried not to notice how sexy her shapely bottom looked in her tight jeans. The living room, although starkly furnished, was spotlessly clean and decorated in desert shades.

From someplace else in the house he could hear the sound of a television playing what sounded like cartoons.

She gestured him to the sofa, and he sat. "The man at the

lumberyard said you were the best carpenter in town," she explained. "He was the one who gave me your name and number."

She perched on the edge of a chair facing the sofa. "So, what will it take to repair the porch?"

"I can't repair it. It needs to come down altogether and a new one built."

A frown creased her forehead, and she caught her lower lip between her teeth. She had luscious full lips, and Luke wondered idly if they would be as soft and inviting as they looked.

"How much is all this going to cost?" she finally asked with a sigh.

Luke stood and pulled a measuring tape from his pocket. "Why don't we go out and get some measurements, then I can give you an estimate." He had a feeling he wasn't going to make much profit on this job.

It was obvious that money was an issue. Anyone who chose to live in this ramshackle place had to have made the decision because they couldn't afford anything better.

"Okay, I'll be right back." She got up, hurried down the hallway and disappeared into the first doorway on the right.

Luke once again looked around the room. On second glance, he saw the work that needed to be done. Windowsills needed to be refinished or painted. The hardwood floor was scuffed and worn. But those things were cosmetic. The rotten porch was something different. She was lucky nobody had been seriously hurt on it.

She returned from the bedroom and they gingerly stepped out on the rotten porch. "This is a bad accident waiting to happen," he said as they stepped off the porch. "If you have me build you a new one, would you want it to be the same size?"

He watched as she gazed at the porch thoughtfully. Lordy, but she was pretty. Her clear, creamy skin looked soft and touchable, and her dark hair was a perfect foil for her startling green eyes.

"It's a pretty good size, isn't it?" she said thoughtfully.

"Sure," he agreed. "It's big enough to hold a couple of chairs and a potted plant or two."

"Then let's keep the new one the same size."

He nodded. "Let's get the measurements."

As she took the end of the tape measure from him, he smelled her fragrance, a soft whisper of something sweetly feminine and clean. It was probably a good thing the woman was married. Otherwise she would be a huge temptation, and Luke was trying not to walk the path of temptation.

"How long have you been here?" he asked as he gestured for her to go to the opposite side of the porch.

"We arrived on Tuesday and have spent the last couple of days having trash hauled off. Apparently my uncle was a bit of a pack rat."

Luke made a mental note of the measurement, then motioned her to the side of the porch. "Arthur was your uncle? Nobody around here knew he had any relatives."

"Actually, he was a great-uncle, but I never met him in person."

"That's all I need," he said and hit the button on the tape measure to retract the tape. "He was a bit of a character, your great-uncle Arthur."

Her cheeks flushed prettily as she met him at the base of the steps leading to the porch. "Poor Uncle Arthur. My father used to say he was a bolt whose nut was screwed on crooked."

Luke laughed at the apt description of the old man. "He was certainly colorful," he agreed. "He sometimes showed up in town with aluminum foil antennas wrapped around his head, said he was picking up signals from space."

She winced, then gave another one of her pretty smiles.

"Well, I hate to disappoint the town gossips, but I don't intend to take up where Uncle Arthur left off," she replied.

Luke grinned. "Don't worry, we've got plenty of other odd people here in Inferno to keep the gossips busy." He hated to think how often in the past he had kept the gossip mill busy.

"Where are you from?" he asked curiously.

"Uh…back east."

He grinned. "Back east as in New York or back east as in East India?"

"Uh…Chicago. We're from Chicago."

Luke didn't know exactly how he knew, but he was fairly certain she was lying. Her gaze didn't quite meet his, and there was a hint of unnatural color to her cheeks that let him know she wasn't being truthful. Again he reminded himself that the lovely lady was none of his business.

At that moment the front door opened. Two children stood in the doorway. The little boy looked to be about five or six, and the girl standing next to him appeared to be slightly younger. Both were dark-haired and dark-eyed, and each of them eyed Luke warily.

"Don't come out here," Abigail cautioned. "We've been using the back door since yesterday," she explained to Luke.

"Who is he?" the little boy asked from the doorway, his voice slightly belligerent.

"Jason, this is Luke Delaney. He's going to build us a front porch that we won't fall through. And Luke, that's Jason and Jessica."

"Hi, kids." Luke smiled at the two rug rats, but neither of them returned his smile. Their dark eyes continued to gaze at him with suspicion.

Luke turned to Abigail. "I'll get some estimates together and call you with them later this evening."

"That will be fine," she replied and again offered him that beautiful smile that ignited a small flame in the pit of Luke's stomach.

Yes, it was definitely a good thing Abigail Graham was a married woman with two children, he thought as he nodded goodbye and headed for his pickup truck. Although he found himself incredibly physically attracted to her, the fact that she was married with children assured him he wouldn't follow through on that attraction.

The last thing Luke was looking for was any kind of a permanent relationship. Even if Abigail were single and available, she had that look in her eyes that told him she probably wasn't a short-term-relationship kind of woman.

He dismissed thoughts of the lovely Abigail and her children from his mind as he pointed his pickup toward the family dude ranch.

Adam Delaney, Luke's father, had passed away a little over five months earlier, leaving Luke and his three siblings as heirs to the successful Delaney Dude Ranch. However, Adam Delaney, who had been a mean bastard in life, had kicked his kids one last time in death.

He'd left them the family ranch with a condition attached, that each of them spend twenty-five hours a week working on the ranch for a year. If before that time any one of them defaulted and didn't spend the required time there, the entire estate would transfer to Clara Delaney, Adam's old-maid sister.

Although Luke had no real love for the place where he'd been born and had spent a miserable childhood, he wasn't about to be the one to make his brothers and sister lose their inheritance.

His plans were to remain here in Inferno for another seven months, then when the inheritance was won, he'd sell his interest in the ranch, take the money and chase after his real dream of being a star in Nashville.

And there was no way that dream included a woman, children or anything that remotely resembled a long-term relationship.

"I don't like him." Jason was tucked into bed, the red Kansas City Chiefs sheet pulled up to his stubborn chin. "I don't think he should be here. I don't like the way he looks."

Abby knew who he was talking about, and she also knew it had nothing to do with like or dislike. It had everything to do with fear.

Men frightened both Jason and Jessica ever since that night a year and a month ago…the night their lives had been irrevocably shattered, the night Abby had lost the one person most dear to her heart.

But Abby couldn't think of that. She couldn't dwell on all she'd lost because then she would be lost in grief. She and the kids were in survival mode now, and the only way to survive was to forge ahead and not look back.

"Jason, Luke seemed like a very nice man. I'm sure he won't hurt your sister or you. Besides, we need him. We can't live here if we don't fix the porch."

Jason frowned thoughtfully. "And if he fixes it we can live here together forever?" His dark little eyes pled with her for assurance.

"That's the plan," she replied and leaned forward to kiss his forehead. "Now, go to sleep. We have a big day tomorrow. We've got all kinds of boxes to unpack and maybe tomorrow evening we'll go into town and eat at a restaurant."

"And I can get a chocolate shake?"

Abby laughed. "If the restaurant has them, then you can get one, but now you need to get to sleep."

Dutifully, Jason closed his eyes. After checking to make certain the night-light was burning brightly, Abby shut off the overhead light and left the room.

She went into the smaller bedroom next door where Jessica awaited a night-time kiss. Five-year-old Jessica smiled as Abby entered her bedroom. It was the bright, beautiful smile of a little angel.

"Hi, pumpkin. All tucked in?" Abby sat on the edge of the bed as Jessica nodded. "You didn't eat very much for supper. Are you hungry?"

Jessica shook her head, and Abby wished for the millionth time that she could hear Jessica's voice. Just one word. It had been over a year since the little girl had uttered a word, and Abby could no longer remember what her voice sounded like.

"Good night, sweetheart." Abby kissed Jessica's forehead, checked on her night-light, then left the room.

She went into the kitchen where she poured herself a cup of coffee, then headed for the sofa in the living room. Curling up on one end, with a television sitcom making white noise, she tried to make sense of the million things that were playing in her mind.

School had already begun, and she needed to get the two kids enrolled, Jason in first grade and Jessica in kindergarten. She hoped the school wouldn't check too deeply into the medical and miscellaneous records needed for enrollment. She'd changed the kids' last name to adhere to their new identity.

She'd done everything she could to cover their tracks, hoped that she'd made no mistakes. Coming here had been a risk, but she'd weighed her options and realized they had no place else to go.

Once the children got settled in school, she'd have to find a job, at least a part-time one. She hoped she could find something that would pay her in cash, where her social security number would not be recorded. She didn't want to leave a trail that somebody might be able to follow.

But eventually a job would become a necessity. It wouldn't be long before their money would be gone, especially with the unforeseen expense of a new porch. It was ironic that there were three trust funds sitting in a bank in Kansas City, each containing enough money to see them living comfortably for the rest of their lives. But she was afraid to access them.

Finding the television noise distracting, she shut it off then went into the kitchen to pour another cup of coffee. She was about to leave the kitchen when the phone rang.

"Mrs. Graham?" a smooth, deep voice inquired.

"Mr. Delaney," she replied, instantly recognizing his voice.

"I've got some figures for you on building a new porch. Is this a good time?"

"Yes, it's fine," she assured him and set her cup on the counter.

As he spoke about the figures and dimensions of the deck, she tried to focus on his words and not on the sexy deepness of his voice. The man had a voice that was positively seductive.

The conversation only took a few minutes. She agreed to the overall price he gave her, and he told her he would have lumber delivered to her home and get started first thing in the morning.

When they hung up, Abby grabbed her coffee cup and headed through the living room and out the front door. Carefully stepping over the hole in the porch, she moved to sit on the rickety steps.

Night had fallen, and the silence was profound. The house was just far enough on the outskirts of Inferno that no city noise was audible. And that was good. The quiet would be good for them all. No ambulance or police car sirens screaming urgency, sounds that always thrust the children into their painful past.

She tilted her head to look at the stars that glittered against the black sky. Instantly she was reminded of Luke Delaney's eyes. His eyes were gray with just enough of a silvery shine and with sinfully black lashes to make them positively breathtaking.

She set her coffee mug aside, wondering if it was the hot brew that was making her overly warm—or thoughts of Luke Delaney.

He'd definitely been a hunk, with his thick, curly black hair and those eyes with their devilish glint. The moment she'd seen him her dormant feminine hormones had whipped into life.

It wasn't just his beautiful eyes, rich dark hair or bold, handsome features that had instantly attracted her. It had also been the lean length of his legs in his tight, worn jeans and the tug of his T-shirt across impossibly broad shoulders.

He'd filled the air with his presence, his scent, his utter masculinity, and he'd reminded her of all the things she'd given up when she'd chosen the path she was on.

She'd hated lying to him, telling him they were from Chicago, but lying was not only necessary, it was positively vital to survival.

She had invented a story for herself that she intended to adhere to. The story was that she was a widow from Chicago who had left the windy city because it held too many painful memories of her husband. A husband who, in reality, had never existed.

Sighing, she wrapped her arms around herself and for just a moment allowed herself the luxury of imagining what it would be like to be held through the night in strong, male arms. She closed her eyes and tried to remember what it felt like to have male lips touching hers in a combustible kiss. Oh, how she used to love to kiss!

She snapped her eyes open, recognizing that she was indulging in a perverse game of self-torture. Those days and nights of Ken were gone, lost beneath family tragedy, lost because he had turned out to be less than half the man she'd believed him to be.

Ken was gone from her life, and there would be no more men for her. The most important things in her life were the two children sleeping in the house where she intended to make a home.

Draining her coffee, she stood and went into the silent house. Although it was still early, she decided to go to bed. Luke had said he'd begin work on the porch early in the morning, and she was exhausted.

She entered her bedroom and stifled a moan as she saw the chaos. Since arriving here, all the unpacking had been done in the kids' rooms, the living room and kitchen. Little had been done in this room.

Boxes were everywhere, and clothes spilled out of an open suitcase on the floor. The only items she'd unpacked were the sheets that were on the bed, her alarm clock that sat on the nightstand and a colorful porcelain hummingbird that was also on the nightstand.

She sank on the edge of the bed and picked up the hummingbird, the delicate porcelain cool beneath her fingertips. It had been a birthday present two years ago, given to her by her older sister.

"You always accuse me of flitting around like a hummingbird," Loretta had said. "So, I figured I'd give this to you and whenever you look at it you can think of me."

Abby's vision blurred with tears as she set the figurine on the nightstand. She couldn't think of Loretta. She didn't have time for grief, didn't have the energy for mourning. The best thing she could do was carry on, remain strong, and that's exactly what she intended to do.

She undressed and got into her nightgown, then turned off the light and slid beneath the sheets. The moonlight poured through the window and painted silvery streaks on the bedroom walls.

The moon seemed much bigger, much brighter here in Inferno, Arizona, like a giant benign night-light chasing away the deepest darkness of the night. She hoped it would keep the bogeyman away.

As always, just before she closed her eyes, she prayed. "Please…please don't let him find us," she whispered fervently. "Please don't let Justin find us."

Justin.

Her personal bogeyman.

The man they'd been running from for the past eleven months. If he found them, then he would destroy them. If he found them, then all would be lost.

Chapter 2

For the thirty-sixth day in a row, Luke woke up stone-cold sober. He opened his eyes and waited for the familiar banging in his head to begin, anticipated the nasty stale taste in his mouth.

Then he remembered. He didn't drink anymore.

He sat on the edge of his bed and looked around. There was no denying it, without the hazy, rosy glow of an alcoholic buzz, the room where he lived in the back of the Honky Tonk looked grim.

The room was tiny and held the battle scars of a thousand previous occupants. It boasted only a single bed, a rickety nightstand and chest of drawers and its own bathroom.

He'd taken the room because he'd wanted to be off the family ranch and because most nights he worked at the Honky Tonk, playing his guitar and singing and, until a little over a month ago, drinking too much.

Until a little over a month ago he'd thought he'd had a

perfect life. He'd had his music and he'd had his booze and there had been nights when he hadn't been sure what was more important to him.

It had taken a crazy deputy trying to kill his sister, Johnna, to change Luke's life.

Luke had stumbled into the scene of the almost crime and, had he not immediately beforehand downed a couple of beers, he might have realized Johnna was in trouble. But, with reflexes too slow and a slightly foggy brain, Luke had become a victim, as well. He'd been knocked unconscious, and it had been up to somebody else to save not only Johnna, but Luke, as well.

He'd awakened in the hospital with a concussion and a firm commitment to change his life. He was twenty-nine years old, and it was time to get his life together. And part of that new commitment included no more drinking, and working hard at his carpentry business, buying time until he could leave Inferno behind forever.

But making the choice to change his life and actually doing it were two different things. There wasn't a moment of the day that went by that he didn't want a drink, had to consciously fight the seductive call of a bottle of Scotch or whiskey.

He gazed at the clock on the scarred nightstand. After seven. He'd shower, dress and get right out to the Graham place to start work. Old Walt Macullough, who owned the lumberyard, liked to get his deliveries done early, before the infamous Inferno heat peaked midday.

It wasn't until he was standing beneath a hot spray of water that he remembered the dreams he'd had the night before. Crazy dreams…erotic dreams of a dark-haired woman with sexy spring-green eyes.

He adjusted the temperature of the water to a cooler spray as his memories of the dream hiked his body temperature higher. In the dream he and Abigail had been splendidly naked and locked in an intimate embrace.

His fingers tingled with the imaginary pleasure of stroking her silky skin, tangling in her length of rich, thick hair. And in his dream her sexy, husky voice had cried out with pleasure as he'd taken complete and total possession of her.

Crazy. He shut off the water and grabbed a towel, shoving away the sensual imaginings. All the crazy dreams proved only that he'd been incredibly physically attracted to Mrs. Abigail Graham, but he certainly didn't intend to follow through on his attraction. After all, she was a married lady, and Luke had never and would never mess with any woman who was married.

But one thing was certain. Luke loved women. Maybe it was because his mother had died when giving birth to Luke's sister, Johnna. Luke had only been a year old.

He'd been raised by a parade of housekeepers, most of whom had stayed only for a month or two before being driven away by Luke's father. Adam Delaney had been a son of a bitch, and keeping household help had been a real problem.

The result was that women entranced Luke. He liked the way they smelled, the feel of their soft skin. He was fascinated by the way their minds worked, but that didn't mean he wanted to bind himself to any woman for anything remotely resembling forever.

Within minutes he was in his truck and headed for the Graham place, pleased to have a big job to keep him busy even though he would have to divide his time between the Graham house and the ranch.

Still, there was nothing Luke liked better than working with his hands. At the family ranch he was in charge of maintenance, mending fences and outbuildings. But what he loved the most was cabinetry work, taking a piece of wood and transforming it into a piece of furniture.

Macullough had already been there, Luke discovered as he parked in front of the ramshackle Graham place. A large pile of supplies had been unloaded by one side of the house.

Before letting Abigail know he'd arrived, Luke walked to the supplies and did a mental checklist, making sure everything he needed had been delivered. In the back of his truck he'd loaded the power tools he knew he would need.

When he was finished with the inventory, he grabbed his bulky toolbox from the truck bed, then approached the front door and knocked. Abigail answered the knock wearing a pink T-shirt and jeans and a warm, inviting smile.

"Mr. Delaney."

"Good morning, and please make it Luke. I just thought I'd tell you that I was here." He tried not to focus on the sweet scent of her that seemed to waft in the air all around him.

"You weren't kidding when you said the lumberyard would probably be here early," she said as she stepped across the hole in the porch and pulled the door closed behind her. "The truck pulled up at six-thirty this morning. How about a cup of coffee before you get started?"

"No, thanks," Luke replied. "I'd like to get most of this porch torn down before the heat of the day gets too intense. Are your kids still in bed?"

She smiled. "Not hardly. For the most part they're on the same schedule as the sun…up at dawn and in bed at dusk. I've got them unloading boxes in their rooms."

Pink was definitely her color, he silently observed. The T-shirt put the hint of roses in her cheeks and made the green of her eyes appear more intense. He couldn't help but notice the firm thrust of her breasts against the cotton material.

He wondered where her husband was, if he'd already left for work or if it was possible he hadn't yet joined his family in their new home. *None of my business,* he reminded himself firmly.

"I think probably the best thing to do is once I get this all torn down, I'll nail your front door shut so your children don't forget and try to exit the house this way," he said in an attempt to focus his thoughts on the task at hand. "You said you have a back door you can use to exit and enter the house?"

"Yes, a door in the kitchen, and I think nailing this door shut is a terrific idea. As much as I like to think I'm always in control of the children, sometimes they escape my radar." She flashed him a gorgeous smile that shot an arrow of heat directly into the pit of his stomach. "Do you have children?"

"Nope. No children, no wife. I'm just footloose and fancy-free."

She nodded. "Well, I guess I'll just go inside and let you get to work. Don't hesitate to come on in if you need anything." She took a step backward and instantly teetered on the edge of the hole in the wood.

"Whoa," Luke exclaimed. He reached out and grabbed her by the upper arms to steady her. Instantly she winced, and he quickly released her. "I'm sorry. Did I hurt you?" he asked, wondering if he'd used more force than he'd intended in grabbing her.

"No…no, I'm fine." She carefully stepped over the hole and flashed him a quick smile that did nothing to reassure him. "I'll just be inside if you need anything." With those words she disappeared into the house.

Luke expelled a deep breath, trying not to think about the fact that her skin had been as soft, as silky, as he'd imagined in his crazy dreams the night before.

And, in that moment when his hands were on her, he'd felt an unexpected quickening of his pulse, an instantaneous surge of heat rising inside him.

She was definitely a sweet temptation, but Luke had fought against temptation before. Besides, he was certain it was because he'd dreamed about her so intimately the night before that he was slightly unsettled around her this morning. Of course, that didn't explain what on earth had prompted him to dream about the woman.

He pulled a sledgehammer from his truck bed. A little hard physical labor, that's all he needed. With grim determination, he set about pulling down the rotting old porch.

For the next couple of hours, Luke worked nonstop. The sun rose higher in the sky, relentless in intensity. It was just before noon when he decided he needed a tall glass of iced water before doing another lick of work.

He walked around the house and nearly ran into Abigail, who was coming out the back door. "I wondered if I could get a glass of iced water," he said.

"Of course. I was just coming around to ask you if you'd like to eat lunch with us," she replied. "I can't offer you anything extravagant, but if you like ham and cheese sandwiches, you're welcome to eat lunch here."

"Sounds good," he agreed. "Normally, I just take a quick break and drive through someplace for a burger."

"Well, as long as you're working here, I'll be more than happy to provide your lunch."

"Thanks, I appreciate it."

Together they entered the kitchen, and again Luke smelled the sweet, floral scent of her. The children stood near the table. He greeted them, but neither of them returned the greeting.

"If you'd like to wash up while I get the food on the table, the bathroom is the second door on the right down the hallway."

He nodded and left the kitchen. As he went down the hallway to the bathroom, his gaze shot into each of the rooms he passed.

The first room on the right obviously belonged to the little girl. It was decorated in shades of pink, and several dolls were on the bed. The first room on the left was the boy's room, with trucks and cars strewn about and a Kansas City Chiefs bed-spread on the bed.

He stepped past the bathroom door to peek at the room at the end of the hallway. A double bed was neatly made up with crisp white sheets, but it was apparent by the stack of boxes that unpacking the children's things had taken priority over Abigail and her husband's creature comforts.

Luke liked that. There had been a time in his life when he'd desperately wished he'd been a priority in any adult's life. It was good and right that parents thought of their children first.

Aware he was out of line peeking into the room, he hurried into the bathroom. The only soap he could find was a bar in the shape of a cartoon character that smelled of bubble gum.

He quickly washed his hands and face, then returned to the kitchen where Abigail was busy pulling things out of the re-frigerator and the two kids were setting the table.

His gaze swept around the kitchen. He noted the wooden cabinets looked nearly as weak and rotted as the front porch. The floor was covered with linoleum that was ripped and faded.

"As you can see, we need some work done inside, as well," she said, apparently noting where his gaze had lingered. "When Jason's foot went through the porch, getting it fixed was a priority. Sturdy cabinets are next on my list. Please, have a seat." She gestured him to the table.

"I really appreciate this, Abigail," he said.

She flashed him one of her gorgeous smiles. "Oh, please call me Abby," she said as he slid into a chair.

Abby. Yes, it suited her far better than the more formal Abigail. Luke sat at the end of the table, and the two children silently slipped into the chairs on either side of him.

He'd never seen two kids so quiet, nor had he ever seen kids with such shadows in their eyes. He thought of the black eye Abby had sported the day before, a black eye that was less visible today. That, coupled with the unchildlike behavior of the kids, caused a knot to twist in Luke's stomach.

He knew all about child abuse. His father hadn't thought twice before backhanding, punching or kicking his kids. The Delaney children had been quiet, too. Quiet and careful, with dark shadows in their eyes.

He frowned and tried to dismiss these thoughts, aware that his own background and experience were probably coloring how he was perceiving things. Besides, thoughts of his father always triggered an unquenchable thirst for a drink of something far stronger than water.

Abby set several more items in the center of the table, then sat across from him. "Please, don't stand on ceremony. Just help yourself."

Luke complied, taking a couple slices of bread and building himself a sandwich. He added a squirt of mustard, then turned and smiled at the little girl next to him. "Jessica, you need some mustard on that?"

"She doesn't talk," Jason exclaimed. "She doesn't talk to anyone 'cept me. She won't talk to you 'cause she doesn't like you."

"Jason," Abby reprimanded softly. Luke looked at the young boy in surprise.

"She probably doesn't like me because she doesn't really know me yet. But once she gets to know me, she'll find out I'm quite lovable." He winked at Jessica, who quickly stared at her plate.

"You know, I noticed this morning when I was checking out the lumber in the yard that there's a big old tree in the backyard that looks like it would be perfect for a tire swing," Luke continued.

"A tire swing?" Jason eyed him with a begrudging curiosity.

"Yeah, you know, a tire on a rope that you can climb in and swing on," Luke explained.

Jason gazed at him for another long moment then frowned at his plate. "I don't think we'd like that," he finally said, but his voice lacked conviction.

"I'll tell you what, why don't I bring the stuff to make the swing tomorrow, then if you and Jessica want to swing on it that's okay, and if you don't want to, that's okay, as well."

"I don't want you to go to any trouble," Abby said, her gaze warm on him.

He shrugged. "No trouble. It will just take a few minutes to tie a tire to that tree." He smiled at her. "I always wanted a tire swing when I was little, but my father wouldn't let us have one."

Once again Jason looked at him. "Is your daddy mean?" he asked.

"My daddy was the meanest man on the earth," Luke replied truthfully.

"No more questions, Jason. Let Mr. Delaney eat his lunch," Abby said to the child, then turned her gaze once again to Luke. "Would you like some potato salad?"

"Sure. Sounds good."

She half stood to pass the bowl across the table to him. As she stretched out her arm, her T-shirt sleeve rode up, exposing a livid bruise on her underarm.

That's why she'd winced when he'd grabbed hold of her earlier, he thought. He took the bowl from her and spooned a portion on his plate, his mind racing.

A black eye, an ugly-looking bruise…was the lovely Abigail Graham being abused by her husband? The bruises, coupled with Jason asking him if his daddy was mean, caused ugly speculation to whirl inside him.

He tried to tell himself it was none of his business. He tried to tell himself to stay out of it. But the thought of some man angrily putting his hands on the delicate, fragile woman before him, or hurting the children beside him, enraged him.

He set his fork down and looked at her. "Uh…could I speak with you for a moment out in the living room?"

She gazed at him curiously, then wiped her mouth with her napkin. "Sure," she agreed. She stood and looked at the kids. "You guys go ahead and keep eating. We'll be right back."

Luke allowed her to precede him into the living room. "Is something wrong?" she asked, a worried frown appearing on her forehead as she turned to face him.

"I don't know. You tell me." Luke drew a deep breath, aware that he was about to invade deep into her personal territory. "I know this is really none of my business, but does your husband have a problem?" he finally blurted.

Her eyes widened in obvious surprise. "What do you mean?"

"I couldn't help but notice that you have the evidence of a black eye and a big bruise on your arm." Luke gazed at her intently. "What I really need to know is if you need some help."

Abby stared at the big, handsome man before her and swallowed hard against the tears that suddenly pressed at her eyes. Help? She needed help in a thousand different ways, but certainly not in the way he meant.

"There is no husband," she confessed. Shock swept over his features. "There's no abusive husband, no abusive boyfriend. I'm a widow, and now it's just the kids and me and I can be incredibly clumsy at times." The lie tripped smoothly off her tongue but left a bitter taste in her mouth.

She wasn't sure he believed her, but her heart expanded with warmth that he'd cared enough to ask. She offered him what she hoped was a reassuring smile. "This moving business has been far more physical than I anticipated. A box fell off a shelf and hit me in the eye, and I'm not sure how I got the bruise on my arm. But we're getting settled in enough that bumps and bruises are at an end."

She reached out and touched his forearm, trying not to notice the hard muscle beneath the warmth of his skin. "But thank you for asking." Self-consciously she dropped her hand.

"I just had to make sure nobody was hurting you."

Abby nodded, finding the fact that he cared far too appealing. "Nobody is hurting me, so that's that. We'd better go finish our lunch."

He nodded, and together they returned to the table. The meal was finished in relative silence, and Abby was grateful when the food was once again put away, Luke was back at work, and she could escape to her bedroom to finish unpacking.

It had been slightly disconcerting to sit at the table across from him and feel the silvery-gray glow of his eyes on her. She was far more aware of him than she should be.

She pulled her bedspread from a box and opened it up to air out. The room would feel more like her own with her sunflower spread on the bed and her favorite knickknacks and perfumes on the dresser top.

She had peeked in on Jessica and Jason before coming into her room and knew they were having a pretend picnic on the floor in Jason's room. As usual, Jason was doing all the talking, but occasionally she heard a girlish giggle from Jessica, and the sound warmed her heart.

As she worked unloading the last of the boxes, she heard the sound of banging coming from the porch. For a moment she allowed her mind to visualize Luke swinging the sledge-hammer. She could vividly imagine the play of the firm muscles in his arms and across his back. Her fingers tingled as she remembered the warmth of his skin beneath her touch.

From the moment she'd told him she was a widow, she'd sensed a subtle change in him. He seemed less standoffish, smiling at her with a gleam in his eyes that made her breath catch in her chest.

She shook her head, as if to dislodge the thoughts. The last thing she could do was invite a man into any area of her life. She was living a lie, and to allow anyone in meant the possibility of danger and heartbreak.

It was nearly an hour later that she heard the sound of the back door opening and closing and knew Luke had entered the kitchen. She left her bedroom and hurried into the kitchen just in time to see him gulping a glass of water.

"Whew, it's definitely warm out there," he said.

Abby nodded, trying to keep her focus on his face. At some point he had taken off his shirt, and his broad, tanned chest shimmered with a light sheen of perspiration. The dark, springy hair that sprinkled his chest formed a valentine pattern, the faint tail disappearing into the waistband of his low-slung tight jeans.

She suddenly realized he was looking at her expectantly as if waiting for her to say something, and a flush of heat warmed her cheeks. She leaned against the table, hoping he hadn't noticed her intense perusal of his firmly muscled, gorgeous chest. "I meant to ask you, I'm going to take the kids out to dinner tonight, but we haven't been in town to really see what's there. Any suggestions on a good place to eat?"

He set the glass on the counter and swiped a hand through his beautiful thick hair. "My personal choice is the diner on Main Street. It's nothing fancy, but the food is good, and it's where most everyone in town eats."

"With two kids, I'm not in the market for fancy. Do they have chocolate shakes?"

He grinned at her, that wide, sexy grin that did amazing

things to his sinfully gorgeous eyes. "Do I feel the kinship of another chocolate shake addict?"

"Not me," she protested with a laugh. "Jason is a chocoholic. I prefer anything with strawberries."

"Hmm, the best way to eat strawberries is lying down on a blanket beneath a big old shade tree." His gaze seemed to hold the glint of blatant flirtation. "And they taste best of all when somebody else is feeding them to you, rather than you eating them by yourself."

"I wouldn't know about that," she said, her insides trembling at the picture he'd painted with his words. "I've never had anyone feed me anything."

"That's an oversight that will have to be addressed," he replied. He studied her for a long moment. "You mentioned earlier that you're a widow. How long has it been?"

There was a gentleness in his voice that made her regret the lies she was about to tell. "A little over a year. He died in a car accident."

"I'm sorry. It must have been tough for you and the kids."

She nodded and averted her gaze from his. She didn't want to see the sympathy there, sympathy for a dead husband who had never existed. "We've managed okay on our own."

"Yeah, well, if you ever need a man around here, you know, to do any heavy lifting or whatever, don't hesitate to call me."

She looked at him again, and something in his metal-flecked eyes made her feel as if he were offering her more than strong arms to lift heavy items. Her cheeks burned with a blush as she wondered if perhaps she was reading more into his offer than he'd intended.

"Thanks, I'll keep that in mind."

"If you really want to eat at the diner, I recommend you go around five. By six the place is packed on most evenings, but Friday night is always the worst."

She nodded, then turned and headed out the kitchen door. She drew a deep breath as she entered her room, wondering why a man she hadn't exchanged more than a hundred words with affected her so. Maybe it was because the sight of him evoked thoughts and images that had little to do with conversation.

"Jason," she said as she entered his room. "Time for a bath, buddy."

"A bath? But it's not bedtime," he protested.

"If I'm taking my best boy into town for dinner, then I want him scrubbed sparkly clean." His face screwed up for another round of protest. "And I hear the place we're going to eat has the most super-duper chocolate shakes in the world." The promise of his favorite drink did the trick, and he headed for the bathroom.

Within minutes Abby had Jason in the tub with Jessica waiting to bathe next. Abby had just pulled Jason from the tub and was fixing fresh water for Jessica when Luke appeared in the doorway.

"Sorry to bother you," he said, "but I'm going to nail the front door shut, then knock off for the day."

She quickly turned off the faucets, gestured Jessica to get in the tub, then stepped into the hallway and pulled the bathroom door closed behind her to afford the little girl her privacy.

The first thing she realized was that the hall seemed far too small. He stood close enough to her that she could smell the masculine scent of him, a mixture of fresh cologne and a whisper of hot male. The heat from his body radiated outward. "You'll be back tomorrow?" she asked.

"Yeah, but before I leave, I wanted to talk to you for a minute about my hours here."

She wanted to move him out of the hallway, step back enough from him that she didn't feel so vulnerable, so overwhelmed by his presence.

"If it's all right with you, I'll work here each day until about three. Then I need to knock off. I work on the family ranch in the afternoons, then in the evenings I work at the Honky Tonk, a little bar on the edge of town."

"Three jobs? You must be an overachiever."

He laughed, a deep, rumbling sound that echoed in the pit of his stomach. "Not hardly. In fact, most people would tell you the opposite is true, that I'm just kind of drifting through life, dabbling here and there."

"And what would be closer to the truth?" she asked curiously.

"I'm not sure. I'm still trying to figure it out," he admitted with a wry grin. He started down the hallway toward the kitchen, and she followed.

"I'll be back around seven in the morning," he said as he reached the door.

"That would be fine," she agreed.

"Then I'll see you first thing in the morning." With another of his beautiful smiles, he turned and left the house.

To Abby, his parting words felt like a nice promise, and that worried her. She closed the door after him and for a moment leaned against it.

What was wrong with her? Why did Luke Delaney make her feel so shaky inside, so vulnerable and needy? And why did she have the feeling that once he'd discovered she wasn't married, he'd been subtly flirting with her?

She knew exactly what was wrong with her and knew she couldn't trust her own perceptions. For the first time in a little over a year, she was feeling relatively safe, anticipating the beginning of a normal life…a new beginning.

For a moment, as Luke had looked at her with his flirting gray eyes, she'd been taken back in time, back to a time of innocence, before tragedy had taken its toll.

She responded to Luke because for the first time in a very

long time she felt the stir of wonderful, frightening hope. But she knew how quickly hope could be destroyed, how fast lives could shatter. She knew better than to hope for anything.

Chapter 3

Abby and the children had driven into Inferno the day they had arrived for a brief visit to the grocery store, but this was their first real foray into town.

As far as Abby was concerned, it was a delightful little town, with a main street typical of hundreds of other small towns across the United States.

When they'd been driving from Kansas City, Missouri, to Inferno, they'd gone through dozens of towns just like this one, and each time Abby had thought how nice it would be to call one of those small towns home.

The businesses were all in one- or two-story buildings, and each had a charming facade that spoke of what lay inside. The barbershop had an actual barber pole just outside its doors, and the floral shop had two barrels of wildly blooming flowers. The sidewalks were wide and shaded with small trees planted here and there.

It was just after five when she pulled her car into a parking spot directly in front of the Inferno Diner. The kids tumbled out of the backseat as Abby stepped out of the car. In the past month, the kids had grown accustomed to diners in small towns.

Stepping inside the establishment, Abby sniffed appreciatively. The air spoke of good home cooking and strong black coffee. She gestured the kids into a booth near the jukebox, knowing they would eventually end up there, feeding coins to the brightly lit machine to hear songs they didn't know.

"I want a cheeseburger, French fries and a chocolate shake," Jason pronounced as they got seated.

Abby nodded and looked at Jessica, who sat next to her brother in the red plastic booth. "What about you, sweetheart?"

Jessica shrugged.

"How about a grilled cheese sandwich with fries and a soda?" Abby suggested, knowing it was the little girl's favorite. Jessica nodded.

"Hi, folks." An older woman with gray hair and a big smile greeted them and handed Abby a menu. "The special today is meat loaf, but I highly recommend you steer clear away from it."

Abby laughed. "Thanks for the honesty."

The waitress grinned. "The cook here does just about everything to perfection, but there's something scary about his meat loaf." She tilted her head and eyed Abby. "You just passing through, or one of the dude ranch guests, or are you new in town?" the woman asked with unabashed curiosity.

"We've just moved into the old Graham place on the edge of town," Abby replied.

"Whooee, you've sure got your work cut out for you. By the way, I'm Stephanie…Stephanie Rogers, head waitress of this fine establishment."

"Abby Graham. The local space alien was a great-uncle of mine."

Stephanie laughed, a loud, robust sound of one accustomed to laughing often. "Ah, honey, every family has at least one in their family. I've got a brother we all try not to claim because he's nuttier than a fruitcake." The laughter in her blue eyes faded and she looked at Abby seriously. "But that old Graham place is kind of a wreck."

"It isn't as bad on the inside as it looks on the outside," Abby replied. "Besides, I've already hired a carpenter to work on the place…Luke Delaney. Do you know him?"

Stephanie rolled her eyes. "Honey, every woman in the four-state area knows Luke Delaney." She leaned closer to Abby. "That man is sin walking on two legs." Her gaze flickered to the children. "Course, if you're married, then you're safe."

"I'm widowed," Abby replied.

"Then you'd better watch yourself. That handsome devil drips charm from every pore in his body, and he can seduce a woman before she knows what's happened."

Stephanie used her order pad to fan her face. "There are days when I see him and wish I wasn't so long in the tooth and could have a go at him."

"At the moment all I want from him is a new front porch," Abby replied with a laugh, although she was more than a little unsettled by Stephanie's characterization of Luke.

"Famous last words," Stephanie replied with a wry grin. "Now, what can I get for you all?"

She took their orders and small talked a moment longer, then left the booth and disappeared into the kitchen area.

"Can we have money for the jukebox?" Jason asked.

"Not until after we eat," Abby replied. "You know the rule, eat first, play the jukebox afterward." It was a rule she'd instigated the first time she and the kids had eaten at a place that had a jukebox.

She'd mistakenly allowed them to play songs before their meals were served and had had to fight with them to get them in their seats to eat.

Before Jason could lodge any real protest, Stephanie returned to their table with their beverages. A thick chocolate shake effectively stilled any complaint Jason might have uttered.

"Cute kids," Stephanie said as she lingered for a moment at their table.

"Thanks, I think so," Abby replied.

"What's your name, cutie?" Stephanie asked Jessica.

Jessica's gaze instantly went to her brother. "She doesn't talk," he explained soberly. "She doesn't talk to anyone but me."

"Shy, huh. My oldest boy was like that," Stephanie said to Abby. "He's twenty-five now and still doesn't talk much unless he's got something really important to say."

"Hey, Stephanie, how about some fresh coffee over here," a guy hollered from the counter.

"No rest for the wicked," she said with a wink, then hurried away.

Abby took a sip of her soda and settled back in the seat. She wished it were just shyness that kept Jessica silent. But she knew it was much more than that, and it ached inside her that after a whole year Jessica still didn't trust Abby enough to speak to her, that the little girl trusted and depended solely on her brother.

Within a few minutes, Stephanie had served them their meals and they were all eating. It was only then that Abby allowed the conversation with the waitress to replay in her mind.

Sin walking on two legs. Yes, that was certainly an apt description, at least physically, of Luke Delaney. From the moment she'd seen him standing at her doorstep, with those gorgeous eyes and that drop-dead lean body with his mountain-broad shoulders, she'd been affected on a purely hormonal level.

But Stephanie's words warned Abby away from what she knew would be foolishness in any case. She could not get involved with any man, not yet…not until she knew for certain they were safe and her secrets were secure.

Even if she was in the market for a relationship with a man, the last kind of man she wanted was a handsome charmer with seduction on his mind.

If and when she decided to invite a man into her life, it would be a man who had the capacity to parent two wounded children, a man who could be a source of strength, support and love for Abby. She certainly didn't need a good-looking cowboy carpenter with a reputation of being a ladies' man.

As they ate, the diner began to fill with people, and Abby was glad she'd taken Luke's advice and come early enough to beat what appeared to be a dinner rush in the making.

She felt the curious gazes of other diners on her and the kids and knew that probably strangers in town were a topic for gossip. It wouldn't be long and everyone would know she was Inferno's newest resident, and not just a passerby who had stopped in for a meal.

"How about some dessert?" Stephanie asked when they had finished the meal. "I've got a fresh apple pie back there that's still warm from the oven."

Abby looked at the kids, who both shook their heads. "I'll take a piece, and a cup of coffee," she said, deciding she could enjoy the pie and coffee while the kids played the jukebox.

Minutes later, the kids stood at the music maker armed with a handful of quarters, and Abby nursed her coffee and cut into the luscious-looking apple pie.

She'd just taken her first bite when Luke Delaney walked into the diner. Instantly, she felt as if the air pressure in the room subtly increased.

He paused inside the door, his long-lashed eyes scanning the room. When his gaze landed on her, a slow smile curved his lips. As he sauntered toward her, she was aware of every other woman in the room watching his progress.

He stopped at her table and smiled. "I see you got here okay." He flickered his gaze to the empty space beside her. "Mind if I join you?"

She wanted to tell him no but found herself scooting as close to the wall as possible to allow him plenty of room to sit next to her.

"Stephanie." He raised a hand to the waitress. "Bring me the usual." The waitress nodded, and Luke slid into the booth next to Abby. "Where are the munchkins?" he asked.

She pointed to the jukebox near the door where the two were feeding in coins and punching buttons. "On the cross-country drive they discovered the joys of the jukebox," she said.

"Do they know what they're playing? I mean, can they read the titles?"

"Jason can read a little, enough to recognize all the Alan Jackson songs."

He laughed. "At least the kid has good taste in music."

"You like country music?" she asked, trying to ignore the clean male scent of him that seemed to wrap around her so effectively. His body warmth seeped to her even though their bodies weren't touching.

He turned sideways so he could look at her, his thigh suddenly pressing against hers. "As far as I'm concerned, there's no other kind of music. What about you? What's your listening pleasure?"

She tried to focus on what he was saying and not on the

sensory overload of his nearness. Despite the material of his jeans and hers, she could feel the heat of his thigh intimately against her own. "I used to enjoy old rock and roll, but when we were driving across country, there were times when we could only pick up country stations, so I have to admit, I've grown pretty fond of it."

"You should come down to the Honky Tonk one night."

"The Honky Tonk?" She was intensely aware of speculative glances being shot their direction from the other diners, particularly the female diners.

"It's a little tavern on the north side of town. I pick a little guitar and sing there most nights."

"Really? So you're a singing carpenter cowboy rancher."

"Yeah, although I'm hoping eventually I can drop carpenter cowboy rancher from my résumé."

She looked at him in surprise. "So, you want to be a performer?" He was certainly handsome enough. She wondered if he had any talent, other than the one of seduction that Stephanie had mentioned earlier.

"In seven months' time I'm Nashville bound," he said, his eyes sparkling with good humor. "And in the meantime, I've got a front porch to build."

She returned his smile with one of her own. "Why seven months? I mean, if Nashville and fame are your dream, then why wait to chase after it?"

Abby knew all about the danger of waiting to reach for dreams. She knew that far too often if you waited too long, fate destroyed any chance of gaining the dreams you might entertain. No, fate hadn't destroyed her dreams, Justin Cahill had seen to that.

She shoved this thought aside and listened as Luke explained to her about his father's will. "Anyway, the short of it is that if I don't want my brothers and sister to lose their inheritance, then

I have to hang around here for the next seven months and put in twenty-five hours a week at the family ranch."

He grinned, that slow, lazy smile that ignited heat in the pit of her stomach. "But, with a new pretty lady in town, hanging around here isn't going to be so bad, after all."

"I already warned her about you, Luke Delaney." Stephanie placed a dinner platter before him and eyed him in mock sternness. "I told her to watch out for you, that you're a charming devil without a heart."

Luke laughed and turned to Abby. "Don't pay any attention to her. She knows the only reason I don't have a heart is because she stole it from me long ago." He turned to look at the waitress. "You know you're the only woman for me, Stephanie."

She slapped him on the shoulder with her order pad. "And you are utterly shameless. You drink too much, you don't take care of yourself and you never take anything seriously." With these words and a wry shake of her head, she turned and left their table.

"She always gives me a hard time," he explained, his features still lit with humor.

"She did warn me about you before you got here," Abby replied. "She said you were a charmer." Abby bit her bottom lip, unwilling to tell him what Stephanie had said about his powers of seduction.

Luke looked at her once again, and she wondered if he had any idea that his eyes seduced by merely gazing at her. "And that's a bad thing?"

"Well, no…" She felt breathless beneath the power of his bedroom eyes. "That is, unless the woman you're charming takes you too seriously."

He grinned. "I take my charming of women very seriously."

She broke the eye contact with him and gazed to where the two kids stood at the jukebox, tapping their feet and wiggling their bottoms in the unself-consciousness of children.

He didn't speak until she looked at him once again, then he smiled that sexy grin that released a million butterflies in the pit of her stomach. "I'll tell you what, I'll give you fair warning before I attempt to charm you, and that way you won't be caught unprepared."

Despite the fact that Abby felt as if she had suddenly plunged into deep waters over her head, she laughed. "Okay," she agreed. "That sounds fair to me." Once again she broke their eye contact and looked at the kids. "And now, if you'll excuse me, it's time for me to get home and get those two ready for bed."

In actuality, it was time for her to get away from Luke Delaney's smile, his body warmth and the heated light that shone from his eyes. He was making her feel things she hadn't felt for a very long time.

She sighed in relief as he stood to allow her to slide out of the booth. "I guess I'll see you in the morning," she said.

"Bright and early," he replied, and in his smooth, deep voice she heard promise that had nothing to do with a new front porch.

She nodded, turned and walked to the cash register, refusing to follow her impulse to turn and look at him one last time.

The man was a definite temptation, but she knew the temptation he offered was not what she needed or wanted in her life at the moment. He could try his talent at seduction with her, but what he would eventually discover was that at this point in her life, she was absolutely, positively unseduceable.

Luke had been in a tailspin ever since learning that Abigail Graham had no husband and no boyfriend. It was as if fate had given him the thumbs-up to follow through on his initial attraction to her.

There was nothing Luke liked more than a challenge and the excitement of a new, fresh relationship. It had been several months since he'd even taken a woman on a date and months before that when he'd last been intimate with a woman.

He knew he had a reputation as a womanizer, and in truth had dated most of the single, eligible women in town. But since his father's death, Luke had not been living up to his reputation.

As he ate, he thought about the lovely Abby, whose clean, lightly floral perfume still eddied in the air around him. A year was a long time to be alone, and there had been loneliness in her eyes, a loneliness that touched something deep inside him.

He shook his head as if to dislodge this thought. He certainly wasn't lonely. His life was merely in a holding pattern until the seven months he had to spend at the ranch were over. And there was no reason he shouldn't spend some of his holding-pattern time with a lovely woman named Abigail Graham.

By the time he'd finished his meal, the dinner rush had come and gone. Stephanie poured herself a cup of coffee and sank down across from him in the booth.

"I shouldn't even talk to you," Luke teased with an affectionate grin at Stephanie. "What are you doing maligning my good name behind my back to the new people in town?"

Stephanie snorted. "You don't need any help maligning your name. I told that pretty lady the truth, that she needs to watch out for you. You're a heartbreaker, Luke Delaney, and you've already broken half the hearts in this town."

"But I'm good friends with every single woman I've ever dated," he countered.

"And that's part of your charm, dear Luke. You somehow

manage to make every woman happy they got a moment of your time even though they wanted a lifetime."

Stephanie took a sip of her coffee and shook her head with a smile. "But, mark my words, Luke. Someday you're going to mess with the wrong woman and you'll have one of those obsessive stalkers on your hands like in the movies."

Luke laughed in genuine amusement. "Ah, Stephanie, you always did have a flair for the dramatic. I'm twenty-nine years old and I'm not cut out for marriage or family life. I play fair and make sure all the women I date know that ahead of time."

Stephanie waved her hands to dismiss his statement. "If anyone in this town wasn't cut out for marriage, it was your sister, Johnna. And look at her now, the picture of happily married bliss." Stephanie finished her coffee and stood. "All you need Luke, is one good woman to tame you and you're finished."

Luke laughed, certain that no woman was ever going to tame and domesticate him. "Trust me, Stephanie. Growing up in my family gave me all the family experience I ever want in my life."

Stephanie frowned. "You can't judge marriage and family by what your daddy did to you kids. Every man needs a good woman, Luke. And that's exactly what you need in your life." With these final words, Stephanie turned and left his booth.

Luke sipped his coffee, thinking of Stephanie's words. It had always amazed him that everyone in town seemed to know what a mean, hateful son of a bitch Adam Delaney had been as a father, but nobody had ever stepped in to help the four children who suffered at his hands.

He shoved away thoughts of his father. Thinking of Adam Delaney always caused a knot of fire to form in the pit of his stomach, a knot that only a good stiff drink could unkink. Instead, he focused on a vision of the lovely Abigail Graham.

Not only did she interest him on a physical level, but she intrigued him, as well. Along with the loneliness he'd thought he'd seen in her eyes, he'd sensed secrets. She certainly hadn't been forthcoming about where they had come from.

Back east, she'd said, then had finally said they were from Chicago. But, when he had gone past the bedrooms, he'd noticed that Jason's room was decorated in a Kansas City Chiefs motif. Why would a kid from Chicago want items from the Kansas City football team in his room? Why not the Chicago Bears?

Luke sipped the last of his coffee and wondered if perhaps he was making too much of nothing. Maybe the kid's father had been a Chiefs fan, or perhaps he'd had a friend from the Kansas City area who had gotten him to follow the team. In any case, it didn't much matter. He didn't really care where she'd come from.

"More coffee?" Stephanie pulled him from his thoughts.

"No, thanks," he replied, and reached in his back pocket for his wallet. "I've got to get out of here. I need to get out to the ranch for a couple of hours before I head over to the Honky Tonk."

"Tomorrow is my night off, and I already told Tom that I want to go to the Honky Tonk and have a drink and listen to you croon a few tunes."

Luke grinned at the older woman. "You and Tom come in, and your first round of drinks is on me." He tossed enough money on the table to pay for his meal and a generous tip.

"Then for sure we'll be in," she agreed.

Luke left the diner, climbed into his pickup and within minutes was headed to the family ranch. He'd surprised himself by telling Abby of his plans to head to Nashville. That was something he hadn't shared with anyone, not even his siblings, who he knew probably didn't give a damn what he did or where he went. To say the Delaney heirs weren't tightly knit was an understatement.

Still, he had a feeling he'd told Abby his plans for a reason. He was interested in her, but he certainly wasn't interested in anything long-term. By telling her that in seven months his plans were to leave Inferno and never look back, he'd subtly told her that he wasn't a man to pin a future on.

Chapter 4

"How about a glass of iced tea?" Abby asked Luke.

"Sounds great," he agreed. "I'm ready to take a break."

It was late afternoon, and Luke had been working on knocking down the old porch since early morning.

The first thing he had done when he arrived that morning was follow through on his promise to hang a tire swing from one of the thick branches of the tree in the backyard. While the kids had played on the swing, Abby had picked weeds and promised herself to buy a lawnmower in the near future.

She had consciously stayed away from the front of the house where Luke was working.

The heat of the afternoon had finally driven them inside. The kids were playing in their rooms, and Abby had guessed Luke would be ready for a tall drink of something cold.

As Luke put down the sledgehammer, Abby tried to keep her gaze focused everywhere but on his broad, naked chest.

She handed him the glass of tea, then stepped back from him and watched as he downed half a glass in long, thirsty gulps.

Condensation from the bottom of the glass dripped onto his chest, and despite her desire to the contrary, she watched the droplet trail down his chest.

"I was hoping I'd be able to salvage some of this wood," he said, and she was grateful for anything that took her attention away from his physique. "But I don't think I'm going to be able to. Most of it is beyond rotten." He took another deep drink, then continued. "I should have the last of this pulled down in the next hour or so, then first thing tomorrow morning I'll start on the new structure."

"It will be nice to be able to walk out the front door and not be afraid of falling through the porch."

"You know, I'd be glad to give you an estimate on some new kitchen cabinets. If I build them from pine, they'd be relatively inexpensive."

"New cabinets would be wonderful," she said thoughtfully. "I've been afraid to put too many canned goods in the ones that are there because they look so weak."

"I'll work up an estimate and you can decide if you want to go ahead then."

"Okay," she agreed, then sighed. "There's so much work here that needs to be done."

"And Rome wasn't built in a day," he replied with one of his killer smiles.

"You're right. And hopefully we'll be here a long time and eventually get the house done the way we want it." She returned his smile with one of her own. "Patience isn't one of my strong suits."

"I've never been one to want to wait for what I want, either," he replied with a wicked grin that instantly drew heat into her cheeks.

He held out his empty glass to her. As she took it from him, their fingers touched and Abby felt a spark of electricity tingle in the air between them. She took another step back from him and clutched the glass tightly in her hand.

There was a silence, an uncomfortable one that she instantly worked to fill. "You mentioned last night at the diner that you had to stay here in Inferno for several months and work on your family dude ranch so your brothers and sisters wouldn't default. So, you have a big family?"

"Two brothers and one sister. And we've recently added a sister-in-law and a brother-in-law." He swiped a hand through his thick hair, and Abby tried not to notice how handsome he looked with the afternoon sun playing on his features.

He had strong, bold features. Midnight dark brows, a straight Roman nose, high cheekbones and a sensual mouth. He was once again clad in customary tight, worn blue jeans that rode low on his hips.

"What about you? Big family? Small family?" he asked.

"No other family. Just me and the kids."

A frown creased his forehead. "I might as well have no family. We aren't very close."

"Do they all live here in town?" she asked curiously.

Luke nodded. "Yeah, Matthew lives at the family homestead. Mark and his wife, April, and son live on a house Mark built on the ranch. Johnna and her husband, Jerrod, live in a house here in town." His frown deepened. "So, we're all here, but we might as well live a million miles away from one another."

"You don't realize how lucky you are to have brothers and a sister," Abby replied. "My sister died a year ago, and there isn't a day that goes by that I don't wish I had spent more time with her, talked to her more often."

As always, thoughts of Loretta brought with them a dark, dangerous well of grief. If only she'd known what had been going on in Loretta's life. If only she'd known the danger. Abby had encouraged her to make the break that had ultimately resulted in her death.

Before Abby could plunge into the dark depths of despair, she mentally shook away thoughts of the sister she missed so much. "Take my advice, Luke and don't waste time where your family is concerned. Enjoy their company while you still have them."

He nodded, his gaze steady, thoughtful as it lingered on her. "So, you lost your sister a year ago. That means you had two tragedies about the same time?"

"Two?" She looked at him blankly.

"Your husband and your sister."

Warmth swept over her as she realized she'd momentarily forgotten all about the husband she'd supposedly lost. "Yes, that's right," she agreed hurriedly, then averted her gaze. "It's been a long, hard year."

He took a step toward her and reached out to grab her hand. She looked at him, surprised by the warmth, the strength of his touch. "I hope Inferno will be good to you and you'll be able to put all the sad times behind you and find happiness here."

For a moment, as she gazed into his beautiful sooty eyes, she wondered if happiness was possible. She hoped so, not so much for her own sake, but for the sake of the two children who meant more to her than anything on the earth.

"Thank you," she replied. She knew she should pull her hand away yet was reluctant to break the warmth and comfort of the contact. It had been so long since she'd felt any kind of masculine touch, even one as simple and uncomplicated as the touch of hands.

He smiled and increased the pressure of his hand on hers. "There's nothing I'd like more than to see those pretty green eyes of yours light up with pleasure, with happiness and laughter."

A dangerous, provocative heat rose inside her as their gazes remained locked, and she saw flickering flames in the depths of his eyes. "Are you trying to charm me, Mr. Delaney?" She forced a light laugh and pulled her hand from his, suddenly realizing his touching her was anything but simple. "Is this the beginning of the seduction that Stephanie warned me about?"

He laughed, a low, sexy rumble that was as disturbing as his touch. "Trust me, darlin', when I start seducing you, you'll know it and you won't have to ask."

His words sent a new flood of heat through her and made the mere act of breathing difficult. "Then trust me, all I really want from you, Luke, is a new front porch and maybe some new kitchen cabinets," she replied quickly, appalled to hear her voice slightly breathless.

Again he laughed. "It's been my experience that women rarely know what they really want."

"And from what Stephanie told me, you certainly have had plenty of experience with women." She shook her head wryly. "Three jobs and an overactive social life. I don't know how you have the strength to get up in the mornings."

Flirting. Someplace in the back of her brain she recognized that's what she was doing. Flirting with Luke Delaney.

He grinned that lazy devastating smile. "My strong suit has always been my terrific stamina."

He laughed as her cheeks grew hot and she knew a blush reddened them. "Besides, my reputation as a womanizer has been greatly exaggerated. You will discover that this town thrives on idle gossip, and I'm not sure why, but I seem to be a favorite topic of that gossip."

Abby certainly knew why. The man was not only as handsome as a pinup model, he had a kind of animal magnetism that she had a feeling could stir the hormones of a female statue.

"So, tell me about your brothers and sister," she said, suddenly desperate to change the topic, get away from the subject of seduction and gossip, neither of which she wanted or needed in her life.

"What do you want to know?" he asked.

"What do they do? What are they like?" She realized she was intrigued by Luke and wondered what kind of family he came from.

"Matthew is the oldest. He's thirty-five and he runs the family dude ranch." Again a frown etched across his forehead. "Matthew is distant and aloof, but he's a good businessman. All that matters to him is the ranch. Mark is thirty-three and he's more easygoing. He's thoughtful and quiet or at least he was until he married April. She's really brought him out of his shell."

The frown disappeared. "Then there is Johnna. She's twenty-eight, a year younger than me." He grinned with obvious affection. "She's stubborn and mule headed, impetuous and opinionated. She's a lawyer who spends most of her time trying to right the wrongs of the world."

"You're close to her," Abby commented.

"I'm closer to her than I am to my brothers, but there's a lot of distance even between me and Johnna."

"Why? I mean, why aren't you and your siblings close?"

He grinned wryly. "What is this? Twenty questions? I don't know the answer to that question." His eyes shadowed slightly. "All I can tell you is that the four Delaney heirs share common parentage, but nothing else. It would take nothing short of a miracle to make us into a real family."

Abby thought she heard a wistful tone in his voice, as if there was a part of him deep inside that longed for a family connection. It echoed inside her, touching a chord of commonality.

Still, as attractive as she found Luke Delaney, she knew she'd be a fool to somehow get the notion into her head that he was the man who could fulfill her dream of a complete and happy family.

Dusk was falling as Luke pulled up in front of the family homestead. He hadn't intended on coming here this evening, but Matthew had called one of the infrequent family meetings, which meant something was amiss.

Luke's stomach tied itself in a knot as he got out of his truck and approached the house where he'd spent the miserable hours and days of childhood.

Family meetings had never been particularly pleasant. Most of the time Matthew called a meeting when something had to be decided, and a final decision among the four very different siblings never came easily.

Each Saturday a late midday meal was served to the guests as a welcome and get-acquainted gathering. But it was late enough in the day that there was no evidence such a gathering had taken place.

The pit fire that cooked burgers and beans had been extinguished, and the tables and chairs put away. The grounds were relatively quiet.

A couple sat at a picnic table beneath a tree, apparently enjoying the sunset that painted the sky in a fiery display of color.

Luke raised a hand in their direction then headed up the stairs to the front door. In two weeks the ranch would go dark for a month. Two months out of the year, one in the spring and one in the fall, the ranch didn't book guests and used the downtime to do major renovation and repair work.

Seven months, Luke reminded himself as he walked in the front door into the airy foyer. Seven months, and then he could leave and never look back. He wouldn't have to worry any more about guests' needs or family dynamics or disturbing memories. He'd blow this place and never look back.

He heard the sound of voices coming from the den and knew that's where the family would be gathered. The knot in his stomach intensified as he stepped into the large room and the first person he saw was Matthew.

As usual, his oldest brother looked as if he'd been chewing on nails. His handsome features were set in a perpetual scowl that evoked in Luke memories of their father.

"Luke." Matthew greeted him with a curt nod.

"Hey, Luke," Johnna said from the love seat where she sat next to her husband, Jerrod. The two of them still had their just-married glow even though their wedding had taken place a little over a month before.

Jerrod had his arm around Johnna, as if she were his most precious possession and he was protecting her from the world at large. Johnna leaned into him, as if in sweet acquiescence. Luke had never seen his sister look as happy as she had in the last month. Marriage to Jerrod definitely agreed with her.

"Would you like a drink?" Matthew asked from the bar in the corner of the room.

Would he like a drink? The siren song rang in his ears, and his mouth grew unaccountably dry. He imagined he could smell Scotch, feel the sweet slide down his throat and the flames as it hit his stomach. Hell, there was nothing he'd like better than a good, stiff drink.

"No, thanks," he forced himself to say, slightly irritated by the question. Shouldn't a brother remember that his brother had quit drinking? "So, where are Mark and April?" he asked as he sat in one of the wing chairs.

"They should be here any time." Matthew carried a drink with him to the chair across from Luke and sat down, the scowl still tugging deep furrows into his forehead.

"Guess what I heard this morning," Johnna said as she shot a coy look at Luke. "I heard that my handsome brother was seen in the diner snuggling up to a new widow who has moved into town."

"I wasn't 'snuggling up' to her," he protested with a laugh. "I'm doing some carpentry work out at her place and happened to see her at the diner last night. I was just being neighborly by sitting down with her and visiting for a little bit."

"Who were you being neighborly with?" Mark asked as he and April came into the room.

"The new widow who has moved into the old Graham place," Johnna answered. "I heard that she's a real looker, with dark hair and pretty blue eyes."

"Green," Luke corrected. "She has pretty green eyes."

"Better watch out, those green-eyed women will get you every time," Mark said with a loving smile to his dark-haired, green-eyed wife, April.

"If we can dispense with the pleasantries, we've got some work to do," Matthew said.

"By all means, let's dispense with any pleasantries," Luke said drily. God, he would really love a drink.

There followed an uncomfortable silence as April and Mark settled on the sofa and everyone turned their gaze to Matthew. He finished his drink in one large swallow, then stood and began to pace the length of the multicolored throw rug beneath his feet.

Instantly Luke was thrown back in time, and for a moment he felt as if he were seven or eight years old again and it was his father pacing the floor, working up a head of steam that would result in a beating for one or more of the four kids. Adam Delaney would slam down a shot of bourbon then slam into one of his kids.

He shook his head slightly to dispel the image. Adam

Delaney was dead and gone, his only legacy the ranch they had to work to keep and enough dysfunction to keep therapy in fashion for years to come.

"We have several things we need to go over and make decisions about," Matthew began. "First of all, April has been asking me for months about renovating the old barn into a sort of a community building." He turned to April. "You want to explain to them what you have in mind?"

April sat up straighter on the sofa. "You all know that as social director here, I'm always looking for ways to offer the guests exciting and wonderful entertainment. If we renovate the old barn, it will make a terrific permanent place for dances and parties." She looked at Mark as if for reassurance. "I had a contractor come out and look at it and it's structurally sound, but still it's a big investment to make."

"And that's what we need to make a decision about," Matthew said. "In seven months the ranch officially becomes ours. If we're just going to sell it and split the proceeds, then I don't see the point in investing any money in renovating the old barn."

Luke looked at Matthew in shock. It was the first time he'd ever heard Matthew even mention the possibility of selling the place.

"I don't want to sell," Mark said. He looked at Luke, at Matthew, then at Johnna. "This is Delaney land. We belong here. I want to pass my part of this ranch on to Brian…and to the child April is carrying."

Everyone looked at April in surprise. "It's true," she confirmed. "I'm pregnant."

Johnna squealed with excitement and quickly ran over to hug April while the men congratulated Mark on the news.

"So, we know that Mark doesn't want to sell," Matthew

said a few minutes later when things had calmed down. "Johnna, what about you?"

She frowned and raked a hand through her boyishly short dark hair. "To be honest, I haven't given it much thought lately. Between my law practice and having to work here twenty-five hours a week, I haven't had much time to think about what the future holds."

"But you always said you hated it here," Luke reminded her. Their mutual dislike for the family homestead had always been a point of commonality between them.

Johnna frowned. "When Father was alive, I definitely hated this place. Now that he's gone, I'm not sure how I feel."

"Look," Mark interjected. "Do we really have to make a decision about selling right now? Can't we go ahead and do the renovations on the barn without knowing for sure what we're going to do in seven months time?"

"Is the money for the renovations an issue?" Johnna asked.

Matthew shook his head. "No, the ranch is doing very well, and we could pay for the renovations without having to take out a loan."

Luke fought a wave of frustration. He didn't want to put any more money in the ranch. More than anything he wanted to convince his brothers and sister that the best thing for all of them was to sell the ranch in seven months, split the proceeds from the sale, then get on with their own separate lives.

He wanted no ties to this place of unhappiness. He didn't give a damn what the others did. The day the year was up Luke intended to sell his share either to one of his brothers or sister, or to an outsider.

With the decision made to go ahead with the renovations, the family meeting broke up. The four of them rarely spent time in idle chatter. They had no idea how to perform the small talk that would encourage a deepening of their relationship with each other.

Luke was the first to leave. After saying goodbye to everyone, he left the house and headed for his workshop in one of the outbuildings.

He didn't have to be at the Honky Tonk until ten and decided he'd work an hour or so on a rocking chair he'd been making. The workshop was the one place he loved on the ranch. Housed in one end of the stables, it smelled of fresh hay, horses and wood chips. Every tool he'd ever need to transform raw wood into useful and decorative items was at his fingertips, bought with money he'd earned at the Honky Tonk.

The rocking chair was complete except for the sanding and finishing, and as he picked up a piece of sandpaper and got to work, his mind whirled with thoughts of his family.

The Delaney children had learned at an early age not to trust one another. Adam Delaney's parenting skills had included a divide-and-conquer mentality. He'd taught his children to trust nobody—particularly each other.

Often before a beating Luke had been told that his transgression had been brought to Adam's attention by one of his siblings.

Luke and his brothers and sister had remained isolated through misery and fear, and now that Adam was dead, none of them seemed to know how to breach those early years of distance and mistrust.

"Luke?" He jumped in surprise as Mark and April appeared at the doorway of his workshop.

"Hey, what's up?" he asked curiously.

"We just thought we'd stop in before heading back to our place," Mark said.

"What a beautiful chair," April exclaimed.

Luke eyed the two of them in suspicion. They had never been in his workshop area before, and he couldn't imagine what had prompted this unexpected visit. "Thanks."

"I saw one of your coffee tables the other day at Susan Milford's house," April said. "You do such beautiful work, Luke."

He grinned, suddenly realizing a possible reason for their being here. "Let me guess, you want me to make you a crib. Sure, I'll be glad to do it."

"Oh, Luke, that would be wonderful, but that's not the reason we stopped." April smiled at Mark, as if to encourage him. "Go on, ask him."

Mark was obviously ill at ease as he looked first at his wife, then at Luke. "Well, you know April is pregnant," he began. Luke nodded. "Since we found out, she and I have been talking and…well…we'd like you to be the baby's godfather."

Luke stared at his brother and sister-in-law in stunned silence. "Is this a joke?" He couldn't imagine why they would want him to hold such an exalted position in the life of their child. Being a godparent was certainly nothing to take lightly.

"Of course it's not a joke," April replied with a sweet smile. "Mark and I both agree that you would make a wonderful godfather. We both know that beneath your superficial charm and bad-boy reputation is the heart of a loving, caring man, the kind of man we want in the life of our child."

Her words caused an unsettling ball of emotion to well up inside Luke, and he instantly swallowed. He didn't want this.

How could he be a good godparent and leave Inferno in seven months? He didn't want chains holding him here, and this felt like an emotional chain of mammoth proportions.

He swallowed again and cleared his throat. "I really appreciate the thought, but maybe it would be better if you asked Matthew."

Luke saw the disappointment in his brother's eyes and instantly regretted his words. But it wouldn't be fair to the baby to have a godparent who wasn't here to share life experiences.

"Okay," Mark said. "Then I guess we'll ask Matthew." He turned on his heels and left the workroom.

April looked at Luke one last time, confusion wrinkling her delicate brow. "You Delaneys are the most complicated people I know," she said, then turned and followed her husband out the door.

In the ensuing silence, Luke got back to work, trying not to think of what had just occurred. The idea that April and Mark would want him as a godfather still stunned him.

For the first time in his life, Luke felt as if his brother had been reaching out to him, trying to make a connection beyond the superficial one they had shared all their life.

And he'd rejected it. And apparently he'd rejected it badly. Luke sank down on a bench and raked a hand through his hair. If he'd wanted a drink before, he desperately needed one now. All he had to do was walk into the house and help himself to the bar stock Matthew kept on hand. A few drinks, and the pain in his chest would disappear.

Yeah, right, he thought drily. His pain might go away but he'd be back on the treadmill that led to nowhere. He'd drink himself into the loser his father had always told him he was.

April's words replayed in his mind. She was a sweet woman but obviously seeing characteristics that weren't there. Beneath his superficial charm and bad-boy reputation wasn't much of anything else. And he was not a good bet for a godfather. Matthew would be a much better choice.

He drew a deep breath and thought of his siblings. His brothers and sister were fools for wanting to keep this ranch alive, for being sentimental enough to want to hang on to a place where they'd endured nothing but heartache.

He was the smart one, the strong one who intended to get away. He had a hunger to be somebody, to make something of himself, if only to prove his father wrong.

Funny, each and every one of the Delaney children had suffered physical and mental abuse at the hands of their father, and the experience had made them who they had been as children and who they had become as adults. His siblings were hanging on here in an attempt to be something they would never be…a normal, happy family.

Luke didn't intend to waste his time or energy on such a fruitless endeavor. Seven months, he told himself. He had seven months here, and then he'd put the past and the bad memories of this place behind him and he'd never, ever look back.

And in the meantime, he had a delightful diversion to occupy his mind for the next seven months. A delightful diversion with dark hair and bright green eyes, a diversion named Abby.

A smile curved his lips as he thought of how delicate and warm her hand had been beneath his earlier that day. And even though she'd told him all she wanted from him was a new front porch, the slight tremor in her voice, the look in her eyes had told him she wasn't as unaffected by him as she'd like him to think.

She knew his reputation, knew his plans to leave Inferno, so she would know exactly what he was offering her and that it had nothing to do with anything long-term.

Yes, indeed, if he had to stick around Inferno for another seven months, it was nice to know that gave him seven months with the winsome Abigail Graham.

Charming a woman was certainly less complicated than family ties and emotional baggage.

Chapter 5

Abby was on edge. She'd been on edge for the past two days while Luke had been working to complete the front porch, but nothing like what she was feeling this afternoon.

She told herself her intense anxiety was due to the fact that early that morning she'd taken the kids to school and enrolled them, then had left them there and returned home alone. She told herself she was worried about how they would fare, that she was afraid the school officials might discover the children weren't named Graham after all and that she was not really their mother.

Although Jessica had been enrolled in an afternoon kindergarten class, Abby had made arrangements for her to attend a morning play group at the school, as well, and she was worried how the little girl would do without her brother for support.

But the truth of the matter was she was nervous because

this was the first time she'd been alone in the house while Luke worked outside. And much of her nervousness was due to the fact that he seemed to be aware of their utter aloneness, as well.

He was in and out of the house more often for drinks of water than on any day previous, and whenever she joined him there, he lingered longer than necessary.

He'd arrived just after nine, and after working only a few minutes had asked where the children were. She'd explained that they had started their first day of school, and from that moment on there had been an overt tension between them that simmered in the air.

It was about two-thirty in the afternoon when he told her that he was taking a break from the porch work and wanted to measure the kitchen cabinets and could use her help.

"It's much easier to get measurements with another person holding the end of the tape," he explained as he pulled a tape measure from his back pocket. He held out the end toward her.

She took a step closer to him, her mouth unaccountably dry. What was it about him that made her feel so alive? What was it about him that seemed to invite crazy feelings and desires?

"Hold the end right here." He pointed to a stop on the end of one of the cabinets. She moved to do as he bid, and he pressed his finger against hers. "Yes, right there," he murmured, his breath warm on her face.

She breathed a sigh of relief as he moved to the other end of the cabinet. The man had a sexual energy that positively seethed from him.

"Okay, got it," he said. "Now I need you to hold it over here." He walked to the refrigerator and waited for her to join him. "Can you reach up here?" He gestured to the bottom of the cabinet over the refrigerator.

She nodded, rose on her tiptoes reaching up. Again he placed his finger over hers, as if to assure himself she was at the right place. "Hmm, you smell good," he said.

He took a step closer to her, so close she could feel his warm breath on the back of her neck, smell the pleasant masculine scent of him.

"Thank you," she murmured breathlessly.

"I was just thinking that with your hand otherwise occupied now might be a perfect time to begin charming you."

Abby turned her head to look at him in panic. "Don't you dare," she exclaimed. "Stephanie told me you charm a woman right into seduction, and I'll tell you right now that even though the other women in this town might find you irresistible, that doesn't mean I do. You just don't have that kind of an effect on me."

"Really?" he replied with obvious amusement. He placed the tape measure on the countertop, then looked at her once again, those sinful eyes of his promising unspeakable pleasures.

"If I don't have any kind of effect on you, then why is your pulse beating so rapidly right here?" With his index finger he touched the pulse point in the hollow of her throat.

Abby swallowed hard, as if in doing so she could dispel the electric jolt his touch sent riveting through her. She knew she needed to step away from his touch, tell him in no uncertain terms that she wasn't about to become another notch on his bedpost.

And yet, there was a crazy, insane, utterly feminine pull in the opposite direction. There was no denying the fact that she was overwhelmingly attracted to Luke, and she suffered a hunger for all the things she saw in his dark, wicked eyes… uncomplicated passion and simplistic desire.

One thing was certain, she had a feeling that the last thing Luke Delaney wanted from her was any kind of real intimacy other than the physical kind. And she certainly wasn't in the position to want any kind of true intimacy with anyone. She harbored too many secrets for that.

"Why is your breathing just a little more shallow than normal?" he asked in his deep, low voice that was as seductive as a voice could be.

"I have asthma," she replied, and he laughed again, seeing through the lie. "Why would I want to get involved in any way with you," she asked lightly and stepped away from him. "From what the gossips in town say, you're rather conceited, you drink too much and you don't take anything seriously."

His eyes danced with brilliant lights of amusement. "I stopped drinking over a month ago, I'm only conceited about the things I have a right to be and I take my lovemaking very seriously."

She wasn't sure how it was possible for him to elevate her body temperature with mere words, but somehow he managed it.

"A year is a long time to be alone, Abby," he said softly, and although he didn't attempt to touch her again, the warmth of his gaze stroked her with the potency of a physical caress.

"Yes, it is," she agreed. "But that doesn't mean I'm ready to fall into bed with the first handsome man who comes along."

"Ah, so you think I'm handsome."

This time it was her turn to laugh. "You know you're handsome. But it takes more than a pretty face and sweet words to seduce me."

He leaned a hip against the counter, eyeing her with a wicked smile. "Really? Then what does it take?"

"You're just going to have to figure it out," she replied enigmatically. In truth, good sense had managed to reign over raging hormones.

She couldn't think about herself, couldn't think about her

wants or needs. She had two children to consider, and it wouldn't be a good idea for her to allow Luke or any man into their life at this time.

Before he could make any kind of response, a horn bleated loudly. Abby checked her wristwatch. "That will be the school bus bringing home the kids," she said, and hurried out the kitchen door.

The bus driver waved as she stepped around the side of the house then opened the bus door. Jason and Jessica tumbled out, their faces lit with the happiness of a success-ful first day of school.

They raced to her, and she leaned down and wrapped her arms around them both. "Did you have a good day?" she asked them.

"We like school," Jason exclaimed. "My teacher is really nice and I got a new best friend and we have a hamster in a cage…."

Abby laughed as the words tumbled from him. "Whoa, slow down." She turned to Jessica. "And what about you? Do you like school?" Jessica nodded, her eyes shining brightly, and Abby wondered how long it would be before she got a call from Jessica's teacher wondering why the little girl refused to speak.

She shoved this worry away. She'd deal with it when it came up. "Go change your clothes, and you can play outside." Luke's swing was a rousing success with the two children, and she knew that's where they would go.

They raced inside the house, and she followed.

"First day of school go okay?" Luke asked as she entered the kitchen.

She nodded and smiled. "It would seem so."

"I always loved school. It was the one place where I could escape from my father."

She leaned against the kitchen table and eyed him curiously. "So your father really was the meanest man on earth?"

"Definitely," he replied, and for just a moment a shadow usurped the sparkle of his eyes. "But thankfully he's gone now, I hope to his just reward."

Abby didn't know how to reply. She wanted to tell him that he was wrong, that his father couldn't be the meanest man on earth. Justin Cahill held that particular honor. Justin Cahill, who had shattered Jason and Jessica, who had stolen so much from her life and had not received his just reward, but rather had escaped the consequences of the heinous crime he'd committed.

"If you'll hold the tape measure for me again, I promise I'll behave," he said, the wicked gleam back in his eyes.

She returned his smile. "I'm not sure I can trust your promises."

"Oh, but you can. I never lie, and I never, ever break a promise."

"Then that certainly makes you different from the men I've known in my lifetime," she replied truthfully, then flushed as she realized she'd said more about her personal life than she'd intended.

They worked in silence for a few minutes, Abby holding the tape where Luke instructed her and Luke taking notes of the measurements needed to construct new cabinets.

They had just finished the last door when the kids raced in to tell Abby they were going out to the swing.

When they were gone, Luke eyed her with open speculation. "Am I to assume from your last statement that maybe your marriage wasn't exactly a happy one?"

The web of deceit Abby had spun seemed to grow more tangled, more complicated. She didn't want to tell more lies. "I'd

To Wed and Protect

rather not talk about it," she finally said. "And if you don't need my help in here, there are some things I need to take care of."

"I'm finished here," he replied, and she was aware of his gaze lingering on her, filled with curiosity, as she fled the room.

Luke stared after her, more curious than ever. He could only discern from her statement that her life had been filled with men who lied and broke promises. When she'd uttered the statement that if Luke did neither, then he was different from the men in her life, she'd looked achingly vulnerable and hauntingly fragile.

He'd had the crazy impulse to take her in his arms and hold her tight. And his desire had nothing to do with anything physical, nothing to do with sex. He'd merely wanted to take away the pain that had momentarily whispered in her eyes.

Crazy, he thought as he left the kitchen by the back door.

He waved to the kids who were taking turns on the swing, then headed around to the front and began to pull down the last of the old porch. As he worked, his mind raced with thoughts of Abby.

Had her marriage been a miserable one? Was it possible her husband had lied to her, broken promises…and even worse?

Once again he thought of Jason asking him if his daddy was mean. Why would a six-year-old ask such a question unless he knew something about mean daddies?

Luke had a feeling what Abigail Graham needed more than anything in her life was some good, old-fashioned fun. She obviously had a good sense of humor. That had been evident as she'd teased him.

But how much fun could her life have been for the past year having the responsibility for raising two kids alone? And how much fun had her life contained prior to her husband's death?

He worked until dinnertime and managed to get the last of the old porch down. He'd just finished loading his tools in the back of the truck when Abby came around the side of the house.

"I was just going to come in to find you," he said. "I've got to get over to the family ranch and put in a few hours, but I'd like to come back later this evening and set the posts. That way they can set up overnight and will be ready by morning."

"That's fine with me, but I thought you worked at the Honky Tonk in the evenings."

"It's closed on Monday nights," he explained. He looked at his watch. "It's almost five now. I'll be back here about eight, if that's okay."

"Sure, that's fine with me," she agreed.

"Okay, then I'll see you about eight." He started to get in his truck, but paused. "Oh…and Abby, I've figured out what you need in your life."

"Oh, really?" She arched one of her perfect brows. "And what might that be?"

He grinned. "I'll tell you later." He slid behind the steering wheel and waved at her, then pulled away from the house.

Within minutes he was at the ranch and spent the next couple of hours repairing a fence that was threatening to topple down.

When he'd finished, he went to the main house, to the bedroom that had been his as a child. Much of his clothing and personal belongings were still here.

When he'd moved into the Honky Tonk, he'd taken very little with him, knowing it wasn't a good idea to store anything of value in the tiny room. The ranch was close enough for him to obtain anything he might need in a short period of time.

He showered, then changed into clean clothes, his mind whirling with memories that being in this room always evoked.

When he'd been growing up, this room had served as both a retreat and a prison cell. There had been times when his father had sent him to this room, and other times when he'd run here to escape his father's rage.

He left the room and the memories behind, heading for the kitchen and a chance to grab something to eat before he returned to Abby's place.

He'd just sat down at the kitchen table with a ham sandwich when his brother Matthew walked in. "I thought I heard somebody down here," he said.

"I stopped by to shower and change clothes."

"And raid my refrigerator," Matthew added drily.

"That, too," Luke agreed affably. "Things seem quiet around here. In a couple more weeks things will really be quiet."

"I've already started a list of things that need to be repaired in the guest cabins," Matthew said as he leaned his back against the refrigerator. He rubbed the center of his forehead with two fingers.

"Rough day?" Luke asked.

"Rough week," Matthew said as he dropped his hand. "We've got a family in cabin four who is driving everyone crazy. I'm tired of dealing with everything. I'm really looking forward to a little downtime."

Luke looked at his oldest brother in surprise. Matthew was always efficient, in control and on top of things. Of the four, Matthew had been the one who had pushed the hardest for them to fulfill their father's will stipulations so they wouldn't lose the ranch. The idea that Matthew's eagerness to hold on to the family ranch might be waning was disconcerting.

They had to hold on to things for another few months…until the terms of the will had been met. After that, it didn't matter.

"I'm heading upstairs. Lock up when you leave," Matthew said.

Luke nodded and watched as his brother disappeared out the door. Luke finished his sandwich, then placed his dish in the dishwasher and checked his watch. Quarter to eight. Time for him to get to Abby's.

As he drove to her house, he told himself Matthew had just had a rough day. There was no way Matthew would encourage them to forget their father's will and the family ranch. Matthew was the son most like his father, and like Adam Delaney, Matthew believed the ranch was the most important thing on the face of the earth.

He pulled into Abby's place and shoved aside thoughts of his brother. Although Luke could definitely use the money that would come from the ranch if they retained control, he really didn't care if they defaulted and lost it.

He'd just raised his hand to knock on Abby's back door when it swung open. As always, at the sight of her, an electric charge shot through him. "I'm back."

"So, you are and right on time," she said.

"I just figured I'd tell you I was here so you wouldn't be frightened when you hear somebody out front. Could you turn on the front porch light for me? Then I'll just get to work," he said and started to turn away.

"Oh, no, you don't," she said, stopping him in his tracks. "What is it you've figured out I need in my life?"

He grinned. "I'm not ready to tell you yet. Maybe after I finish setting the posts."

"I'm going to hold you to it," she exclaimed.

He grinned, then turned and left. By the time he reached the front of the house the front light was shining on the space where there was now no porch.

He'd dug the holes for the posts earlier in the day, and it didn't take him too long to mix the concrete, then set the posts into the holes. In the arid heat of the night, they would set up quickly, and by morning he should be able to start constructing the new porch.

He'd finished setting the last post then walked to the back door, surprised to find Abby seated on the stoop and gazing at the stars.

"Stargazing?" He sat next to her on the stoop and instantly caught a whiff of her evocative perfume.

"Yes. I can't seem to get enough of the stars out here. They all look so much closer, so much bigger and brighter."

"That's because they are tools the cowboys use."

She eyed him ruefully. "Let me guess. Cowboys use the stars to seduce young women."

He laughed. "You brought it up this time, I didn't. I was going to say that the cowboys used to use the stars for direction."

"I'm impressed," she said with a teasing tone. "You can talk about things other than charming women."

He smiled. "Where are the munchkins?"

"In bed. I tucked them in about an hour ago. Apparently the first day of school was rather exhausting. Neither of them gave me a bedtime argument."

"I wouldn't give you a bedtime argument, either," he said, unable to help himself.

"You're terrible," she replied, and he knew the color of her cheeks had deepened to a bewitching pink.

"That's not true," he countered. "I've been told I'm very good."

She laughed and shook her head, causing her hair to dance like a silken waterfall around her slender shoulders. Luke liked the sound of her laughter and guessed that she probably hadn't had much laughter in her life the past year.

"Okay, I said I'd tell you what I think you need in your life," he said.

"And what might that be?" she asked cautiously.

"Just some good, old-fashioned fun."

Her gaze held his for a long moment, and in the depths of her beautiful, soft green eyes he saw he had touched a vulnerable area.

He fought the impulse to throw his arm over her shoulder, pull her tight against his side. He was afraid he might spook her by moving too fast.

"I get the feeling that there hasn't been much fun in your life for the past year," he finally said.

"That's true," she agreed softly, her eyes holding a wistful yearning.

"You should come down to the Honky Tonk some night," he said.

"To watch you perform?" she asked.

"Nah. You need to come in and kick up your heels, do a little boot-scoot boogie."

She laughed. "I don't know how to do a boot-scoot boogie. In fact, I can't remember the last time I danced."

"You're kidding. Your husband didn't take you out dancing?"

She broke eye contact with him and once again gazed at the star-studded skies. "No, he never took me dancing."

Luke stared at her in amazement. If he had a wife who looked like her, he'd take her dancing every chance he got just for the opportunity of holding her close and swaying in rhythm to whatever music played. Her husband must have been a fool.

Luke wasn't a fool. Before he could stop himself, he stood, grabbed her hand and pulled her off the stoop and into his arms in a traditional dance position. "Ever danced with a cowboy carpenter beneath a starlit sky?"

"Never," she replied, her voice slightly husky.

"Then you're about to experience one of life's little joys." And with these words, he whirled her around, tightening his grip on her waist as they spun.

She held herself rigid and unyielding for a few moments, but when he didn't try to pull her tightly against him, he felt her relaxing by degrees.

As he hummed a familiar ballad, she continued to become more fluid, stepping and swaying with him as a night breeze danced in her hair and the moonlight kissed her features. And as he felt the rigidity leaving her, he pulled her closer... closer...and closer still.

Finally she was where he wanted her, so close her thighs pressed against his and her breasts snuggled against his chest. Her warm breath fanned his collarbone, producing a heat inside him that had nothing to do with the warmth of the night air that surrounded them.

Suddenly they weren't dancing anymore. They stood in the embrace, and when she turned her face to look at him, the tune he'd been humming died on his lips.

Just a whisper of invitation lit her eyes as her mouth parted slightly. It was all the invitation Luke needed. He captured her mouth with his, stealing a kiss that was freely given.

Her instantaneous response surprised and enflamed him. He'd intended for the kiss to be a light, sweet gesture, but her mouth was too hot, too hungry, and stirred a wild hunger inside him.

He dipped his tongue into her mouth, at the same time pressing his hand into the small of her back. Her tongue met his, deepening the kiss to explosive heights.

She moaned deep in the back of her throat and lifted her arms, wrapping them around his neck as their bodies pressed more tightly against each other.

A scream shattered the moment, a scream of such childish terror, it raised the hairs on the nape of Luke's neck. "What the hell?" he exclaimed as a new source of adrenaline shot through him.

Abby whirled out of his arms and raced up the steps to the back door. "It's Jason," she said and disappeared into the house.

The scream came again, high-pitched and frantic. Luke hurried into the house and down the hallway to the little boy's room.

He stepped into the doorway to see Abby trying to control a flailing, fighting Jason. It was obvious the little boy was still asleep, but that didn't stop his churning arms and legs. As Luke stood hesitantly, he saw one of Jason's elbows crash into Abby's chin. He took a step forward, intent on helping her, but she stopped him.

"Please...just go," she said, her eyes begging him to comply. Still he hesitated, wanting to help. "For God's sake, Luke. Leave," she said more forcefully. "We'll talk tomorrow."

As she focused her attention on the flailing child, Luke hesitated another moment, then complied with her wishes. He left the bedroom and went down the hallway toward the door. The childish screams had stopped, but he could hear Jason sobbing. They were deep, rending sobs that tore at Luke. And beneath the sobs he could hear Abby's soft, soothing voice.

Luke stepped onto the back stoop and drew a deep, unsteady breath, allowing the momentary burst of adrenaline to slide away. The transformation from desire to panic had been abrupt, and the result was confusion.

He suspected he knew the source of Abby's black eye and the bruise on her arm. In trying to soothe Jason, she apparently became a battle-scarred warrior.

He got into his truck, his thoughts whirling. It was obvious Jason had been suffering a horrendous nightmare. What could a little boy possibly dream about that would cause such obvious terror?

A little boy who had nightmares, a little girl who didn't talk and a woman whose kiss had shot wildfire through his veins. Luke had a feeling if he didn't take care, he'd be in way over his head with this woman and her children.

Chapter 6

Sleep was a long time coming for Abby after she finally got Jason settled into a peaceful sleep. She undressed and got ready for bed, but her thoughts whirled chaotically.

She'd hoped that in settling here, in building a home and establishing some semblance of normalcy, Jason's nightmares would finally stop.

She knew they'd only been here a little over a week, and she was probably expecting way too much, way too soon. But she couldn't help the deep depression the little boy's latest nightmare had instilled in her.

How long would he suffer the remnants of that night? Somehow she had to figure out a way to heal the two children who had been left in her care by the sister she'd loved and lost.

Sliding between the sheets, she knew she needed to seek professional help for the kids. They had been seeing a therapist before they'd left Kansas City, and on their last visit, the therapist had told Abby she thought a physical move from the city would do as much to heal the kids as anything.

But Jessica was still not talking, and Jason was still having horrendous nightmares. No healing appeared to be taking place.

She had a feeling finding a good therapist who specialized in traumatized children would be impossible in the small town of Inferno. She'd need to go to Tucson or another big city to find them help.

Too tired to think about it anymore, she closed her eyes, and instantly a vision of Luke filled her mind. Luke, with the moonlight stroking his bold, handsome features. Luke, his lips curved in a smile as he hummed and twirled her around in his arms.

For one sweet moment, the cares of the world had fallen from her shoulders and she'd felt young and desirable and carefree. And then there was the kiss. The kiss.

She pushed the sheet aside. Heat swirled through her as she remembered the hunger, the fire, the utter desire that she'd not only tasted in his kiss, but had felt inside herself as she'd responded to him.

Abby was no virgin—she'd been engaged to be married before the crime that had destroyed her world. But none of Ken's kisses, none of his caresses had ever stirred her like Luke's kiss had done.

When he'd stood in Jason's doorway and seen her struggling with the frantic little boy, she'd seen his desire to help in his eyes, and that had been nearly as powerful as his kiss in managing to creep in beneath her defenses.

She closed her eyes, too tired to think about any of it tonight. Tomorrow she would get on the phone and try to find a therapist for the kids. Tomorrow she would figure out exactly how much she was going to tell Luke about Jason's nightmares. She was going to have to decide if it was safe to divulge any of her secrets to Luke Delaney.

Morning brought few answers. She had just put the kids on the school bus when Luke's familiar pickup approached.

She stood in the front yard as he pulled up and got out of the truck, looking as handsome, as strong and masculine as she'd ever seen him. "Hi," she greeted him as he strode toward her.

"Hi, yourself," he returned easily. "You look tired."

"I am," she admitted. "It was kind of a long night."

He stepped next to her, the gray of his eyes soft and his smile gentle. "I wanted to help but didn't know how." He threw an arm around her shoulder. "You got the coffee on?"

She nodded, fighting the impulse to lean into him, to spill the events that had shaped her life for the past year, to share the pain that radiated inside her and she feared would always exist inside her.

Together they went into the house and to the kitchen, where Luke gestured her into a chair at the table while he took it upon himself to pour them some coffee.

"I guess I owe you some sort of an explanation," she said when he was seated at the table next to her.

"You don't owe me anything," he countered with the same gentleness of tone, the gentleness that reached inside her and stroked a tiny piece of her pain. "It's obvious from what I saw last night that your son suffers terrible nightmares or night terrors."

"He's not my son." Horror swept through her as she realized she'd spoken the words aloud.

Luke's eyes widened. "Excuse me? But they call you Mom and you introduced them as your kids."

Abby wrapped her hands around her coffee cup, recognizing that this was the moment she had to decide if she could trust Luke or not. She quickly decided she would trust him with some of the truth. "Jason isn't my son, and Jessica isn't my daughter. They are my nephew and niece."

"Your sister's kids?"

Abby nodded. "I took custody of them when their mother was murdered."

Again Luke's eyes widened. "Murdered?"

Emotion rose inside Abby, a wave she felt helpless to fight against. She nodded again, then took a sip of coffee in an attempt to steady herself. "In order for you to understand, I guess I need to start at the beginning." She frowned, wondering if she knew what had been the beginning.

"My sister, Loretta, was married to a man named Justin Cahill. Neither my parents nor I particularly liked Justin. He was a braggart and never held down a job. He was verbally abusive to her and the kids. But Loretta seemed to love him so we all tried our best to make him part of our family."

She drew a deep breath and stared into her coffee mug. "A month before her murder, I realized Justin was being more than verbally abusive to her, and I convinced her the best thing to do was divorce him. I helped her find a little apartment, and she and the kids moved into it. Three weeks later Justin came to the apartment and beat her to death. Jessica and Jason were in the apartment when it happened."

"Oh, God, I'm so sorry." His hand instantly sought hers in a warm grip of comfort. "And that's why Jason has nightmares." It was more a statement than a question.

"Actually, what he's doing is replaying that night in his dreams. And, according to the therapist Jason was seeing before we moved, in his sleep he tries to fight with his father to save his mother's life."

"That poor kid," Luke said, and she heard the wealth of sympathy in his voice as his hand tightened around hers. "Jessica stopped talking at the same time?"

"Yes. That night the police removed the kids from the apartment and brought them to me. Jessica told me about how her daddy had hurt her mommy, and that's the last time Jessica said anything to anyone except Jason."

She cleared her throat. "Anyway, so now you know the explanation for Jason's nightmares." But there was a wealth of information she hadn't given him, like the small fact that she didn't have legal authority to have the children in her custody and that they were on the run from Justin...and possibly the law.

"So why the story of you being a widow? Are you or were you married?"

"No." Abby pulled her hand from his and once again wrapped both hands around her coffee mug. "I'm not, nor have I ever been married. I made up that story so we wouldn't have to explain to people what had happened. I thought it would make things easier on the children. It was Jason's idea to call me Mom. He said I would be his mom on earth, but we always talk about their mother in heaven." Her voice cracked on the last sentence, and she drew a deep breath to steady herself.

He nodded, his eyes curiously opaque. "That it makes things easier on the children is the best reason to tell a lie. What about their father? Where is he?"

"Nobody knows. Apparently he's disappeared off the face of the earth, and that's just fine with me." But Abby knew Justin was looking for them, hunting them down like prey. And she hoped he never, ever found them.

"When you told me you'd had a rough year, you weren't kidding. How are you holding up beneath all this?"

She looked away from him, unable to see the compassion in his eyes and not fall apart. "My sister was my best friend. It was me who encouraged her to leave Justin in the first place." She fought against a wave of killing guilt. "But I'm all right. I'm strong."

She drew a breath and squared her shoulders. "I have to be for the kids. They're the ones I worry about. They have to live not only with the memory of that terrible night, but also with the knowledge that their father is a bad man."

Luke leaned back in his chair. "Kids are fairly resilient, and I'm a perfect example that kids can grow up and eventually deal with the fact that their father is a bad man."

"But your father didn't kill your mother," she replied.

"That's true," he agreed easily. "But there were times I thought sure he was going to kill one of my brothers, or my sister, or me."

"He was really that mean?" she asked even though she could tell by his somber expression and the heavy tone of voice that he wasn't exaggerating.

"I thought he was the devil."

"How did you survive?"

He shrugged. "We just did." This time it was his turn to take a sip of his coffee before continuing. "Actually, the four of us all had our own way of coping with Father. Matthew was the good son who never broke the rules and worked from sunup to sundown with the single goal of pleasing the old man. Mark became invisible, never talking, trying to blend into the woodwork so he wouldn't do anything to upset the old man."

He took another sip of his coffee and grinned. "Johnna, on the other hand, did just the opposite. She met my father with rebellion and rage and kept him stirred up most of the time."

"And what about you?" Abby asked.

"Me? I learned how to sing. It was the one thing I did that pleased the old man. My dad used to play Jim Reeves all the time when we were growing up. By the age of six I knew all the words to all the songs. One day my dad heard me singing in my room, and he called me down to his study and demanded I sing for him."

He drew a deep breath, and Abby saw the pain of memories cross his features. She reached for his hand, as he had done to her earlier. His hand was cool, as if the force of these memories had stolen all his body heat.

"I went down to the study, knowing that if he didn't like my singing he'd smack me or take off his belt and whack me. I was so scared that while I sang for him, I wet my pants."

"Oh, Luke." All thoughts of Abby's problems and worries fell aside as she grieved for the little boy who had sung for a monster and been so afraid he'd wet his pants.

Emotion swam in the air, inside her, a depth of emotion for him and for the children she now claimed as her own.

She released his hand only long enough to leave her chair, and as she stood, he did, as well. Together they met in an embrace. His arms wrapped around her, and she allowed herself to accept the comfort, the warmth and the strength she found there.

Leaning her head against his broad chest, she could hear the pounding of his heart. "Your kids will be okay, Abby," he said softly. "They're lucky to have you. With your love and support they're going to be just fine."

She'd hungered to hear those words from anyone, and for a moment her fears about the kids were soothed. She lifted her head from his chest and looked at him. She'd meant to thank him, to say how much his words meant to her, but the moment she saw the fire in his eyes, anything she might have meant to say left her mind.

His lips crashed down on hers and instantly Abby knew she was going to make love with him. Not tomorrow. Not next week. Today, at this moment, while they had the house to themselves and their depth of emotion had been transformed into lust.

She wanted to be held, heartbeat to heartbeat, skin against

skin. She needed to lose herself in the flames that lit his eyes and scorched her lips as his kiss sent electric currents racing through her.

Luke didn't have to be the right man in her life to be the right man at this moment. She gave herself to him, pressing against him with need, meeting his tongue with her own, stoking the flames of desire between them until they were totally out of control.

Making love to Abby had been the last thing in Luke's mind when he'd reached out to her. He'd been shocked by the information she'd shared with him, and equally shocked by how candid he'd been with her about his past with his father.

But holding her, feeling her soft curves against him as her sweet scent filled his head, desire had unexpectedly awakened.

When her lips met his with the same intense fever coupled with a yielding surrender, he was lost…lost despite the fact he knew they were moving too quickly and on the wave of heightened emotions.

He finally pulled his mouth from hers. He stared at her, and in her eyes he saw a hunger that matched his own. "Abby." He knew one of them needed to take control of the situation before it spun crazily out of control.

"Shh." She pressed two fingers to his lips then took his hand in hers and led him out of the kitchen. "Don't stop this, Luke. It's what you want, and for right now it's what I want."

As she pulled him down the hallway toward her bedroom, Luke's heart boomed rapidly. He'd wanted her from the first minute he'd laid eyes on her, and that desire had grown with each and every moment he'd spent in her company.

The morning sunlight streamed into her bedroom window, and he noticed that her room had been transformed since the last time he'd peeked into it. The bed was neatly made with a bedspread that was a splash of yellow sunflowers.

Where before there had been a stack of boxes in the corner, there were now only two waiting to be unpacked.

He scarcely had time to take all this in before his attention returned to Abby, who stood next to the bed. As he watched her, she pulled her T-shirt over her head.

His breath caught in his chest at the sight of her. Clad in her jeans and a wispy, pale pink bra, she appeared fragile and more vulnerable than before. But the glow in her eyes as she unfastened her jeans and slid them down her slender legs was anything but vulnerable.

He drank in the sight of her in the few seconds he had before she pulled down the spread and disappeared beneath the sheets on the bed.

"Do you always keep your women waiting?"

Her husky voice broke his inertia, and he ripped his T-shirt over his head and threw it on the floor. He felt as if his fingers had all turned to thumbs as he worked the buttons on his fly. Before he allowed his jeans to fall on the floor, he took out his wallet, opened it and withdrew a foil package.

When he was naked, he hesitated at the edge of the bed. He knew they had stirred up powerful emotions as they'd talked of their pasts, and he wanted to give her a chance to change her mind, didn't want to in any way be accused of taking advantage of her vulnerability.

"Luke, I promise, no recriminations, no expectations."

Her words removed the last barrier between Luke and his desire for her. He placed the foil package on the nightstand, then slid beneath the sheets and reached out to her.

She came willingly to meet him, her body pressing against his as their lips sought each other in frenzied need. Luke had thought he'd spent the last week quietly seducing her, but he realized she'd been doing some seducing of her own. She'd stoked in him a fire of desire he'd never felt before.

When he finally broke the kiss, he moved his lips down her jawline into the hollow of her throat. She wrapped her arms around his neck, pulling him more tightly against her.

His hands crept up to cup her breasts. Despite the silky material of her bra, he could feel her taut nipples beneath his fingertips. He raked his thumb across the tips and reveled at the sweet moan that escaped her.

It took only moments for him to grow frustrated by the material that kept their bodies separate. With a groan, he reached behind her and unfastened her bra, then swept his hands downward to steal away her panties.

She aided him in his efforts, shrugging the bra from her shoulders and raising her hips, then kicking off the lacy panties.

He knew he wouldn't be able to last too long, that the moment he entered her all control would be lost. And before that happened, he wanted to make love to her, to taste her sweet skin, to touch her in ways that made her wild with wanting him.

And that's exactly what he did. With the golden shine of sunlight slanting into the window, he threw back the sheets and made love to her.

He loved the scent of her, the taste of her skin and the way she responded to each touch, every caress. She was an active lover, matching him touch for touch, kiss for kiss, caress for caress.

Although he would have loved to make love to her throughout the morning hours, all too quickly he felt himself reaching the point of no return.

"Luke," she said, her voice taut with need. "Please...I want you."

That's all he needed to hear. He picked up the foil package, surprised when she took it from him. Her eyes glittered with anticipation as she tore open the foil and removed the protective sheath.

Her fingers were hot and radiated urgency as she rolled the condom onto his throbbing member. Immediately, he got on top of her and she parted her legs to welcome him. With one smooth motion he entered her, sliding into her tight warmth as a groan of intense pleasure escaped him.

Her fingers dug into his back as he remained motionless, overwhelmed by sensation and momentarily afraid to move. He drew several deep breaths, fighting for control, then slowly, almost imperceptibly began to move his hips against hers in the age-old rhythm of need.

He meant it to be slow and easy, building to a shattering conclusion. But it was impossible to go slow and easy. The sensations that rippled through him demanded faster…frenzied. And Abby demanded it, as well, setting the pace with hip thrusts that took him higher and higher.

It wasn't until she stiffened and cried out in splendor that he allowed himself the final release. Wave after wave of pleasure swept over him until he was gasping and spent.

He rolled to her side, pulled her against him and waited for their breathing to return to normal. She curled against him, and he was vaguely aware of how well their bodies fit together. With her head on his shoulder, they fit together like puzzle pieces.

He stroked a hand through her hair, marveling that it was, indeed, just as soft and silky as he'd imagined. "You okay?" he asked softly.

"At the moment, I'm better than okay. I feel simply marvelous."

"That's because I'm a marvelous lover," he teased. "Hadn't I mentioned that before?"

She laughed. "I believe you might have mentioned it

before. I guess I can tell Stephanie that your legendary charm overwhelmed me," she said lightly.

He grinned. "I think I was the one that was overwhelmed by your considerable charm. Besides, one single occurrence does not a success make," he countered.

For a long moment they remained quiet, neither seemingly eager to break their embrace. "I'm sorry about your father being so mean," she finally said.

He leaned on one elbow and looked at her. The sunlight painted her face in golden tones, making her eyes appear a striking green. "And I'm sorry about your sister." He gazed at her curiously. "What about your parents? Were they good ones?"

Her lips curved into a smile that shot a new wave of desire through him. "They were the best. They were kind and loving and wonderfully supportive." A tiny frown creased the center of her forehead. "What about your mother? You've never mentioned her."

"She died giving birth to Johnna. I was only a year old at the time, so I never really knew her."

She reached up and placed her palm against his cheek. "I wish you would have had the kind of parents I had."

"Are they still around?"

A dark shadow stole the sparkle of her eyes. "No. They died four years ago in a car accident. I'm just grateful they weren't around to know about Loretta. I think her death would have killed them." The shadow disappeared. "And now we'd better get out of this bed."

In one fluid movement, she left his arms and rolled out of bed. He sat up and watched as she grabbed her bra and panties then disappeared into the adjoining bathroom.

He remained in the bed as he heard the sound of a shower starting, deciding that when she finished, he'd jump in for a quick cleanup.

His body still retained her fragrance, a scent that would be distracting as he worked the remainder of the afternoon. Even now, as he breathed deeply, he felt a renewed stir of desire for her.

He frowned, not particularly pleased to find himself wanting her again so quickly, so strongly. It also bothered him that he had confided so much of his past to her. He'd never, ever told anyone about singing for his father and wetting his pants. Why on earth had he told her of that particular little embarrassing incident?

He was still ruminating over this when she entered the bedroom clad in a bathrobe. "Abby…about what just happened…" he began, feeling the need to somehow insert a little distance between them.

She held up her hand to silence him. "I told you, Luke. No recriminations and no expectations. What happened, happened. It's over, it's done."

She sat on the edge of the bed and gazed at him somberly. "When Loretta was murdered, I was engaged to a man who professed to love children and value family above all else. When he realized I was taking on two scarred, frightened children, I expected him to be by my side, but he ran for the hills. When my sister left her husband, I thought that finally she was going to get a chance to live a happy, normal life, but I was wrong."

She got up from the edge of the bed and grabbed her jeans and her T-shirt. "I've learned the hard way to expect nothing from life or from people. I take it one day at a time." She offered him a strained smile. "Don't worry, Luke. As far as I'm concerned, we can forget this happened at all. The bathroom is all yours. I'll finish dressing in one of the kids' rooms." With these words she left the bedroom.

Luke stared after her, oddly disturbed by her words, and bothered that her words had disturbed him.

Chapter 7

Abby was almost grateful the next morning when Luke called her and said he wouldn't be able to work at her place that day.

She needed the day without his magnetic presence to get the ground firmly beneath her feet and deal with the embarrassment the events of the day before had created in her.

She had probably been the easiest seduction the man had ever successfully completed. She'd practically thrown herself at him, insisting that he make love to her. Her cheeks burned at the memory of how forward she'd been and how glorious being in his arms had felt.

She'd known from the moment she'd met Luke, when he'd teased her with those sooty eyes of his, that he would be a magnificent lover, and she hadn't been wrong.

He'd been gentle yet masterful, sweeping her into the heights of delight with hungry kisses and hot caresses. When his dark eyes had gazed at her, he'd made her feel more beautiful and more desirable than anyone had ever made her feel.

With utter mastery and confidence, he'd known just where to touch, just how to kiss to produce a fiery hunger for him inside her.

She spent the entire day trying to forget the power of his kisses, the warm comfort of his arms, the utter splendor of his naked body against hers.

He called the next morning and told her once again that he had other business that wouldn't allow him to get to her place that day. She wondered if perhaps he was trying to avoid her, and that only increased her embarrassment over the intimacy that had occurred between them.

It was early Thursday morning, and she was standing at the edge of the road with the children waiting for the school bus, when she saw Luke's familiar black pickup heading in their direction.

She couldn't help the small lurch of her heart as he parked the truck and stepped out. He was so darned sexy in his tight, worn jeans and the white T-shirt that pulled provocatively across the width of his chest.

His thick, dark hair gleamed in the sun and despite herself her gaze swept across his chest to his bulging biceps, and she remembered how good it had felt to lay in his strong arms.

He waved but didn't approach. Instead he walked to the back of the truck and unloaded several pieces of lumber.

"What's he doing now?" Jason asked, his dark eyes focused on Luke.

"He's going to finish building us a nice, new porch," Abby explained.

Jason eyed her somberly, a tiny frown on his forehead. "When I'm in school, is he nice to you?"

Abby saw the worry in his eyes and leaned down to draw

his little body closer to hers. "He's very nice." Jessica stepped closer, as if she, too, momentarily needed the warmth of Abby's arms around her.

"There are good men and there are bad men," she said to them. "Luke is a good man. He's making our house nice, and he's nice to me. He makes me smile."

"If he's mean to you, I'll kick him," Jason exclaimed with a burst of little-boy bravado.

"You know that kicking somebody is unacceptable," Abby chided softly. "Besides, Luke would never do anything to hurt me. He's a nice man."

At that moment the school bus lumbered into view. She gave each child a hug. "Now, you have a great day at school and I'll see you later this afternoon. We're safe here, and nobody is going to hurt me or either of you."

She saw them safely on the bus, then as the big yellow vehicle pulled away, she waved to them until they were out of sight.

Jason's concern for her safety was not surprising, but it was heartbreaking nevertheless. A six-year-old boy should never have to worry about the physical safety of an adult.

Surely they were all safe. It had been two months since the debacle of a trial, two months in which she'd heard no word from Justin Cahill, the man who'd murdered her sister and who was the father of the children.

As she turned to walk toward the house, she steeled herself for interacting with the man she'd made love to three days before.

"Morning," he said as he opened his toolbox and began to lay out what he'd need to begin work. "I see you got the munchkins off okay."

She nodded, aware of the uncomfortable tension that thickened the air between them. "Can I get you anything before you get started? A cup of coffee or something?"

"No, I'm fine," he replied briskly. "This is going to take a lot of work so I'd better get right to it."

She hadn't realized how much she'd enjoyed his easy company or his lighthearted banter until now with its conspicuous absence. "Okay, just let me know if you need anything," she replied then went into the house.

It's better this way, she told herself as she went into Jason's room to begin the morning task of making beds. A business relationship was all she'd ever wanted from Luke Delaney to begin with, and things had just careened out of control the afternoon they'd made love.

It was obvious from his distance that he was done with her, had accomplished his mission, and that was fine with her. He'd given her an afternoon of sweet warmth, of intense pleasure, and all she expected from him now was carpentry work.

She spent the morning on chores, making beds and picking up clutter the children had left around the house. She consciously tried to stay away from the front of the house where she could hear the sounds of a man at work. She fought the desire to stand at the front window and watch him work, to hide behind the curtains and drink her fill of him.

However, at noon, with her stomach growling for lunch, she left the house by the back door and walked around front to see if Luke wanted to join her for lunch.

He was nowhere in sight, and his truck was gone. Apparently he wasn't interested in eating lunch with her. She fixed herself a sandwich, knowing he'd be back.

She ate the sandwich then decided to unpack the last two boxes that were in her bedroom. She'd put off unpacking them because she knew the boxes contained mostly items that had belonged to Loretta.

A half an hour later she sat on the floor of her bedroom, surrounded by an array of items that held no real monetary value but things she'd thought the children might want someday.

Each item Abby pulled out brought with it a pang of grief and yet a wealth of happy memories. There were several photographs of Abby and Loretta together as children and a couple of them as teenagers. There was a book Loretta had loved to read aloud to the younger Abby. Knickknacks, a stuffed bunny missing its nose—the box was filled with treasures. There was even a guitar with broken strings.

"Abby?"

She jumped at the sound of Luke's deep voice and looked up to see him standing hesitantly in the bedroom doorway. "Sorry, I knocked but apparently you didn't hear me." He stepped into the room, curiosity lighting his eyes. "Hey, where did you get the guitar?" He stepped closer as she held it out to him.

"It was my sister's," she explained as he took it from her and examined it. "Loretta was always looking for ways to expand her horizons, better herself and her education." She gestured to a stack of CDs nearby. "She learned French in ten easy sessions, painted an oil painting with DVD instructions. At one time or another she took guitar lessons, ballet classes and played the drums."

"Sounds like a fun person," Luke said softly.

Abby offered him a full smile. "She was the best. She had a lust for living that was enviable. I thought maybe Jason or Jessica might decide to play the guitar so I packed it along with this other stuff to bring with us."

"They won't be able to play it without strings." He handed the guitar to her, the expression in his eyes inscrutable. "George Marley at the general store always orders strings for me. I could pick some up and string it for you."

"Thanks, I'd appreciate it." She got up off the floor, suddenly far too aware of the two of them alone in her bedroom, the place of their recent indiscretion. "Were you looking for me for something?" she asked, then felt the heat of a blush sweep over her cheeks as his gaze flickered to the bed, then quickly back to her.

"I could use your help outside for a few minutes. I need another hand, that is if you don't mind helping."

"Not at all." She hated the stiff formality between them, the uncomfortable tension that filled the air, but was too embarrassed to broach the subject in order to break the ice.

She followed him outside, and with him showing her what to do, helped by balancing two two-by-eights in place so he could nail the support beams.

"Sorry I couldn't make it the last couple of days," he said as he grabbed a hammer. He hammered in a nail. "We had a fence go completely down at the ranch, and it required immediate attention."

"You don't have to apologize," she replied. "Besides, it really worked out well because yesterday I kept the kids out of school and drove into Tucson for a counseling appointment."

"How did it go?"

She shot him a quick smile. "I don't know how much help one session offered the kids, but it certainly helped me just knowing we've started getting them some help."

He hammered in another nail, then looked at her. "I told you before, they're lucky to have you on their side."

"It's the least I can do for Loretta. She and I were so close, and she was my strength when our parents died. I'm just giving back to her kids all the love she gave to me when she was alive."

He nodded and worked for a few minutes in silence, a frown creasing his forehead. She could smell him, the scent that had by now become familiar. It was the scent of maleness and bright sunshine and a faint wisp of woodsy cologne.

Instantly it brought to mind the sensual pleasure of their morning spent in her bed. Not only had his fragrance wrapped around her, but his body had, as well, warming her from the outside in.

"Do the kids like to ride?"

"Ride?" She stared at him blankly as she consciously worked to dispel the images of making love to him.

"Horses?"

"I don't think either of them have ever been on a horse," Abby replied.

"What about you? You like to ride?" For the first time since he'd arrived, she was grateful to feel the tension between them ebbing somewhat.

"I used to love to ride, but I haven't since I was a kid."

"If you want, I could set it up so you and the kids could take a trail ride over at the ranch some time. I've never met a kid who didn't want to ride a horse."

"Thanks." She smiled at him warmly. "That would really be nice."

"It's no big deal. We've got plenty of horses that are real sweet-tempered for kids." He hammered another nail. "Okay, you can let go. I can handle it from here."

She nodded and turned to hurry into the house, away from him. She knew that making love to him three days earlier had been a mistake. What she couldn't understand was why on earth she was thinking of how nice it would be to repeat the error of her ways.

The moment Luke had seen Abby's smile, he'd wondered why he had stayed away from her for the past couple of days.

When he'd left after making love to her, he'd felt off balance, out of sorts. Although she had said all the words about no expectations he'd wanted to hear after he'd made love to her, something had bothered him.

He'd figured it out that evening as he'd nursed a soft drink at the Honky Tonk. It wasn't the lovemaking that had bothered him. That had been magnificent. It had been the emotional intimacy they'd shared just prior to falling into bed that had disturbed him.

Never before had he given quite so much of himself to a woman. Telling her about the first time he'd sung for his father, sharing with her the enormous emotional turmoil the incident had created, had shocked him and left him feeling oddly vulnerable.

Luke didn't like feeling vulnerable. He'd been vulnerable as a kid and had vowed he'd never feel that way again.

And so he'd distanced himself, taking the last couple of days to find his balance once again. He'd put in his hours at the ranch for the week and had finished the rocking chair for Rita Sue Ellenbee to sell on consignment in her craft store. He had kept himself busy and tried to keep his mind off Abigail Graham.

He straightened and swiped a hand across his brow as the school bus pulled up and Jason and Jessica got off. Jessica raced directly into the house, but Jason walked over to Luke.

He peered into Luke's toolbox with interest. "What's that?" he asked, pointing to a blue-handled Sheetrock knife.

"It's for cutting Sheetrock," Luke explained.

Jason tilted his head to one side and moved closer to Luke, bringing with him that special scent of boyhood. It was the smell of sweaty hair and sunshine, an earthiness that wasn't unpleasant. "What's Sheetrock?" he asked.

Luke thought of what Abby had shared with him about the horror the kids had been through, and despite his reluctance, he felt a certain kinship with the little boy.

Luke hadn't had an Abby to take control and make things

right. He hadn't had an Abby to provide stability and love in his childhood. Admiration for the woman who had taken in the two kids fluttered through him.

"Sheetrock is the stuff that makes the walls in a house," he said to Jason.

"Why would you want to cut the walls?" Jason asked.

"Sometimes you get a hole in a wall accidentally and you use the knife to cut a new piece to fit into the hole," Luke said.

Jason eyed him soberly. "My mom says you're a good man, that you wouldn't ever hurt her."

Compassion swept through Luke. "I always try not to hurt anyone," he replied. He crouched so he was eye to eye with the boy. "And I promise you I'll never, ever hurt your mom."

Jason held his gaze for a long moment, then nodded as if satisfied. "But, if you ever do hurt her, I'm gonna kick you really hard."

"There you are," Abby said as she rounded the side of the house. "I was wondering where you disappeared to. Come on inside, honey. You don't need to be bothering Luke."

"He's not bothering me," Luke replied as he straightened. "We were just talking about tools and man kind of things."

Jason's little chest puffed out. "Yeah, man things," he agreed.

"Well, I just thought a certain little man might want some chocolate chip cookies and milk with his sister," Abby said. Jason frowned, obviously torn between the allure of cookies and the appeal of watching Luke work.

"I know if I had the chance to eat cookies, I'd jump on it," Luke said.

"You could come in and eat a cookie with us," Jason said.

Luke could tell that Abby was as surprised by the boy's invitation as he was. Until this afternoon, Jason had remained suspicious, downright wary of Luke.

Luke set down his hammer. "I suppose I could choke down

a cookie or two," he agreed. He was only agreeing because he could use a little break, he told himself. The sun was hotter than a firecracker, and a few minutes of coolness in the house would revive his flagging energy.

Minutes later the four of them sat at the kitchen table, milk in front of each and a platter of cookies in the center of the table.

"Robert Goodman has a pet lizard," Jason said. "He brung it to school today so we could all see it."

"He brought it to school," Abby corrected.

"That's what I said," Jason replied impatiently.

Luke grinned and listened as Jason extolled the virtues of owning such a creature. He tried not to notice how pretty Abby looked in a forest green T-shirt that did amazing things to her eyes.

He wanted her again. Sitting across from her at the table, seeing her laughing and interacting with the kids, the hint of a milk mustache above her upper lip, desire slammed into him. And just as suddenly, he couldn't remember why he thought he needed distance from her in the first place.

"I think we should get a pet lizard," Jason said, drawing Luke's attention to the conversation.

"Sorry, there is positively, absolutely no way I'm having a lizard in this house," Abby exclaimed. "Personally, I think they're a little creepy."

"Then how about a dog?" Jason replied and Luke could tell by the expression on the boy's face that this had been the ultimate goal to begin with.

"A dog?" Abby looked at Jason, then at Jessica, who nodded eagerly, her eyes shining with excitement.

"I think they're ganging up on you," Luke observed with a grin, then shoved back his chair. "And this sounds like a family kind of decision, so I'll just scoot outside and get back to work."

Luke left the house to the sound of Jason promising all

the things boys for an eternity had promised about taking care of a dog.

He'd wanted a dog when he'd been young, but he'd been afraid to get one, afraid that his father would hurt the pet to punish him.

He shoved the thought out of his mind and returned to the work at hand. It was dusk when he finished for the day and packed up his tools. The porch was slowly taking shape but would require at least two or three more full days to complete. Normally he hired a high school kid to help him on the bigger jobs like decks, but with school in session, Luke had decided to do this job alone.

Besides, if he'd had a high school kid working with him he wouldn't have had the opportunity to make love to Abby. If he had a high school kid working with him, he'd probably never get an opportunity to make love to her again.

With his tools packed away, he walked to the back of the house and knocked on the door.

She stepped onto the stoop, the fading sunlight kissing her features with a golden hue. "Knocking off for the day?"

He nodded and grinned. "But I couldn't leave without knowing who won the battle."

"The battle?" She looked at him, those green eyes of hers lit with curiosity.

Again he was struck by a swelling wave of desire for her as he remembered how her green eyes had shimmered beneath half-closed lids as he'd made love to her. He jammed his hands in his pockets to stymie his desire to grab her and pull her close, capture her kissable lips with his.

"The dog battle," he replied, trying to focus on the conversation and not on his pulsing, pounding, crazy need.

She smiled. "The verdict is still out where the dog is concerned."

"Dogs are good for kids," he replied. He could vividly re-member the taste of her lips…hot, sweet honey that had flowed through his veins as his mouth had possessed hers over and over again.

He took a step away from her, consciously willing his mind to stop its thoughts. "If you decide you want to get them a dog, let me know. There are a couple of breeders in the area, some that are reputable and some you should stay away from."

"Thanks, Luke. For everything." For a brief moment he saw in her eyes that she wasn't just talking about his carpentry work, that she, too, was remembering the morning they'd spent in one another's arms.

He nodded and took another step backward. "I'll see you in the morning." He turned to leave, then whirled to face her. "How about on Saturday I come and pick up you and the kids and we go into town. We could get those guitar strings and maybe have lunch at the diner and I could show you and the kids the joys and secrets of our little town."

The smile that lit her face nearly stole Luke's breath away. "That sounds nice," she agreed.

"Great, we can finalize the plans tomorrow or the next day when I'm here." He stepped off the porch.

"That sounds fine," she returned.

He nodded and waved, then hurried toward his truck, wondering what on earth had possessed him to issue such an invitation.

Chapter 8

It was a perfect day for an outing. Overnight a cool front had passed through, and the weathermen were forecasting a comfortable eighty degrees for the day's high temperature.

Abby tried not to dwell on the pleasure that swept through her as she discarded first one outfit, then another in an effort to dress for the trip into town. She couldn't help but look forward to spending the day in Luke's company.

She told herself it was because she had very little interaction with adults, that most of her days and nights were spent in the company of the children. It was only natural that she would be looking forward to a little adult conversation.

Looking at the clock and seeing it was a quarter to ten, she quickly decided to wear a pale pink sundress that she knew was both becoming and comfortable.

She checked her reflection in the bedroom dresser mirror, making sure her lipstick wasn't smudged and her hair was brushed, then left her room to make sure the kids were ready to go.

They sat in the living room on the sofa, wiggling and squirming with suppressed eagerness. Abby realized they were just as eager as she was for a trip into town. They had dressed themselves with care, and their faces were scrubbed shiny clean and their hair neatly brushed.

"You two look terrific," she exclaimed.

"You look pretty, too," Jason said, and Jessica nodded in agreement.

"Thank you, kind sir," she said and curtsied. "We'll be the best-looking family in Inferno today," she said, and the two kids giggled.

At that moment a knock fell on the front door, and Abby knew Luke had arrived. He'd finished the porch the day before, and the last thing he had done was open the front door so it was once again functioning. She opened the door to greet him, and her breath caught in her throat.

Always before, she'd seen him dressed for work, wearing worn jeans and faded T-shirts or jeans and no shirt. This morning he was again clad in a pair of tight jeans, but instead of his customary T-shirt, he was wearing a gray dress shirt. The sleeves were rolled up to expose his strong forearms, and the color of the shirt enhanced the black-lashed beauty of his eyes.

"Good morning," he said, his gaze sweeping over her with obvious approval. "Wow, you look terrific," he said, and the heat that flowed from his eyes caused a warmth to sweep into her cheeks.

"Thank you," she replied. "You look really nice, too."

He grinned. "When you go to town on a Saturday morning, it's good to clean up a bit. And I must say, Ms. Graham, you clean up damned fine."

Again heat suffused Abby's cheeks, and at that moment the kids pushed past her and flew out the door.

"Let's go!" Jason exclaimed. "We want to go shopping and eat lunch at the diner and see all the stores."

Luke laughed and gestured Abby out the door. "Looks like somebody is eager for a trip into town."

Abby locked the house, then stepped off the porch, following Luke and the kids, who were just ahead of her. "Where's your pickup?" she asked as she realized a blue van awaited them.

"At the ranch. We use this to transport guests, and I figured it was better to drive it than have the kids ride in the back of the pickup." His eyes twinkled with humor. "Of course, if anyone sees me driving this thing, it's going to totally destroy my image. A black, shiny pickup is a babe magnet. A blue minivan just isn't the same."

"I'll tell you what, if we see any babes along the way, you can duck down and I'll pretend like I'm driving."

Luke laughed.

Abby got into the front passenger seat while the kids got into the back. "Buckle up," she reminded them as Luke slid behind the wheel.

Within minutes they were on their way.

"Nice day," she said, fighting a wave of unaccountable shyness. She'd slept with this man, knew most all the parts of his body intimately and yet at the moment felt nervous and shy.

"Gorgeous," he agreed. "It's always nice when autumn brings cooler temperatures."

"I guess cooler is relative. Back home, autumn just meant the beginning of winter."

"That's one thing we don't have here," he replied. "The winter months are our best months at the ranch. We stay fully booked from November through February with people wanting to escape winter."

"It will sure be nice not to have to worry about shoveling snow or driving on icy roads." She settled back in the seat and tried to relax. "So, you mentioned the other day you're going to show us all the joys and secrets of Inferno. What kind of secrets are there?"

"Is there buried treasure?" Jason asked from the backseat.

Luke laughed, the deep rumble shooting pleasure through Abby. "Not that I know of, Jason. If I knew there was buried treasure somewhere in Inferno, I would have dug it up long ago."

Luke shot Abby a conspiratorial wink. "But I can show you real bullet holes in the side of the bank where a band of desperados tried to steal the bank's money."

"Wow," Jason exclaimed. "I can't wait to see that."

"And what are the holes really?" Abby asked, keeping her voice low so Jason and Jessica couldn't hear her.

"Oh, they're real bullet holes, all right, but they weren't put there by desperados," Luke said, keeping his voice low, as well.

"So, how did they get there?" she asked, leaning slightly toward him in an effort to hear his quiet voice. Instantly she could smell the familiar scent of him, the woodsy, spicy male scent that had driven her half wild when she'd made love with him.

"Burt Holloway used to work as one of the tellers in the bank before he retired last year. One day his wife called him outside and held him at gunpoint against the side of the building. Seems she was miffed because she'd heard a rumor that he was flirting with one of the waitresses down at the Honky Tonk."

"So she shot him?" Abby asked incredulously.

"She unloaded a six-shooter into the wall behind him but didn't hurt him none. Just put a touch of fear into him. Old Burt, he hasn't been back to the Honky Tonk since."

"What are you guys whispering about?" Jason asked, a touch of indignation in his voice.

Luke wheeled into a parking space in front of the diner, shut off the car, then turned to look at Jason. "We were trying to decide if you were going to drink one or two chocolate shakes at lunch."

"Two!" Jason exclaimed.

"Then we'd better get sightseeing so we can work up an appetite," Luke said.

The four of them got out of the car, and Abby and the kids looked at Luke for direction. "Let's see the bullet holes first," Jason said.

"Is that okay with you, Jessica?" Luke asked, his tone infinitely gentle with the little girl.

She nodded affirmatively and grabbed Abby's hand.

"Then we'll begin our tour of the lovely town of Inferno at the bank."

Minutes later the four of them stood in the alley beside the bank, eyeing the six holes in the adobe building. "What are desperados?" Jason asked curiously.

"Bank robbers…bad guys," Luke replied. "But don't worry buddy, bad guys go to jail."

"And they stay there forever?"

Jason's question hung in the air for a moment, and Luke looked at Abby, as if wanting help in answering the question. "Most of the time bad guys stay in jail forever," she replied, the tiny white lie told to still a little boy's fears.

"What you have to remember, Jason, is that we're the good guys," Luke said. "And the good guys always win." In one smooth movement he picked Jason up and placed him on his shoulders.

Jason squealed in delight as his arms locked beneath Luke's chin. "Look at me, I'm tall as a tree," he said and laughed.

And that set the tone for the day. Luke took them in and out of quaint little shops. He took them to the fire station manned by volunteers where the kids got to sit on the shiny red fire engine and play with a litter of kittens that had taken up residency there.

Everywhere they went Luke was greeted with friendliness. It was obvious he was adored by the women of the town, and liked by the men, as well.

And throughout the town tour, Abby found herself fighting the enormous attraction that had drawn her to Luke from the moment she'd first met him.

It didn't help that he seemed to have endless patience with the kids. He was sweetly gentle with Jessica and abounding with good humor in the face of Jason's endless curiosity. And to Abby's surprise she found those traits sexy as hell.

She couldn't help but realize that this was the way a family interacted, that to strangers on the street who didn't know either her or Luke, they appeared to be a perfectly normal, happy family.

And she knew the danger of those kinds of thoughts. She hadn't lied to Luke when she'd told him she had learned to expect nothing from men.

Certainly Justin Cahill had shown her the epitome of cruel indifference, and Ken…he had simply shown her that words of love spoken when blue skies abounded meant nothing when stormy seas lay ahead.

At least Luke had been honest with her, telling her that in seven months he was out of there, and he had no intention of allowing anything or anyone to stop his pursuit of his dream.

It was midafternoon when they finally stopped for lunch at the diner. The meal was accompanied by lots of laughter as Jason pled his case, once more, for a dog.

"I would clean my room twice every day," Jason said.

"And Jessica told me she would, too." Jessica nodded vigorously in eager agreement.

"And we'd make you breakfast on Saturdays…your favorite, pancakes. And if we had a dog, Jessica and me would feed him and take him outside for walks and take care of him so you wouldn't have to ever do anything. We'd do everything around the house and you could just stay in bed if you wanted and—"

"Whoa." Abby laughed and held up a hand to still the promise-spewing Jason. "I'll tell you what." She grabbed her purse and got out a handful of change. "Why don't you and Jessica go play the jukebox and let me think about it for a few minutes."

Jessica and Jason scrambled from the booth, leaving Abby and Luke alone for the first time that day. Luke smiled at her across the table. "You know they aren't going to be happy until you get them a dog."

"I know," Abby agreed with a small laugh. "Jason has been unrelenting in his quest, and there's a small part of me that thinks it wouldn't be such a bad thing. I mean, I know the bulk of the work for a pet would fall on my head. But on the other hand, having a dog seems so wonderfully normal and right."

"And you want wonderfully normal and right for the kids," he said.

She nodded. "I do."

He took a sip of his soda and gazed at the children, then back to her. "My offer still stands to help you find a good dog."

"You've done too much for me and the kids already," Abby replied.

"You keep wearing that killer dress and I'll keep trying to do nice things for you." His eyes glowed with a familiar heat that she hadn't seen since before they'd made love.

"And you keep looking at me like that and I'll try to do nice things for you," she returned, her voice slightly breathless.

He laughed, not the full-bodied laughter he'd shared with the kids all morning, but rather a low, seductive laugh that held a promise that momentarily swept away her ability to breathe.

She broke eye contact with him and grabbed her glass of water, her mouth suddenly achingly dry.

"You feel it, too, don't you, Abby?" His voice was whisper soft, and again she looked at him, into the heat of his sexy eyes.

"Feel what?"

He smiled knowingly. "The desire to repeat what we did the other day." Like powerful twin magnets, his eyes held hers, making it impossible for her to look away. "That dress is lovely on you, Abby, but all I've been able to think about all day long is taking it off you."

Flames of heat warmed her cheeks at his words. "I must say, that surprises me." She fought to control both her blush and the raging turmoil his words created.

He lifted a dark eyebrow. "And why should that surprise you?"

"If I am to believe that you are the womanizer people in this town have told me you are, then half the excitement of getting a woman in bed would be in the chase. I'm afraid I didn't give you much of a chase."

"Abby." He reached across the table and drew one of her hands into his. "I'm the first one to admit that I like women and I've dated a lot of them. But I don't sleep with all the women I date and I definitely don't like to play the kind of head games so many people like to play."

"I don't play head games, either," she replied. "I just... I'm not very exciting and..."

He squeezed her hand to still whatever other protest she was about to make. "Abby, you have no idea how exciting I find you, and I'd like to make love with you again."

"Let's change the subject. You're making it difficult for me to think."

He grinned and released her hand. "Okay, tell me what you were doing before you started taking care of Jason and Jessica."

"My life was okay. I was a third grade teacher."

"That doesn't surprise me. It's obvious you love children. Okay, so during the day you were a teacher, and in the evenings?"

She shrugged. "I visited with Loretta and the kids a lot and I was dating a man named Ken Masters."

Luke's eyes were opaque. "Were you in love with him?"

"No." The answer came swiftly and with assurance. "I wanted to be in love and I tried to fool myself that I was in love with Ken. He was a high school coach and we had school in common. We attended school functions together, and it just seemed sort of natural that we'd eventually be together forever."

"But he let you down."

She nodded her head. "He was great initially in the days immediately following Loretta's death. It wasn't until he realized I intended to keep the kids with me that he started to freak out."

She paused a moment and took a sip of her tea, grateful that thoughts of Ken no longer hurt at all. "He tried to talk me into putting them into foster care. He said they required more than I could give them, but what he meant was their presence in my life cramped his style. I realized then that I'd been fooling myself about my feelings for him. The easiest thing I've ever done in my life was tell him goodbye."

Before he could respond, the kids returned to the table.

"So, do we get to have a dog?" Jason asked eagerly.

Abby gestured the kids into the booth. Jason slid in next to Luke and Jessica next to her. She eyed them both soberly, grateful to be on less treacherous ground talking about a dog with the kids instead of the past or Luke's desire for her.

"I've given this a lot of thought, and I've decided that next week, if Luke could take us to some of the dog breeders he knows, then we'll see about getting a dog."

Jason yelped with excitement, and Jessica clapped her hands together, her button eyes shining with delight.

"Oh boy, a dog! That's a lot better than a lizard," Jason exclaimed.

Abby checked her watch and realized it was almost three. She knew Luke played his guitar and sang at the Honky Tonk on Saturday nights and probably had other things he wanted to do besides spend all his free Saturday time with her and the kids.

"We probably should be getting back home," she said to Luke.

He checked his watch and nodded. "Yeah, I've got a few things to take care of before I go to work tonight." He stood and pulled out his wallet.

"Please, let me get lunch," she said, fumbling quickly in her purse.

"I'm not accustomed to my date paying my way," Luke protested.

"We aren't a date," Jason exclaimed.

Abby laughed. "That's right. We aren't a date, and I insist I pay in return for your fascinating tour of town."

Luke grinned easily and stuck his wallet back in his pocket. "I never argue with a headstrong woman."

Luke and the kids stood nearby while Abby paid for the meal, then together the four of them left the diner. They had just reached the car when Luke snapped his fingers. "Hey, we almost forgot what we came to town to get—the guitar strings."

"You said the man in the general store orders them for you?" Abby asked. She knew the general store was a couple of blocks away, and she could also tell that the kids were growing tired.

"Why don't you guys go ahead and get in the car. It will just take me a couple of minutes to run and get them," Luke suggested.

"Let's go in here and look," Jason said, pointing to the craft store in front of where they were parked.

"Okay, if you aren't in the car, then I'll know you're in there," Luke said, then turned and began to walk in long, even strides away from them.

"All right, we'll take a peek around and by that time Luke will be back," Abby said as she guided the kids to the quaint shop's door.

Inside the air was cool and sweetly fragranced by candles and potpourri. The shelves held an array of items—knitted booties and crocheted blankets, hand-sewn dolls and wooden painted trucks.

There were hand-painted bird feeders and intricate yard ornaments, flower arrangements and paintings and cross-stitched towels and T-shirts.

"Hello…hello. Welcome to My Place." A dainty, gray-haired woman approached them, beaming a smile and bearing a platter full of cookies. "I'm Rita Sue Ellenbee, the proprietor of this establishment."

"Hi, I'm Abby Graham and these are my children, Jason and Jessica," Abby replied.

"Ah, yes, the town has been buzzing with the news of the pretty new widow and her lovely children. Would you like a cookie? My own special recipe of honey and oatmeal." Rita Sue held out the platter.

"None for me, thank you," Abby replied, then nodded at the kids, who each took one.

"Feel free to wander around. We have something for everyone in here."

"We're just waiting for Luke," Jason said around a mouthful of cookie.

"Luke? Luke Delaney?" Rita Sue asked, and Abby nodded.

"He's such a nice young man…a bit of the devil in him, but just enough to make him fun. His work always sells the quickest here."

"Really? What kind of things does Luke sell here?" Abby asked curiously.

Rita Sue placed the platter of cookies on a shelf and gestured for Abby and the children to follow her. "I haven't put out his newest work yet. He just dropped it off to me a couple of days ago."

She led them into a back room that was obviously used for storage. Boxes and crates lined the walls, and in the center of the room set a gorgeous, solid oak dressing table. "That's Luke's work," she said.

Abby ran her fingers across the smooth, glazed wood in surprise. "It's beautiful," she said, awed by the workmanship displayed in the intricately carved lines and decorative etching. "He's been doing some work for me around my place, but I had no idea he was so talented."

"Luke could make a good living just building furniture, but he doesn't seem to have any real ambition that way," Rita Sue said. "He brings me a piece every couple of months, and it usually sells the first day I put it out on the floor. I'm always harping at him to make them faster, but he just grins that devilish grin of his that tells me he's going to do it in his own time, his own way."

Abby smiled. "Thank you for showing it to me. And now we'd better get outside. Luke will be looking for us."

They walked toward the front door, where a young couple

was just entering. Rita Sue grabbed her platter of cookies and went to greet the new couple.

Abby gazed out the plate-glass window as the kids stopped to look at a display of tissue-paper flowers. She didn't want Luke to have to come in search of them.

Main Street was busy, and it was obvious many people had come out to enjoy the pleasant day. Several men sat outside the barbershop on a bench, and a young couple walked leisurely hand-in-hand, apparently window-shopping.

At the corner, the sheriff stood chatting with another man, and as Abby's gaze swept over them, her blood froze and her breath.

No. Her mind screamed in denial as she stared at the man with the sheriff. It couldn't be. Her heart banged painfully in her chest.

She drew a deep breath and forced herself to calm down. She could only see the man's profile. She had to be mistaken. It couldn't be him…just somebody who resembled him.

"No," she whispered. No, it couldn't be him. Fate wouldn't be so cruel, and she had tried to be so very careful. When he turned, she'd see that it wasn't him at all.

Then he turned, and she saw him fully. It was him. Her heart once again boomed in frantic rhythm as her blood turned icy cold in her veins.

Somehow, some way, Justin Cahill, the man who had murdered her sister, the father of the children she claimed as her own, was here in Inferno.

And he could only be here for one reason. He knew they were here. He had found them.

Chapter 9

The minute Luke saw Abby sitting in the van, he knew something was wrong. She wasn't just pale—she looked positively ill.

The kids both seemed okay. They were buckled into the backseat, each of them looking at books Abby had bought for them earlier in the day.

But Abby definitely was not okay. He threw the guitar strings on the floor between them and slid behind the steering wheel. "What's going on?" he asked.

"Nothing. Everything is fine…just fine," she replied, a sharp edge in her voice. "I just really need to get home right away."

"All right, let's go." He started the engine and pulled away from the curb, aware of her gaze darting frantically out the front window, then out the side.

The tension rolling from her was thick enough to cut, and he could hear her taking shallow little breaths, as if she were fighting off sheer hysteria. As they drove away from town, she constantly turned in her seat to check the road behind them.

"Abby, what's going on?" he asked again, unease rising in him as he recognized that the emotion that darkened her eyes appeared to be fear. "Did somebody say something to you? Did something happen while I was gone?"

"Is something wrong?" Jason asked from the backseat.

"No, honey. Everything is fine…just fine," Abby said to him. "I'll tell you later," she said in a low voice to Luke.

The drive was finished in silence. Abby continued to twist in her seat and look out the rear window as Luke tried to figure out what might have happened in the space of the few minutes he'd been getting the guitar strings.

When they reached the house, Abby opened the front door and told the kids to go inside and turn on the television or play in their rooms, then she stepped out on the porch with Luke.

Her eyes still held an edge of panic, and her delicate hands worried themselves, clenching and unclenching, twisting and wringing.

"I have to think," she said absently and paced the front porch. "We have to go… We have to leave here."

"What are you talking about?" He stepped closer to her and grabbed her hands in his. "What do you mean, leave here? Where are you going?"

"I don't know… We just…we just have to go. We have to get out of here." Her hands were cold as ice and trembled unsteadily. She tried to pull them away, but he held on tight.

"Why? Why do you have to leave? For God's sake, Abby, tell me what's going on."

Tears formed in her eyes as she gazed at him. "I can't tell you. I can't tell anyone. I'm afraid…" The tears trickled from her eyes and fell down her cheeks. "Please, let me go so I can get the kids ready to leave. If we stay here, I'll lose everything, and the children will be lost."

"I'm not going to let you go until you tell me what's going on." Luke squeezed her hands. "Abby, you can trust me. Maybe I can help."

She drew a deep breath. "You can't help," she said with an edge of bitterness. "Nobody can help."

"Try me," Luke exclaimed. "Trust me." He dropped her hands and grabbed her shoulders.

For a long moment she gazed into his eyes, as if assessing him to see if he was worth her trust. Finally, he felt the tension in her ebb slightly. "Justin Cahill has found us." The words were whispered hoarsely as if torn from enormous force.

"Justin Cahill?"

"The kids' father."

Luke frowned in confusion. "But I thought…you said he'd disappeared." He dropped his hands from her shoulders.

"He's not disappeared anymore. He's here in Inferno, and he can only be here for one reason. He wants his children," she exclaimed, her voice laced with undisguised bitterness. "I put all my faith in the judicial system, and it let me down." She moved to the porch railing and stared into the distance.

She looked so fragile, so small and helpless, Luke's heart ached for her. He moved to stand next to her. "What happened?"

"Justin was arrested for the murder of my sister, and I was granted temporary custody of the children. The murder case was handled by an overeager assistant district attorney. She charged Justin with first-degree murder and refused to consider including any lesser charges. She was so certain she'd get him."

"But she didn't."

Abby turned to face him, her eyes tortured pools of emotion. She worried a slender hand through her hair. "No, she didn't. In her defense, it looked like an open-and-shut case. After all, she had two little eyewitnesses to the crime, and even though Jason and Jessica were horribly traumatized, she was certain that by the time the trial took place they would be able to testify."

"But they weren't."

"Jessica quit talking altogether, and whenever Linda, that was the assistant DA, tried to talk to Jason, he'd fly into rages and tears. Finally I told her she couldn't use them, that she'd have to figure out the case without their testimony. She remained confident. They had Justin's fingerprints in Loretta's apartment and a neighbor's testimony that he'd thought he'd seen Justin lurking around just before the murder took place."

"And that wasn't enough to see him convicted?"

"At the last minute Justin produced an alibi witness for the time of the murder." Abby's voice rang with festering anger. "A young woman came forward to testify that Justin was with her the entire night of the murder. The case fell apart after that."

Once again she directed her attention to the distance, and her fist hit the porch railing in barely contained rage. "I had told Linda from the very beginning that first-degree murder wasn't the right charge. She couldn't prove premeditation, and I begged her to include lesser charges for the jurors to consider. But she didn't want to hear it. She was so damned confident that she could turn the jury her way."

"But she didn't," Luke concluded softly.

All the anger, all the bitterness seemed to fall away from her, leaving her looking painfully vulnerable, achingly defenseless. "No, she didn't."

As Abby's eyes filled once again with tears, Luke drew her into his arms and held her tight.

"Two months ago the verdict came in…a hung jury, a mistrial. I was at my apartment with the kids when Linda called to give me the bad news." She shuddered, her voice muffled by his chest. "And Linda told me unless new information came to light, they weren't going to try him again. I knew the moment he got released he'd come looking for me… Come looking for his kids. So I packed up and ran, and I've been running every since."

She lifted her head and through the haze of her tears a steely strength shone. "By taking the kids and running, I know I broke the law. But I had no other choice. I will not allow him to have Jason and Jessica. He's a brutal, hateful man, and he'll destroy them. I had to break the law in order to save them from him. He's a murderer, and he only wants them for two reasons—actually, two million and one reasons."

"Two million and one?"

She nodded and stepped out of his embrace. "First and foremost, I know he wants them to make sure they continue their silence about the night of Loretta's death. But the main reason he wants them in his custody is that each of them has a trust fund of a little over a million dollars apiece."

Luke whistled, shock sweeping through him. "I guess that gives him a little over two million reasons to want to be a good daddy."

"Justin was never a good daddy," she said, her eyes flashing with a renewed burst of anger. "He was cold, and brutal, and authoritarian. The kids were terrified of him before the night he killed my sister, and I'll do whatever it takes to make sure they stay safe from him." Once again she threaded her fingers through her hair, then turned toward the front door. "I can't waste any more time. I've got to get the kids packed, and we need to get out of here."

She started for the door, but Luke stopped her by grabbing her arm. "So that's it? You just run?"

"That's right," she replied, her chin raised in mute defiance.

"And when he finds you again?"

"We run again…and we keep running until we find a place where he won't be able to find us." Her chin went a notch higher. "I don't care how many laws I have to break to keep those babies safe."

"And what kind of a life is that for your kids?"

The chin that had a mere moment before been raised in stubborn bravado lowered, and her eyes flickered with a haunting deep pain. "It's better than what Justin will give them," she said softly, her voice quivering with the depth of her emotion.

"But is it good enough? Always in hiding, afraid if Justin doesn't find you the law will? What kind of a life is that?"

She attempted to jerk her arm from his grasp. She obviously didn't want to hear what he had to say, but he held tight. "Abby, there's got to be another way. You can't condemn those kids to a life on the run."

"I tried the other way," she cried and this time managed to tear her arm from his grip. "I trusted the system to do the right thing, to put him in prison and keep him away from the children. But it failed me. It failed them. The day he walked out of that courtroom acquitted, he regained the right to have his children. And he's a murderer. He beat my sister to death in a fit of rage!"

"But the children have a right to have a normal life, with a permanent home and the same school, the same friends and a dog."

A sob caught in her throat as she slumped against the front door, utter defeat on her features. "Don't you think I know that? Don't you think I want that for them? But I don't know what to do. Justin could show up here at any minute and demand I give him his children, and legally, he'd have that right."

Luke had never wanted to help anyone more than he

wanted to help her and the children at that moment. "Maybe it's time you stand and fight."

She sniffled and straightened. "But I have no tools, no weapons to fight him."

"Yes, you do," Luke protested. "You have two very power-ful tools. You have Jason and Jessica. Even though they might not be ready or willing to talk about the night of their mother's murder, surely they'd be willing to tell a judge they want to remain living with you. And I happen to be related to the best lawyer in the state, my sister, Johnna. I can call her right now, and she'll start the ball rolling in getting you permanent custody."

For the first time since they'd left town, a tiny ray of hope shone from her eyes. Once again Luke placed his hands on her shoulders, felt the warmth of her sun-kissed skin beneath his fingertips. "Abby, stay. Fight. Give Jessica and Jason a chance for a normal childhood.

Luke wasn't sure why, but it suddenly seemed overwhelm-ingly important that the children got the opportunity to have good childhoods, the kind Luke had never had.

"You'll call your sister?" she said, the first real sign that she was contemplating his words.

"Right now, if you want me to."

Again tears welled in her eyes. "I'm so scared, not for me, but for Jessica and Jason."

He pulled her to his chest, and she came willingly into his embrace. He stroked a hand through the shiny silk of her hair and hoped to hell he hadn't just given her the worst advice in the world.

The attractive woman with boyishly short dark hair flew through the front door when Abby opened it, bringing with her a dynamic energy that Abby found oddly comforting.

"Johnna McCain," she said and grabbed Abby's hand in a strong grasp.

"I'm Abby. Abby Graham."

"Nice to meet you, Abby." Johnna's gaze shot to her brother, who was seated on the sofa. "You said it was an emergency, so I got here as fast as I could."

"Please, have a seat," Abby said as she gestured Johnna toward the chair across from the sofa. As she sat, Abby sank down on the sofa next to Luke, her nerves raw and on edge.

For the past hour, while they'd waited for Johnna to arrive, Abby had expected at any moment a knock on the door and the unwelcome presence of Justin Cahill demanding his children.

She was also more afraid than she'd ever been in her life that she was making a bad decision, trusting when she should be running. What if she didn't win this fight? What if this was the biggest mistake she'd ever made in her life?

"So, what's going on?" Johnna asked, looking first at Abby, then at Luke. "What's the big emergency?"

Abby drew a deep breath and for the second time that day bared the secrets that had driven her actions for the past two months. She told Johnna about the debacle of a trial, how when the verdict of a mistrial had been announced, Abby had packed the kids up and spent the next six weeks traveling from motel to motel, seeking anonymity and safety.

After six weeks, disheartened by the lifestyle of constantly being on the move and living out of boxes and suitcases, Abby had remembered her inheritance from her crazy uncle Arthur and had come here.

"Didn't you think Justin Cahill might be able to trace you here?" Johnna asked as she looked up from the notes she'd been taking on a legal pad.

"Uncle Arthur died when Justin was already in jail. This

place was left to Loretta and me, and since Loretta was dead, it all became mine. I didn't think Justin knew anything about the inheritance."

"Apparently he learned something, otherwise there would be no reason for him to be in Inferno," Luke said.

"Where is Justin's home? Where were you all living when the crime occurred?"

Abby was grateful for the way Johnna phrased the question. It was easier to think of it as the crime than the murder of her sister. "We were all living in Kansas City, Missouri." She shot an apologetic look at Luke. "I told you Chicago, but that was a lie."

He nodded, appearing unsurprised by this information.

"Okay, let me get this straight," Johnna said. "Legally you were granted temporary custody when Justin was arrested and put into jail."

"That's right," Abby replied.

"And legally, you have received no notice that the temporary custody was terminated."

"No, nothing. But it would have been difficult for me to get notice since we were on the run."

Johnna nodded and took a moment to make several more notes on her pad. "The first thing I'll need to do is check to see if anything has been filed in the state of Missouri. I want to get the trial record and take a look at that… See if there's anything I might use in a custody battle."

She looked at Abby. "I have to ask you a question that might make you angry, but I need all the facts if I'm going to help you."

"What question?" Abby asked, tensing in preparation for something unpleasant.

"You told me these kids have over a million dollars a piece in a trust fund. I need to know what your financial status is. I need to make sure that Justin Cahill can't use the fact that you're after the children's money and that's the only reason you want custody."

Abby nodded, unsurprised by the question and pleased she had an answer that would erase any argument that might be made concerning her motives for gaining custody. "I have my own trust fund, more than both of the children put together and more than I could ever spend in a lifetime." She smiled self-consciously. "My father was something of a financial wizard and wanted to make sure we were all taken care of."

"Great," Johnna exclaimed. "You have some sort of documentation of that?"

Abby rose from her chair and went into the kitchen, where she grabbed her purse off the table. She returned to the living room and withdrew a business card from her wallet.

"This is my lawyer in Kansas City. He's the executor of the trust funds. I'll contact him and tell him to send you any pertinent paperwork. I haven't accessed any of my money since we left Kansas City. I was afraid of leaving any kind of a paper trail that Justin might try to follow. But apparently he found us anyway."

Luke reached out and grabbed her hand as he heard the wealth of emotion in her voice. "You're doing the right thing," he said, as if he'd heard the doubts swirling around in her head.

She nodded, although she was no longer certain what the right thing was. She was putting her children's safety and well-being in the hands of a woman she'd never met before today and a man she'd made love with, but didn't know much better.

"What kind of work does Justin do? Can he physically provide a stable environment for the children?"

Abby frowned. "He never held down a job when he was married to Loretta. I know he was beneficiary of a small insurance policy, and I suppose when he was found not guilty he got that, but he probably has a wealth of attorney fees to pay." Abby shrugged helplessly. "I don't even know where he might be living now. When he and Loretta split, he was living in a small studio apartment."

"Okay," Johnna said. "I'll get my investigator checking into his background and find out what ammunition we can use." She closed her pad and eyed Abby somberly. "Unfortunately, I can't do anything about this until Monday morning. First thing Monday I'll file the paperwork requesting permanent custody of the children."

She stood, and Abby and Luke did the same. "I have to be honest here with you, Abby. Family courts generally like to keep kids with their biological parents. But I'm a fighter, and it's obvious you are, too."

Abby and Luke walked with her toward the front door. "I'll do my damnedest to make sure those kids remain with you. In the meantime, if Justin shows up here, under no circumstances do you allow him to have the children. Call Sheriff Broder and tell him at the present time you have legal custody."

"Don't worry," Abby said. "There's no way I'd allow him the kids."

At that moment Jason called Abby from his room, where he and Jessica had been playing. Abby smiled at Johnna. "And speaking of kids, I better go see what's going on."

Johnna nodded. "Too bad you aren't married. Family court also loves two-parent families. Go…" She waved Abby away. "Go see to the kids. Luke will see me out the door."

Abby nodded and hurried down the hallway, aware that she had just set into motion a battle of mammoth proportions. She was gambling, and the stakes were high, the well-being of the two children she loved more than anything else in the world. She had to win. If she didn't, they would all be destroyed.

Chapter 10

"What are you doing, brother?" Johnna asked as she and Luke stepped out of the house.

"What do you mean?"

"Playing Sir Galahad is not your usual style," Johnna said drily.

"Maybe I'm changing my style," Luke replied more sharply than he intended. He drew a deep breath to steady the emotions that had rolled through him from the moment Abby had spilled her secrets. "She's a very nice lady, and she needs help."

"And you talked her into getting help."

He hesitated, then nodded. "She was set to run again."

"But you convinced her to stand and fight." Johnna's gaze lingered on him thoughtfully. "Are you involved with her?"

He shrugged, breaking eye contact. "Sure, I've been doing some work for her around the place. I built her the new porch, and she wants her kitchen cabinets replaced."

Johnna elbowed him in the ribs. "You know that's not what I meant."

"What difference does it make?" he asked as they reached her car.

"I was wondering what might happen if you talked her into staying and fighting, then I lose the custody battle."

Luke smiled at his sister, a smile that held little humor. "Then I guess you'd just better be sure you win the battle."

"Sure, no pressure there." Johnna opened her car door, but instead of getting in she turned to face Luke. "Be careful, Luke. Abby seems nice enough, but she's trouble. I can tell you that if everything she told us is true, this custody battle has the potential to get very ugly. You don't need to get yourself involved in something like this. You're fighting your own personal demons."

Luke looked into the distance, knowing his sister was talking about his drinking problem. "At the moment the happiness of those kids seems a lot more important than a drink. They have suffered enough. All I want is for them to get a chance to have a normal, happy childhood."

He turned to Johnna as she placed a warm hand on his arm. "The kind of childhood we never had?" Her gray eyes were filled with emotion, and Luke knew she was remembering the kinds of horror they'd suffered at the hands of their abusive father.

"Yeah, something like that," he finally replied.

Again Johnna studied him, her brow creased thoughtfully. "You know, Luke, by fixing their childhood you won't be fixing your own."

"I know that," he scoffed, uncomfortable by her piercing gaze and speculative expression. "What is this? Psychology one-oh-one? I'm just trying to help out a woman who is alone and trying to do something good for a couple of kids. Don't make it into any more than that."

"Okay." Johnna dropped her hand from his arm but remained standing next to her car. Her gaze swept around the area. "It's kind of isolated out here, isn't it?"

"Yeah, it is."

Johnna frowned. "Maybe I should get in touch with Judd and see if he'll kind of keep on eye on things out here until we get something legal going on. If Justin Cahill has killed once in the heat of anger, there's nothing that says he won't kill again to get what he wants."

Judd Walker was the private investigator Johnna used in her law practice. "No, that's okay. I'll take care of it," Luke said. "I'll stick around here until we've got a handle on Cahill."

Johnna reached up and laid a palm on Luke's cheek. "Be careful, Luke. I don't want to see you getting hurt."

She didn't wait for his reply, but got into her car and started the engine. As she drove away from the house, Luke stared after her.

Johnna had been angry for as long as Luke could remember, rebelling against the cruelty of their father, railing about the injustice of their lives. But somehow when she'd married Jerrod McCain a month before, she'd found a kind of peace.

It was as if in Jerrod's love, she'd found self-worth and the ability to put the past firmly behind her. And in doing that, she was becoming a softer, more caring person.

Luke raked a hand through his hair and stared at the sun, which had begun its descent. Things were changing. His sister and brother Mark had changed. It unsettled Luke.

He turned and faced the house, thinking of what Johnna had said. He'd put in motion events that might ultimately lead to Abby's destruction. And how would he feel if that happened and she looked at him with dead eyes, or with eyes filled with blame?

What difference did it make, he asked himself. Abigail

Graham meant nothing to him. They'd made love and spent some time together, but it wasn't like he intended to have any kind of a long-term relationship. In seven months he'd be gone from here.

Still, the thought of her losing the kids to the man who had killed their mother, the man who had killed Abby's sister, tore through him. If she lost the kids it would be his fault because he'd encouraged her to stay and fight.

He dragged his hand down the side of his face, trying not to think that he might be instrumental in Abby's ultimate undoing. He had to think positive. He'd help her through this and do anything to help Johnna and Abby win the battle for the kids.

With this thought in mind, he went to his truck and retrieved the guitar strings he'd bought, then walked into the house. He found Abby in the kitchen preparing the evening meal. She flashed him a surprised, taut smile. "I thought you'd left with your sister."

"What made you think that?" He tossed the strings onto a countertop.

She dropped an unwrapped package of hot dogs into a pot of boiling water. "You have to play tonight. I figured you'd need to get going in order to make it to the Honky Tonk on time."

"I'm not going to play at the Honky Tonk tonight." He sank down in a chair at the table. "In fact, I'm not going anywhere tonight."

Her dark, perfect eyebrows rose in confusion. "What do you mean?"

"I mean I'm going to stay here for a few days. I don't want you here alone with just the kids in case Justin shows up."

"I can't ask you to do that, Luke," she protested weakly.

"You didn't ask, and I insist," he replied. "Don't worry, everything will be aboveboard. I'll bunk on the sofa."

"I'm not going to protest," she said, and turned to the stove to stir a pan of beans. "To tell the truth, Justin has always scared me more than a little bit. I don't want to be here alone if he shows up."

Luke saw the tense set of her shoulders, knew the emotions that had to be rolling through her. Panic, uncertainty, fear... She had to be experiencing them all.

He shoved back from the table and moved to stand behind her. He placed his hands on her shoulders, and she stopped stirring the beans and leaned back just a little bit.

"You're going to win this, Abby," he said softly. "Johnna is smart and tenacious, and she'll use every tool at her disposal to win for you."

She turned to face him, her eyes sparkly bright with unshed tears. "I hope you're right. I can't imagine what their life would be with him. And I can't imagine my life without them."

At that moment Jason and Jessica raced into the kitchen, and Luke dropped his hands from Abby's shoulders. "We're starving," Jason exclaimed.

"Then I guess we'd better eat," Abby exclaimed with what Luke knew was forced cheerfulness. "Jason, why don't you get the plates and set the table. Jessica, you do the silverware and the napkins."

"And what about me?" Luke asked.

"Drinks," Jason replied. "You can get us something to drink for supper."

They all worked for a few minutes in silence, then sat down at the table to enjoy a simple meal of hot dogs, beans and potato chips.

Jason provided suppertime chatter, recapping their time spent in town as if none of his three dinner companions had been with him.

Abby and Jessica were silent, and Luke worked overtime to fill the dead silences, rattling about the dude ranch and all the horses they owned.

Abby's tension didn't seem to dissipate throughout the meal. When the supper dishes were done, she called the two kids into the living room. She sat on the sofa and motioned for Jason to sit on one side of her and Jessica on the other. Luke realized she had to tell the children something of what was going on.

Thinking she needed some time alone with them, he excused himself and stepped out on the front porch. Night had fallen, and silence reigned. The sky, as usual was clear, filled with the sparkling of thousands of stars.

Luke leaned against the porch railing and stared into the thick blanket of darkness that surrounded the house. He was vaguely surprised Justin Cahill hadn't shown up. It wouldn't take the man long to find out where the new woman in town lived.

Maybe Abby had been wrong. Maybe it hadn't been Justin, after all, just a man who'd resembled him. Maybe she'd panicked over nothing.

And maybe Justin Cahill was biding his time, setting up an offensive assault, secure in the fact that Abby didn't know he was anywhere near her and the kids.

It was difficult to believe a day that had been so good could be transformed into such a mess. Luke had enjoyed their trip into town and had been taunted and teased by Abby's loveliness throughout the day.

She'd been a vision in that pink sundress that had emphasized her small waist and displayed her slender, shapely legs. He'd been on a slow sizzle all day, but the sizzle had been effectively doused by the appearance of Justin Cahill back in her life.

He'd been leaning against the porch railing for about a

half an hour when the front door opened and Abby stepped outside.

"How did it go?" he asked.

She shrugged. "They're frightened, but I did my best to reassure them. I couldn't not tell them. What if Justin does show up here? I didn't want them to be taken by surprise."

She moved to stand next to him, and instantly the sizzle was back. Her scent surrounded him, and her body heat radiated toward him. "What are they doing now?" he asked, trying to concentrate on anything that would take his mind off his desire to take her in his arms and kiss her.

"Getting ready for bed." She sighed, a whisper soft sound of weariness.

"It's been a long day, hasn't it?" Again he had to fight his impulse to embrace her, to pull her tight against his chest. She didn't need any further complications at the moment, and he certainly was savvy enough to know that now wasn't the time for sex or romance.

"Yes, it has been." She turned to face him, her eyes luminous in the moonlight that spilled down. "And I never thanked you for what was a lovely trip into town."

He shrugged and jammed his hands into his pockets. "You don't have to thank me. I thoroughly enjoyed myself."

"I just can't believe this is happening. I guess I should have never come here. I should have driven into Mexico and started a new life there."

"But then you wouldn't have had the good fortune of meeting me." Although Luke's voice was filled with teasing humor, she didn't respond but merely uttered another weary sigh.

They stood in silence for several long minutes, and Luke wondered if she sensed his growing need to touch her. The moonlight loved her features, the soft glow appearing to magically erase any tension.

She sighed one last time and rippled her hair with her fingertips. "I'd better get the kids tucked in."

"If you have a chance to get that guitar for me, I'll be glad to string it this evening."

She nodded and disappeared inside. Luke followed a moment later. He sank down on the sofa and closed his eyes, listening to the soothing sounds of her voice drifting from Jason's room.

His mind played and replayed the conversation with his sister. What were the odds of them winning custody for Abby? Certainly Luke knew enough about the law to understand that if Justin Cahill had been found not guilty in Loretta's murder, then they couldn't use the murder as a reason for a judge to terminate his parental rights.

But surely a judge couldn't ignore the expression of fear in the kids' eyes at the mere mention of their father. Surely their desire would be taken into consideration.

He snapped his eyes open as Abby came into the living room, the old guitar in one hand and a set of sheets in the other. A pillow was tucked under one arm.

He jumped up, grabbed the bedding from her and set it on the coffee table. "I didn't know if you'd need a blanket or not," she said. "The house stays fairly warm at night."

"This is fine," he assured her, then grinned. "I'm an old, seasoned cowboy. I've got my horse to keep me warm." He didn't realize how much he'd missed her smile until it flashed, bright and carefree, for a brief moment.

"Just keep your horse outside. I'm having enough problems contemplating a dog in the house." Her smile disappeared as quickly as it had come. "And now, if you don't mind, I think I'm going to call it a night. I'm more than exhausted." She placed the guitar on the coffee table next to his bedding.

"Go on, get a good sleep. Things will look better in the morning."

"Do you promise?"

Those green eyes of hers held his, and more than anything he wanted to promise her that morning sun would bring hope and happiness. "I told you once that I don't make promises I can't keep. To be perfectly honest, I don't know if things will look better in the morning or not."

She smiled again. "Thank you, Luke."

"For what? For telling you tomorrow might be just as crappy as today?"

"For everything. For being kind and for staying here and for making me see that a life on the run isn't what the kids need." Again for a long moment her gaze held his, and he thought she wanted to say something more...or needed something more from him. Then she broke the gaze and turned away. "Good night, Luke. I'll see you in the morning."

She disappeared down the hallway and into her room. Luke watched her go, then went into the kitchen to retrieve the strings he'd tossed on the countertop earlier. Before leaving the kitchen, he checked the back door to make sure it was securely locked.

He returned to the living room, grateful for any task to take his mind off everything that had happened that afternoon. Before he began to string the guitar, he checked the front door, as well, to make sure it was locked up tight.

He sat on the sofa and began to string the guitar, his thoughts whirling chaotically in his head. Surely Justin Cahill wouldn't be foolish enough to try to take the children by force.

He'd want to present himself as a poor, beleaguered man who'd been wrongly accused of his ex-wife's death, acquitted of the crime and now wanting, needing to be reunited with his children.

His role as victim wouldn't work if he stormed this place and took his children by force.

It didn't take Luke long to string the guitar, then he worked on tuning it, strumming the strings softly so as not to disturb the other occupants in the house. When the guitar was tuned to his satisfaction, he placed it on the coffee table and set about making his bed for the night.

Keeping in mind that there were two kids in the house, he decided to sleep in his jeans. In the morning they'd all have to take a trip to the ranch so Luke could get some spare clothes.

Luke yawned, surprised to find himself exhausted. Normally on a Saturday night he'd play at the Honky Tonk until three in the morning, but on this Saturday night he was exhausted despite the fact that it was just a few minutes after ten.

Within minutes of keeping his eyes closed, he fell asleep.

A scream awoke him. He sat straight up, for a moment disoriented as to his surroundings and what had pulled him from his sleep. A sliver of moonlight slid through the windows, and as he looked around the room he remembered. He was at Abby's.

The scream came again, a familiar, high-pitched expression of abject terror. Jason. Luke sprang from the sofa and raced down the hallway to the little boy's room.

Abby was already there, and just like last time Jason's arms and legs were flailing wildly as he suffered the throes of an unspeakable nightmare.

"Shh, baby, it's all right. I'm right here," Abby said as she fought to control Jason's gyrations.

This time, instead of giving Abby an opportunity to send him away, Luke strode into the bedroom and sat on the end of the bed. Gently but firmly, he grasped Jason's ankles so the little boy couldn't kick Abby and she could concentrate on dodging his windmilling arms as she tried to wrench him from his nightmare dreamscape.

"Jason, sweetie, wake up. It's just a dream. You're safe here."

Within minutes Jason had awakened and sobbed in Abby's arms. "I don't want to live with my daddy," he cried. "I want to stay here with you forever."

"And that's exactly what you're going to do," Abby assured him. "Don't you worry, Jason. I'm going to do everything I can to make sure that you live with me forever."

Luke remained seated on the foot of the bed as Abby stroked Jason's brow and attempted to send the little boy back into a peaceful slumber.

She was a terrific mother. Luke's admiration for Abby fluttered through him. These kids needed her. They needed her patience and her love. And he once again silently vowed to do anything it took to help her win her case.

As the minutes passed, Luke became aware of several things, like the fact that Abby's sweet scent filled the room and that she was clad only in a pale pink frilly nightgown.

With the light shining from the night-light in a nearby wall socket, the gown almost appeared translucent. Luke couldn't tell if he could really see the faint, dark circles of her nipples beneath the thin fabric or if it was just his imagination.

He knew every inch of her, had lovingly studied her body the single time they had made love, but now he had an overwhelming desire to learn every inch of her body all over again.

His body reacted to his thoughts, filling with a tension that seemed almost unbearable. But it was a tension he wouldn't, couldn't follow through on.

He'd told her that everything would be aboveboard, that he would sleep on the sofa. He couldn't very well tell her he'd prefer to sleep in her bed each night and make love to her from dusk until dawn. He couldn't very well tell her he'd really like to ease the tension that simmered in him by kissing her, touching her, making slow, sweet love to her.

He stood, and with a nod to Abby left the bedroom. He turned on the lamp on the coffee table in the living room and sat down on the sofa, too wired to fall back asleep just yet.

Picking up the guitar, he willed the tension to leave his body, willed away the desire that had momentarily struck him. He strummed the strings in a soft, melodic tune, allowing the music to physically relax him even as his mind whirled.

Apparently Abby's talk with the children had stirred the demons in Jason's head, resulting in another of his nightmares.

Luke knew all about nightmares. He'd suffered horrendous dreams until he was about thirteen years old. In his dreams he hadn't been fighting to protect his mother against his father, but rather himself. He'd dreamed often that his father was trying to kill him and suffered the knowledge that if his father succeeded, nobody would care.

He mentally shook himself to dispel thoughts of his miserable childhood and instead thought over the conversation he and Abby had had with Johnna earlier that evening.

The most difficult thing for Luke to accept was that he was as helpless in this situation as he'd been as a young child dealing with his father. What he wanted to do was fix it, fix the whole thing so Abby would be happy, fix it so the kids would be assured a good life.

He set the guitar down as Abby came into the living room. She'd pulled on a short coral-colored terry robe that was belted tightly at her slender waist.

"I finally got him back to sleep," she said. She stood in the doorway between the hall and the living room, looking as fragile as Luke had ever seen her.

And in that instant, something Johnna had said replayed

in his mind and he knew exactly what he wanted to do. It wouldn't solve the problem, but it might just give her a fighting chance.

"Abby." He stood and faced her. "Marry me."

Chapter 11

"Excuse me?" Abby wondered if the stress of the day coupled with a lack of sleep had affected her ability to hear accurately.

"Marry me."

Luke strode over to where she stood and took her hands in his. He pulled her to the sofa, where they both sat. "Think about it, Abby. You heard Johnna this evening. She said it was too bad you weren't married, that judges liked to put children in stable two-parent homes. So let's make this a two-parent home."

She pulled her hands from his, her head reeling with his crazy suggestion. And it was crazy…wasn't it? "Luke, I… That's crazy," she finally managed to say.

"What's crazy about it?" His gray eyes bore into hers intently. "We get married and fight for custody. Once the custody battle is decided, then we have an amicable divorce. You get the kids, and I go to Nashville. Everybody goes away happy."

Abby frowned, finding it hard to think with him sitting so close to her, with his naked, muscular chest inches away from her. Everybody goes away happy, he'd said, and she'd love to believe that it was exactly what was going to happen.

But could she ask this man to give up his single status, even temporarily, for her? Confusion whirled in her head, and she felt the dull throb of a headache at the base of her skull. She stared at the coffee table, unsure what to do, what to say.

"Abby, this might provide the edge that you desperately need," Luke continued. She looked at him once again, saw in his eyes a burning need she wasn't sure she understood.

She rose. "I need to think about it," she said. She offered him a faint smile. "Your offer has thrown me for a loop. This is too important to decide at a moment's notice. I need some time to assess things."

He nodded. "Go to bed. We can talk about it in the morning."

Abby drew a deep breath. "Yes, we'll talk about it in the morning." She murmured a good-night, then went into her bedroom and crawled into bed.

She'd hoped that sleep would claim her quickly, but it remained elusive as she tossed and turned, thinking and re-thinking everything that had happened during the day.

She thought of Jason's terror and Jessica's silence. She thought of how much she had grown to love the two kids, how much she wanted to shower them with the love she would never get a chance to give her dead sister.

More than anything, she wanted to protect them…protect them from the kind of life they'd have with their father. Loretta had been married to Justin for six years at the time of her murder, and in those six years Abby had learned enough about Justin Cahill to know he was dangerous.

As she'd stood at the grave, burying the sister she'd so

loved, she'd vowed to herself that she would do anything to make certain the kids never had to live with that man again.

But did *anything* mean a temporary marriage to a man she didn't know that well? Would a marriage to Luke really help her or hurt her in the end?

"Okay, I'll marry you," she said the next morning as she walked into the kitchen and found Luke seated at the table with a mug of coffee before him. "Unless, of course, you've changed your mind," she hurriedly added.

He grinned and pointed her to the chair opposite him. "Sit," he commanded. "I think it's only right that I pour a cup of coffee for my wife-to-be."

"Are you sure about this, Luke?" she asked as she sat at the table.

"I've never been more sure about anything in my life," he replied.

She watched as he poured her a cup of coffee. It was obvious he was freshly showered—the scent of fresh soap hung in the air, and his hair was still slightly damp.

He set a mug of the hot brew in front of her, then returned to his chair across from her. "Don't look so scared," he said. "I promise you a temporary marriage to me won't be too painful."

She smiled and wrapped her hands around her mug. "I want you to understand that if we do this I won't expect anything from you. I mean, it won't be like we'll be a real husband and wife."

"You mean you promise you won't henpeck me or make me account for every hour I'm away from you, or spend all my money on foolish female things?"

She laughed, his teasing tone calming her nerves and oddly enough shooting strength through her. Her laughter died and she eyed him somberly. "But I'm serious, Luke. If we do this

I want you to understand that I don't want you to change your lifestyle in any way. I will expect nothing from you during or after the marriage."

"Okay," he agreed easily.

"And I don't think we should say too much about this in front of the kids. I don't want to confuse them. I mean, I don't want them to think that you are going to be a part of their lives forever." She felt a blush warm her cheeks and knew she wasn't making the point she'd intended to make. She looked into her coffee mug. "Just so as not to confuse them, I think the sleeping arrangements should remain the same even after the wedding ceremony."

"Okay." Once again he agreed easily, and she looked at him gratefully, only to see the charming, devilish sparkle in his eyes. "But I have to warn you, that doesn't mean I'm not going to try to talk you into a conjugal visit once in a while."

Abby's cheeks grew hotter, and she was saved from having to make a reply by the appearance of the kids. It wasn't until after breakfast, when the kids had gone outside to play, that she and Luke got a chance to talk alone once again.

"I spoke with Johnna while you were dressing the kids," Luke said, patting the sofa next to him for her to sit. "I told her what we have planned and made the arrangements to meet her and Jerrod at the church at noon tomorrow."

"Noon tomorrow?" Abby echoed faintly and sank down beside him. Suddenly it seemed so real, and she felt a nervous fluttering in her stomach. In less than twenty-four hours she would be Mrs. Luke Delaney.

"Johnna is going to take the kids into a playroom at the church while her husband, Jerrod, performs the ceremony. My brother Mark and his wife, April, will be our witnesses, and as far as all of them are concerned, this is a love match, not a temporary arrangement."

Abby looked at him in surprise. "But don't you want your family to know the truth?"

He shook his head. "I don't want anyone to know the truth. I don't want a whisper of this to get to Justin. As far as everyone in this town is concerned, you bowled me over with your charm, captivated me with those luscious green eyes of yours."

"And remind me again what I'm supposed to tell everyone when they ask why I married you," she said teasingly.

He leaned toward her, his eyes bewitching, his smile the sexy one that shot heat through her. "You can tell everyone that I stole your heart one night when we danced together under the stars."

Abby's heart stepped up its rhythm as she worked to think of something fun and sassy to say in return. But her mouth was too dry to speak as her head filled with the magic of those moments when they'd danced together in the moonlight.

Luke reached out a hand and ran his fingertips down the side of her jawline and across the hollow of her throat. His touch was warm and soft and sent a shiver racing up Abby's spine.

She forced a light laugh and leaned away from him. "I think I'll tell them that I felt sorry for you."

He sat up straighter and eyed her in surprise. "Sorry for me?"

She nodded. "Because before you met me you were just drifting through life without a purpose, without knowing real happiness, and I came along and saved you from yourself and your wayward lifestyle."

He laughed. "Ah, so you're one of those rescuing women."

"Not really," she replied more soberly. "There are only two people on this earth I really want to rescue…Jason and Jessica."

Luke leaned toward her once again and laid a hand against her cheek. "I know," he said softly.

Suddenly Abby needed to get away from him, gain some

physical distance. "And speaking of the kids," she said as she jumped up from the sofa. "I'd better go check on them."

A few moments later, she breathed deeply of the mid-morning air as she watched the kids playing on the tire swing. The emotions that whirled inside her confused her.

She had once believed herself head over heels in love with Ken Masters, but Ken had never made her feel the way Luke did. And she certainly wasn't in love with Luke Delaney.

She was just feeling an exceptional amount of warmth toward Luke because of what he was doing for her and the kids. Surely that explained the way her heart fluttered at his merest touch, the way her pulse stepped up its pace when he looked at her.

It was intense gratefulness she felt toward Luke, and nothing more. After all, the man who had professed to love her with all his heart had walked out on her when she'd taken custody of the kids. And Luke, a man who didn't even pretend to love her, was willing to go the extra mile in order to try to help the children she so loved. Of course she'd be feeling grateful and warm toward him.

At eleven the next morning, Abby, Luke and the kids headed into town. Their first stop was the courthouse, where Abby and Luke obtained their marriage license.

"I can't believe you can get a license and get married all in the same day," Abby said as they got into the car to drive to the church.

"We don't believe in wasting time in Arizona, so there's no waiting period," Luke replied.

Within minutes they were at the church, and Abby fought a wave of nervousness that was nearly nauseating. Everything had happened so quickly. She almost wished there were a waiting period in Arizona so she would have time to think…to make sure that she was doing the best thing for everyone.

Johnna greeted them at the door of the small, quaint-looking church. She introduced them to her handsome husband, Jerrod, the minister who was going to perform the ceremony, then whisked the kids away to a back room where she said she had all kinds of fun awaiting them.

"We'll just wait a few minutes for Mark and April to arrive," Jerrod said.

"Is there someplace where I can freshen up a little?" Abby asked, trying to still the nerves that jangled inside her.

Jerrod pointed the way to the ladies' rest room, and Abby slid inside the door, grateful for a few moments alone. She stared at her reflection in the mirror above the sink. The pale-faced bride-to-be who returned her stare was a stranger.

Was she doing the right thing? There had been no word from Justin, although Johnna's private investigator had confirmed that he was, indeed, in town. Still, he'd made no move to contact Abby or the children.

Maybe they were jumping the gun. Maybe they were over-reacting to the situation. Maybe this whole wedding thing was not necessary.

A vision of Jason's face, of Jessica's face exploded in her mind, and she knew it was impossible for anyone to be over-reacting where their safety was concerned. Justin's silence was ominous, and she couldn't fool herself into thinking otherwise.

She smoothed her hands down the sides of her dress. For her wedding gown, she'd chosen a knee-length, sleeveless beige dress. It was cotton, nothing real fancy, but she'd never worn it before and felt it was perfect for a simple wedding ceremony.

And Luke…Luke looked magnificent in a pair of charcoal dress slacks and a white shirt. They had gone the day before to his family ranch so he could pick up clean clothes. There, Abby had met his oldest brother, Matthew. Matthew had been curt but civil and obviously surprised by the news that his baby brother was getting married.

Luke. His name rang inside her, creating a heat that had no source. He'd teasingly told her he would do his best to talk her into a conjugal visit or two, and she wasn't sure he would have to talk too hard to get what he wanted.

"Abby?" Luke called to her through the door. "Mark and April are here. It's time."

It was time. Time for her to temporarily bind herself to Luke. She would become his wife in the eyes of the law and before God, but she had to remember that her marriage wouldn't last until death did them part…but would end in seven months when Luke left Inferno forever.

She left the rest room and was greeted by Luke, who introduced her to his brother Mark and Mark's pretty wife, April.

April took Abby's hands in hers and smiled warmly. "I'm so pleased," she said. "Luke is a wonderful, warm, caring man, and I'm so pleased you were able to see beneath his facade and find and fall in love with the man within."

Abby made what she hoped was an appropriate response, enormous guilt sweeping through her. She wanted to confess to April that this wasn't really a marriage of love, but rather a marriage of survival—her children's survival. But she knew Luke was right. Nobody must know the truth until the custody issue was settled.

"Every bride needs some flowers," Luke said, and surprised her by handing her a nosegay of sweet-smelling baby white roses.

"How did you manage this?" she asked, the gesture touching her more deeply than she cared to admit.

He grinned. "I have my ways."

With Jerrod orchestrating, they all got into their positions,

April standing next to Abby and Mark standing next to Luke in front of the small altar.

A sense of numbness swept through Abby as Jerrod began speaking the words that would make her and Luke husband and wife.

She'd once dreamed of this moment, of a long white dress and a lacy veil, of splendid flowers and golden bands. Most of all, she'd dreamed that her wedding would be the beginning of a lifetime of love and passion and laughter.

Maybe someday she would still have her dream wedding, but at the moment she was binding herself to Luke in a temporary arrangement in the best interests of Jessica and Jason.

"Will you join hands and face one another," Jerrod instructed.

Abby's cold, slightly trembling hands were clasped in Luke's bigger hands. The warmth and strength that radiated from his hands somewhat calmed the nerves that danced inside her.

She looked into his dark-lashed, smoky eyes and repeated the vows that would make him her husband. As she said the words, she was struck with a sense of horror as a jolt of realization struck her. There was more than a little bit of her heart that wished this was for real…forever. There was more than just a little bit of her heart that was in love with Luke Delaney.

As Luke said his vows, he knew the mixed emotions that had to be fluttering inside Abby. Her eyes were windows to those emotions, first darkening with a hint of anxiety, then lighting and sparking with something that pulled a ball of emotion into Luke's chest.

For the first time in his life, Luke felt as if he were doing something that was positively right. If he did nothing else for the rest of his life, at least he would have the knowledge that he put himself on the line to help two innocent kids. And that made him more than the loser his father had always proclaimed him to be.

It was crazy, but as he spoke the promise to love, honor and cherish Abby, he felt the words deep in his heart, deep in his soul. The emotion in his chest grew to mammoth proportions. Although he knew the vows they spoke were only temporary, he silently vowed to do whatever he could for Abby and her children for the time he would be in their lives.

"You may kiss your bride," Jerrod said, bringing Luke back to the moment at hand.

Once again he gazed deeply into Abby's eyes as he leaned forward to deliver the kiss that would seal their bond. Although the kiss was swift and light, the feel of her sweet lips beneath his sent a wave of heat cascading through him.

With the ceremony done, there were congratulations all around, then Luke and Abby gathered the children and left the church.

"I've got a surprise for us all," he said when they were in Abby's car after the ceremony had been completed.

"A surprise? What kind of a surprise?" Jason leaned over the seat.

"Sit back and buckle up and I'll tell you," Luke replied. Jason did as he requested, and Luke continued, "How would you all like to go on a picnic?"

"A picnic? Cool!" Jason replied.

"I've got everything we need for a successful picnic in the trunk," Luke said, then grinned at Abby who was looking at him in surprise. "I was busy early this morning while you were still in bed."

"A picnic sounds nice," she agreed.

"I'm going to take you to one of my most favorite places

in the world," he said softly. "It's a perfect place for a wedding day picnic."

She smiled and nodded, then cast her gaze out the car window. She'd been unusually quiet since the ceremony, and he wished he could read her thoughts, wondered if she was already regretting their decision.

She looked as pretty as he'd ever seen her. The beige dress was a perfect foil for her shiny dark hair and displayed her slender curves to perfection.

His wife. Under the laws of the land and in the state of Arizona, he'd just bound his life with hers, promised to love and honor her in sickness and in health, until death do them part. Or until the custody issue was resolved, he reminded himself.

He'd planned the picnic because he thought that with the tension of the last two days, a little relaxation and fun would be good for her.

It was another beautiful day, warm but not overly hot. A faint breeze stirred the trees as Luke turned onto Delaney property. He drove past the main house and the guest cabins, following a dirt road into a pasture.

"Look, I see horses," Jason exclaimed. "Look, Jessica, there's a black one and a brown one."

"That's Mabel and Betty," Luke said. "We don't ride them anymore. They've been retired, but maybe later we can coax them over here to get a bit of an apple."

He pulled in near a grove of trees and parked the car, and they all got out. Luke popped open the trunk and began to unload the items he'd packed earlier.

"A blanket, a basket of food, a ball, a Frisbee…" Abby smiled at him. "It would seem you've thought of everything."

"I believe in the Boy Scout motto, be prepared."

"Were you a Boy Scout?"

"Nah, I got kicked out of Boy Scouts for playing with the Girl Scouts," he teased. He was rewarded with her laughter. "Jason," he called. "Heads up." He threw him the ball, then tossed the Frisbee to Jessica.

While the two children played, he and Abby spread the blanket beneath a shady tree. "Stretch out here and relax and I'll unpack the food," he said.

With Abby sitting on the blanket, Luke began to unload what he'd packed for their lunch. "I hope you don't mind that I raided your refrigerator," he said. "We've got balogna and cheese sandwiches, chips, apples and cookies."

She tilted her head and eyed him curiously. "You must have been up before dawn."

He nodded. "Prewedding jitters, I guess."

As he pulled out a blue plastic container, she placed her hand on his arm. "Are you sorry we went through with it?" Her eyes, the beautiful green of spring, were filled with concern.

He leaned over and touched her cheek. "Now how can I be sorry about marrying the prettiest woman in Arizona?" he teased, then realized she wanted, needed more than that. He pointed to where the children were throwing the Frisbee back and forth.

"How can I be sorry for trying to help them? How can I be sorry for stepping up to the plate when all my life I wish somebody had done that for me?"

Her eyes held a compassion that made a curious ache in his chest. "I wish I would have been there for you, saved you from your mean, wicked father."

Luke smiled, consciously shoving aside all thoughts of his past. "I survived." He pulled a dark blue bowl covered with foil out of the basket. "And your kids are not only going to survive, they are going to thrive under your love and care."

Her eyes darkened. "I hope so. It's been three days and

there's been no word from Justin. I don't understand why he hasn't contacted me yet."

"Conversation about that man is strictly off-limits today," Luke replied. "We aren't going to let him ruin our picnic."

She drew a deep breath. "You're right." She pointed to the blue plastic bowl. "What's in there?"

"It's a surprise. You'll see later." He set the bowl aside and called the kids to eat.

As they all sat on the blanket and enjoyed the food Luke had packed, their laughter ringing through the trees, Luke felt a strange sense of peace. He could see the main house in the distance, the house that had held his childhood bogeyman, and it was strange to him that the unhappiness he'd experienced there, at the moment, seemed distant and long ago.

It was as if Jason's boyish, braying laughter and Jessica's sweet little giggles chased away the ghosts of his past.

As they ate, to the delight of the children, Mabel and Betty drew closer. When Jason and Jessica had finished eating, Luke cut up a couple of apples into horse-bite-size pieces.

"Just go stand in front of them and hold a piece of apple out in your hand and they'll take it from you," Luke instructed. "Don't worry, they won't hurt you." Jason led the way, Jessica hiding behind him as they approached the horses with the apples.

"And now, dear Abby, I told you once what the best way to eat strawberries was…." He popped the top of the bowl to display ripe, red strawberries.

Abby's face lit with surprise. "Where did you get them?" she asked in obvious amazement.

He grinned, pleased that she was pleased. "I raided them from the ranch yesterday when we came to pick up my clothes. Now, stretch out and let me feed them to you one luscious berry at a time."

"Luke," she protested with a charming blush. "It isn't necessary that you feed me."

"Ah, but it is." He took one of her hands and gently pushed against her shoulder, guiding her down to the blanket on her back. "I promise to be a good and dutiful husband for the duration of our marriage if you'll just indulge me this one whim."

Her eyes twinkled merrily. "And this is the only whim of yours I'll have to indulge?"

Heat swept through Luke as he thought of all the whims he would like them to indulge together. He stretched out on his side next to her, the bowl of strawberries between them.

Jason and Jessica had finished feeding the horses and were playing a game of hide-and-seek as Luke fed Abby the first plump, juicy berry.

The moment her mouth closed not only around the berry, but the tip of his finger, as well, Luke knew he was in trouble. White-hot desire swept through him.

He fed her another strawberry, unable to speak as he worked to staunch the flow of heated blood through his body. Abby seemed to sense his sudden mood change from teasing to tormented.

Her eyes deepened in color, and once again a blush stained her cheeks. Her lips were rosy red with berry juice, and what Luke wanted to do more than anything was kiss her long and hard.

"Oh, boy, strawberries." Jason's delight tore Luke from his growing fog of desire. "Can me and Jessica have some?"

"Sure," Luke agreed and sat up. Abby also rose to a sitting position. He wondered if she had any idea how precariously close he'd come to losing it…how he was both grateful and disappointed that Jason had quelled the mood of the moment.

The four of them polished off the strawberries in no time.

But it wasn't until the sun was slowly sinking in the sky that they packed up and headed back to the house.

As they drove home, they sang old childhood songs. Jessica didn't sing, but clapped her hands in rhythm, her eyes sparkling with happiness.

It had been a good day. The issue of the custody battle ahead, the specter of Justin Cahill had remained at bay for the duration.

They'd ended their time in the pasture by the four of them playing Frisbee. Abby had kicked off her high heels and taken off her panty hose, then chased after the flying disc like a wood nymph chasing a butterfly.

She placed a hand on his arm, her eyes sparkling. "Thank you, Luke. It was an absolutely perfect day."

"It was nice, wasn't it?"

"And I know two little people who will sleep very well tonight," she added.

Luke nodded. He knew one good-size man who would probably sleep quite poorly. He wondered how many newly-wed grooms spent their wedding night alone on a sofa.

But this wasn't really a marriage, and he wasn't really a groom, he reminded himself. They had entered into this arrangement for the children. Abby wasn't in love with him, and he certainly wasn't in love with her.

"I can't believe how much the kids took to the horses," Abby said, breaking into his thoughts.

"Next week, we'll take them over to the ranch and let them ride. We'll ride in the morning, then take the afternoon to find that dog you've promised them."

Luke had never expected such mundane things like a promised horseback ride and finding the perfect dog would bring him a sense of joy. But he was actually looking forward to them. He could easily imagine Jason and Jessica's faces the first time they were put on the back of a horse or the first time their new dog licked them.

"Let's sing Bingo," Jason said from the backseat, and once again the car rang with song and laughter.

All laughter died as they pulled into Abby's driveway and saw a patrol car waiting there. "Oh, no, what now?" Abby said softly.

Luke parked the car and they all got out.

"Evening," Sheriff Jeffrey Broder greeted them, his features set in sober lines.

"Sheriff." Luke nodded, then spoke to Abby. "Why don't you go open the door and let the kids go on in the house."

She nodded, lines of tension that had been gone all day appearing on her lovely face.

"What's up?" Luke asked the sheriff softly as Abby went to unlock the front door.

"I hate like hell to be out here," Broder said. "But you know part of my job is serving papers for the county."

"So, you're here to serve papers?"

Broder nodded, then offered Abby a tight smile as she rejoined the two men. "Abigail Graham?"

She nodded, trembling like a leaf precariously clinging to a tree in a stiff wind. Luke placed an arm around her shoulders.

Jeffrey held out a large, official-looking envelope. "You are hereby served."

Abby took the envelope from him but didn't open it right away.

"On a more pleasant note, I hear congratulations are in order," Jeffrey said. He offered a gentle smile to Abby. "Maybe your influence can keep this guy out of my jail."

Abby shot Luke a surprised glance.

Luke smiled. "Don't worry, I'm not a habitual lawbreaker. There's been a couple of times that Jeffrey allowed me the use of one of his jail cells to sleep off the effects of too much alcohol, but that was a long time ago."

"It has been a long time," Jeffrey agreed. He shifted from one foot to the other, obviously uncomfortable. "Well, I guess I'll just get out of here. Again, my congratulations on your marriage. I never thought you'd bite the bullet, Luke."

"Me, neither," Luke replied and pulled Abby closer against his side. "It took one very special woman to capture me."

Luke held tight to Abby even after Jeffrey's car had disappeared into the distance. Her fingers trembled as she opened the envelope and pulled out the legal papers that told them Justin Cahill was attempting to legally reclaim his parental rights to his children.

And so, the battle had begun.

Chapter 12

"This is where we stand so far," Johnna said to Luke and Abby. It was Wednesday morning, and the three of them sat at Abby's kitchen table. "Judd has been terrific in getting us good information on Justin Cahill. Right now we know he's staying at Rose's Bed and Breakfast in town."

"Maybe we could get Rose to poison those homemade muffins she offers her guests in the mornings," Luke said drily.

Abby smiled at him. "Or at least short sheet his bed," she replied.

Luke returned her smile, and she felt a rivulet of warmth flood through her. It frightened her just a little, how much she'd come to depend on his strength, on his sense of humor and on his neverending optimism in getting through all this.

Johnna ignored their little asides and continued. "Judd has learned that Justin has no visible means of support. He lives in a small, one-bedroom apartment in Kansas City and he's a loud complainer about how the judicial system screwed up his life with false murder charges."

"So right now Abby and I have the upper hand as far as where is the best physical place for the children to be," Luke said.

"That's true," Johnna agreed. "But that could change at any moment. All Justin has to do is tell the judge that he intends to get a bigger apartment or rent a house. Judd was able to get into his bank records and has discovered that Justin is not rolling in the dough, but he's certainly not destitute."

"Who is this Judd?" Abby asked.

"He works as a private investigator for me," Johnna explained.

"He's in his mid-thirties, moved to Inferno a couple of years ago," Luke explained further. "All anyone really knows about him is that he's a loner, used to work for the FBI and lives like a hermit in an old house on the north side of town."

"Justin has retained the services of Gordon Clemens, an attorney from Tucson. He's supposed to be a real shark."

Abby's heart fell. "Can you handle him?" she asked Johnna.

Johnna flashed her a full grin. "I eat sharks for breakfast. Now this is what's going to happen. We've filed all the appropriate paperwork, and I've talked to a children's services social worker to line up a home study."

"What exactly does that mean?" Luke asked.

"Her name is Sonya Watkins and she's going to come out here Saturday morning and look around the place. She'll speak with both you and Abby and talk to the kids." Johnna placed the woman's business card on the table. "Her report will hold a lot of weight with the judge. And we have a court date in two weeks."

"So quickly?" Abby shot a panicked gaze to Johnna.

"The quicker, the better, Abby," Johnna said gently. "You don't want this hanging over your head… Over the kids' heads. We're a small county, and unlike the rest of the country, our children's services department isn't overworked. And I think that's it for now," Johnna said, and closed the folder in front of her.

She stood, and Luke and Abby did the same. "I think it's obvious that Justin intends to use the court system to get what he wants and has no intention of storming this place to take his kids by force."

"Good luck if he tries," Luke said grimly as the three of them walked to the front door.

"Oh, and something else," Johnna said. "I think it's best if you stay away from the Honky Tonk until this is all settled," she said to Luke. "We'll play up the ranch and your woodworking abilities to the judge."

"I'd already made that decision," Luke said. "Although I have to play there this Friday night for just a couple of hours. It's Jim Grogin's birthday, and I promised him months ago that I would sing a couple of his favorite tunes at his party at the bar that night."

Johnna frowned. "Okay, but after that, stay away from that dive. And for goodness sake, Friday night, don't do anything stupid." She flashed a smile at Abby. "I'll be in touch." And with that, she flew out the door.

Abby turned to look at Luke and instantly realized he was angry. A pulse throbbed in his tensed jaw muscles. "Luke? What's wrong?"

She followed him to the sofa, where they both sat. "Nothing," he said, his voice curt.

She placed a hand on his thigh. "Luke, you've been so good the last couple of days listening to my fears, my sorrows, almost everything that is in my heart. Why won't you share with me what has your jaw twisted into knots and your hands clenched into fists?"

He sighed and raked a hand through his thick, dark hair. "I just get so irritated because my sister and my two brothers always seem to expect the worst from me. It irritates me that they don't believe in me."

"But I believe in you," she said softly.

He turned to look at her, his eyes deep pools of smoldering flames…flames that threatened to instantly consume her.

He didn't say a word, but rather took her in his arms and captured her lips in a hot, hungry kiss. Just that quickly, they were out of control.

From the moment he'd fed her those strawberries on the blanket in the pasture, in the back of Abby's mind she'd yearned to make love with him once again.

And she'd known it had been on his mind, as well. She'd seen the hunger in his eyes when he gazed at her, felt the electricity flowing from him when their hands brushed or their shoulders bumped.

In the instant their lips met, any and all reasons they shouldn't make love again fled Abby's mind. All she knew, all she could comprehend was the hunger for his touch, her need for his body against hers.

He deepened the kiss, his tongue touching hers as his hands tangled in her hair. As he pressed her closer she could feel his heartbeat banging, racing in rhythm with her own. And she could feel his obvious arousal.

"Abby, sweet Abby," he murmured as his lips left hers and trailed down the side of her jaw to the sensitive skin just below her earlobe.

He gently tugged her hair, tilting her head back to give him better access to the hollow of her throat.

His mouth nipped and kissed, shooting fire through her, filling her with a heat she knew only he could stanch. He raised his head to look at her, to see the assent in her eyes, then he stood and scooped her into his arms and carried her into her bedroom.

Johnna had arrived early enough that morning that Abby hadn't had an opportunity to make the beds. Luke deposited her gently in the middle of the jumbled sheets, then stepped back and pulled his T-shirt over his head.

As Luke undressed, Abby did the same, driven by a fever of need, of want. She wanted to be naked with him, for him. She wanted immediate skin-to-skin contact.

When he joined her on the bed, she moaned in pleasure as his warm flesh made contact with hers and she was surrounded by that woodsy, spicy scent that always drove her half-wild.

He gathered her into his arms, the hairs on his chest teasing her nipples, the length of his legs wrapping around hers. Once again his mouth sought hers in a kiss of fiery intensity.

When the kiss ended, his eyes bore into hers. "I feel as if I've been on fire for months…years…and the only thing that can put the fire out is you."

"I've felt the same way," she replied, her voice husky to her own ears. She tangled her fingers in his hair and pulled him closer for another kiss, lost in splendid sensual pleasure, lost to everything but the magic of Luke.

And it was magic…every stroke of his hands, each touch of his lips created an enchantment that momentarily swept away all the cares of the world, banished all fear and uncertainty.

Time seemed to stand still as he stroked the length of her body in slow, languid, torturously wonderful caresses. His mouth found every erogenous zone, lingering here and there to bring her the most exquisite pleasure.

He took her to the peak over and over again, but held back giving her the ultimate release. Over and over again he left her trembling with need, until finally he paused to put on a condom, then entered her.

Slowly, he moved deep within her, then pulled back slightly, hot friction sending Abby again to the peak of pleasure. Again and again Luke repeated the give and take, stepping up the rhythm as his breaths became short and shallow.

She felt Luke's rising tension, felt his muscles growing more taut, his body filled with immense heat that only served to enflame Abby.

As Luke cried out her name and stiffened against her, she tumbled over the edge, every nerve ending in her body tingling in splendid delight as she gasped breathlessly.

For long minutes afterward they lay in one another's arms, in an embrace so close Abby could feel Luke's heartbeat slowly resuming a normal rhythm.

"I'm sorry Johnna upset you," Abby finally said as she lay with her head on his chest.

He stroked a hand down her hair and drew a deep sigh. "She upset me because she reminded me that I'm probably an alcoholic."

Abby raised her head and looked at him. Despite the sunshine pouring into the room, his eyes were dark with more than a hint of self-loathing. "But Luke, you haven't drunk the whole time I've known you."

"I'm a recovering alcoholic, and Johnna's words just reminded me that I'll always be only one drink away from failure."

Abby placed a hand on his jaw. "But until you take that drink, you are a success. And I know you're brave enough, smart enough to stay strong."

He grinned, the darkness in his eyes lifting. "You are something else, Mrs. Abigail Delaney. I think in the next couple of days I'm going to build you the most beautiful kitchen cabinets in the entire state of Arizona."

"Luke, you don't have to do that," she protested.

He smiled again. "I know I don't, but I want to."

"I can pay you for your work," she said. "Now that Justin knows where I'm at, there's no reason for me to not access my trust fund."

"I don't want your money," he replied. "It will be enough for me to know that when I'm in Nashville, you and the kids will be living in a place that's nice." He pulled her to his chest and stroked her hair. "But for the moment I just want to stay here with you in my arms."

When I'm in Nashville. His words swirled around in her head, filling her with a profound sadness. She knew she shouldn't be sad. She'd gone into this arrangement with her eyes wide open.

Luke had never promised to love her, to set aside his dreams of singing for her and the children. He'd never promised to spend the rest of his life with her. He was here only until the custody battle was decided.

Two weeks. Johnna had said the trial was set for two weeks. There was both pleasure and pain in the short waiting period. She was glad the custody issue would be over, that she didn't have to wait an eternity to find out if she would be able to raise the children she loved.

Two weeks. It wasn't enough time for her to spend with Luke. She wanted more. She was in love with Luke and she wanted a lifetime with him.

She wouldn't make love to him again, knew that to do so would just make it that much more difficult when the time came to tell him goodbye. And she would have to tell him goodbye.

In six and a half months he would leave Inferno, but in two weeks he would leave her. She squeezed her eyes tightly closed against a sudden burning of tears.

She wasn't sure what was worse—the possibility that in

two weeks she would lose the children or the absolute certainty that in two weeks she would lose Luke.

"I really hate to leave you and the kids," Luke said as he and Abby stood on the front porch. The sun was dying in the west, splashing the horizon with vivid colors.

"But you promised you'd do this," Abby replied. "We'll be okay, Luke. Justin hasn't shown hide nor hair around here. There's no reason to believe he'll suddenly make an appearance."

"I know, but I still don't like it." Luke sighed, his gaze lingering on Abby. "I wish I hadn't promised Jim Grogin that I'd sing tonight." He wondered if there would come a day when he tired of looking at her, when the scent of her didn't stir him to distraction.

"But you did promise." She reached up and straightened his collar, then brushed a piece of lint from the navy shirt he wore. "This Jim Grogin is a friend of yours?"

"He was a peer of my father's. When I was thirteen, he talked my father into letting me work a couple hours a day at his ranch. I don't think he really needed me, but I think he knew I needed a couple hours a day to escape from my old man."

Once again Luke directed his gaze away from her and toward the quickly setting sun. "He's a good man, and those hours I spent on his ranch were good ones."

It was a vast understatement. Jim was quick to praise the young Luke, and it was Jim who had taught Luke a love of wood and the basic elements of woodworking.

"Anyway, the six months I worked for him were the happiest months of my adolescence."

Abby tilted her head slightly and looked at him curiously. "Why only six months?"

"My father refused to let me work for him any longer than

that. I think my old man saw that I was developing some pride and some independence, and he wasn't about to let that happen."

"Then it's important that you go. And if you don't leave now you'll be late." She smiled at him. "I swear we'll be fine here until you get home."

"I've got my key, so lock up tight and don't open the door for anybody. If you hear anything odd, anything at all, don't hesitate to call Sheriff Broder. He can be out here in minutes."

"Would you get out of here?" She laughed and gave him a nudge to move him off the porch.

"I'll be home by midnight," he said as he walked backward toward his truck.

"I'm sure the kids and I will be asleep, but Peaches will greet you with her puppy enthusiasm."

Luke grinned, waved, then got into his truck. On Wednesday afternoon when the kids had gotten out of school, Luke had taken Abby and the kids to a dog breeder he knew. There they had discovered Peaches, an eight-week-old golden retriever who had greeted Jessica and Jason as if they were long-lost best friends.

Peaches had come home with them, along with a bag of dog food, water and food dish and a large cage for housebreaking and nighttime sleeping.

When the two kids had fought over who got Peaches in their bedroom for the night, it was decided that Peaches' cage would stay in the living room with Luke.

Three days that week, Abby had gone with Luke to the ranch so he could get his twenty-five hours for the week in. She spent the hours sitting at a picnic table in the shade, watching the guests and reading a book.

However, it wasn't the dog or working at the family ranch that was on Luke's mind as he drove toward the Honky Tonk. He was nervous about leaving Abby alone.

There was absolutely no reason for him to be nervous. Justin had given no indication that he intended to do anything but battle them in a court of law, so there was really no reason to be worried.

It felt strange to be worried about somebody else. Luke had spent all his life until this point not worrying about anyone. But Abby pulled out of him feelings he'd never felt before.

Still, that certainly didn't change his plans for himself. He was going to be somebody, become somebody important. In six and a half months, he'd be gone from here, on his way to his destiny.

He parked his truck in the lot in front of the Honky Tonk. For a moment he sat and stared at the gawdy neon sign, the dusty, smoke-filled curtains that hung in the window. He hoped this was one of the last dives he'd ever have to work, that when he got to Nashville he'd be working better places.

He also knew this place was one of his greatest temptations. The moment he walked through the doors, he'd smell the booze in the air, get that old sweet yearning as each and every bottle in the place sang a siren song.

He thought of Abby's words, of her assurance that he was strong enough to make good choices. Funny, but he wanted to make good choices for her. He wanted to be a better man…for her. Sighing, he got out of the truck, slightly disturbed by thoughts of Abby.

Although it was only a few minutes before nine, the place was already jumping. As Luke grabbed his guitar from the back of his truck and headed toward the front door, music drifted out along with the sounds of raucous laughter and the clinking of beer bottles.

Luke entered the large, dimly lit bar and was greeted by half a dozen of the regular customers. He returned their greetings as he wove his way through the crowd toward the tiny stage.

The guest of honor, Jim Grogin, was seated with his wife and grown children at the table just in front of the stage. He stood as he saw Luke approach. "Luke, I'm so glad you could make it," he said as he slapped Luke on the back. "When I heard that you'd gone and gotten yourself married, I wasn't sure you'd be here at all."

"I wouldn't miss it," Luke replied, and smiled warmly at the gray-haired man. He nodded to Jim's wife, Sadie, and to their two sons and their wives. "Looks like you've got the whole gang here."

Jim nodded. "All except the grandbabies." His pale blue eyes twinkled merrily. "Can't have my sweet grandbabies in a dive like this."

"And the only way he got me into this dive is by promising me I would get to hear you sing," Sadie said.

"Let me buy you a drink, son," Jim said, and motioned for the waitress. "What will it be?" he asked. "As I recall, you used to be a Scotch man."

"Used to be, but now I'm strictly a soda man. I'll take a ginger ale," he told the cute little waitress.

"So, tell me about the woman who finally managed to capture your heart," Jim said. "I haven't seen her, but I heard through the grapevine that she's quite a looker with long dark hair and blue eyes."

"Green," Luke corrected. "Her eyes are green." He smiled as he thought of those lovely green eyes. He'd learned to watch her eyes, knowing that her moods and feelings would be reflected there. She would make a terrible poker player— her eyes would never allow her to bluff.

"And I understand she's got a couple of children," Jim continued. "I got a feeling she couldn't have picked a better stepdad for her babies. You learned firsthand about bad fathers. I got a feeling you're going to be a great one."

His words filled Luke with a crazy kind of guilt. He wanted to confess to Jim that fatherhood wasn't part of the deal, that the whole marriage thing was merely temporary. Instead he excused himself, telling them he needed to get set up and ready to perform.

Setting up required little more than positioning the microphone and a chair in place on the stage. He'd just finished doing that when the waitress came with his drink. "Just put it there on the edge of the stage," he said, then did a quick tune-up of his guitar.

It was nearly ten when Luke began his first set. He sang for twenty minutes, singing songs requested by people who yelled out their favorites.

He set his guitar aside, downed his soda and grinned at the waitress, who instantly replaced it with a fresh one. He took a ten-minute break, visiting with people who had become acquaintances over the years, then he began another set that included a rousing version of "Happy Birthday" for the guest of honor.

He was into his third set when he noticed the stranger watching him intently from the back of the room. Although Abby had never given him a physical description of Justin Cahill, Luke instantly recognized him. Jason and Jessica had the dark eyes of their father and the same cheekbones and slender face.

The man had the shoulders of a steroid freak, thick and bulging, made more apparent by the tank top he wore. There was a challenging glint in his dark eyes as he held Luke's gaze from across the room.

Luke was unsurprised when he finished the set and Justin Cahill stood at the foot of the stage. "Thought it was time I introduced myself to you. I'm Justin Cahill." He held his hand out for a shake.

Luke looked at his hand, the hand that Abby believed had killed her sister, and he deliberately shoved his own hands deep into his pockets.

Justin's eyes flared with the heat of suppressed rage. "So that's the way it is," he said tightly.

"It would appear that's the way it is," Luke replied.

Justin took a step toward him, invading Luke's personal space, but Luke didn't give the man the satisfaction of stepping back. "I just thought I'd stop by and let you know that there is no way in hell you're getting my kids. They belong to me."

Not "with me" but rather "to me." A definite indication that the man had no right to have his children. "We'll just have to wait and see about that, won't we?" Luke replied, refusing to rise to the man's baiting tone.

"I'm just giving you a friendly heads-up. I don't intend to lose this fight." With those final words Justin spun on his heels and headed for the exit.

Luke grabbed his soda and downed it, feeling as if he needed to wash a very bad taste out of his mouth. He set the empty glass down and headed for the back office of the tavern, where he knew there was a telephone.

"Toby, can I use the phone?" he asked the owner of the Honky Tonk, who sat at his desk going over paperwork.

"Help yourself." Toby waved toward the phone on the corner of the desk, not taking his gaze from his work.

Luke grabbed the receiver and quickly dialed. "Abby," he said when he heard her voice at the other end of the line. "Justin was just in here and just left. That means he knows you and the kids are there alone. He probably won't bother you, but I'm leaving here now and should be there in fifteen minutes."

"I'll keep the doors locked until I hear your voice," Abby said.

"Trouble?" Toby asked.

"Nothing I can't handle," Luke replied. "Would you do me a favor and lock up my guitar? I'm just going to sneak out the back door."

"Sure, no problem," Toby replied.

Luke started out of the office, but hesitated in the doorway, a wave of dizziness overtaking him. He shook his head, thinking he must have moved too fast, then headed out the back door.

He stepped into the night air, and the ground seemed to be moving, twisting and undulating beneath his feet. He slammed his back against the building and closed his eyes, drawing deep breaths and fighting against the blackness he sensed descending.

His drink. Justin must have put something in his drink. He shook his head again and took several steps forward. The blackness reached out, insidiously pulling Luke in.

Abby, his mind cried. It was his last conscious thought.

Chapter 13

Abby sat in the darkened living room staring out the front window, watching for Luke's truck. The house was quiet around her except for an occasional tiny whine from Peaches in her cage.

It had been almost thirty minutes since Luke had called, and she expected to see the headlights of his truck at any moment.

Luke hadn't gone into any real detail about seeing Justin, and curiosity burned inside her as she wondered what had happened, what had been said between the two men.

Peaches whined again, and Abby made her way through the darkness to the cage. "What's the matter, baby?" she asked softly. The dog nudged her cold, wet nose against her hand.

She knew if the light were on she would be able to see Peaches' beautiful liquid brown eyes gazing at her adoringly.

She opened the cage, lifted the puppy into her arms and was instantly rewarded with a wet lick along her neck.

She returned to her chair and put Peaches on her lap. The dog wiggled and squirmed for a moment, then settled down, snuggling against her with a sigh of contentment.

As Abby returned her gaze to the window, she stroked the silky fur. The dog had already wrought a miracle of sorts earlier that evening. As the two kids were playing with her in the living room, Abby had heard Jessica tell the dog she loved her.

"I love you, Peaches," Jessica had said loud and clear. The first words Abby had heard her speak since her mother's murder. Abby hadn't said anything, hadn't even indicated she'd heard, but her heart had expanded with joy as she realized there was a healing taking place in both the children.

First thing in the morning the social worker was to arrive to look around. Abby had spent most of the evening making sure everything was neat and clean, looking at each room with an objective eye.

Although there was work that needed to be done in several areas of the house, she didn't think the social worker would count any of that against them. The house was clean, but had a lived-in feeling. It was obviously a home filled with warmth and love.

Making love to Luke again had deepened her feelings for him, and she knew eventually she'd be left with a heartache. She suspected that Luke's confession of being a recovering alcoholic had been an effort to warn her away. Just as he'd distanced her the first time they'd made love, she had a feeling he'd attempted to do the same the second time they'd made love.

But she knew in her heart, in her soul, that Luke was a good man, and she prayed that he would continue to stay strong and sober. Whether he was with her or not, she wanted that for him.

She sat straighter in the chair as she saw twin headlights pierce the night, heading in the direction of her house. Luke. Finally. She breathed a sigh of relief. She didn't realize how tense she'd been until some of that tension seeped out of her.

As the vehicle drew closer, her anxiety returned, exploding through her veins. It wasn't Luke's familiar pickup making its way toward the house, but an unfamiliar compact car.

Who was it? It was certainly too dark for her to be able to see the occupant of the car. Who would be driving to her house in the middle of the night?

Justin.

His name rang in her ears as fear turned her icy cold. Peaches, who'd fallen asleep on her lap, lifted her head and growled deep in her throat.

Abby put the dog on the floor and raced to the front door, assuring herself that it was locked tight. She grabbed the cordless phone and ran to the door, peering through the small diamond-shaped window in the wooden door.

The car pulled up directly in front of her porch and sat there idling for several long, torturous minutes. Knowing that Luke should be pulling in any minute, Abby was hesitant to call the sheriff, especially since at the moment she wasn't even positive it was Justin.

As she watched, the driver got out of the vehicle and stretched his arms overhead, as if he'd been driving a long distance and was stiff. As the moonlight fell full on his features, Abby recognized that it was, indeed, Justin.

Abby remained at the door and quickly punched in the numbers she had memorized that would ring the phone in the sheriff's office.

Sheriff Broder answered on the first ring.

"This is Abby Graham. Please come to my place quickly. I need help."

"On my way," Sheriff Broder responded.

As Abby punched the phone off, Justin sauntered to the front door. Heart pounding frantically, Abby put her weight against the door even though she knew in the back of her mind that no lock and certainly not her inconsequential body weight would keep Justin out if he wanted in.

"Abby." He knocked lightly on the door. Peaches growled, then barked low and deep in her puppy throat.

"Get out of here, Justin," she said, trying to keep her voice low enough so she wouldn't awaken Jason and Jessica. She didn't want them to experience the pulse-pounding fear that rocked through her.

"What's the matter, Abby? Do I make you nervous?" He chuckled, the sound once again turning Abby's blood to ice. He banged a fist against the door. Abby jumped and swallowed the scream that nearly escaped her.

"You bitch. You stole my kids. Did you think I wouldn't find you? Did you really think you could get away from me?" He banged the door again, then laughed. "Loretta always said I made her nervous."

White-hot rage swept through Abby as he spoke her sister's name. He was the monster who had stolen Lo-retta from the people who loved her. "I've called the sheriff, Justin. He'll be here any moment."

Again he laughed, a wicked, evil sound that sent icy fingers up Abby's spine. "Don't worry, Abby. When I decide to get you, you won't have time to call the sheriff. You won't have time to do anything." He didn't wait for her to reply, but walked off the porch and back to his car.

She watched as he drove off into the night, the darkness eventually swallowing the taillights of his car. She sagged against the door, hot tears scalding her cheeks.

They were tears of fear, tears of relief, and most of all,

they were tears for the sister who was no longer with her. She was almost sorry Justin hadn't done something violent, something totally out of control that would see him permanently behind bars.

He'd only come for one thing, to mentally terrorize her. It had been a cat-and-mouse game. Damn him. Damn him to hell. And where…where was Luke?

She returned to her seat, Peaches once again in her lap, and stared out the window. At that moment she saw the whirling red lights that indicated Sheriff Broder was coming toward the house.

She met him on the porch and quickly explained to him what had happened. He seemed already to know that Luke was playing at the bar and assured Abby he would keep an eye on the place until Luke got home.

Abby went inside, assured by the presence of the sheriff but disturbed by Luke's absence. Where was he? Why wasn't he home yet? If he'd left as soon as he called, he should have been home by now.

As the seconds and minutes ticked by, her mind whirled with possibilities. Maybe he'd gotten held up at the party. One of the things she'd made clear to him was that she didn't expect him to change his lifestyle because of their marriage. But he said he'd be right home, a small voice niggled inside her head.

When an hour had passed, she fought the edges of panic that attempted to creep into her mind. She thought of calling one of Luke's relatives, but knew if nothing was wrong Luke would be angry at her decision.

And so she did nothing. She sat in the chair, staring into the darkness, a sentry guarding her children and waiting for the man she loved to return home.

She awakened with a start, torn from a horrible nightmare. She gasped and opened her eyes to brilliant morning sunshine pouring through the window and a wet tongue licking her cheek.

A new sense of panic ripped through her as she gazed at her watch and saw that it was seven-thirty and Luke still hadn't come home. The sheriff's car, which had been outside her home when she'd fallen asleep, was gone.

With a groan, she unfolded her stiff body and stood. The social worker would be here in an hour and a half, and somehow Abby had to act like everything was normal.

The first order of the day was to let Peaches outside. When Peaches was finished with her business, Abby and the dog returned to the house. Abby checked on the children, who were still sleeping soundly, fed Peaches, then headed for a shower.

As she stood beneath the hot spray of water, her mind raced frantically. She thought of everything she had heard about Luke when he'd first come to work for her.

He drank too much, lived too fast, didn't take care of himself and took nothing seriously. He loved women and had a reputation as a charming rake. But she had come to see him as nothing like the man the rumors had portrayed.

She'd seen his innate warmth both with the children and with herself. She knew there was far more to the man than his reputation or the face he showed to the people in this town. Otherwise she wouldn't love him.

So, why hadn't he come home? And what should she do about it? She was nothing to him but a pleasant diversion. Theirs certainly wasn't a real marriage, it was a marriage created for the good of Jessica and Jason. What right did she have to set in motion a search? And how would such a search by the sheriff affect the custody suit?

But what if there had been an accident? What if Luke was hurt somewhere? What if he needed help? Oh, God, she was so confused.

By the time she got out of the shower, she'd made a decision. She would do nothing about Luke's absence until after the social worker left. She'd meet with Sonya Watkins and make a vague excuse about Luke having to work. She'd pretend that everything was fine and pray that it would be.

But when Sonya Watkins left, Abby intended to tear up the phone lines, seeking Luke's whereabouts, no matter what the repercussions.

By the time she and the kids were dressed and had eaten breakfast and cleaned up the kitchen, Sonya Watkins had arrived.

Sonya was a plump woman in her mid-fifties who radiated confidence and warmth. She greeted Abby and the two children with a smile that was obviously meant to put them all at ease.

But Abby wasn't put at ease. She was aware that this woman with her cheerful smile and twinkling blue eyes was here to do a job and held an enormous amount of power as to the future of the children.

"What I would love to do first is see the children's bedrooms," she said. "Jason, would you like to show me your room?"

"Sure," Jason replied easily. He led the way down the hall to his room, Sonya following him and Jessica and Abby following Sonya.

Abby and Jessica stood in the doorway as Jason showed Sonya all the treasures his room contained. When Sonya had seen his book collection, his favorite truck, his ant farm and the rest of his goodies, she moved on to Jessica's room.

It was obvious she'd been told that Jessica didn't talk, for she asked no questions that would demand a reply from the little girl. She oohed and aahed over Jessica's stuffed animal collection and pretended to drink a cup of tea from a tiny plastic cup.

Abby returned to the kitchen and waited for Sonya to join her there. "Nice house," she said.

"Thank you. We still have some work to do, but my husband has already accomplished a lot."

"Yes, I expected to see your husband here this morning," Sonya said.

"Unfortunately, he got called away on business," Abby said, hoping the woman wouldn't pursue the subject. She didn't. She spoke to Abby about the children's routine, their school and their therapy.

Abby tried to stay cool and calm and answer all the questions, address any concerns, but her heart cried out. Where was Luke? Why wasn't he here? She prayed that wherever he was he was safe and unharmed.

Luke opened his eyes and instantly closed them to shut out the glare of the mid-morning sun. Dreaming. He had to be dreaming that he was in the alley behind the Honky Tonk.

He closed his eyes, for a moment drifted in a kind of foggy reality, then opened them once again.

It was still the alley. What was he doing here? What had happened? His mouth was dry, achingly dry. He started to sit up, then moaned and grabbed his head.

Hellfire, had he tied one on? He plucked at his shirt and wrinkled his nose. He certainly smelled like a brewery.

He'd never had a hangover like this. His skull felt as if it had been stuffed with rocks, and he felt disoriented, drugged.

Drugged.

Suddenly the fog fell away and he remembered. He'd had a restrained confrontation with Justin Cahill. Then he'd done something incredibly stupid—he'd downed a drink that had been sitting on the edge of the stage unattended.

Abby! Her name exploded in his head, and this time, ignoring the utter agony of his head, he jumped up from the ground and headed for his truck.

Let her be all right. Let Abby be all right. The words were a litany that raced around and around in his head as he pressed his foot firmly on the gas pedal.

Had Justin planned this? Had he drugged Luke to make certain he'd be out of the way, incapacitated? Had he left the Honky Tonk and driven to Abby's? Stormed the house and taken the children by force? Had Abby been hurt…or worse?

The fear that ripped through him was suddenly joined with a new emotion—rage. His rage was directed at the man who was at the bottom of all this.

Justin Cahill. If Luke discovered that he'd harmed Luke's wife or children, then Luke would personally hunt the man down and kill him with his bare hands.

As Luke turned into the driveway of the house, he was met by a car leaving. The driver of the car was a plump, gray-haired woman. She waved as they passed one another.

Relief made him gasp aloud as he saw Abby standing on the porch. He parked the truck, and before he got the door open, she was there.

He stepped out of the truck, and she threw herself into his arms. "Oh Luke, I've been worried sick," she said, her face buried in his chest. "I was so afraid something bad had happened to you."

"And I was so afraid that something had happened to you and the kids." He held her tightly for a moment, thanking the forces that had kept her safe through the long night.

She finally raised her head and gazed at him. "What happened, Luke? I was going to call the sheriff the minute the social worker left."

The social worker. In all the chaos, Luke had forgotten that Sonya Watkins was scheduled to do a home study that morning. He guessed she had been in the car that had passed him as he'd turned into the driveway.

"I'm sorry. How did it go with Mrs. Watkins?"

"I think it went okay, but what about you? Tell me what happened."

"Come on, let's go inside and I'll tell you what happened," he said. With his arm still around her shoulders, the two of them headed for the front door.

As they reached the door, she turned to him again, her nose wrinkled. "You stink," she exclaimed.

"Trust me, there's definitely more booze on me than there is in me. In fact, before I do anything, I want to take a shower."

"And while you shower, I'll make a pot of strong, hot coffee," Abby replied.

They parted in the living room, Luke heading for the bathroom and Abby for the kitchen. As Luke went into the bathroom he heard the sound of Jason and Jessica's laughter and Peaches' excited barking. No sound had ever sounded so good to his ears.

In the bathroom he stripped off his stinking clothes and jumped beneath the hot spray of water. What was Justin up to? Initially, Luke had thought the man had drugged him in order to gain access to Abby and the children. But Abby and the children appeared to be fine. So, what had been the point of drugging Luke? What had been the point of pouring alcohol all over him?

Almost as soon as the question zipped through his mind, the most logical answer followed. Luke knew the town of Inferno well enough to know that if one person had seen him in that alley, then most everyone in town would know he'd tied on a drunk and slept it off through the night.

He also knew that nobody in town would doubt the story. After all, a leopard didn't change its spots, and Luke had been known to drink too much before. But never before had it bothered him...what the town thought of him.

And now, Justin would be able to use where Luke had spent the night last night in the custody trial. All he'd have to do was call anyone in town who'd known that Luke had passed out.

That would certainly make an impression on a judge. And how devious and smart Justin had been to even think of such a thing. And how stupid Luke had been to be caught so off guard.

When he was dressed in clean clothes, he went into the kitchen where Abby had a mug of hot coffee waiting for him.

How on earth was he going to convince Abby he hadn't gotten stinking drunk and passed out? Given his reputation and the fact that he'd confessed to her that he was a recovering alcoholic, how was he going to convince anyone what really happened?

"You want to know where I've been all night?" he asked as he sat down next to her at the table. "I passed out and spent the night in the alley behind the Honky Tonk."

Her forehead wrinkled as she stared at him. "What do you mean, you passed out? I don't believe that for a minute," she said flatly.

He looked at her in surprise. "You don't believe me? Why not?"

"You aren't telling me everything," she said, her gaze holding his intently. "Something else happened. You didn't just get drunk and pass out."

"What makes you think that?"

She smiled and reached across the table to take his hand in hers. "Because I know you, Luke. Because you knew how important it was that you be here this morning for the home study…because you thought I might be in danger last night. And because I know you aren't the kind of man to blow off those things and just get drunk."

If he didn't believe her words, then he would have found

it impossible to discount the light of belief that shone from her eyes. She believed him. She believed in him.

He pulled his hand from hers as emotion clogged his throat, making it impossible for him to speak. The idea that this woman who hadn't known him so very long, who'd heard all the rumors about his character yet believed in him filled him with a sense of awe he'd never before experienced.

He took a drink of his coffee, swallowed against the unfamiliar emotions, then explained to her what had happened. He told her about his meeting with Justin, the fact that Justin had had an opportunity to put something in his drink, and the moment he'd awakened remembering nothing after attempting to leave the Honky Tonk and get home to her.

"He came here. Last night Justin came here."

Luke sat up straighter in the chair. "What happened?" he asked as his blood began a familiar boil, the boil that had begun as he'd driven home.

"Nothing, really. I called Sheriff Broder, and he arrived just after Justin left." Although she looked perfectly calm and collected, there was a slight tremor to her voice that let him know she must have been terrified.

This time it was Luke who reached for her hand. Her hand felt small and vulnerable in his, and a wave of fierce protectiveness welled inside him.

"He didn't try to get in? He didn't try to hurt you?"

"No, nothing like that." She drew a deep breath. "He just frightened me," she confessed in a small voice.

Luke rose and pulled her into his arms, wanting…needing to shelter her, even though it was after the fact. She pressed against him in comfortable familiarity, and as always, her very nearness stirred Luke's senses.

Suddenly he was glad the custody suit would be resolved

in ten days. The simple marriage agreement he'd entered into for the sake of the children all of a sudden didn't seem so simple anymore.

Chapter 14

"How about we go over to the ranch and take a trail ride?" Luke suggested the evening before the custody hearing. "The ranch went dark today, so we'll have the trails all to ourselves."

"Yeah, let's do that," Jason said with excitement. Jessica nodded eagerly.

"Even if I said no, it appears I would be outvoted," Abby said with a tired smile. "Go put on your jeans," she said to Jason and Jessica, who flew out of the room almost before the words were out of her mouth.

"Would you rather not go?" Luke asked.

"No, it sounds like fun. Anything to keep my mind occupied is welcome."

Luke fought the impulse to go to her, to pull her into his arms and assure her that everything would be all right. He hated seeing the tiny stress lines across her forehead, the lackluster of her eyes that indicated too little sleep.

Things had been tense since the night Justin had come here and Luke had been drugged. They had contacted Johnna and told her what had happened. Luke wasn't sure his sister had believed him, but she'd believed Abby that Justin had come to the house.

Johnna had filed for a restraining order against Justin, and since that day none of them had seen the dark-haired man whose appearance in Inferno had so dramatically changed their lives.

Within minutes the children were in the living room and ready to leave. They got into Abby's car and headed for the Delaney Dude Ranch.

Abby was quiet on the drive. She'd grown increasingly quiet and distant over the past week, and it was a distance Luke didn't know how to breach.

If he'd been a real husband, he would have held her through the darkness of the nights, forced her to talk about the fear and anxiety he knew filled her up. He would have shouldered as much of her burden as he could…if he'd been a real husband.

He'd already decided that if by some cruel trick of fate she lost the children tomorrow, he'd stick around her place for a couple of days to see that she was going to be okay. If she got custody, he'd pack up his things and move out tomorrow afternoon. Then in six months he'd leave Inferno and head to Nashville.

He waited for the burst of adrenaline he always felt when he thought of his future, but it was slow in coming. He chalked up his lack of enthusiasm to too much on his mind.

Tension had ripped through him, as well, for the past couple of days. He didn't trust Justin Cahill, kept waiting for the man to do something evil or underhanded.

Just as Luke had suspected, it hadn't taken long for the news of Luke's fall off the wagon to make the rounds of gossip.

Still, Johnna was optimistic about the hearing the next day, but Luke was worried what Justin might do if he lost. When he'd looked into Justin's eyes that night at the Honky Tonk, he'd sensed a man who would do anything…anything to get what he desired. And he wanted the children. Not because he loved them. Not because he wanted to make their lives better. But because he wanted the two million bucks that parental rights would put in his hands.

Even if Abby won custody, Luke decided he'd better hang out at the house for a couple more days to make certain that everything was all right.

He pulled into the ranch and parked near the stables. As the kids tumbled from the backseat, Luke reached across and grabbed Abby's arm to halt her exit from the car.

"Abby, we've done everything we can. There is absolutely nothing more we can do but try to enjoy today, all of us together."

Those green eyes of hers gazed at him, and in their depths he thought he saw an emotion that shouldn't be there. He thought he saw love.

He turned from her and exited the car, disturbed by what he thought he'd seen. Love had never been a part of this bargain. Love was the last thing that was supposed to happen.

As Abby climbed out of the car and the kids danced with excitement, Luke dismissed the craziness he thought he'd seen. He had to be mistaken. Abby was grateful to him. She loved what he had done for her. But she certainly didn't love him. Hell, even his own father, his own siblings had never really loved him.

Matthew, who was in the process of saddling up his horse, Thunder, met them outside the stables. He greeted them with his usual curt restraint.

"I thought I'd take Abby and the kids for a little trail ride," Luke explained.

"I'm getting ready to ride the fence lines and see what work needs to be done in the next month while we're dark," Matthew replied. He climbed on the back of the tall, spirited horse. "I understand tomorrow is an important day for you and your family. Good luck." With these words, he rode off.

Luke stared after his brother, wondering if any of them would ever be able to feel close to Matthew. Matthew seemed to be so tightly wound, so isolated.

It took thirty minutes for Luke to get everyone's horses saddled and ready to go. They'd ridden once before, earlier in the week, so the kids had overcome their fear of that first ride and were eager to get started.

It had been another perfect day, and the warmth of the sun had lingered into the evening hours, but it was not uncomfortably warm. There was just enough of a breeze to stir the air, kicking up the scents of earth and flowers and clean air.

They rode with Luke in the lead, then Jason, then Jessica, then Abby bringing up the rear. When they hit open pasture, the kids rode side by side, and Luke fell back to join Abby.

She shot him a warm smile. "Thank you. This is just what I needed. The warmth of the sun, the sound of the kids laughing and a good and steady horse beneath me."

He returned her smile, feeling some of the tension that had gripped him in the past week easing. "I think we all needed this," he said. "It's been a long couple of weeks."

"And in some ways it's been the best couple of weeks in my whole life," she said.

He looked at her in surprise. "Why?"

She raised a hand from the reins and threaded it through her hair, and her beauty ached inside Luke's chest. "Three times in the last week I heard Jessica speak out loud to Peaches. Jason hasn't had a single nightmare in the last two weeks."

She frowned thoughtfully and returned her hand to the

reins. "I don't really know quite how to explain it, but everything has seemed sweeter, more intense these last weeks." She sighed. "Maybe it's because I know there's a possibility that I'll lose everything tomorrow." She flashed him a bright smile. "But I'm not going to think about that today."

They rode for a few minutes in silence. It was a pleasant silence, broken only by Jason's chattering and an occasional burst of giggles from Jessica.

Tails switching, the horses plodded along the familiar trails at a sedate walk. The horses used for the guests were sweet-tempered and rarely spirited.

When they had been riding for about forty-five minutes, Luke insisted they stop and take a break. He knew that people who were unaccustomed to riding found muscles they didn't know they had after a brief time on the back of a horse.

They stopped at the same place where they had enjoyed their picnic the week before. The two children instantly began a game of tag while Abby and Luke sat in the shaded area beneath the trees. Luke allowed the horses to roam free, knowing they wouldn't go far and would return to him when he whistled.

As he stretched out his legs, Luke watched Abby watching Jason and Jessica as they played. The expression of joy that lit her face, the love she so obviously felt for the two, made her appear even more beautiful.

Luke knew he wouldn't make love to her again, that it wouldn't be right at this point in time. She was consumed with the custody fight, frightened about the future, and he had no intentions of being a part of that future.

He had two beautiful memories of the two of them making love together, memories that stirred him to distraction whenever he thought of those moments of passion. And he had a feeling making love to her one more time would only make their parting more difficult.

For the first time, he wondered what her life would be like after he was gone. "So, what are your plans once the custody issue is behind you?" he asked.

She pulled her knees to her chest and wrapped her arms around them. "It depends on what the outcome is of the custody fight."

He smiled. "I'll rephrase the question. After you win custody of the kids tomorrow, what are your plans?"

She returned his smile, then frowned thoughtfully. "To be honest, I haven't given it a lot of thought. I've been so focused on tomorrow."

"Are you going to stay here in Inferno? Now that you can access your funds, you could live anywhere you want."

"We'll stay here," she said immediately. Her gaze shot to the two children playing tag. "Jason and Jessica love it here, and I must confess, I've fallen in love with Inferno."

She stretched her legs out before her. "I'll probably spend the next year while Jessica is in kindergarten not working. I'll get the rest of the house in order, then when she's in school full-time, I'll see about taking a teaching position."

"Sounds like a good life," he said softly.

"We're going to have a wonderful life." She said the words fervently, ferociously, as if she was less concerned in him believing them as believing them herself.

"I know you will," he replied, fighting a tiny bit of sorrow that he wouldn't be here to share it with her.

He stood and reached a hand out to pull her up. "We'd better get started back. The sun has started to go down."

She nodded and put her hand in his. He pulled her up, and for just a moment their bodies came together, her breasts against his chest, her thighs against his. An instantaneous burst of heat swept through him, and he wondered if he'd ever again find a woman who stirred him on such a primal level.

She stepped quickly away from him, as if she'd felt the same flame of heat he had. Once again he thought he saw something flicker in the depths of her eyes, something tender, something that unsettled him.

"Jason, Jessica, come on, we're heading back," he called to the kids who were playing hide-and-seek nearby. It took ten minutes to get the kids settled on their horses and ready to head to the stables.

They had only ridden a short distance from the grove of trees when the sound of a gunshot split the air. Jessica and Jason screamed as adrenaline exploded inside Luke.

"Get off the horses! Get down on the ground," he yelled as another shot cracked resoundingly.

He slid off his horse and pulled the two kids down, keeping the horses between them and the area where he thought the shots had come from.

"Abby…Abby, get down," he commanded. She appeared to be in a daze, as if he wasn't making sense. Still holding the horses, with the terrified kids clinging to him, he grabbed Abby's arm to pull her down.

She slid off the horse and to the ground, and it was then Luke saw the red stain spreading out to take over the white of her T-shirt.

"Abby!" he cried in horror as she slumped to the ground.

"Mommy! Mommy!" Jason wailed, and Jessica screamed as Luke tried to calm the kids and assess Abby's wound, all the while trying to keep behind the shelter of the horses.

"I'm all right," Abby said. "It's just my arm."

"Are you sure you're okay?" Luke asked urgently.

She nodded, her lower lip caught in her teeth.

"Stay here behind the horses. I'll be right back."

"No, Luke. Wait," she exclaimed as the children huddled by her side.

But he didn't listen to her. He left the cover of the horses and raced for the nearest grove of trees, a deadly rage rising inside him. Somebody had attacked his family. Somebody had shot his wife, and Luke knew who that somebody was. He wasn't about to let Justin Cahill get away.

He knew the general area where the shots had come from, and he raced swiftly, as silently as possible through the woods. He'd only run a few seconds before he heard the noise of somebody crashing through the underbrush, racing through the trees.

Cahill. The name pounded in his head and stoked the fires of anger to a fever pitch. He stopped long enough to listen, then followed the noise of running footsteps.

A figure ahead of him spurred him faster, and with a roar of rage, he hit Cahill in the back, tumbling both men to the ground. As Justin smashed down, the shotgun he'd been carrying flew out of reach.

Justin rolled to his back, and Luke jumped on top of him. "You son of a bitch. I'll kill you," Luke thundered as he smashed a fist into Justin's jaw.

Justin bucked and kicked in an attempt to escape, but Luke straddled his prone body and delivered another blow, and another, and another.

"Luke…Luke, stop, you're going to kill him." Matthew's voice pierced the red haze that had descended in Luke's head.

Matthew grabbed Luke's arm as he reared back to deliver another hit. Luke stared up at his elder brother, his vision blurred by tears. "He attacked my family. Matthew…he shot Abby."

"I know, and you need to get Abby medical help. Go on. I'll take care of this scumbag," Matthew said, and for the first time Luke noticed he had a revolver in his hand.

Luke stood and Justin sat up, his eyes burning with hatred.

"I hope I killed the bitch," he said. "She talked my wife into leaving me. She ruined my life."

Luke would have smashed the man's face again if Matthew hadn't cocked his gun. "Keep your mouth shut, you piece of dirt, and I'll try my best not to accidentally shoot you," Matthew said. "Go, Luke. Your family needs you."

His family needed him. Yes.

Abby. As he raced to where he'd left Abby and the children, his heartbeat frantic, the thudding rhythm of rage being replaced with the anxious beat of fear.

When he reached them, his fear grew overwhelming. A white pall had stolen the color from Abby's face, and her eyes were dull.

"Luke," she said weakly.

"It's all right. Everything is going to be just fine." He didn't take the time to explain. "We need to get you to the hospital." He tried not to focus on the blood that had completely soaked the white sleeve of her T-shirt.

"Jason…Jessica… I need you to stop crying and listen to me. I'm going to put you both on Abby's horse. Jason, you hold tight to the saddle horn, and Jessica, you hold tight to your brother, okay?"

Still sniffling, they nodded. He put the kids on the back of the horse, then went to Abby. "Abby…Abby, honey, we've got to get you out of here. I'm going to have to lift you up and put you on my horse. Can you lift your arms around my neck?"

She nodded, a faint movement of her head, then with a deep, wrenching moan, she lifted her arms and weakly clung to him.

It took him three attempts to mount the horse with her in his arms, but he finally managed to get up and hold her tight against his chest.

He grabbed the reins of the children's horse, and they took

off, moving as fast as possible, the blood pounding in Luke's head as it seeped from Abby's body.

He was terrified that the jostling motion of the horse would make her wound worse, but the alternative was for her to bleed to death.

"Hang on, Abby…hang on," he said over and over again. But she didn't hang on. By the time they reached the car, she'd passed out.

Thirty minutes later Luke sat in the hospital waiting room, Jessica on his lap and Jason seated in the plastic chair next to his. They were waiting for the doctor to come out and tell them Abby's condition.

Luke barely remembered the drive to the hospital. He'd never been so terrified in his life. She'd looked dead when he'd carried her into the emergency room, both he and the children screaming for help.

He held Jessica closer, realizing the little girl's hair smelled like Abby's. Abby's children. What would happen to them if Abby… He couldn't think about it. He couldn't imagine anything more horrible.

"Luke."

He looked up, surprised to see Sheriff Broder approaching him. "Heard you had some excitement out at the dude ranch," he said.

Gently Luke stood and put Jessica in his chair, then took Broder's arm and led him away from where the children were seated.

"Your brother came to see me about twenty minutes ago. He had a little surprise for me."

Luke nodded. "Cahill."

"Yup." A whisper of a grin lifted the corner of the sheriff's mouth. "Matthew had him trussed up like a calf. Told me that Cahill took a couple of shots at you and your family." Broder gestured toward the children. "I see the kids are okay."

"My wife. He shot my wife." Luke had never felt such bleak despair as when those words left his lips.

"Is she going to be all right?" Broder placed a hand on Luke's shoulder as if to steady him.

"I…I don't know. We're waiting to hear from the doctor."

"I need to get a report from you," Broder said, but at that moment Dr. Johnny Howerton entered the waiting room and strode toward Luke.

"We'll have to do this later," Luke said, his heart banging in his chest as he anticipated what the doctor might say. "How is she?"

"She's weak and she was in shock, but she's stabilized. The shot was clean and took a dozen stitches, but she's conscious and she wants to see you."

"I'll stay here with the children," Sheriff Broder said.

Luke walked to Jessica and Jason. "This is the sheriff. He's going to wait here with you while I go in and see Mom for a minute."

"But I want to see her," Jason said, his little face streaked with dirt and tear tracks.

"I know, buddy. But for now she is in a place where only grown-ups can go in. I'll tell her you and Jessica love her and to get well real soon, okay?"

"Is she going to be all right?" Luke asked a moment later as he followed Dr. Howerton down the hallway.

"She was incredibly lucky. An inch one way or the other and that bullet would have done tremendous damage. As it is, she's going to have a sore shoulder for a while. I'd like to keep her a day or two for observation." He stopped outside the door to a semidarkened room. "Just a few minutes, okay?"

Luke nodded and entered the room. Her eyes were closed and her face was as pale as the sheet that covered her. He wanted to see her eyes sparkling with life. He wanted to hear her laughter ringing in the air.

Luke sat in the chair next to the bed and gently took her hand in his.

"Abby? It's me, honey. It's Luke."

Her eyes fluttered open, and to his immense relief her fingers tightened slightly around his. "Luke. I have to… I need to…"

"Shh," he whispered softly. "You're going to be all right. You've lost a lot of blood, but you're going to be fine."

"I have to go home," she said, a grimace twisting her features as she tried to sit up.

"You aren't going anywhere," Luke protested and gently pushed her against the pillows. "The doctor wants to keep you overnight."

"Overnight?" Her face was even paler than before, and a frown etched its way across her forehead.

"What?" he asked.

"The custody hearing…it's first thing in the morning. You have to go. You have to be there for me. Dress the kids nice…make sure their hair is combed…"

"I will. I promise," he said. He squeezed her hand once again. "You just rest and don't worry about a thing. Everything is going to be just fine."

"Justin? It was Justin, wasn't it?"

Luke nodded. "He's in jail now, and there's no way in hell he's going to get custody of those kids tomorrow. The son of a bitch took a gamble and he lost, Abby."

She closed her eyes, the grimace of pain momentarily easing. When she opened her eyes and looked at him again, her gorgeous green eyes were awash with tears.

"It's going to be all right, Abby," Luke said, his chest tight with emotion. He leaned forward and stroked a strand of her hair. "You want me to sit here with you for a while?"

"No, I want you to take the children home, feed them supper and tuck them into bed. I know they must be terrified and I want things as normal as possible for them. Please, Luke…promise me you'll take them home right now."

"I promise," he said, unable to deny her anything at the moment.

She closed her eyes, and her fingers went lax around his. He waited a moment or two, to see if she would speak or open her eyes again. She didn't, and finally he stood, leaned over and kissed her cheek, then left the room.

After telling Dr. Howerton to call him if any problems arose, he left the hospital and took his kids home.

They ate hot dogs and beans for supper, and while they ate, Luke explained to Jason and Jessica that Abby was fine, but the doctor wanted to keep her for a couple of days.

When they'd finished eating, Luke told the kids to get ready for bed and he would tuck them in. He let Peaches out to run, then let the dog back in and went into Jason's room.

"You all tucked in, buddy?" he asked as he sat on the side of the bed.

Jason nodded. "Can we go see Mom tomorrow?"

"You know we've got to go see the judge tomorrow morning, but after we're finished there, we'll go see your mom." Luke ruffled the little boy's hair, kissed him on the forehead, then moved to Jessica's room.

Jessica's big brown eyes pierced Luke's heart. He saw in their depths fear, and although he repeated that her mommy was going to be fine and would be home in a couple of days and that in the meantime he'd keep her and her brother safe, he wasn't sure the little girl believed him.

After tucking in the kids, Luke went into the living room, where Peaches curled up next to him on the sofa.

Over and over again he replayed that moment when Abby had slumped from her horse to the ground, her T-shirt seeping blood. And over and over again he was filled with a sense of horror.

He never again wanted to see her so lifeless, so still. Never again did he want to see pain etching lines into her forehead, stealing away the sparkle of her eyes.

And never had he wanted a drink more than he did at this moment. He knew Abby had a bottle of wine in one of the cabinets in the kitchen. Although wine certainly wasn't his drink of choice, he knew a couple of glasses would take the edge off, relieve some of the tension that racked his body, erase some of the fear he felt each time he thought of Abby lying so pale, so lifeless.

He got up from the sofa and went into the kitchen, Peaches at his heels. He sat at the table and stared at the cabinet where he knew the wine was stored.

The kids were taken care of and sound asleep in their beds. Abby wasn't home. Nobody would know if he fell off the wagon.

Just one drink. It would make him feel better, dull all the emotions that thundered inside him. A vision of his father filled his head, a mental picture of the old man pacing the floor, bourbon splashing from the glass in one hand, a belt ready to strike in the other.

The beatings had always been worse when the old man had been drinking. Luke leaned back in the chair and dragged his hands down the sides of his face. Just one little drink. Nobody would know.

Except him. Until he took that drink, he was in charge of his life, his destiny. As Abby had told him, until he took that drink, he was a success.

Abby. He remembered her unshakable belief in him when

he'd stumbled home one morning, reeking of alcohol Justin must have poured over him after he'd passed out in the alley. She hadn't questioned his story, had believed in him like no other person ever had in his life.

Suddenly the thirst he'd entertained was gone, vanished beneath the need to be the best he could be, not only for Abby, not only for the children, but also for himself.

"Come on, Peaches, it's time to go to bed. We have a big day tomorrow." He put Peaches in her bed, then, instead of stretching out on the sofa, went into Abby's bedroom. He wanted to sleep in Abby's bed with her sweet scent surrounding him.

As he walked into her bedroom, he spied the guitar he'd strung leaning against the wall next to her bed. He pulled down the sunflower bedspread, pulled off his T-shirt, then got in beneath the sheet.

He kept his jeans on, fearing that Jason might very well have one of his nightmares tonight. As he'd expected, the sheets smelled of Abby, and the room seemed filled with her spirit.

Closing his eyes, he tried to find sleep, knowing he'd need to be alert and clearheaded in the morning to face the family court judge. But sleep remained elusive. He was still too keyed up, too wired by the evening's events.

Abby white-faced, falling to the ground. Abby worried about her children despite her wounds. Abby… Abby…Abby.

He turned on the bedside lamp and grabbed the guitar. Strumming the strings in soft tones, he felt himself start to relax. He'd nearly finished the first tune when Jason appeared in his doorway.

"What's up, buddy?" he asked softly.

Jason shrugged his little shoulders. "I can't sleep." He rubbed his eyes. "Could I sleep in here with you, Luke?"

Luke patted the mattress next to him, and Jason eagerly jumped into the bed. Within minutes Jessica had joined them, cuddling up on the opposite side of Luke.

"Sing us a lullaby," Jason said. "Our mommy in heaven used to sing us lullabies…before our daddy hurt her."

Luke's heart skipped a beat. Abby had told him the kids had never talked about that night, the night they had seen their father kill their mother.

"You saw your daddy hurt your mommy?" he asked lightly, still strumming the strings of the guitar.

"Mommy and Daddy were fighting, and she told us to go to our room, but we didn't," Jason said.

"Mommy was crying and Daddy hit her until she wasn't crying anymore," Jessica said.

"Remember that your mom and I talked about going to talk to the judge tomorrow?" Luke asked. He continued to strum the guitar in soft, soothing tones. They both nodded. "You think you could tell the judge what you saw your daddy do to your first mommy that night?"

They both frowned, obviously disturbed by the idea.

"It would really help your mommy now if you could do that," Luke continued. "And the judge would make sure you never, ever had to see your daddy again."

"And we could live together here forever?" Jason asked.

"You and Jessica and your mommy and Peaches could live together forever, and you'd never have to be afraid again," Luke said.

Jason frowned for another long moment, then he shook his head. "Then I'll tell the judge tomorrow."

"Me, too," Jessica said softly.

"Now will you sing us a lullaby?" Jason asked.

As Luke began to sing, Jessica and Jason snuggled against his sides. The scent of childhood clung to them, and he was awed by the fact that they had trusted him enough to tell him about the night of their mother's death.

Somewhere in the back of his mind, Luke wondered if Nashville could possibly be better than this.

Chapter 15

Abby awoke that morning knowing nothing on earth was going to keep her away from that custody hearing. In spite of the doctor's protests, despite an overwhelming lethargy and muscle aches that ripped through her, she left the hospital wearing a hospital gown tucked into her jeans and took a taxi to the courthouse where the hearing was going to take place.

She was early so she sat on a bench outside the courthouse, waiting for her family to arrive. Her family. Please God, let them continue to be her family.

She remembered Luke telling her that Justin was in jail for shooting her, but she was afraid he might somehow wiggle out of that, that even if they settled the custody issue today it would only be a temporary settlement and eventually she'd have to face Justin…and again and again.

The sun was warm on her face, and the heat penetrated the gown where her shoulder was bandaged. It felt good, like the warmth of Luke's hands when they made love…like the warmth of his smile when he gazed at her.

Luke. Her time with him had been magical, and she wished the magic could go on forever. But he had big dreams, big hopes for finding magic in Nashville, and his future didn't include her.

After the hearing, it was time for her to set him free. He'd never intended the marriage to be permanent, and she'd promised him no strings, no regrets.

She would never let him know how much she would miss him, how much it would ache inside her when they said goodbye. She would never let him know how much she loved him…that she had a feeling she would always love him.

"Mommy!"

The cry called her from a half-sleep, and she opened her eyes to see Jessica and Jason racing toward her, Luke, handsome as a devil in a suit, following just behind them.

"Easy," she said to the kids as they raced into her arms. She hugged and kissed them, then stood and faced Luke.

"What on earth are people going to say? My wife sleeping on a bench in a hospital gown?" His eyes were teasing as he drew her against him. She welcomed his support, leaning against him for strength.

"I've never cared much what people say," she replied.

"I can't believe you're here. Did the doctor say it was okay?" he asked worriedly.

She smiled sheepishly. "Let's just say he was not particularly enthusiastic about letting me go. But I couldn't miss this. I had to be here."

At that moment Johnna arrived, gray eyes twinkling as she eyed the group. "This is going to be a cakewalk," she said merrily. "I can't believe that man was so stupid as to get himself arrested the night before this hearing."

"I just wish it was on a charge that would put him away forever," Abby said softly.

Luke held her closer, and Abby fought a sudden burn of tears. She'd once believed she couldn't live without her children, and now she had to figure out how she was going to live without the man she loved.

"Come on, let's go get this done," Johnna said. "I have a feeling the judge won't look kindly on a man who would discharge a firearm in the direction of his children. I believe what he did to you is considered attempted murder, and there's no way he isn't going to face that charge."

Abby nodded, somehow not assured by Johnna's words. He'd gotten away with murder before…why not attempted murder?

Together the five of them entered the courthouse.

Abby wasn't sure what she'd expected, but the hearing was surprisingly short and rather informal. The judge, an elderly man with a snowy head of hair and piercing blue eyes, indicated that he had a favorable home study report from Sonya Watkins.

Shock riveted through Abby when Sheriff Broder arrived with Justin in tow. The children became obviously upset, and the judge took them back with him to his chambers.

As they waited for the judge to return, Luke's hand grabbed hers, and in a whispered tone he told her what had happened with the children the night before, how they had indicated that they would tell the judge what had happened the night their mother was killed.

Abby said nothing, but her heart filled with an amazing joy and an intense pain. Luke had proven to Jessica and Jason that he was a good man, and they had trusted him with their secrets.

They would miss him when he was gone, this man who

had sung them lullabies. And her heart would break when it came time for her to say goodbye to him.

She glanced at Justin, who cast her a cocky smile. The man had tried to kill her. Without a doubt she knew that had been his intention. He'd wanted her out of the children's lives, permanently out of the way. And she saw in his eyes a promise... the promise that this wasn't over.

A wave of hopelessness shot through her. How much time would he get for shooting her? Enough time so that when he got out of jail the children would be grown? Somehow she didn't think so. She had long ago lost faith in the judicial system and knew it was possible Justin would get off with a slap on the wrist and probation.

Luke wrapped his fingers around hers, as if sensing her anguished thoughts. Again she wondered what she was going to do without him. Since their marriage, for all intents and purposes they had interacted like a real family. And more than anything, Abby wished they could continue to be a family forever.

As the minutes clicked by, Abby wondered what was going on between the judge and the children. What if despite what they'd told Luke the night before, they simply couldn't bring themselves to talk to the judge?

Finally the judge returned to the bench, his features sternly forbidding. "I have just spoken to the children at length. I find them to be bright and articulate, and you are to be commended, Mr. and Mrs. Delaney, for their adjustment to life after their mother's death."

"Your Honor, I appreciate everything that Abby has done for my children in my absence from their lives, but I am their father and I have a right to have my children back with me," Justin said.

"Mr. Cahill, even if I were to discount the circumstances involving the shooting last night, even if I were to believe your story that the shooting was accidental and you had no intention of harming anyone, I cannot discount what the children told me concerning the night of your wife's murder."

Justin looked stricken, and Abby knew he had been confident the children would remain too traumatized to ever discuss that night with anyone.

"I have been in touch with the district attorney in Kansas City, Missouri," the judge continued. "And in light of this new information, they inform me that they intend to go to trial once again and charge you with first-degree murder. Therefore, in the best interest of the children, I terminate your parental rights and grant permanent custody to Luke and Abby Delaney." The judge banged his gavel. "Court dismissed."

Justin erupted with shouted curses and threats. Luke grabbed Abby and hugged her, and Johnna did the same. Abby clung to them both, unable to believe that it was over.

Broder led a still screaming Justin from the courtroom, and the judge released the children from his chambers. Again there were hugs all around as Abby told them they were going to live with her forever.

"I'd love to continue a long celebration," Luke said. "But we need to get this woman back to the hospital."

"No…please. I just want to go home," Abby said. "I'll call the doctor from there and get all his instructions. Please, Luke. Let's all go home."

Now that the drama of the moment was over, Abby was beyond weary, and her shoulder ached with an unrelenting, throbbing pain.

But they had won! Tears of joy spilled down her cheeks as she realized the children would never have to spend a day…a minute with their father. She and the children could build a good life together without looking over their shoulders, without being afraid.

And if what the judge had said was true, Loretta's murder would finally be vindicated. Justin would be returned to Kansas City to stand trial again, and this time she knew the children would be strong enough to voice what had happened on that horrible night. It was over. Finally.

For the next four days, Abby spent most of her time in bed as Dr. Howerton had instructed. Luke insisted that he cook the meals, and it was one of the few things Abby realized he did not do well. Each evening at supper they all spent the first few minutes of the meal trying to guess what the ingredients were of whatever he had cooked.

And every night Abby lay in bed, dreading the day when Luke would leave, knowing the time was coming far too quickly for her. With each day that passed, she felt Luke subtly distancing himself from them all. Not in big ways, but in small ways that told her he was preparing both her and the children for his absence.

Exactly one week after the custody hearing, the day after they got the news that Justin had been extradited to Missouri to stand trial again, Luke began to pack what few belongings he'd brought to the house.

His truck was packed and ready to go just minutes before it was time for the children to get home from school. Abby wondered if he'd timed it that way on purpose. He would leave as the children arrived home, giving her no time to grieve his leaving.

"It's not like we'll never see each other again," Luke said as the two of them stood next to his truck. "It's still months before I leave town."

She nodded, her mind embracing the vision of him. Those strong, bold features of his would be forever emblazoned in her memories. Her fingertips would always retain the feel of his wide, muscular shoulders, the springy hair of his broad chest, the warmth of his skin.

Her heart would treasure forever the laughter they had shared, the dramas and joys of their time together. Her soul would always cherish and remember her love for him.

For a long moment his gaze held hers. She didn't want him to go, yet she couldn't stop him. She'd promised and, just like he always kept his promises, she always tried to keep hers.

It was he who averted his gaze first, staring toward the road where a cloud of dust indicated the approach of the school bus. "You and the kids will be fine," he said, and it sounded like he was assuring himself more than her.

"Yes, we'll be fine," she agreed softly. And they would. Abby was strong, stronger than she'd ever believed herself to be, and she knew she would survive this even though her heart was breaking into tiny, shattered pieces.

"Johnna will send over the divorce papers. They should be cut and dried."

Again Abby nodded, unable to speak as emotion rose in her throat.

With a squeal of brakes, the big yellow bus lumbered to a halt, and Jason and Jessica got off. They raced toward Luke and Abby, their faces lit with happiness.

Jason's smile fell first as he saw Luke's things in the back of the truck. "Where are you going, Luke?"

Luke bent on one knee and drew Jason and Jessica close to him. "It's time for me to go back to my own house. I was just staying here with you guys while I worked on the place and while we were waiting for the judge to make a decision."

"Where's your house?" Jason asked.

"You know the ranch where we ride the horses? That's where I'm going to be living now."

Jessica's lower lip quivered slightly. "But Peaches is gonna miss you," she said softly and put a little hand on Luke's cheek. "You're our lullaby man. Who is gonna sing us lullabies?"

Luke stood, as if needing to distance himself from the children. "Your mommy can sing you lullabies," he said.

"No, she can't." Jason wrinkled his nose. "She doesn't sing good at all."

A burst of half-hysterical laughter left Abby's lips. "Now you know the last of my secrets. I'm pretty much tone-deaf." The laughter died on her lips, and she swallowed hard against a sob that threatened to erupt. "You two better go see your dog. She's been waiting for you all day long."

Jason and Jessica gave Luke one final look then headed for the house.

"Then I guess this is it," Luke said, his gaze once again not meeting hers.

"Yes."

"But we'll see each other around." His beautiful gray eyes looked at her for a long moment. "This is for the best, Abby. You don't need a man like me in your life."

"You mean I don't need a strong, wonderful, loving man?"

He didn't reply, but instead climbed into his truck, started the engine and took off.

Abby watched his truck pull away, the tears she had tried so hard to contain once again burning…oozing uncontrollably down her cheeks.

Luke. Luke. Her heart cried out for him. Her soul mate. The children's lullaby man. Gone.

She turned, stumbled to the porch and sank down, half-blinded by the tears that continued to flow down her face. She'd known all along that this day would come, had believed she was prepared for it.

What she hadn't been prepared for was the utter, profound, intense heartache of loving Luke.

"Mom, can we have some cookies?" Jason asked as he flew out the front door.

"Sure," she replied, not turning to look at him. "You can each have two cookies and a glass of milk."

"You sound funny." Jason sat next to her and looked at her. "You're crying."

Abby hurriedly swiped at her cheeks. "Maybe just a little," she replied.

"Are you hurt?" He looked at her worriedly.

"No, I'm not hurt on the outside, but my heart hurts."

Jason's eyes narrowed. "Did Luke hurt your heart?"

"Maybe just a tiny little bit," she said, then swiped her eyes. "But Luke didn't mean to hurt my heart." She gave Jason a hug and forced a wide smile. "But don't you worry. I'll be fine. We're all going to be fine. Come on, let's go get some cookies and milk."

Luke had believed that in making the break, in packing up and leaving Abby, he'd feel relief. After all, it had never been intended to be a lasting marriage. They had accomplished their goal, and now it was time for him to focus on his future.

But as he drove away from the house, he felt no relief, and he felt no real thrill of anticipation when he contemplated his future.

The lullaby man. He remembered the night Abby had been shot, when he and the children had been together in her bed and he'd sung every lullaby he could think of to the two worried children.

There had been a special peace inside him as he'd smelled the scent of childhood clinging to them, had watched their eyes grow heavy with sleep and had seen their smiles of pleasure as he'd sung them to slumberland.

Would he ever have a better audience? All he had ever wanted to accomplish in his life was to prove to his old man that he could be somebody important…be somebody special. And wasn't he that to Abby's children? He was their lullaby man.

He hadn't expected to hurt when he walked away from them, and yet pain radiated through his chest directly into his heart.

It was a familiar pain, the pain he'd felt as a child when he'd realized no matter what he did, his father wouldn't love him. It was the same ache he'd felt as a young man, displaced and alone despite his family. It was the gnawing agony that always in the past had made him reach for a drink.

He pulled his truck to the side of the road and shut off the engine, needing to think. Everything suddenly seemed all jumbled up in his head.

He hadn't expected to fall in love with Jason and Jessica, and he told himself it was saying goodbye to them that had confused him, unsettled him. He hadn't realized until this moment just how deeply they had crept into his heart.

Abby loved him. He knew it as surely as he knew his own name. As he'd told her goodbye, in those moments when their gazes had locked, he'd seen her love…unabashed, unadorned and unhidden. It had flowed from those beautiful eyes of hers and momentarily filled up every dark space and every lonely place in his heart.

She loved him and she believed in him. He leaned his head back and closed his eyes, thinking of that morning when he'd come home stinking of booze. She had believed his story without reservation because she knew what kind of man he was and believed the best of him.

Now all he had to figure out was what kind of a man he was and what he really wanted for himself.

* * *

Abby and the two children had just finished their cookies and milk when a knock fell on the front door. "I'll get it," Jason exclaimed, flying from his chair and racing for the door with Peaches and Abby at his heels.

Jason pulled open the door, and Luke stepped in. "Hi, Jason," he said.

Without warning, Jason drew back his leg and kicked Luke hard in the shin.

"Jason!" Abby yelled as Luke yelped and Peaches barked.

"I told him," Jason said, his little chin raised defiantly. "I told him that if he ever hurt you I'd kick him really hard. He hurt you and made you cry."

"Go to your room, young man," Abby exclaimed, appalled by Jason's actions. As Jason stalked off down the hall, Luke hobbled to the sofa and sank down.

"Don't be too hard on him," Luke said as he rubbed his shin.

"I'm so sorry," Abby exclaimed, trying to figure out why he was back, trying to ignore how her heart leaped at the sight of him. "Did you forget something?" she asked.

He straightened up. "Yeah, I did. I forgot that I promised you I'd build you new kitchen cabinets. I never got them finished."

"That's not necessary now," she murmured. "Besides, it wasn't a real promise. It was just something you mentioned."

"No." He stood with a shake of his head. "I distinctly remember it was a promise, and I told you I never break my promises."

Abby felt as if she were involved in some sort of emotional warfare. Didn't he realize she didn't want him coming here everyday, working in her kitchen, indulging in flirtatious banter, then leaving each night to go back to his own life?

She didn't want him to build cabinets. She didn't want him to wash the windows or take out the trash. All she wanted was for him to love her. She held her tongue as Jessica came into the living room from the kitchen.

"Sweetie, why don't you go get your brother and the two of you can play outside on the swing for a little while," she said.

Jessica nodded, and Luke and Abby said nothing until the kids had disappeared out the front door. "Luke, I don't think it's a good idea, you coming back and forth here to do any work."

She was pleased at how unemotional she'd managed to sound, pleased that her voice didn't betray the tumultuous emotions his mere presence had stirred in her.

"You're right. I don't think that's a good idea, either." He advanced toward her, his gaze holding hers. "I think it's best if I just stay here until all the work around this place is completed. And I figure with the hours I have to put in at the ranch and my woodworking business, the work around here should take about thirty or forty years to complete."

She frowned and looked at him in confusion. "What are you talking about?" she asked. This time her voice caught with emotion.

He stood mere inches from her, the familiar masculine scent of him surrounding her. "I'm talking about forever, Abby. I'm talking about making love to you every night and waking up with you in my arms every morning." He placed his hands on either side of her face. "I'm talking about watching Jason at his first Little League game and taking Jessica to her first dance recital."

Abby's heart had begun the rhythm of hope, of love, but she knew of Luke's dreams and would not, could not be the reason he didn't pursue them. "But…what about Nashville?"

Luke dropped his hands from her face and stepped back from her. He grabbed her hand and led her to the sofa where they both sat down.

"Nashville was the dream of a boy," he said. "A boy whose father had told him thousands of times how worthless he was. So that boy dreamed of being a star, of being rich and famous…somebody important to show his old man."

He smiled and tightened his fingers around her hand. "And then an amazing thing happened. He looked into the eyes of a beautiful woman and saw that he *was* somebody important. I love you, Abby. And when you look at me, I feel like I'm king of the world. And if I turn my back on our love, then I truly am the fool my father always told me I was."

"Oh, Luke." Tears sprang to Abby's eyes, and she started to reach for him but paused as he held up a hand to stop her.

"I want you to understand something, Abby. I'm an alcoholic, and I'll always have to fight that battle one day at a time."

"When I had Justin hanging over my head, that's how I learned to survive," she said softly. "One day at a time. I couldn't anticipate the future, nor could I dwell upon the past."

His eyes, those beautiful, long-lashed eyes gazed at her intently. "I realize now I drank to forget instead of working to heal the wounds left by my father. But you loving me…the kids trusting me, that's done more to heal me than I ever thought possible. I love you, Abigail Delaney."

Abby threw herself into his arms, unable to stand not being there for another minute. "I love you, Luke. I have never loved anyone as much as I love you. But I want you to be sure. You're giving up your dreams."

"Darlin', I've never been more certain of anything in my entire life." His smoky eyes gazed into hers with an intensity that threatened to steal her breath away. "And all I'm doing is trading dreams. I'm trading in the dreams of a child for the dreams of a man. You and the children, you're my real dream."

She leaned into him and touched her lips to his, needing

to kiss him, wanting to show him just how very much he meant to her.

Their kiss was hungry, fevered with emotion, salted by Abby's tears of happiness. He was the man she'd dreamed of in the darkest, most lonely hours of the night. He was not a knight and not a knave, but simply the man she wanted to spend the rest of her life loving.

She'd hoped…she'd prayed that eventually she'd find a man strong enough to lean on, yet gentle enough to parent the two children who would require plenty of patience and understanding. And fate had delivered Luke to her doorstep…the answer to her prayers.

"I think I fell in love with you that very first day I met you," he said when their kiss finally ended.

"That was lust, not love," she said teasingly.

He grinned. "Trust me, I lust for you and probably will continue to lust for you until we're both old and gray. But I know the difference between lust and love. And I love you, Abby. I don't want a divorce. All I want is to be a good husband to you and a good father to Jason and Jessica." And with these words he claimed her lips again in a kiss of infinite love.

Tears of joy coursed down Abby's cheeks. He ended the kiss and smiled at her. "Please…please wipe those tears away. If Jason sees them, he's liable to cripple me for life."

Abby laughed through her tears, and with his fingertips he gently wiped the tears away. "Promise me…" she began, her love for him so intense it shimmered inside her like a million brilliant lights. "Promise me we'll weather the storms of life together. Promise me that you'll love me forever."

He grinned, that lazy, sexy grin that always lit a fire in the depth of her soul. "That's the easiest promise I've ever made." Again he placed his palms on the sides of her face. "I promise that I'm going to love you until the day I die, and even in death, we'll find each other and share eternity loving each other."

"And I promise the same thing," she replied, wondering if it were possible for her to be any happier than she was at this very moment.

"I'm not singing down at the Honky Tonk anymore," he said. "The only singing I want to do now is for Jessica and Jason. They are the best audience I could ever have."

"We need to go tell them that you're going to stay, that you're going to be their daddy from now until forever."

"Yeah, we need to tell them. But first…" He stood and pulled her into his arms for another kiss, this one filled with passion, with commitment, with love.

Abby's heart sang with the knowledge that this was only the beginning for them…the beginning of a life together and of dreams realized. They were now, truly and forever, a family.

* * * * *

THE HARLEQUIN
BESTSELLING AUTHOR
COLLECTION

CLASSIC ROMANCES IN COLLECTIBLE VOLUMES
FROM OUR BESTSELLING AUTHORS

On sale
NOW!

--✂------------

SAVE
$1.00

on the purchase of 1 or more books
from the HARLEQUIN®
BESTSELLING AUTHOR COLLECTION

Coupon expires March 31, 2011.
Redeemable at participating retail outlets. Limit one coupon per customer.
Valid in the U.S.A. and Canada only.

5 2 6 0 9 4 5 1

Canadian Retailers: Harlequin Enterprises Limited will pay the face value of this coupon plus 10.25¢ if submitted by customer for this product only. Any other use constitutes fraud. Coupon is nonassignable. Void if taxed, prohibited or restricted by law. Consumer must pay any government taxes. Void if copied. Nielsen Clearing House ("NCH") customers submit coupons and proof of sales to Harlequin Enterprises Limited, P.O. Box 3000, Saint John, NB E2L 4L3, Canada. Non-NCH retailer—for reimbursement submit coupons and proof of sales directly to Harlequin Enterprises Limited, Retail Marketing Department, 225 Duncan Mill Rd., Don Mills, Ontario M3B 3K9, Canada.

U.S. Retailers: Harlequin Enterprises Limited will pay the face value of this coupon plus 8¢ if submitted by customer for this product only. Any other use constitutes fraud. Coupon is nonassignable. Void if taxed, prohibited or restricted by law. Consumer must pay any government taxes. Void if copied. For reimbursement submit coupons and proof of sales directly to Harlequin Enterprises Limited, P.O. Box 880478, El Paso, TX 88588-0478, U.S.A. Cash value 1/100 cents.

5 65373 00076 2   (8100)0 11701

® and TM are trademarks owned and used by the trademark owner and/or its licensee.
© 2010 Harlequin Enterprises Limited

BSCCOUP0910

REQUEST YOUR
FREE BOOKS!

2 FREE NOVELS
FROM THE ROMANCE COLLECTION
PLUS 2 FREE GIFTS!

YES! Please send me 2 FREE novels from the Romance Collection and my 2 FREE gifts (gifts are worth about $10). After receiving them, if I don't wish to receive any more books, I can return the shipping statement marked "cancel." If I don't cancel, I will receive 4 brand-new novels every month and be billed just $5.74 per book in the U.S. or $6.24 per book in Canada. That's a saving of at least 28% off the cover price. It's quite a bargain! Shipping and handling is just 50¢ per book.* I understand that accepting the 2 free books and gifts places me under no obligation to buy anything. I can always return a shipment and cancel at any time. Even if I never buy another book, the two free books and gifts are mine to keep forever.

194/394 MDN E7NZ

Name	(PLEASE PRINT)	
Address		Apt. #
City	State/Prov.	Zip/Postal Code

Signature (if under 18, a parent or guardian must sign)

Mail to **The Reader Service:**
IN U.S.A.: P.O. Box 1867, Buffalo, NY 14240-1867
IN CANADA: P.O. Box 609, Fort Erie, Ontario L2A 5X3

Not valid for current subscribers to the Romance Collection
or the Romance/Suspense Collection.

Want to try two free books from another line?
Call 1-800-873-8635 or visit www.morefreebooks.com.

* Terms and prices subject to change without notice. Prices do not include applicable taxes. N.Y. residents add applicable sales tax. Canadian residents will be charged applicable provincial taxes and GST. Offer not valid in Quebec. This offer is limited to one order per household. All orders subject to approval. Credit or debit balances in a customer's account(s) may be offset by any other outstanding balance owed by or to the customer. Please allow 4 to 6 weeks for delivery. Offer available while quantities last.

Your Privacy: Harlequin Books is committed to protecting your privacy. Our Privacy Policy is available online at www.eHarlequin.com or upon request from the Reader Service. From time to time we make our lists of customers available to reputable third parties who may have a product or service of interest to you. If you would prefer we not share your name and address, please check here. ☐

Help us get it right—We strive for accurate, respectful and relevant communications. To clarify or modify your communication preferences, visit us at www.ReaderService.com/consumerschoice.

MROM10R

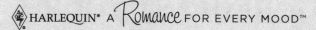

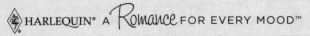

HARLEQUIN® A *Romance* FOR EVERY MOOD™

CLASSICS

Quintessential, modern love stories
that are romance at its finest.

Harlequin Presents®

Glamorous international settings…
unforgettable men…passionate
romances—Harlequin Presents
promises you the world!

Harlequin Presents® Extra

Meet more of your favorite Presents
heroes and travel to glamorous
international locations in our regular
monthly themed collections.

Harlequin® Romance

The anticipation, the thrill of the chase
and the sheer rush of falling in love!

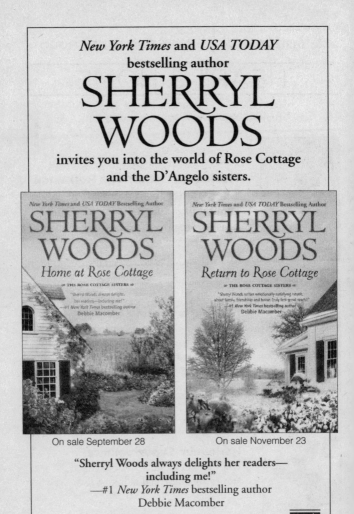